The Reckless Rescue

Marc B. DeGeorge

MuseMarc Studio, LLC.

Acknowledgments

A story may be written by one person, but it takes many to turn it into a novel.

To the following: I am truly grateful for your efforts. Thank you for your continued willingness to help make my dreams a reality.

First, my dedicated and awesome reading group, Brennan Bishop, Ben Pick, Saloni More, and Tracey Canole—all authors in their own right. Thank you for your critical commentary, positive support, and friendship.

My amazing editors, Savannah Gilbo, Brittany Dory, and MPeters. The quality of your efforts have enabled me to tell a compelling story—with no errors!

Also to my wife and family, for giving me the time to forge this next work...and all the ones that come after. Forgive me. There's going to be lots.

.

Chapter One

YOU MIGHT BE THINKING that rescuing the planet and saving our Empire from total collapse would make our lives easier or even better. You'd be wrong.

We found out real quick that fame isn't all it's cut out to be. It brought way more headaches than it did benefits. Even my mom says so.

For instance:

Did we make any money from it?

Nope.

Do we have lifetime positions with some big company?

Nope. Though only Grady wanted that.

Do I get to spend more time with Kayley?

Definitely not. She's been on a whirlwind tour with Captain Teddy and Sergeant Cortell. The Angelcanis government wanted to use their current celebrity status for an international morale booster. Great for the planet, not so great for me. I haven't seen her for six months.

I am happy for her, though. She gets to be exactly where she deserves to be. Every night, when we talk via Sergo, I can hear the excitement in her voice. Kayley'd never admit it, but she's in heaven. Who am I to impede her dream? If anything, I need to pull myself back up to her Goddess-like level.

So, to build up my hero points, I'm going to see Grady. He needs to get some sun—it's not healthy for him to be inside that much—so I want to get him to come to the beach with me. That's a big ask. Grady has hated the beach ever since he was young. It has something to do with the fact that he almost drowned when he was five. As his friend, I've decided it's time he got over that fear.

Grady's been burying himself in every piece of data the military engineers would let him get his greedy eyes on. He's been avoiding the crowds of fanboys and fangirls by trying to invent the next big thing. Personally, I think he's building a new engine for space travel with the help of the Teddys—one that doesn't freak him out when it pushes the ship up past light-speed. Maybe it'll even hit record speeds, but no one is ready for that. Humans already dislike FTL travel.

Parrish has been hanging with me when he's not sporting around. He and Afton got invited to a high-profile marathon, and he had to spend most of the last six months training. Afton, too, though she was less serious about it. I think she was just killing time until her dad returned. Now she stays home a lot. I guess I can't blame her. If I had a dad that I hadn't seen for a while, I'd want to be around him too.

"Yo, Rance!" It's Parrish. He waves at me as I turn the corner onto Grady's street. I didn't expect him to be meeting up with Grady too, but this could be a good thing. Parrish is beach friendly and might take my side when I go to tear our mutual buddy from his hidey-hole.

"Hey, what's that?" I ask, nodding to the rectangular wooden box he's holding. "Are you bin-picking now?"

"No, I found it while I was out on a run," Parrish says. "I brought it with me because I figured you'd know what it is. You seem to be the resident expert ever since you got that shuttle-cook thing."

"Shuttlecock, you mean, but it's actually called a Jianzi. A shuttlecock is for a different game. And Grady's the real antiques expert. I just got my one heirloom."

"Yeah, well, that thing. Such a strange name for a toy. I sound like I'm cursing every time I say it." Parrish holds the box out to me so I can have a closer look. It's got some metal twangy-thingies on one side with a hole underneath. It's also got a big crack on the bottom, and patches of black dirtying up its rough finish. "Maybe you can look it up in that Imperial database you've been playing around on lately. Or even ask the doc."

Parrish means Doc Elizabeth. Elizabeth Chapman, that is. She's the only other one of us that's got little to do these days since the Teddy ship had to blink back to their homeworld for repairs, taking with it her little home on their ship. She didn't really want to get back on so soon, anyway. After however long being cooped up with no one but Teddys, the doc is enjoying the air and the sun just a little too much. I expect we'll see her at the beach today.

"Sure." I take it from him and give it a once-over. "Looks like one of those things you use to take the husk off of corn."

"Could be." Parrish shrugs. "Hey, you going to Grady's too?"

"Yep. I'm going to practice saving someone," I reply with a grin. "Someone who needs to get out of his house and get some sun, preferably at the beach."

"Oh, no." Parrish shakes his head. "No way. Grady has permanently cemented himself to his workstation for the rest of his life. Or until he develops something that he thinks his parents will be proud of him for. You're dreaming if you think you can get him to step foot outside."

"We'll see." I smirk. "I might have a chance if I had some backup. You up for it?"

"Yeah." Parrish grins back. "I'm always down for a rescue."

"You still trying to rub that in?" I give him a playful shove. "Remember, it was *I* who sacrificed himself so the rest of you could sneak off the *Mursilis*."

"And not you who went the wrong way and got caught?"

I could try telling him the truth, but there's little point in it now. No points getting scored on this one.

"Hit a guy when he's down, why don't you?"

Parrish chuckles and pats me on the back. As the only other person —that I know of—that's dated Kayley, he knows how much I'm missing her. I'll bet he's missing her too, in his own way. At one point not that long ago, our little gang was almost split apart due to differing college plans, but a fake war with the Teddys kept us together, and not only did we stop the war, but we caught the bad guy behind the whole thing too! Now the Empire and the Teddys are in the process of starting a new relationship between species.

And because of all that, our gang is split, anyway. If I ever figure out how that went down, I'm going to travel back in time and make some corrections. There is the minor problem of figuring out time travel, though. Parrish and I also have a more immediate priority.

We get to Grady's townhouse, newly restored and sporting a new top level. It was a much bigger mess than we had originally thought, but the Imperial government, in its haste to cover up the actions of Minister Crowley and his associates, took care of his place as well as mine. Now they're both a little bigger than they used to be.

I press the buzzer, but there's no answer. It's a good thing Grady gave us the pass code, otherwise this mission would end in complete failure. Parrish and I step into a darkened foyer and proceed through the living room to get to the stairs. As the sun shines through a crack in the heavy curtains, a fog of dust creates a wall of reflected sunlight. The stench of an overflowing waste bin in the kitchen is a sign that We've gotten here just in time. We hit the stairs towards our first rescue of the new year.

"Grady, you're a bit paler than usual," I say, glancing around his new workspace up on the fourth floor. There are reference manuals intertwined with empty automeal trays everywhere. I'm surprised the pages of each book aren't dyed in beet juice. "I was thinking—"

"No dice, dude," Grady mumbles as he pulls the coverlet tighter around his shoulders. "I'm not going anywhere until I finish this, and I'm a long way off."

"Finish what?" Parrish asks, picking up a cup with a suspicious brown liquid in it. It might just be tea, but tea doesn't usually stick to the sides of a cup like that. Parrish glances around for a trash bin, but when he doesn't find one, he places it down on a table and pushes it as far away from himself as he can.

"I've almost got it," Grady says, a manic smile coming to his face. "After getting a close look at the Teddy drive, I think I can solve the problems that my dad was having with his FTL drive."

"That's great, buddy. Why don't we celebrate? I hear the water's nice today."

"Water?" Grady spins on me, his faux cape flying in the air like he's some vampire from the cine. His eyes narrow. "Are you asking me to go to the beach?"

"Maybe?" I turn to Parrish for support with a hopeful curl of my mouth. "Sure, if that's what you want to do. What do you say, Parrish?"

"Yeah, sounds like a good idea." Parrish nods, pretending to consider the idea. I appreciate the backup.

"What's wrong with you, dude?" Grady snarls. "Did you forget I hate the ocean?"

"It's no different from taking a bath."

"I don't take baths."

"You don't take showers either," Parrish says, wrinkling his nose and waving a hand across his face. "Seriously, dude, you need to clean yourself."

"I'm too busy. Besides, I'm the only one here."

"Yeah, that's kinda obvious, dude," I say. Grady's parents are away on a big project off-planet. It's been three months already and they won't be back for at least another three. If the Teddys share some of their tech with the Empire, they might never get back home. I've offered him to stay over my place plenty of times already, so he wouldn't be lonely, but ever since he started working on this project, I've been just as alone.

Well, mostly. My mom is home, and she's good company. When she's not on her Sergo with Kayley's mom, that is. Ever since Kayley and I told our respective parents about us getting together, our moms have been closer than ever. I wonder if they're conspiring something that neither Kayley nor I would approve of. Knowing my mom, I'd say the chance of that is high.

"Hey Grady, did you know that sunlight helps you grow brain cells?" Parrish asks.

"Does not," Grady replies. "There's no data published that ever came to that conclusion."

"No," I say, "but sunlight helps your mental state. Which means it helps you think. That's kinda the same as growing brain cells. You definitely need a good mental state to solve whatever you're trying to solve, dude. So you should totally come with us."

"I already said no, dude," Grady says. "I appreciate you guys coming over, but I got to get back to this."

"We're just trying to help you out, Grady," Parrish says, walking up to him. "I mean, look at you. I've never seen you so...well, dude. You need to get out, or you're gonna get sick, and if you get sick, then what are you gonna do? You can't work on your project then, can you? You don't want that to happen, and Rance and I don't want that to happen to you either. I mean, who are you working on this for, anyway? Your dad? He doesn't—"

"I'm working on this for *me*, dude!" Grady spins on Parrish so violently that Parrish takes a step back and puts his hands up. "No one else! This is my thing, and I'm gonna finish it, even if it kills me! Now would you both get lost so I can get back to work, please?"

Grady stomps back to his workstation and drops himself into his chair with a sniffle. I've never seen my friend so uptight. I know he wants to show his parents just how capable a designer he can be, but he's got his whole life to do that. I wonder if his parents said something to him to get him into this frenzied state.

Parrish motions to me to join him over by the top step, and I nod. With a quick glance back at Grady, I tiptoe over to him, and we turn our backs on our overly pale friend.

"Grady's in a bad place, Rance. I'm really worried about him," Parrish whispers.

"Yeah, me too."

"So what do we do?"

I take another look at Grady. He's already returned to immersing himself in whatever thing he's working on. I'll bet he's already forgotten his best buds are still here, which is good because we can talk about him without him even noticing. Still, when I see my friend withering away, my stomach turns. We have to do something, or else Grady will get sick. Or worse.

"I think it's time for intervention, dude," I say and turn around slowly until I'm facing Grady again. "We've got to help him understand there's other things in life besides pleasing his parents."

"I'm with you," Parrish says. "So, how do we go about it?"

"Follow me, and be ready," I say, shuffling quietly towards Grady. I raise my hands, preparing for—something. What I'm not sure yet, but I'm hoping I'll have an answer once I get to Grady.

"Okay, get ready," I hiss at Parrish. He leans his athletic frame down close to me, his hands coming up to mimic my stance. We come to a stop just behind Grady's chair. He's still typing away frantically and taking no notice of us. That's a definite sign of how messed up he is right now. How could someone take no notice of two people creeping up behind them?

"And…" Parrish eyes me sideways as I slip to the other side of Grady's chair.

"Get him!" I pounce onto my startled friend while my other startled friend tries to follow along. "Quick, wrap him up!"

"What in the—" Grady cries. "What are you doing?"

"This is for your own good, Grady! You're getting some sun today!" I say as we swaddle him in the coverlet. "I'll get his feet!"

Parrish slides him off the chair, and we pick up our wildly protesting bud and prep him for a long haul to the beach. Grady wriggles like a caterpillar in his cocoon as he struggles to get free. He won't, though. We've got him too tightly packed.

"You guys are nuts! I'm not going to forgive you for this!" Grady shouts. It could be just me, but I think I hear a small hint of amusement in his voice. That's what I'm hoping, at least.

"You can be angry all you want, Grady, but we're doing this because we care!"

"Make sure that file's saved!" is Grady's last plea before we haul him down the stairs like a gigantic summer roll.

Chapter Two

AH, THE BEACH. ANGELCANIS' sun dearly loves its daughter planet. Our town is by the ocean and has great weather nearly year-round. You only get gray skies and hard downpours when you go farther inland. Which means it's almost always a good time to go to the beach.

Our favorite beach, White Orchid, is also the most popular of all the beaches in town. Anyone who wants to be social comes here to see and be seen. The soft white sand, gentle wind, and mild waves make it a perfect place to take a dip without getting roughed up by the ocean. The sport-heads go down to Break Beach for any sort of aquatic challenges.

We're sitting on the coverlet we carried Grady in, which Grady nearly exploded over once we unrolled him and spread it out on the sand. He's calm now and sulking underneath the shade device we got for him. It's unlikely he'll move, but I'll take it as a small step forward. Parrish and I will make sure he doesn't attempt to escape. We don't have our suits with us anyway, so there's not a whole lot more to do other than enjoy the sun and the sights.

Which apparently includes Teddys, our fuzzy alien friends.

"Greetings Rancid, Gratin, and Parrish," Original Teddy says, strolling up with two of his blue buddies. We call him that because he was the first Teddy we met. "Littoral is recommended for alleviation of discomfort."

"Speak for yourself, Teddy," Grady growls, and he pulls the sun visor we loaned him down over his face.

I grin and shake my head at him and then turn back to Original Teddy to answer. As I take his short, big disk-eyed form in, I have to stop and blink. I have no idea why I didn't notice it before, but around his waist are three circular tubes. If that was the only unusual thing, I'd be okay with it. But he and his blue buddies also have several foam wraps around their short stubby arms and tentacles. They look like someone took a drink cooler and made it able to walk.

"Teddy...what are you wearing?"

"Requirements for littoral recreation."

"Those are life-preservers, Teddy." I point to his tentacles. "And those are arm floaties, for kids. You don't need those to have fun at the beach."

Original Teddy turns to the nearest blue buddy, and an instant cacophony of clicks, whirrs, and whistles ensues. The heated debate goes on for a good minute, then Original Teddy whips his tentacles, and the floaties go flying in all directions. A second later, the blue buddies do the same.

"Teddy has decided not to recreate."

"Oh, sorry to hear that." I glance at Parrish, who shrugs. "What will you do then? Return to the ship?"

"That is not accurate, Rancid. Security is paramount. Conclave must occur."

"What? Danger?" I glance around, searching for some assailant.

"That is not accurate. Contingency is forthcoming."

I sigh. Well, at least we won't have to dash to safety. Getting Grady here was enough exercise for one day. He might not seem like the type, but Grady can put up a serious struggle if he wants to.

"So, you wanted to talk to us about something, then?"

"That is accurate. Requisition for appointment. Rancid and compatriots will reconnoiter to determine contingency."

I tilt my head at him, taking a moment to process his meaning. While I try to run the possibilities through my brain, Original Teddy focuses his saucer-sized eyes on Grady, who's likely dozed off at this point. I hope so. I don't think he was getting much sleep either. Never again will I leave him on his own like that.

"Awaiting commencement of conclave," Original Teddy says, turning back to me.

Shoot, I spaced out, worrying about Grady, and I totally forgot to translate the Teddyspeak in my head. We came out here for Grady's sake. But if the Teddys want to talk, I'm fine with that too. I just need to figure out what they want.

"So, what was it you wanted to discuss, Teddy?"

"Dude," Grady says from under his visor. "They want us to investigate something for them."

"Oh." I glance at Parrish again to see if he had gotten that too. He just turns a hand up and shrugs his shoulder. Well, there's his answer. I turn back to Original Teddy. "What did you want us to check out?"

"Menace is occurring. Reconnoiter to determine menace and terminate."

"Terminate?" I ask.

"Abolish menace to insulate Teddy."

Phew. Abolish sounds much less extreme than terminate. I really hope that Teddy isn't asking us to assassinate someone. They're not a violent species, at least not in my experience so far. They do eat live animals, so there's that, but I've never seen them attack someone.

So, if I understand this correctly, they want us to check out someone or something that's worrying them and then get rid of the problem. That doesn't seem difficult, and I'd be happy to help, but we came here for Grady. Maybe they could wait a little while.

Before I can ask, I spy a pair of familiar legs approaching and blush a bit because I shouldn't be looking at the body parts of other women. Still, I'm a guy in his prime, and even though I'd never kiss anyone but my KayKay, I can't help but notice things like legs. Goddesses help me.

"Well, fancy meeting the three of you here," Doc Elizabeth says as she strolls up to us, hands on hips. "Hello, boys. Out for a little fresh air and some sun?"

The beach may be busy, but three dudes in street clothes chatting with three fuzzy aliens aren't going to be hard to notice. We stand out like a supernova in the middle of a patch of dark matter.

"Hey, Doc," Parrish says. "Yeah, that's kinda the plan." I see him jerk his head back towards Grady. It draws the doc's gaze over to our bud, and she presses her lips together when she gets a solid look at him.

"You leave this to me, boys. Good job convincing him to come out."

"Convincing?" Grady grumbles. "They kidnapped me!"

"Ah, well, good show either way." Doc Elizabeth steps under the shade and puts herself down next to him. "How are we, Mr. Grady?"

Teddy and his blue buddies follow the doc onto our coverlet and drop themselves down around Parrish and me. As I watch them, I wonder how they're going to get the sand out of their fuzz. It can't be easy. At least now I can give the Teddys my full attention. Our reinforcement is here, and she'll cover for us while we handle the newest crisis to hit our lives.

"Okay, Teddy, why don't you start from the beginning. Let me see if I can get this."

"Agreed, Rancid. Inception is best." Original Teddy slides himself forward so he can address Parrish and me at the same time. "Conclave with human organization has commenced. Teddy welcomes conclave. Humans welcome Teddy apparatus."

"Of course they do, Teddy," I say. "Your ships are more advanced than ours. The Empire definitely wants your drive tech."

"Teddy welcomes distribution. Deviant is also available. Teddy does not recommend distribution to deviant."

Okay. So the Teddys don't want their tech falling into the hands of some bad guy. That makes perfect sense. I'm glad that I've been able to get through the Teddyspeak with ease. I'm also glad Original Teddy isn't trying to throw any complex ideas at us. At least, I don't think these are complex ideas.

"So you're worried about your tech getting into the wrong hands? Is that it?" I ask.

"That is accurate. Menace is forthcoming. Teddy has encountered deviant. Menace is imposing."

"Of course, Teddy. We don't like the bad guys either. That's why Minister Crowley had to go."

"Menace is menace," Original Teddy says. "Reconnoiter is possible. Termination of appropriation is recommended."

I stare at my fuzzy friend, wondering if we're just talking concepts or if an actual threat exists. It's more than possible, but if we're only discussing in theory, it's going to be difficult to find a place to search for said theoretical menace.

A quick glance over at Parrish gets more than a shrug this time. He's leaning forward, fully engaged in the conversation. He notices my attention on him and he nods. "We need to help them out, Rance. Whatever it is."

I agree. There's no question in my mind that we'd say yes if the Teddys are asking for our help. We won't get much from it, however. Teddys can't pay, and we aren't likely to get more work from this mission. That's okay. I'm still confident that something will come our way.

Before we can decide, however, we need to get down some concrete facts.

"Teddy," I start, "have you identified a person or an organization that is a threat to you?"

"That is accurate."

"You have?" My heart picks up its pace. "Can you show us?"

"That is accurate."

Great. Now we're getting somewhere. If the Teddys really have a person under suspicion like they're saying, then we've got our place to start. At least partially, anyway. Kayley's got to come back so we can pull Afton out of her house and get back to being a team. Once we're at full power, then we'll be able to get rid of this troublemaker.

We can at least investigate this bad guy...if it's a guy at all. It could be a woman, an organization, or even another alien species! How cool would that be? Provided they weren't out to eradicate humans from the universe, we might even turn them over to our side. Our popularity would be Commonwealth-wide then, and that's when the actual jobs start coming in!

I hate to be selfish, but that would absolutely lift me up to Kayley-deserving status. I'd be wealthy and famous, and that's exactly who she deserves to have by her side. So I need to get moving the achievement meter into the green. I'm not taking for granted that I'm her boyfriend.

"Okay, Teddy," I say. "We'll help. If you can point us in the right direction, I doubt we'll have much trouble checking this menace out. Termination might be another story, but we can figure it out as we go, right?"

"Better we have a plan, plus a backup plan," Parrish says. "When I play ball, I never go into the game without at least ten plays I can call right off the bat if I need to."

"When's the last time you even played a match, dude?" Grady's taunt comes to us from out of the shelter. It's followed by a well-timed yelp, which I can guess is Doc Elizabeth keeping things straight back there. Parrish just smiles. He knows his best play here is to say nothing.

"So when do you want us to start, Teddy?" I ask.

"Recommendation is immediate."

"But can we get something to eat first, at least? I'm starving," Grady calls.

"Agreed," Original Teddy says. "Nutritional is possible."

"Great!" Grady says, popping out of the shelter like he just woke up from an eon of great sleep. "Noodles it is. You're buying!"

All I can do is glance back at the doc while Parrish vocalizes exactly what I was thinking.

"What did you just do to him?"

Chapter Three

THERE'S AN AMAZING NOODLE place not far from the beach that only the locals know about. It's hidden in between the back streets of an area that was formerly an industrial park. Now enterprising individuals are rediscovering the area and setting up shop in the abandoned buildings. It's great for us because we're locals. Plus, the food is crash-your-ship-into-an-exploding-star good.

The four humans wait in line while the Teddys find a cooler spot to rest in. As much as they seemed to like the beach, they must have been melting in the sun. Teddys aren't exactly built for hot weather. Not that I've heard any complaints from them.

"So, what's good here?" Doc Elizabeth asks, glancing around, presumably for a menu.

"Noodles," Grady answers.

"Right, yes, I got that they serve noodles here, but what are the options?"

"Well, you can have the noodles, or, if you're really hungry, you can have the noodles," I explain with a small smirk. "I know it's a difficult choice, but trust me, they're both really good."

"Ah." The doc presses her lips together and stands up straight. "I think I get it. Well, then...I think you know what I want to order."

The small puffs of steam coming from the booth smell so stomach-rumblingly good that I rub my belly just to stop it from becoming a runaway boulder. Grady and Parrish are equally as famished. They both shuffle back in that primitive hunger dance that only happens when a young person is past due for their caloric intake.

"Excuse me, but is this spot any good?" A man's voice, from behind us. I pivot and I catch its owner—a lanky man, tall and stiff, dressed head to toe in the dullest browns ever experienced in the Empire: tan pants, a peanut-colored shirt, a cedar tweed jacket, and a less than exciting wheat-hued overcoat. Even his eyes and his scruffy hair are brown.

"Depends," Grady replies.

"Depends upon what?"

"If you like noodles or not."

"I suppose I do. Are they savory or spicy?"

"Savory."

"Excellent. I think I will try them."

Before I turn around, I take another glance at him. He's completely out of place. Not just here at the noodle stand, and not even in our town. He's unrelated to anything on Angelcanis at all. Who wears an overcoat in the summer? My guard is already up as I turn back to him.

"New here, are you?"

"Ah, just in town for some business, actually."

"Oh? How did you hear about this place?"

"My local contact recommended it."

I nod understandingly, but I know that's the largest payload of nonsense this side of the long-haul freight route that goes from Bradbury to Yeomanry. This dude is definitely some kind of Imperial agent. I can't tell yet if this guy might be our menace or not. But it is just way too coincidental that ten minutes ago we were chatting it up with the Teddys, and now this guy shows up wanting to eat a hot bowl of noodles in an overcoat.

I glance towards the darkened alley where the Teddys are cooling off. They haven't moved or otherwise made themselves known. The blue buddies are well camouflaged against the slate blue of the corrugated metal walls that envelop the courtyard we're in. I hope they're wise enough to stay that way.

"I'm sorry, but could I ask you a question?" Mr. Brown-and-Lanky asks. "Were all of you living in this town during the attack?"

"Why do you ask?" I shoot back.

"Well." Mr. Lanky scratches his head. "I sell insurance, and I was just wondering how extensive the damage was around here. I've been searching around town, and I can't seem to find any evidence that there ever was an attack! Now, I know the people of this planet are very resourceful, but I have to say, I'm very impressed they cleaned everything up so quickly."

I let out a small breath and relax. Okay, so that's feasible. He could be an insurance salesman. They might dress like him. He acts geeky enough to be an actuary or something like that. Still, I'm not quite sold on his story.

"There are two buildings under construction on the main avenue that runs through town. Both blew up on the day those—on the day we were attacked."

I pause because I don't know if he's who he says he is, or part of the Empire-wide conspiracy that saw a hidden faction of the military attack and kill innocent members of the Empire. We caught the guy —a former Minister Crowley—who gave the order to attack the Teddys, and then to bomb our planet. But there's still members of that faction out there. We've got to be careful.

"I see, but I suppose there's not much to see there now."

"No. Why didn't you come sooner?"

"Well, unfortunately"—Mr. Lanky's cheeks redden a little—"I was just assigned this planet about two months ago. This being a colony and all, the company only recently added it to the vetting list."

I should ask him what company that is, but with the thousands of insurance companies likely out there, it would take us a year of searching to find his name in the right one. Besides, if he was a government agent, he could have already planted his name in said company. Nope, not going to happen that way.

With no other obvious recourse, I smile and turn back to my buds. We're next in line anyway, and I can't keep questioning him without him getting suspicious of me. Better to leave him alone for now. Besides, I'm starving.

We get our bowls and find a table to inhale our food. As hungry as we are, one bowl might not be enough. At least they're cheap enough for me to afford seconds. I'm not destitute, but I worry that one day my mom won't be able to support the two of us financially. If I really want to protect the people of Angelcanis, I need to earn money to start my business of fighting the good fight. Otherwise I'll have to go get a job flipping veggie filets down at the local diner.

"Hey, are you gonna finish that?" Parrish says, pointing at my bowl. I lift my head and blink at him, then glance down at my bowl. It's still full.

"This is a no-fly zone for you, buddy," I reply, covering my bowl with my hands. "Get more if you're still hungry."

"I thought you were hungry too," Doc Elizabeth says.

"Don't mind him," Grady says, sneering. "He's just pining over his long-lost girlfriend."

"I am not!"

"Well, you were pining over something."

"Yeah, our long-lost financial award the government promised us but never gave."

"Give it up, dude. Our government's got no money."

"Speaking of government," Doc says, glancing around then leaning in. "Who was that gentleman you were chatting up on the line? He seemed a bit...lost."

I glance around and spot him sitting on a bench on the other side of the courtyard, away from the other patrons. All of a sudden, he glances up and catches me looking at him. He smiles and lifts his bowl to me as if to show how much he's enjoying his meal. All I can do is smile and give him a thumbs-up.

"I'm not sure." I shoot my eyes in his direction again, careful not to move my head. "He says he's an insurance salesman, but he smells more like an Imperial stiff."

"Ooh." The doc raises her eyebrows. "Do you think he's the menace the Teddys were talking about?"

"No idea, but we can't take any chances."

"That guy's no threat," Grady says, sliding back in his chair and rubbing his stomach. "He doesn't even look like he could investigate someone stealing a kid's candy bar."

I crush my lips together. Grady's assessment is wrong. At least, that's what my gut says. I don't have any proof that disproves his statement, and I'm not exactly trusting of the government when they took my father away from me.

"I don't know, dude, I think we should check him out, just for the sake of the Teddys."

"Well, that's going to be difficult," Doc Elizabeth says. "He's gone."

Shoot! I jump up and spin around—he's nowhere to be seen. I push my seat back and run to check the main alley that leads back to the beach. Not there either. That's just strange. No one with his height and poor fashion sense could blend in with the locals.

This could all be in my head, but I have to find out. No one pokes around our town and gets away with it!

"Get the Teddys back to their shuttle," I say to Grady and Parrish. "I'm going to go look for him."

"What?" Parrish frowns at me and stands. "No way. I'm going with you. It's too dangerous to go alone."

"Yeah, you guys go have fun," Grady says and grins. "I'm going back home and doing what I do best. But first, I think I'm going to have Rance's noodles there."

"Like hell you are!" I grab the edge of my bowl before he can get his greedy hands on it. Then, pressing it to my lips, I gulp the remainder down in seconds flat. I wipe my mouth with my forearm and let out a satisfied sigh.

"Now, that's not very polite table manners, Mr. Rance," the doc chides me with a shake of her head.

"Don't worry, no one's keeping score. Parrish, let's go."

We race down the far alley opposite the main entrance. Out of all the other possibilities, this one seems most likely. It's also the most difficult to follow. We wind and turn through the passage until I'm sure that we've come the wrong way.

I spot a small café or bar just up ahead. A pair of patrons are sitting outside. Good—they might have seen him pass by.

"Tall feller, right?" answers one patron, taking a long sip of his drink. "Yeah, he went down that way about a minute or so."

"Thanks!"

Parrish and I continue down the alleyway at a more cautious pace. If we suddenly smash into him, there's going to be a lot of hard questions flying our way. A low profile is a better option, especially if we're trying to spy on him.

The passageway gets narrower. A safety net hangs above us, blocking out the sunlight and bringing the light down to cozy restaurant level. We're going to need some artificial light if it gets any darker.

"Hey, there he is!" Parrish whispers and points. Sure enough, Mr. Lanky is doing us the favor of making himself obvious. He's got his Sergo out and appears to be tapping furiously on its screen. Parrish and I cut our slow jog down to a tiptoed advance.

"Can you make out his screen?" I ask, squinting to try.

"From here? Use your lens!"

"Good idea." I pull my own Sergo out and turn the camera on, zooming in to catch a good angle.

The problem is, at our distance, everything is so dark and shaky that his screen just shows up as a white blur. I turn on the lens enhancements, but even they're not much help. They don't design Sergos to make award-winning cine.

Parrish grabs me suddenly, shoving me back against the wall. I wince, preparing myself for a hard slam and a big noise, but Parrish is an athlete and skilled at moving himself and others around. Still, I'm shocked.

"What was that for?"

"Sorry, he was about to look our way."

Whoa, okay. I didn't notice that at all. I was trying to see his screen. Now we'll have to check to see if he saw us. I drop to the ground and crawl to the edge where the alley bends. Mr. Lanky was in a small alcove at the end of that run.

But now he's not.

"Parrish, he's on the move again. We've got to catch up to him."

After a solid half hour of racing around to check the connecting alleys and any other little spot we could find, we double back. Another half hour after that, Parrish and I find ourselves out of energy and ready to give up. How he managed to elude us is a mystery. But it does tell me one thing.

"Dude," I say, catching my breath. "I don't know who this guy is, but he's no insurance salesman."

Which means we'd better watch our backs.

Chapter Four

WE HEAD BACK TOWARDS the noodle shop to find the others. There's a profound sense that we've accomplished very little in our chase. Mr. Lanky is after something, for sure, but he might not even be after the Teddys—or us, for that matter. We may have just outed ourselves as persons of suspicion. Not that we weren't before.

Now that I've had a chance to think about it, the Teddys coming to us for help was odd. A lot of their tech is a hundred years ahead of anything the Empire has. But I would still say yes, even if their tech was a thousand years beyond what we could do. They're my buds, and buds look after each other.

As Parrish and I get ready to turn down the back passage that leads to the main beach entrance, a woman with blonde- and black-striped hair bursts out of the alley with a scream. She shoves her way past us and darts around the corner.

We stare at each other, then shrug and continue on our way. I doubt it's any real trouble. Everyone uses this area as their own amusement park.

And then two monster-sized men in black suits and helmets come charging at us, guns in hand.

"Out of the way!" growls one of them. We comply as fast as we can. Neither of us wants to be flattened by rampaging, gun-toting simians. They hit the end of the alley then split up, each of them heading around a different corner.

"What the heck was that about?" I ask, glancing back down the alley after them.

"No idea," Parrish replies, "but we shouldn't wait around to find out."

I nod but don't move. The image of those two gorillas flashes back in my head. They were dressed like soldiers, but something was off about them. I've seen enough uniforms at this point to know. If that woman was a criminal, the constabulary would be chasing her, not a pair of heavily armed soldiers. Our town isn't a breeding ground for unlawful behavior—nowhere on Angelcanis is.

A gun goes off, the shot echoing through the alleyway. Then another scream. This time I clearly hear a plea for help, followed by another shot.

"Dude, something isn't right about this," I say through gritted teeth.

"No kidding, but we'd better stay out of it, Rance. Guns, as you know, mean trouble."

"Well aware, but we wouldn't be doing our job if we just stood by. This is what we signed up for."

"Signed up for? That's not how that works. People are supposed to come to us."

"That woman needs help," I say, "so I'm going to see if I can help."

"Last I checked, Rance, you weren't some superhero."

Parrish makes a solid point. We're not vigilantes on patrol. Sure, our mission is to solve people's problems, but as of late, that's been about finding lost pets. Despite that and the large men with guns, I still want to go. Something about this situation tells me that's exactly what I need to do.

"I'll be careful," I say and jet down the passage towards the next intersecting alley and dart left towards the sound of the scream. At least, where I thought I heard it coming from.

"Rance! Wait!"

I don't wait. Parrish will catch up. In fact, I pick up my pace, throwing a glance through windows and open doors as I pass by. This area's different from the way we just came, and it's less occupied, which doesn't make me feel better about my decision.

I come to a junction and slide to a stop. Which way? I already know my luck with choosing a direction—it's bad. If I choose one or the other, it will be wrong, which means it doesn't matter which way I go.

So I choose to go right.

It's wrong. Definitely wrong. It's a dead end. I sigh and throw my hands up. I'll have to turn back, but first, I really need to catch my breath. I lean back onto the corrugated metal of the former factory behind me. Its coolness is relaxing, and I close my eyes. Just for a moment, and then I can resume my search.

A footstep crunching on the gravel that covers the ground wakes me from my chill mode. I pop my eyes open.

It's her!

She freezes, and her hands come up. She's watching me as I regard her. The woman's eyes narrow a bit, but then her gaze goes soft. With a quick glance behind her, she dashes towards me, panting. I push myself up off of the wall and try to appear confident.

"Please, help me!" she cries as she crashes into me. I step back and throw my arms wide so I don't fall over. The woman keeps pressing me back, trying to find some way to wrap her arms around me. I try to gently hold her off, but she's stronger than I expect. So much so that she forces me back against the wall, her body crushing against me. I get squeezed between her and the wall, and my elevated sense of inappropriate contact is screaming at me to get away. I'm having difficulty finding a place to look that doesn't feel wrong. Her low-cut, skintight jumpsuit isn't helping much either.

"Hey, miss! Miss!" I say, attempting to push her off while not touching her somewhere improper. "It's okay! I'll help you! Just tell me what's going on!"

"Oh, thank you! Thank you!" She squeezes me into a hug, then pulls back, still panting. "Those men—"

"Are they trying to kill you?"

"No, they..." Her head spins back towards the alley entrance as a shot goes off. "Listen, I need your help...please."

"Of course." I shrug. "That's what I do."

"Oh, thank you. Thank you." She takes my hands in hers and pulls them to her chest with a hopeful smile. I return the smile and try to take my hands back, but her grip is like iron. "What is your name?"

"Rance."

"Rance, you have to find...my husband. I think those men who are chasing me might be after him too. I'm worried that he is in serious trouble."

"What about you? Don't you need help?"

"No, I..." She turns and drops her gaze. A hint of redness comes to her cheek. "I'll be fine."

If Kayley were here, she'd be smacking me up, down, right, and left and then she'd throw me into the nearest trash bin. Not for appearing to be intimate with another woman, but for making decisions without really thinking them through. I'm aware that's what I'm doing, but my gut just tells me this is the right choice. At least, I'm pretty sure it's my gut.

"Okay, don't worry. We'll find him," I say, wondering why I believe her. "What's his name?"

"Freddie...Freddie Espy." As if her voluptuous body pressed up against me wasn't bad enough, I notice a sweet smell about her that mixes with her perspiration. It's...alluring.

No, stop that!

I have to keep focused, but I can't move away, and she's still got my wrists locked against her bosom. Maybe I just tell her we're on the job to get her off me?

"Um, can I have my hands back?"

"Oh, sorry. It's just that...I'm so worried about him. I just need someone to hold me."

"Yeah, miss, I get it, but that might not be me?" I feel my own cheeks reddening now. "Can we get back to your *husband*..."

"Yes, please," she says in that breathless voice she's been using this whole time, "you have to save him. I'll do anything. Please. I have money. I can pay."

"Money?"

Another shout comes from down the passage. It's Parrish, looking for me. I take in a breath to call back to him so he can find us, but before I can, her hand flashes out and covers my mouth.

"No, you can't, they'll hear you," she says, checking down the alley again.

After hearing the word *money*, the idea of running from two thugs is trivial. This could be our first real rescue! Wait until Parrish finds out!

"Okay, we'll do it," I say. "You can count on us. Now, if you don't mind—"

"Rance," she says, cutting me off with a caress of my cheek. There's a tingle down my spine, and I really have to find a way to move this to a more professional environment. I don't want to lose our first client because of some misunderstanding. "Please, when you see him, give him a message. Tell him Danny loves him very much."

"Sure, but that's all you want to tell him?"

"No, tell him this too." Before I can evade her lips, they find mine. I go stiff at the uninvited assault on my person. What a sucker I am— always trying to please until I get myself into trouble.

I am not enjoying this. I am not enjoying this. I am not enjoying this.

"Rance!" I hear Parrish yell. I break off the kiss and turn to look down the alley. He sees me, then freezes. I swallow hard, wondering what this must look like to him. I really hope he gives me the chance to explain.

A second later, I realize she's gone. I blink and glance around. She's nowhere. How is that possible?

"Dude," Parrish says as he trots up to me, a severe frown covering his face. "What just happened? Who was that?"

"Honestly, I have no idea, but I think we've got our first actual client." I check around for her again. How did she just evaporate into thin air? Did I hallucinate the whole thing?

Parrish's mouth drops open as he stares at me, lost for words.

"You saw her too, right?"

"Didn't..." Parrish shakes his head. "Are you okay? I thought you were getting assaulted!"

"Not exactly." I touch my fingers to my lips and come away with a greasy red residue. No hallucination, but did we just get hired? I'll forget everything else that just happened if there's some real money at the end of this.

"Well." Parrish puts a hand on my shoulder and examines my face. "As long as you're okay, that's what's important."

"Yeah, I'm good. Let's get back to the others."

Chapter Five

I WAKE UP THE next morning with the worst stomachache I've ever had. I sit up in bed, clutching my belly, feeling like I really need to get to the bathroom, stat. The welling in my throat tells me I'm not likely to make it. I need to find a trash bin straight away.

To the shock of Grady and Parrish, I burst from Grady's guest bedroom and fly into the kitchen like a missile homing in on its target. I spot the bin in the corner and rocket to it. But my foot slips, and I end up landing flat on my tummy—and my upset stomach releases its contents onto the floor.

"Dude! Nasty!" Grady says. "Have some self-control!"

"Hey, Doc!" Parrish calls. "Rance needs your help!"

I sigh and shut my eyes, relieved that the emergency is over. I feel a bit bad about messing up Grady's nice kitchen floor, but once I recover, I'll clean it up before it starts to smell.

"Rance, you alright?" Parrish lifts me by my arms and turns me over to sit, resting me against the cabinets under the countertop.

"What's wrong with him?" Grady asks as Doc Elizabeth rushes into the kitchen and drops next to me. "Was he poisoned?"

The doc puts her wrist to my forehead, then checks the pulse on my neck. There's a noticeable relaxing of her body after that. Doc Elizabeth even smiles a little as she takes my head in her hands and checks my eyes. Once she's done, she nods once and hums lightly.

"Well, boys, what we have here is a serious case of lovesickness, but don't worry, it's curable. A kiss from this young man's paramour ought to do him right."

"So," Grady says, and his forehead wrinkles as he tries to compute the meaning of that, "he's okay, or not?"

"I'm sure he'll be fine," Doc Elizabeth replies. "Likely, something he ate just irritated his stomach. It's not like you boys find the most sanitary of food outlets to eat at."

"Could that be what bothered his stomach?" Parrish points to a small white capsule within the brown ejecta of my stomach's former contents. Doc Elizabeth glances at it, raising an eyebrow.

"Well, now, that's suspicious."

After a bit of cleaning and a nap—they cleaned, I napped—we hike up to Grady's workspace and jump right into studying the mystery capsule, this time with me wrapped in a blanket.

"Hey, check this out. There's a circuit inside," Grady says. He's got it in the particle scanner so we can see through the capsule's casing before we try opening it. It's not a good idea to just open something up when you don't know what's inside. Especially when it comes from your stomach.

"Can you tell what it does?" Parrish asks, leaning over Grady's shoulder.

"No, but I'm sure it's not going to blow up."

"Famous last words," Doc Elizabeth says and takes a seat next to me on the small sofa in the back of the room. I'm not sure if you could call it a room. It's more of a platform. First off, there are no walls. Well, there's one wall. It's the side where the stairs come up. Other than that, only the sides of the building and the roof surround it. It's even possible to slip through the rail and jump down to the next floor below.

"Try higher magnification," I suggest.

"Go back to sleep," Grady replies. "I'm already there."

It's true. He does already have a larger projection up. I was too busy admiring the stained glass windows surrounding his space to notice. They are amazing. There are all sorts of nature scenes from around the planet—water lilies in spring, red-crowned cranes in winter, rice fields in summer. Our government really spared no expense for Grady's high-profile parents. My mom got an empty room.

"So, what do you see, then?" I ask.

"Might be a communications device."

"Communications?"

"Let's open it up!" Doc Elizabeth says.

"Fine, but Rance is doing it," Grady replies. "It's his puke all over the capsule."

"No one thought to clean it off first?" I snort and get myself over to the tray that Grady just ejected from the scanner. Without further debate on the subject, I pick up the capsule and raise it up to the light from a sconce on the wall.

"Check the seam for any sort of switch, don't just—"

Grady stops when I ignore his direction and just pull the thing open. It slides apart easily, exposing the microcircuit inside. There's a short chirp, and a light turns on from inside the componentry. I flinch and drop the circuit back onto the tray, then step back a few steps, just to be safe.

"You're sure it's not going to explode?" I ask.

Grady responds in the negative with the most *you're dumb as dirt* tone he can muster, but I don't think he's right. See, when I find secret electronics in my stomach—which would be never—I tend to get a bit restless.

Another chirp comes from the device, and a three-dimensional projection takes form right in front of me. At first it's just a white cylinder, but a moment later the form takes shape. It's human, for sure.

The form becomes clearer, and I can see a body. Female, almost familiar. She turns around in a circle as if she's scanning Grady's room. I notice she's wearing a skintight jumpsuit. Could it be?

"It's her!" I cry. The hair gives her away. She turns to face me as the image comes to its final resolution. "The woman from yesterday!"

"Oh, hi there, darling." She smiles sweetly and waves with a twinkle of her fingers. "I was wondering when you were going to call me. No trouble with the AIC unit, I hope?"

"Who the hell are you?" I growl.

"Oh, honey, don't get upset. This is the only way we could speak privately without those two goons breathing down my neck. Besides, you seemed to enjoy how I passed it to you."

"Wait." Parrish steps in next to me, squinting his eyes at her. "You mean you kissed Rance just so you could slip the capsule into his mouth?"

"Beats going the other way, sugar." She tilts her head and shrugs with one shoulder. Parrish turns on me and frowns.

"How did you not feel that?" he asks. I also give him a shrug. I could say it was because she had her tongue jammed down my throat, but that's not going to appease my bud in any way. He's barely on the right side of the *I believe Rance* equation. No need to push him back in the wrong direction.

"So, you wanted to talk to me? Away from those thugs?" I ask.

"Yep. You never know who's listening, and besides, I prefer to stay away from violence. It always makes my hands all rough."

"First, tell me who you are."

"I already did, honey." She turns a finger on herself. "Danny. Danny Lecker. Are you going to introduce me to your friends, Rance baby?"

By now, Doc Elizabeth, forming a hard scowl, and Grady, with a bit of head-scratching, have gathered behind me. I introduce the three of them in order, starting with Parrish. Danny beams at my buds, but the doc only gets a polite nod. I wonder what that's about.

"So, are you really looking for your husband, or was that just a lie to get close to me?" I say, folding my arms.

"No, no, Rance honey—"

"Can you *not* with the honey, please?"

Danny drops her chin and pouts. If I wasn't already fully familiar with this tactic from Kayley, it might move me.

"Fine, you want to get down to business? Let's get down to business." Danny's cute act disappears, and her true self comes out. Now she's looking as canny and ruthless as I suspected her to be.

"What business do you have with us?" Doc Elizabeth challenges.

"I saw your ad on the local boards, and I want to hire your little team—if you're up for it."

"No thanks, we're not interested," Parrish says.

"Your friend already told me you would. Unless you're okay with doing nothing but saving little kitties from trees and helping old ladies cross the street? How much does that pay?"

Parrish has no answer. We have been making nothing but pocket change doing our little rescue missions. One lady even paid us with a cake. Sure, the locals are willing to support us to get our fledgling business off the ground, but other than the attacks, which turned out not even to be alien, our planet doesn't really have much going on.

"Well, what I'm willing to pay you is going to be more than enough to set up shop and get yourselves out there to make some real pay. All you have to do is find my husband and bring him back to me."

"It can't be that easy," Doc Elizabeth says.

"Of course it is," Danny replies. "I can even tell you where they're holding him. It's not even—"

"Holding him?" Grady catches the phrase just like I did.

"That's what I said, hot patootie. They're *holding* him at the Imperial prison for political prisoners on Exodus. It's the nicer part of the station. You've already proven you can break into a military facility, so this should be easy-peasy for you."

"We had a lot of help, and it wasn't under very tight security," I say. "No one was expecting an attack on that base. It was nowhere near the front...and by the way, how do you know that?"

"So, get help then." Danny ignores my question. While that's not common knowledge, it's also not a secret either. We did do an interview with a local media group where I, well, kinda bragged about it.

"What if we refuse?"

My Sergo buzzes suddenly and twitches. It's Kayley, calling right on time. I curse under my breath and pull the device from my pocket, but hesitate to answer it. I glance at Danny, then back to the call.

"Oh, who's that?" Danny asks, lifting herself up on the tips of her boots to sneak a peek at my Sergo. "Don't tell me. It's time for your call with your girlfriend. Aren't you going to answer it? It's not nice to keep a girl waiting."

I mutter something and turn my back on Danny to answer the call. As I hit the answer button, it hits me that Danny not only knew it was Kayley, but that we call each other at the same time every night. If this woman knows that, what else does she know? I get a chill down my spine, and its effect must be all over my face because when Kayley comes on, her sunshine smile dims significantly.

"Rance, everything okay? Are you sick?"

"I'm fine. I'm here with Parrish, Grady, and Elizabeth. We're just finishing up a meeting."

"Oh? What about?" Before I can respond, Kayley demands that I show her the others, which I do. All of them take their turns with the pleasantries and a quick chat.

"Not going to introduce me?" Danny asks.

"No."

"Rance, is someone else there?"

"Yes! Hi, Kayley! How are you? Loved your speech yesterday!" Danny hops up and down and waves as if Kayley can see around the entire space instead of her Sergo-lens-limited viewing angle.

She can hear everything, though.

"Who's that?" Kayley asks with eyebrows raised. I sigh and tilt the screen so she can see, knowing that this will lead to a torrent of questions.

Danny twinkles her fingers and does her sweetness routine when Kayley catches sight of her. My girlfriend tries to be cordial but is frowning at the same time. Danny takes notice and smirks, to which Kayley seems to have no idea how to respond. I need to disengage the two of them before it gets ugly.

"Okay, so, KayKay, let me finish here, and I'll call you back, okay?"

"Not too long. We're getting picked up to go to the amphitheater soon."

When I turn back to Danny, she's got her arms clasped behind her and is grinning ear to ear while rocking back and forth on her feet.

"I bet you really care about her, don't you, Rance?"

"Of course."

"I bet you'd do anything for her, wouldn't you?"

"Absolutely." My eyes narrow, wondering what she's getting at.

"Well then, you take me up on this job, and with the kind of money I'm willing to pay, you *could* do anything for her."

"Such as?"

"Oh, honey, have some imagination!"

"Sorry, I would, but I'm not feeling well. Someone jammed a capsule down my throat, and I got sick."

"Come on now, tell me you didn't enjoy that."

I roll my eyes at her, but I have a feeling that won't be enough to put this woman off. I made a mistake yesterday telling her we could help. We've already got to help the Teddys, and that might take up most of our time. Even so, this could be big money! Having funds would allow us to do all sorts of things, like some real advertising. The sooner we get up and running, the better I will feel about my own personal situation as it relates to my girlfriend.

"So, my little love bugs, what's your answer? And remember, if you say nothing, you're as good as saying yes, so just say yes, and I will love you forever."

"Please don't," Parrish says.

"So, then, I think that's a yes from all of you! Great! I'll be sending you the info on Exodus shortly."

Danny signs off before I can contradict her. I sigh. We may have to go through this after all. It's not like I can just Sergo her back. There's no personal code attached to a pill that I vomited. What's becoming painfully clear is that if we're going to pull off two jobs at once, we're going to need the whole team.

"Oh, dude, what are we going to do?" Grady asks.

"Yes, Rance, best you come up with something," Doc Elizabeth says. "That woman seemed fairly insistent that you help her."

I pull my Sergo out and call Kayley back. She answers almost immediately, as if she was doing nothing other than waiting for my call. That's the dream I'm going with, anyway. It's helping me not to erupt into a fiery ball at the moment.

"Kayley, we're coming to see you," I say.

Chapter Six

AFTON SAUNTERS IN, NOT pausing a moment to check for us. That's because we're always in the same spot. Or we were until Wylde Thyme was blown up and rebuilt to better specs. The quick-serve counter used to be right by the entrance, but now it sits on the other side of the bar. They chopped that in half to make way for the new, larger kitchen.

Other than that, it looks the same: mirrors all around, large plants in large planters in the sunniest corners and vines everywhere else, wood and polished chrome furniture in the spaces in between. It's like we've stepped inside a large plant, and that seems to be the exact impression the owners wanted to give.

"Long time, boys, what's the special occasion?" Afton says, clapping her hands on my shoulders and Parrish's, then grabbing Grady on the sides of his head and placing a sloppy kiss on the top of his head. He whines and squirms, but Afton is gone before he can even turn around.

"We've got a gig!" I say, hoping to get right down to business.

"Actually two," Parrish corrects. "Well, maybe two."

"So." Afton takes a stool next to Parrish on my right side. "You can't do it without my amazing skills, is that it?"

I grin and start to answer, but there's a commotion coming from the bar. Two men whistle and applaud as the bartender turns on the vid screen. A second later, my heart melts as Kayley appears. She's dressed in a subdued government uniform, but her signature smile is its own source of luminance. There's no doubt in my mind—Kayley belongs in front of the camera lens. It's like she could merely raise her arms and wish for whatever she wanted, and the world would follow her command. That's exactly why the government chose, and only her, for the tour. She's like a light in the darkness.

As much as I believe she deserves the spotlight, I don't watch her speeches. They just remind me of how much I miss her, and that sets me in a dark mood until I can speak to her after her presentation. Those two guys cheering for her at the bar are just two of the millions of her adoring fans. Sure, the rest of us would get a pat on the back and a "good job" or two if we reminded them of who we were, but that's just adding another boulder on my shoulders while I try to swim in the river that is Kayley's fame.

Good thing I have friends that will throw me a flotation device when they see me sinking.

"Just remember," Parrish whispers in my ear, "that's the girl who's only got eyes for you."

And then there's Afton, who'll shove my head under before pulling me out and demanding I thank her for it.

"Don't you have a lot to live up to, huh, buddy?" Afton jabs a finger into my shoulder. "Good thing you've got the best friends around."

"Plus some who aren't even human," Grady reminds me. "Which is why we're here...isn't it?"

"And here I thought you guys just missed me."

"We do!" Parrish says.

"Nice save, Parry." Afton leans forward on the counter. "So, what's this about a gig? From Grady's comment, it's got something to do with the Teddys?"

I tell her about our strange meeting with the Teddys, how they think someone is after their technology, and the mysterious Mr. Lanky who could be a part of all of it. Afton listens as she chews on her nail, interested but not at all concerned.

"Don't forget to tell her about Danny," Parrish says. "That's important too."

"Danny?" Afton shrugs. "I don't know any guy named Danny."

"You'd never mistake her for a dude," Grady says, waving the counter steward over. For someone who never seems to gain any weight, Grady is often as focused on food as Afton or Parrish. Still, it's a good call. The steward arrives and takes our order. He's new, so we each have to explain our specific orders, hoping he remembers them for the future. Of course, he could just save our account in the system like the last guy did.

"So, a chick," Afton says, "intriguing. Is she sexy?"

"That's not important," I growl. "The fact is that she could be offering us a lot of money."

"It must be to you. Your cheeks are going all strawberry. So what's the 'could' part about it?"

"She's trouble, guaranteed," Grady says.

I elaborate on Grady's statement while Afton frowns and then wrinkles her nose when I reach the point where the communications capsule decided it was time to remove itself from my stomach.

"First of all, eww," Afton says. "Second, how did it get in there in the first place?"

I freeze and throw Parrish and Grady a glance, trying not to make it obvious that I'm caught in a serious conundrum. Where Kayley might hear my story out in full and then scold me for being stupid, Afton will certainly bash me first and ask questions after.

"We think she must have put it in his food somehow," Parrish says.

I let out a silent sigh and thank the Goddesses twice over for a friend like Parrish. We're usually pretty straightforward with each other when it comes to the truth. This seems like a reasonable time to tell a small little lie.

"Rance, just how out of it do you have to be to not see some well-endowed lady try to dump a bright white capsule into your bowl of noodles?" Afton snorts and shakes her head.

I barely hear her. My brain acknowledges her voice and the fact that she wants my attention, but I'm focusing on the vid screen, where my girlfriend is winding up her speech. I've watched them once or twice, but they're basically the same thing—inspirational drivel the government wants her to say. It's not the words that are captivating. It's how she delivers them.

"And so, my fellow Angelicans, before I end my time here with you, I want to leave you with one final thought. But before I do that, I would like to humbly thank you, from the bottom of my heart, for all of your care and

support tonight. That you've chosen to spend your evening here, with the other members of the tour and me, says much more about you than it does about us. It means you truly love this planet and want to see us prosper as one of the Empire's greatest communities."

Kayley added in that last bit. Right at the moment she says it, they turn the cameras on the audience. So many are affected by Kayley's message. It's as if everyone in the crowd takes a collective gasp. I, too, am taken in by her words, but for a different reason. That girl—no, that amazing and wonderful woman—is dating me! Someone should pinch me so I can really know I'm not just dreaming this.

Someone does.

"Ouch! Hey!" I glare at Afton, who's grinning at me.

"Serves you right for going all moony-eyed on us. Besides, I just did you a favor." Afton points to the plate of veggie fries in front of me. "Parrish was about to steal half of them."

I nod my thanks to her, but I find my eyes drifting back up to the vid screen.

"So, can we get back to the important conversation we were having before your brain melted?" Afton asks, raising her voice enough to stop me from going into another Kaydream.

"Sorry, yeah." I rub the spot on my face where Afton tried to rip a chunk of my skin off. "So, the dilemma that we are havingthat we need the whole team for—is that we've got two important gigs we need to cover. How we juggle both at the same time is going to be the question."

"I thought the question was whether we ignore the flirty lady or not," Grady says.

"We are not ignoring her, dude," I reply. "She's offering money. Big money."

"How much, exactly?" Afton asks, reaching around me to snatch a handful of fries.

"Well, she didn't mention the amount, but she's insisted a few times that she is willing to pay."

"Smells fishy. Are you sure she's legit?"

"She went through the trouble of shoving a capsule down my throat."

Afton narrows her eyes at me, and I realize my poor choice of words.

"I thought you said she snuck it into your noodles?"

"Parrish said that. I didn't."

"And I only said we think that's how she did it," Parrish adds.

"Well, how else could she have done it?"

None of my male buds want to answer that. Thank the Goddesses for some mercy. And good friends.

"We're getting off-topic," I say, attempting to channel some of my girlfriend's voice into my own. "We're talking about how we get both gigs to run smoothly. I suggest splitting up, at least initially."

"I don't know, dude," Grady says. "We may be burning a lot of fuel on a gig that doesn't offer any real reward. It might not even be real."

"Not real?" If I could only mention how real Danny's tongue in my mouth felt, Grady might not be so doubtful.

"Grady's right, though," Parrish says. I raise an eyebrow at him. "The Teddys are our friends, and remember, Rance, if it wasn't for them, you might still be in prison."

He had to bring that up, didn't he? I guess I deserved it.

"It's not like I'm saying no to the Teddys, guys. I totally want to help them. It's just that..."

"Just that what?" Afton asks, hands on her hips. "No, seriously, what?"

I sigh. How do I explain the complexity of how I don't feel like I'm stacking up as Kayley's boyfriend in a way that my buds take me seriously? I bet they're exhausted hearing me whine about that all the time. I can't help it. I just want the best for Kayley, and that includes me, maybe not as her equal, but at least someone she doesn't have to look down to see all the time.

"No answer is the default for letting us decide for you," Afton says, "and this time, I'm taking the boys' side. Sorry, but Teddys first. Then if this lady drops some real numbers on us, we talk to her again."

"I don't know." I shake my head. "She's not that easy to get rid of, Afton. She's very insistent on having her way."

"Yeah, well, no lady is having her way with you, just because she insists on..." Afton frowns. "Why are you going all strawberry again?"

"Never mind," I reply quickly. "Just forget it. You guys win. We help the Teddys first."

Afton glares and takes a step closer. I try to remain as neutral as I can. One wrong move and I get the executioner's block. Afton is likely thinking right now that I'm trying to hide something from Kayley, which isn't the issue. I'm just agreeing with my buds to get them off my back. If I have to, Kayley and I will go find Danny's husband by ourselves. If I can convince Kayley to help, that is.

"Remember, buddy," she says, poking a finger into my chest. "She's my friend too, and I'm watching you."

"Well then." I smile. It's a legit smile. "You'll like what I'm going to suggest next."

"What?"

"That we hop on the Teddy shuttle and go get Kayley. We're going to need her for this." We already told Kayley that we're coming to get her, but anyway, this is kind of the same thing.

"We can do that." Afton nods and turns to go back to her seat, and I swivel around on mine, satisfied with the outcome of our conversation. But now, something else is seriously wrong.

"Guys...what happened to my fries?"

The roar of applause hits me like a detonation as we step out of the shuttle, just behind the temporary stage. As I come off the ramp, I catch the tips of Kayley's fingers waving to her admirers—all twenty-five thousand of them. Even with that considerable number of competitors, I'm undeterred. It's been six months, and now I get to hold her in my arms for real.

As soon as she gets through the mass of reporters and fans, that is. I can't believe what some of these people bring to her, items that are somehow enhanced when she puts her signature stamp on them. One parent even holds his baby daughter out to be gently branded. Kayley, the consummate celebrity, doesn't miss a beat as she inks the baby's shoulder and kisses her forehead.

Sergeant Cortell, who is nowhere near as surrounded as Kayley, breaks through the crowd and heads straight for us, with Captain Teddy right behind him.

"Hey! You guys made it!" he says, grabbing us each by the shoulders. "So great to see you all!"

It is good to see him. He was right in the thick of everything when we lost his boss, Colonel Nelson, in our first attempt to secure the evidence to take down Minister Crowley. Since then, the Sergeant has committed himself to getting rid of all the bad seeds in the Imperial government. I'm glad he's on our side.

"Yeah," I reply with a smile, "thanks for the last-minute clearance for the landing. The nearest landing pad is almost an hour from here. We would never have made the end of her speech."

"Kayley would have waited, I'm sure. You wouldn't believe how excited she was that all of you were coming." The Sergeant chuckles. "She almost repeated the same line when we saw the shuttle pass overhead."

"Felicitations," Captain Teddy—leader of the first Teddy ship we ever set foot on—says and heads right up the ramp and into the shuttle. I guess he really misses his own people. I can't blame him—I get tired around humans too.

"Guys!" Kayley shouts and charges us, her arms wide. "I can't believe it!"

She squeezes together with Parrish and Afton in a tight embrace, with Parrish's arms wrapping around the others. Kayley giggles and wriggles her way out between the two of them. Next is Grady, who feigns terror as Kayley grabs his face and plants kisses all over it. I smile at all the hijinks, my heart beating faster with every moment because I know what's coming next.

"Hey you." Kayley smiles slyly at me as she slides her arms around my neck. What comes next is six months of pure bliss packed into five seconds of the most groundbreaking kiss Kayley and I have ever shared. Better than our first, even. She's so warm, and her aroma that hits my nose—one part perfume and one part Kayley—nearly makes me faint. Kayley chuckles lightly and playfully smacks my cheek to return me to the planet.

"I missed you so much, KayKay. I—"

Kayley puts a finger on my lips and gives me her signature smile, keeping her eyes connected with mine. As she gazes at me, her smile flattens out, and an eyebrow rises as she turns to scan the others.

"So, you want to tell me what's going on? Why did you guys decide to hijack the Teddy shuttle and fly across the planet to come see me? Not that I'm not happy to see you, but I'm coming home in just a few weeks, anyway. Is everything okay?"

"Kayley, so much has happened." I take a breath to stop myself from exploding with every word that I need to say to her and nod to the Teddy shuttle. "But we should talk inside."

She fixes her gaze back on me, chewing the inside of her cheek. Her thumb rubs against the back of my hand. I know I'm making her worried, but it's not like someone died. We've got a mission, and that's a good thing. I just wonder why I don't feel so confident about how she's going to react.

All of us pile back into the shuttle and take seats in the cabin, with Kayley and I sharing a corner so we can look at each other. Captain Teddy and Original Teddy come from the cockpit and join us, both deciding that the floor is more comfortable for them while all the humans find edges of things to perch on.

"Okay, now that you've successfully scared me, why don't you explain what this is all about?"

"Well, it's about the Teddys, mostly," I reply.

"And a chick that's got the hots for Rance," Afton adds.

Kayley turns to Afton, blinking.

"Hey, let's not overwhelm her," Parrish says, stepping in. "Let's start at the beginning."

"KayKay," I say, "the Teddys need our help. They think someone's after their tech to use for bad reasons."

"Okay...explain bad reasons."

"Well—"

Before I can continue, Grady lifts a hand to stop me. "Think of it this way. What would someone or some group do with the ability to blink through space, showing up anywhere they wanted in the Empire?"

"Right." Kayley nods with uneasy haste. "That's bad."

"This blink tech can send ships or people, right?" Sergeant Cortell asks.

"Not people by themselves, yet," Grady says, "but ships, armored vehicles...bombs."

The sergeant puts on a grim face, which is mirrored by everyone else in the room. After we took down Minister Crowley, we discussed this possibility amongst ourselves. But like most things that don't require our immediate attention, we tossed it away in the "never going to happen" file. We should have given it the attention it needed then.

"So, have you identified a person or group that's actively looking to steal Teddy tech? How would they even go about that, anyway?"

"Hacking into their systems is unlikely, even though we've done the reverse," Grady says.

"True," the sergeant adds. "We had an in-depth knowledge of the systems we were hacking into...the colonel did, that is. There's no equivalent on our side, and I'm in a position to know."

"I think whoever it is would want to get their hands on an actual piece of equipment." Grady's eyes dart around the cabin. "Like this shuttle...or, even try to kidnap a Teddy."

"We know that wouldn't work," I say. "The Teddys could just locate their missing friend in an instant."

"But that wouldn't stop the person from trying to get information from that Teddy." Kayley presses her lips together. "They might even try torture."

"Right, so the Teddys have asked us to help find the menace, I mean, the person or people who are after them."

"Any leads?"

"Not yet, but there was some government stooge poking around the other day. Parrish and I tried to follow him, but he somehow gave us the slip."

Kayley drops her gaze, thoughtful for a moment. I watch her, hopeful that she'll come to the same conclusion I did and put her tour on hold to come and help us. She can even take charge if she wants. I've got no issues with that. This is a serious enough reason for her to come back with us.

"Okay, it seems like you guys have it well under control." Kayley lets out a sigh. "Thanks for telling me, but you really didn't have to come all the way here to do it. I know we're worried about secure lines of communication and all that, but we could have figured something out."

Grady slumps, and Afton pushes a finger into her cheek. They've got my feeling down exactly—we really need her help. Our team needs its leader.

"No, KayKay," I say. "We didn't come here just to tell you. We want you to come back with us."

"Go back with you?" Kayley sits up, shaking her head. "No, I can't go back. I've twelve more cities to complete before we end up in Yeomanry for the final event. You guys can handle this without me."

"If you're worried about letting the Prime Minister down, I'm sure he'll understand if you give him the reason. This is way more important than giving speeches, anyway."

Kayley pulls her hand back from mine and folds her arms. As she stares at me, her eyes take on a hard edge, and that's when I realize my mistake. That was the absolute wrong thing to say at the exact wrong time.

"Why don't you tell me about this other problem, then?"

"Which other one?"

"She means the one about the wo—"

Afton claps a hand over Grady's mouth and pulls him away from us. I catch her eyes for a moment, wondering why she's stopping him. Kayley does too, but a moment later she turns back to me.

"Is this the woman you were talking to when I called the other day?"

I nod.

"And what's so special about her?"

This is like walking in a minefield where even the path you've cleared can suddenly grow mines again without a hint that they're there. I've already said the total wrong thing once, which is causing this current intensity from Kayley aimed right between my eyes. I could just cut my losses right now and tell her that Danny Lecker is old news, like my buds are expecting me to. But then we'd lose that opportunity and the potential payout that comes with it.

No, I need to think positively here. The others might not want to bother with Danny, but if I can get Kayley on my side, then I'll be on the right track again, headed towards fame and fortune, and most importantly, a girlfriend I deserve.

Of course, this could all unravel right in my face, and everything I hope for crashes down on me. Ah well. Here goes nothing.

I explain about Danny, leaving out the points where she got too close and things were shoved down my throat with her tongue. That would capsize this entire boat ride in an instant.

"I don't know, Rance," Kayley says after hearing my explanation. "This woman sounds dangerous. She *looks* dangerous. I saw her on the AIC projection. She's a con, no doubt about it. She's just trying to take advantage of you because you were nice to her. I doubt she even has any money, and this *husband* of hers is probably just her partner in crime who got caught."

"I thought that too," Grady says, returning, "but after I thought about it, she's more sophisticated, tech-wise, than she seems at first. That AIC device isn't easy to get, and she risked damaging it by shoving it down Rance's throat so she could talk to us after she escaped from the government thugs."

Uh-oh.

There's a bit of a pause from Kayley as she digests what Grady just said. I really hope she doesn't connect any dots. None of us want to get into the details of how that happened, exactly.

"She attacked Rance?" Kayley asks. "What happened?"

No one answers her.

"Rance." Kayley shakes me. "Rance, what happened? Were you hurt?"

"No, I'm fine," I answer.

"She tricked him into swallowing it," Parrish says, glancing at me. "I saw the whole thing. But she didn't hurt him. Not at all."

"Are you sure?" Kayley rubs my shoulder.

I give her a smile and sit up straight. A quick glance at my buds tells me they're backing my play, whatever that might be, and for whatever reason—something we may have to discuss later so we can get everyone on the same page. I think that for the moment, if I can get Kayley to come back with us, they won't care how it happens. And I would be well positioned to get what I want.

"Yeah, but..." I drop my head and gaze at the floor in front of me. "This is a tough one, Kayley. I don't think she's going to go away so easily, and I don't think she's going to take no for an answer. That could seriously jeopardize our chances of solving the Teddys' problem."

"Harry," Kayley says, looking at the sergeant. "Do you think you can get some of your people on this?"

"Well"—he thinks for a moment—"as much as I'd like to, I don't think that's going to happen. This is really a situation for the local constabulary. It's not a military matter, and if I pull resources from another mission, someone will get suspicious. That could mess up their investigation with the Teddys."

Kayley looks at me with a somewhat despondent expression. I try to look sympathetic, which isn't hard—I am. We still need her, and I'll bet she's missing us just enough to say yes.

"Okay." Kayley takes in a deep breath. "How about this? Since you need me so badly, I'll ask for a two-week postponement, and then we can take care of this. But after that, I have to finish what I committed to doing." Kayley looks around at all of us. "You guys may not realize this, but what I've done for this planet is a big deal. Angelcanis needed a morale boost, and it's really improved the Teddys' reputation too, right, Captain?"

"That is accurate. Teddy is welcome," Captain Teddy replies.

"So." Kayley takes my hand and squeezes it. "I'm here for you guys, but then I need to take care of Angelcanis. Deal?"

I take her hand in both of mine and kiss it. It's a deal, alright.

Chapter Seven

THE ROAR OF APPLAUSE hits me like a detonation as we step out of the shuttle, just behind the temporary stage. As I come off the ramp, I catch the tips of Kayley's fingers waving to her admirers—all twenty-five thousand of them. Even with that considerable number of competitors, I'm undeterred. It's been six months, and now I get to hold her in my arms for real.

As soon as she gets through the mass of reporters and fans, that is. I can't believe what some of these people bring to her, items that are somehow enhanced when she puts her signature stamp on them. One parent even holds his baby daughter out to be gently branded. Kayley, the consummate celebrity, doesn't miss a beat as she inks the baby's shoulder and kisses her forehead.

Sergeant Cortell, who is nowhere near as surrounded as Kayley, breaks through the crowd and heads straight for us, with Captain Teddy right behind him.

"Hey! You guys made it!" he says, grabbing us each by the shoulders. "So great to see you all!"

It is good to see him. He was right in the thick of everything when we lost his boss, Colonel Nelson, in our first attempt to secure the evidence to take down Minister Crowley. Since then, the Sergeant has committed himself to getting rid of all the bad seeds in the Imperial government. I'm glad he's on our side.

"Yeah," I reply with a smile, "thanks for the last-minute clearance for the landing. The nearest landing pad is almost an hour from here. We would never have made the end of her speech."

"Kayley would have waited, I'm sure. You wouldn't believe how excited she was that all of you were coming." The Sergeant chuckles. "She almost repeated the same line when we saw the shuttle pass overhead."

"Felicitations," Captain Teddy—leader of the first Teddy ship we ever set foot on—says and heads right up the ramp and into the shuttle. I guess he really misses his own people. I can't blame him—I get tired around humans too.

"Guys!" Kayley shouts and charges us, her arms wide. "I can't believe it!"

She squeezes together with Parrish and Afton in a tight embrace, with Parrish's arms wrapping around the others. Kayley giggles and wriggles her way out between the two of them. Next is Grady, who feigns terror as Kayley grabs his face and plants kisses all over it. I smile at all the hijinks, my heart beating faster with every moment because I know what's coming next.

"Hey you." Kayley smiles slyly at me as she slides her arms around my neck. What comes next is six months of pure bliss packed into five seconds of the most groundbreaking kiss Kayley and I have ever shared. Better than our first, even. She's so warm, and her aroma that hits my nose—one part perfume and one part Kayley—nearly makes me faint. Kayley chuckles lightly and playfully smacks my cheek to return me to the planet.

"I missed you so much, KayKay. I—"

Kayley puts a finger on my lips and gives me her signature smile, keeping her eyes connected with mine. As she gazes at me, her smile flattens out, and an eyebrow rises as she turns to scan the others.

"So, you want to tell me what's going on? Why did you guys decide to hijack the Teddy shuttle and fly across the planet to come see me? Not that I'm not happy to see you, but I'm coming home in just a few weeks, anyway. Is everything okay?"

"Kayley, so much has happened." I take a breath to stop myself from exploding with every word that I need to say to her and nod to the Teddy shuttle. "But we should talk inside."

She fixes her gaze back on me, chewing the inside of her cheek. Her thumb rubs against the back of my hand. I know I'm making her worried, but it's not like someone died. We've got a mission, and that's a good thing. I just wonder why I don't feel so confident about how she's going to react.

All of us pile back into the shuttle and take seats in the cabin, with Kayley and I sharing a corner so we can look at each other. Captain Teddy and Original Teddy come from the cockpit and join us, both deciding that the floor is more comfortable for them while all the humans find edges of things to perch on.

"Okay, now that you've successfully scared me, why don't you explain what this is all about?"

"Well, it's about the Teddys, mostly," I reply.

"And a chick that's got the hots for Rance," Afton adds.

Kayley turns to Afton, blinking.

"Hey, let's not overwhelm her," Parrish says, stepping in. "Let's start at the beginning."

"KayKay," I say, "the Teddys need our help. They think someone's after their tech to use for bad reasons."

"Okay...explain bad reasons."

"Well—"

Before I can continue, Grady lifts a hand to stop me. "Think of it this way. What would someone or some group do with the ability to blink through space, showing up anywhere they wanted in the Empire?"

"Right." Kayley nods with uneasy haste. "That's bad."

"This blink tech can send ships or people, right?" Sergeant Cortell asks.

"Not people by themselves, yet," Grady says, "but ships, armored vehicles...bombs."

The sergeant puts on a grim face, which is mirrored by everyone else in the room. After we took down Minister Crowley, we discussed this possibility amongst ourselves. But like most things that don't require our immediate attention, we tossed it away in the "never going to happen" file. We should have given it the attention it needed then.

"So, have you identified a person or group that's actively looking to steal Teddy tech? How would they even go about that, anyway?"

"Hacking into their systems is unlikely, even though we've done the reverse," Grady says.

"True," the sergeant adds. "We had an in-depth knowledge of the systems we were hacking into…the colonel did, that is. There's no equivalent on our side, and I'm in a position to know."

"I think whoever it is would want to get their hands on an actual piece of equipment." Grady's eyes dart around the cabin. "Like this shuttle…or, even try to kidnap a Teddy."

"We know that wouldn't work," I say. "The Teddys could just locate their missing friend in an instant."

"But that wouldn't stop the person from trying to get information from that Teddy." Kayley presses her lips together. "They might even try torture."

"Right, so the Teddys have asked us to help find the menace, I mean, the person or people who are after them."

"Any leads?"

"Not yet, but there was some government stooge poking around the other day. Parrish and I tried to follow him, but he somehow gave us the slip."

Kayley drops her gaze, thoughtful for a moment. I watch her, hopeful that she'll come to the same conclusion I did and put her tour on hold to come and help us. She can even take charge if she wants. I've got no issues with that. This is a serious enough reason for her to come back with us.

"Okay, it seems like you guys have it well under control." Kayley lets out a sigh. "Thanks for telling me, but you really didn't have to come all the way here to do it. I know we're worried about secure lines of communication and all that, but we could have figured something out."

Grady slumps, and Afton pushes a finger into her cheek. They've got my feeling down exactly—we really need her help. Our team needs its leader.

"No, KayKay," I say. "We didn't come here just to tell you. We want you to come back with us."

"Go back with you?" Kayley sits up, shaking her head. "No, I can't go back. I've twelve more cities to complete before we end up in Yeomanry for the final event. You guys can handle this without me."

"If you're worried about letting the Prime Minister down, I'm sure he'll understand if you give him the reason. This is way more important than giving speeches, anyway."

Kayley pulls her hand back from mine and folds her arms. As she stares at me, her eyes take on a hard edge, and that's when I realize my mistake. That was the absolute wrong thing to say at the exact wrong time.

"Why don't you tell me about this other problem, then?"

"Which other one?"

"She means the one about the wo—"

Afton claps a hand over Grady's mouth and pulls him away from us. I catch her eyes for a moment, wondering why she's stopping him. Kayley does too, but a moment later she turns back to me.

"Is this the woman you were talking to when I called the other day?"

I nod.

"And what's so special about her?"

This is like walking in a minefield where even the path you've cleared can suddenly grow mines again without a hint that they're there. I've already said the total wrong thing once, which is causing this current intensity from Kayley aimed right between my eyes. I could just cut my losses right now and tell her that Danny Lecker is old news, like my buds are expecting me to. But then we'd lose that opportunity and the potential payout that comes with it.

No, I need to think positively here. The others might not want to bother with Danny, but if I can get Kayley on my side, then I'll be on the right track again, headed towards fame and fortune, and most importantly, a girlfriend I deserve.

Of course, this could all unravel right in my face, and everything I hope for crashes down on me. Ah well. Here goes nothing.

I explain about Danny, leaving out the points where she got too close and things were shoved down my throat with her tongue. That would capsize this entire boat ride in an instant.

"I don't know, Rance," Kayley says after hearing my explanation. "This woman sounds dangerous. She *looks* dangerous. I saw her on the AIC projection. She's a con, no doubt about it. She's just trying to take advantage of you because you were nice to her. I doubt she even has any money, and this *husband* of hers is probably just her partner in crime who got caught."

"I thought that too," Grady says, returning, "but after I thought about it, she's more sophisticated, tech-wise, than she seems at first. That AIC device isn't easy to get, and she risked damaging it by shoving it down Rance's throat so she could talk to us after she escaped from the government thugs."

Uh-oh.

There's a bit of a pause from Kayley as she digests what Grady just said. I really hope she doesn't connect any dots. None of us want to get into the details of how that happened, exactly.

"She attacked Rance?" Kayley asks. "What happened?"

No one answers her.

"Rance." Kayley shakes me. "Rance, what happened? Were you hurt?"

"No, I'm fine," I answer.

"She tricked him into swallowing it," Parrish says, glancing at me. "I saw the whole thing. But she didn't hurt him. Not at all."

"Are you sure?" Kayley rubs my shoulder.

I give her a smile and sit up straight. A quick glance at my buds tells me they're backing my play, whatever that might be, and for whatever reason—something we may have to discuss later so we can get everyone on the same page. I think that for the moment, if I can get Kayley to come back with us, they won't care how it happens. And I would be well positioned to get what I want.

"Yeah, but..." I drop my head and gaze at the floor in front of me. "This is a tough one, Kayley. I don't think she's going to go away so easily, and I don't think she's going to take no for an answer. That could seriously jeopardize our chances of solving the Teddys' problem."

"Harry," Kayley says, looking at the sergeant. "Do you think you can get some of your people on this?"

"Well"—he thinks for a moment—"as much as I'd like to, I don't think that's going to happen. This is really a situation for the local constabulary. It's not a military matter, and if I pull resources from another mission, someone will get suspicious. That could mess up their investigation with the Teddys."

Kayley looks at me with a somewhat despondent expression. I try to look sympathetic, which isn't hard—I am. We still need her, and

I'll bet she's missing us just enough to say yes.

"Okay." Kayley takes in a deep breath. "How about this? Since you need me so badly, I'll ask for a two-week postponement, and then we can take care of this. But after that, I have to finish what I committed to doing." Kayley looks around at all of us. "You guys may not realize this, but what I've done for this planet is a big deal. Angelcanis needed a morale boost, and it's really improved the Teddys' reputation too, right, Captain?"

"That is accurate. Teddy is welcome," Captain Teddy replies.

"So." Kayley takes my hand and squeezes it. "I'm here for you guys, but then I need to take care of Angelcanis. Deal?"

I take her hand in both of mine and kiss it. It's a deal, alright.

Chapter Eight

AFTER WE GET BACK home, the first thing we do is ditch our friends and go for a walk, just Kayley and me. Sure, we're beat from all the convincing we had to do to get Kayley's government agent to agree to a two-week pause. We should have started with "a matter of Commonwealth security." Then it would have taken us five minutes to get the agent to agree. Instead, I tried to hide the issue, and that only made the woman suspicious. Thank the Goddesses Kayley stepped in.

All that's in the past now, and I'm happy to live in the moment. We stroll, my hand in Kayley's, headed to our favorite spot in the park. Our little grotto, where no one else will bother us. I might even tell Kayley those three little words, which are at once so simple to say, but take so much effort to get out. Even when I have no doubt in my mind that I love her. I just want the moment to be special the first time I say it.

"Oh, you bad boy!" a familiar voice interrupts. We spin around, and all my senses explode in alarm. "You are a very, very bad boy, Rance! I'm really upset with you!"

There, in a full-powered armored suit, is Danny Lecker. She is absolutely mad, and what's worse, she's holding a very big gun.

"That's her, isn't it?" Kayley says in a low voice, though I'm not sure why she does. Danny is glaring at us with eyes like a nuclear furnace. She can see and hear every word we say.

"Yeah, that's her," I mutter in reply.

"Why haven't you started looking for my husband?" Danny shouts. "I sent you all the information! I expected you to have at least gotten your plan together...didn't you get my message?"

"Er." I glance at Kayley and scratch my head. "Yeah, sorry, haven't been checking my messages. We've been preoccupied. Um, is there some reason you're dressed like that?"

"Preoccupied? Oh, sorry, you little lovebirds sharing a moment?" Danny asks, powering up her rifle. "You know, that's all I'm asking for! Is it really too much to ask?"

The whine of the weapon draws attention, and everyone near the park entrance makes a sharp turn away and walks as fast as they can. Danny doesn't notice. Either that or she doesn't care. Her eyes are laser-focused on Kayley and me as she takes a few steps closer.

"Well?"

"Well, what?" Kayley responds in a sharp tone. Danny pauses and frowns.

"Well, answer my question!"

"Everyone is entitled to be with the one they love," Kayley replies, her voice flat.

"So glad you agree! Now, honey, if you would." Danny motions with her gun. "Come get your pretty little self over here so I can fire on your boyfriend."

"No," Kayley replies. Danny's mouth drops open.

"What do you mean, no? You do see the big weapon here, honey, don't you?"

"I do, but I'm not going to do as you say. You'll just have to shoot me too."

"And if you shoot her," I add, "then I'm definitely not helping you."

"Dammit!" Danny stomps her foot, and it puts a big crack in the concrete as the gate above our heads shakes. "Why do the two of you have to be so cute together?"

Kayley and I share a look. Is she really angry at us for being a cute couple? I didn't even realize we qualified for such a category. No one has ever said that to us before. Does that mean she's jealous of our relationship? Jealous enough to blow us both to high heaven?

"Okay, well," Danny says, raising her gun at us, "if that's how it's going to be—"

"Put your weapon down!" Four constables dash towards us. They've got guns of their own, and they're leveling them at Danny. I do hope they realize how seriously outgunned they are.

"Do you mind?" Danny shouts over her shoulder. "This is a private conversation!"

"Drop the gun and surrender!"

This is going to turn into a stand-off. Or it won't, and there's going to be a bunch of bullets and energy bolts flying in a moment. Either way, we don't want to be here when it happens. I tilt my head towards the short steps leading down to our grotto. Kayley nods in agreement, and we inch our way towards them.

"Oh, no, no, no, no, *no!*" Danny spins on us. "We are *not* done talking!"

That's when the soldiers open up with their weapons. I shove Kayley forward, and we tumble down the short flight of stairs and land hard on the concrete path. Kayley lets out a squeak, and I reply with an *oof* of my own.

We force a quick recovery and jump to our feet. The firefight continues above us, but we don't wait. I grab Kayley's hand and we race down the path together. The more distance we can put between us and that powered suit, the better.

It gets quiet, and I get nervous. Did she beat them, or did they manage to knock her out? I hope nobody got hurt. Danny included. I have no idea why that is—it would just bother me if she got hurt.

"On the left, up ahead!" Kayley says. I glance that way and get what she sees. There's a small shed, and the door is open. It's perfect. Hopefully. I remember what happened the last time I tried to hide in a shed—it didn't go so well.

We slip in and slide the door gently, so we don't give away our hiding spot. The inside is cramped and dark. If I were in here with anyone else, it might be awkward.

With some difficulty, Kayley wraps her arms around my body and snuggles into me. She even giggles a little.

"You know? We haven't been this close since..." Kayley pauses and tries to remember the moment. I, on the other hand, can't forget it.

"Since we were on an alien ship that was dangerously speeding out of control?"

"I don't think of it that way," Kayley said. "You said something really sweet to me then."

"I did?"

"You did. You know, this wouldn't be a bad time to say something sweet to me again."

"Shouldn't we keep silent so she doesn't hear us?"

"Rance, don't worry. Even if she's still alive, she won't find us in here."

I want to say something to her, but I wasn't expecting it to happen like this. I was picturing a much more relaxed and romantic moment, moonlight streaming down on us while I hold her hands and get lost in her eyes. I've got a few of the required elements, but it's not yet perfect.

A heavy thump shakes the entire shed and sends us both slamming into the wall. The jangling of tools swaying on hooks makes a cacophonous sound in this tiny space. Kayley matches my yelp, and we struggle to stay upright.

"Rance, honey! Where are you?" It's Danny, very much alive. "Come out come out, wherever you are!"

"You were saying?" I ask Kayley. She shushes me and covers my mouth.

The heavy stomps of Danny's power suit rumble the ground around us. With every step, another tool in the shed shakes from its holster and clatters to the ground. We stay as silent as we can, unmoving. Hopefully she'll give up looking and we can run home. And maybe hide out there for a year or two.

Danny's thunderous steps approach. I hear the whine of the motors in her suit—she must be right next to us. Kayley buries her face into my shoulder, and I squeeze her tighter.

I'm wondering where she got such a thing. Isn't it military issue? Who is this woman, anyway?

We stay frozen together, clutching one another as if letting go means certain death. It could, but for me, holding on to her like this is the simplest thing I've ever done. I could do it for eternity if required. Though, I should shower first.

The pounding steps die away, and we both let out a sigh. She's gone, or at least I think she is. We should think about making our own getaway.

"KayKay, let's get out of here."

"Good idea."

There's a clank and a ping as one of us, I think me, knocks into a tool and sends it down to the floor. Kayley stifles a cry, and we do our statue routine again and let the moments pass by. No hurry. We can wait it out.

Until we can't.

A tap comes on the door. It's no random noise—someone deliberately knocked. If we were dead silent before, we're now making a negative amount of sound. We hold our breath until neither of us can stand it any longer. I don't know which one of us gasps first, but the sound is obvious.

The shed door flies open, ripped free of its hinges by a power stronger than any human could muster. We're blinded by a spotlight that illuminates us in the flood of its glaring beam.

"This is the best you naughty little kids could do?" Danny says. "I mean, really. Did it not occur to you that I might have some enhanced optical ability on this machine?"

"Well, I think we were just kinda trying to not get shot, so I suggested—"

"No, Rance," Kayley interrupts, "I suggested this. You were behind me, remember? Or did you forget you pushed me down the stairs?"

"I was just trying to save your life, KayKay!" I whine, but then look her over. "Did you get hurt?"

"No, but you could have at least given me a warning."

"Hey, hey! Save the marital spat for later!" Danny interjects.

"You stay out of this!" Kayley hisses at her. Danny takes a step back, her eyes widening as she shakes her head. I can't believe it either. Doesn't Kayley remember the woman has a big scary weapon in her hands?

"Kayley, I really don't think you should..." My eyes dart towards the quickly recovering Danny. Her eyebrows begin to draw together as her weapon rises until the dangerous end points towards us.

"You are a really rude little girl. You know that?" Danny growls. "And you want to know what else? Your boyfriend is a terrible kisser! I think the two of you deserve each other!"

Kayley turns on me with eyes blazing. I can't look back, or she'll reduce me to ashes with the flames shooting from her eyes. It's much easier to look at Danny, though she's not much of a safer choice.

"Rance." Kayley's voice is low and intense. "What does she mean by that?"

"She's just a bit annoyed at us, KayKay, because we tried to hide from her. Though, to be fair, she did kinda force us to do it."

"Darling," Kayley continues, the edge of her voice getting sharper, "that's not what I'm asking."

"Oh, get over it," Danny says. "He couldn't resist me. No man can. Besides, I had to give him the AIC somehow. Delivery with my tongue was the best way."

"You couldn't have just handed it to me?" I ask, blinking at her.

"Where's the fun in that?"

Kayley turns on Danny, her cheeks turning the color of her hair, but Danny shoves her rifle in Kayley's face. Kayley pauses, but her glare keeps its sharpness.

"Now, back to business," Danny says. "When are you going to get my husband?"

"Who said we were going to do that?" Kayley shoots back.

"Girl!" Danny shouts, shaking her weapon. "*Big* gun in your face? Do you not see it?"

When Kayley doesn't answer, Danny twists around to fire her gun into a tree. There's a screech and a second later there's a hole straight through its trunk that I could probably fit through. Oh, boy.

"Danny," I say, raising my hands, "maybe we need a moment to discuss it? You know, just a quick chat with my girlfriend to consider our options?"

"No. You. Can. Not!"

"Then." I pause, catching some pink fuzzy movement from the corner of my eye. I smirk, and add, "shoot us with your *big* gun and set us free from your annoying chatter."

"Fine." Danny grins, taking aim. "Have it your way."

"Teddy! Popsicle!"

I turn and see Parrish and the gang racing towards us. A sharp static sound crackles, and the smell of burning electronics wafts through the air. Original Teddy jumps down from somewhere above and lands in front of the others. I have never been more ecstatic that our fuzzy little buddies can zap things. Now it's not strong enough to do more than stun, but I just found out that it works well on electronics.

"What the hell?" Danny looks down to see smoke pouring from her suit. Her face reddens and her forehead wrinkles. "What did you do to my suit?"

"Popsicle," Teddy replies, catching Danny's attention. She raises an eyebrow at our fuzzy friend.

"And what does that mean, exactly?"

"For us to know and for you to find out," Afton says, reaching a hand out to Kayley. My girlfriend goes to take it, but then turns back to Danny and steps right up to the woman.

"If you *ever* touch Rance again, you're going to have a big problem." With that, Kayley spins on her heel and saunters away. Afton smirks at her, then puts an arm around Kayley's shoulders.

Parrish waves me over, and with one last glance at the glaring Danny, we all head home. Parrish copies Afton and directs me up the path with his arm about me. Grady does the same on the other side.

"How did you guys know to come?" I ask, seriously glad to see them.

"Well, it was Afton's idea. She thought we were going to discuss the Teddy situation, but you guys took off so quickly. So, Afton wanted to play a joke on you by having Teddy popsicle the two of you, and then we were going to set you up in the pool or something. I don't know if she had thought it through fully."

"Well, thanks for being such jerks," I say with a sarcastic grin. "If it wasn't for you guys, we would have been in big trouble."

"Oh, sure!" Danny shouts after us. "You think this is over? I'm not even close to quitting! Do you want to know how much this suit cost me? A lot! Now you owe me! And I plan to collect! Let me tell you, Danny Lecker *always* gets what's she's after!"

Chapter Nine

MY HOUSE ISN'T FAR from the park, but instead of going there, Afton insists on heading to Grady's so we can do what she was expecting us to do and figure out a plan to investigate the Teddys' menace. She's, of course, correct in her expectation that we should be doing what we agreed to do. I know I was selfish when I begged Kayley to go for a walk with me. She readily agreed though, so I'm not the only guilty party here.

I had totally planned to confess my love for her and tell her all the things I wanted to do so I could be worthy of her, minus the part about Danny, of course. But that's out in the open now, and it doesn't look like that's going to be a viable case for us, anyway. The Teddys are now my main priority—and hope.

Good thing, then, that our first person of interest has decided to come to us.

"Hello there!" Mr. Lanky waves and increases his pace towards us. "Fancy seeing you again! How are we all this fine evening?"

If he's really a government agent, I would hope that he'd realize visitors to our town are never found on this side street. Then again, he might just be who he says he is. Best if we get to the bottom of it now.

"Oh, it's you," I say. "Strange to see you this far outside of downtown."

"Yes, well." Mr. Lanky rubs his chin. "I seem to have gotten lost. You see, I was thinking about how I could pick up some new accounts here, and I must have been so deep in thought I did not realize where I was."

"Which hotel are you staying at? We could tell you how to get there, or I could point you to the nearest taxi station."

"Thank you. That's quite generous of you!" Mr. Lanky smiles at me, then all of a sudden, his eyes catch on one of my companions. "Say...is that a Teddy?"

"That is accurate," Original Teddy replies.

"Oh! It can speak Common! Amazing!"

Shoot. If there was any hope of shooing him away quickly, we just lost it. He was going to notice Original Teddy sooner or later. A short, fuzzy, pink alien with tentacles walking with a group of humans tends to stand out. Now we'll have to disengage with this guy without rousing his suspicions.

"So, what's your name, little fella?" Mr. Lanky bends down, putting his hands on his knees.

"I am Teddy."

"But..." He raises a finger.

"They're all called Teddy," Afton says, cutting off any more questions about the origin of Original Teddy's designation.

Mr. Lanky stands up straight again, the sides of his mouth turning down. I catch him giving Afton a sharp look. Then he returns to his overly pleasant self.

"So, I thought I heard some commotion coming from down that way." He points in the direction of the park. "Any idea what it was? This isn't a dangerous area or anything, is it?"

That gets a snort out of a few of us. Mr. Lanky searches our faces, keen for an answer. Since the others are too polite to give him one, I think I might just step up to the plate. If I can't nicely get rid of him, then maybe I can scare him away.

"Oh yeah, this is a dangerous area for sure. Lots of crime around here. What you heard was likely the gangster shoot-out that happened by the park earlier."

Kayley presses against me and gives me a *what the hell are you doing* pinch. I just press my lips together so I don't crack a smile in Mr. Lanky's face.

His widened eyes and slight pause are well worth any risk I'm taking with Kayley, which is likely small. She wants him gone as much as any of us. The only difference is Ms. World-Famous would choose a more highbrow way to achieve it.

"I suppose the rumors are true about this planet," Mr. Lanky says.

"What rumors?" I feel my forehead wrinkle.

"Well, about Angelcanis being a breeding ground for the criminal underground and a potential headquarters for a building resistance against the Emperor."

They've called our little colony planet a few things, but never a home base for terrorists. My ears get warm around their edges. I take a step forward, but Kayley grabs my hand, halting me from going any farther.

Kayley's tug on my hand does more than stop me from doing something stupid. I realize that he's not talking about the Teddys any longer. I can cool off knowing that I've achieved the first step in my goal. Now, how to signal the others to get Original Teddy out of here?

"Sir, our peaceful planet of Angelcanis is not a host to radicals, and I take insult that you would think that!"

At the same time I make my ridiculous statement, I point towards Original Teddy behind my back. I can only hope my buds understand my archaic signaling and wait for the right moment to get our fuzzy friend out of here while I keep this brown tent pole occupied.

"No, no," Mr. Lanky says and raises a hand. "This isn't what I believe at all. Certainly not since I've arrived here. They're merely rumors! No need to take insult."

"Well, sir, I would advise you against spreading disgusting rumors such as those! They belittle the people of my planet, and they might just get you into some trouble. Our people are proud of what we've accomplished, and nobody is going to take that away from us!"

"Yes, I understand." Mr. Lanky bows acquiescence towards me. I return the bow as is polite, but I could care less if he understands. "May I ask you a question?"

"Sure." If it keeps his attention off Teddy, then I'll answer anything. Kayley's quick tap on my back tells me that Teddy is safe. I'd like to see for myself, but I've got to keep this going.

"I heard that a group from this planet was responsible for the assault on the staging base off Herdewyke. There might have been some, ah, Teddys involved as well. Have you heard anything about that?"

Kayley's grip on my hand gets tighter. I fight myself not to react despite the chill that traces down my spine. One thing is clear: this guy is a government agent. I might have doubted it before, but if he knows about our little jailbreak, then he's got to be a part of the military. I consider how his little charade has kept me off-balance, and how he's just taunting me with that fact now.

It's not the first time I've been in a situation like this. Minister Crowley tried to bait me a few times too. It didn't work, and neither will this guy's stunt. But my priorities have switched. I need to find out who he works for and if he's after the Teddys or me. Or both.

"An assault against one of the largest military stations in the Empire?" I laugh and shake my head. "That would be impossible!"

"All the same, it happened."

"But"—I tilt my head—"how would someone like you know about something that happened on a military base?"

"Ah." He smiles and raises a finger. "I bet you didn't know the military buys insurance."

"Why would I know that? And why ask me, anyway? I'm nobody special."

"Perhaps not," Mr. Lanky says, tilting his upturned finger towards Kayley. "But she is! An excellent speech, young lady. I saw it just the other evening on one of the local stations. You have great potential, you know."

"Thanks." Kayley smiles, but it's fake. I know because her teeth aren't showing at all. Plus, her grip on my hand just got painfully tight.

"Could I, perhaps, trouble you for a stamp?"

"Oh, I don't have my official stamp on me."

Shoot. This guy is way more sophisticated than I expected. It just occurred to me that he's now trying to distract me from prying. It might be best to retreat and regroup. As long as the others are gone, with Original Teddy right with them.

A quick glance to my right confirms my hopes. Great. A small win for us. Now for Kayley and me to extricate ourselves from this conversation. I wouldn't put it past Mr. Lanky to have noticed our amateur ploy and turned the tables on us. All that means is that he's a pro, and we need to get out of here.

"I'm sorry, Mr...." Kayley says.

"Brownrigg."

That can't really be his name, now can it? Wearing all of those earth tones like that? No way.

"Yes, thank you. Mr. Brownrigg." Kayley pulls out the real smile now. "Perhaps you could provide me a forwarding address, and I can have someone send it to you?"

Oh, I am so glad I'm dating this girl. I should have chosen the sophisticated approach, but my cosmopolitan girlfriend is already making it work.

"No." Mr. Brownrigg smiles back—I know he can't help it—and presses a hand against his heart. "I appreciate it greatly, but it's unnecessary."

"Are you sure?"

"Yes, thank you so much."

"Well then, Mr. Brownrigg. You'll have to excuse us as I currently have a curfew per my agreement with the government."

"Of course, thank you for stopping to speak with me. I wish you a pleasant evening."

"You as well."

Once we get out of sight of him I stop, realizing something.

"KayKay, we never gave him directions on how to get back to his hotel."

"Come on now, darling, do you really think he's lost?"

I glance behind us, considering her question. I don't know who this guy is yet, but he is going to complicate our lives from here on out.

"No," I reply, taking another look over my shoulder. "I think he knew exactly where he was going."

Chapter Ten

THE WATER IN THE shower at Grady's house is so cold, my muscles are tighter now than when I stepped in. For such an expensive home, I can't believe they'd skimp on a solar heating system like that. Maybe somewhere in his parents' empirical philosophy of life, cold showers are a good way to focus the mind. I have to say, if that's true, it works very well. I can't remember a moment when I've been sharper.

Which makes it interesting that my thoughts turn to Danny Lecker. I have no doubt that she escaped whatever trouble we left her in. That woman is not one to stop at no. That was obvious the moment I met her.

I get dressed and meet the others in the dining room for breakfast. Parrish is trying his hand helping Kayley burn—I mean, cook—the corncakes they went to get earlier. The two of them appear to be having fun, and that sends a jealous streak flashing through me. But I clamp down on it. My plan to attain worthiness is underway. A little smile between the two of them won't get to me.

"Did Danny really threaten to shoot you?" Grady asks as I lean on the back of the chair at the head of the table. It's late enough in the morning now that the sun isn't blasting its rays through the window, but I bet there's still a good amount of dust flying about.

"She could have, but she didn't for whatever reason."

"That's because she still wants our help," Afton is astute to observe. "She never intended to shoot anyone, just scare us into thinking she would so we'd help."

"I don't think she's as dangerous as you guys think she is," I say, drawing immediate scrutiny of my person. Some of it is considered, and some of it is full of contempt.

"Says the guy who kissed her," Afton says.

"I did not—" I shoot back, but Kayley cuts me off.

"We're not discussing that," she says in a short tone of voice.

"Thanks, honey." I beam at her for backing me up, but all I get is a glare in return.

"Busted," Afton says through a faked cough. She also gets the eyes of death from Kayley and throws a bath towel over her wet head, pretending to hide.

"Hey, did you just take a shower? Was it cold?"

"No, why?" Afton lifts the towel from her face to stare at me as if I just asked her if her hair was really black.

"We don't need to worry about her," Kayley says, getting us back on track. "I'm here to help protect the Teddys, and I'm on a limited timeline, so we should get to making a plan."

"She'll just call if she wants us, anyway," Grady says. I don't think he realizes he's throwing grenades in my direction. "Or we can also call her."

"What do you mean *we* can call her?" Kayley's eyes narrow.

I reluctantly pull the capsule from my pocket and hand it to her. Kayley accepts it, holding it between her fingers as if it's some kind of insect.

"So, this is the thing she jammed down your throat...while she was kissing you."

"Uh, that's the AIC device, yeah." And that is all I'm confirming.

"She tricked him into it, Kayley," Parrish certifies. I know he's trying to be helpful, but when her forehead wrinkles, I know he's failed.

"Not what we're discussing right now, Parrish." She goes back to examining the device. "How does it work?"

As if in answer to her question, the capsule chirps, and the light comes on. Startled, she fumbles the capsule before she recovers, cupping it in her hands as if it were a live animal.

"She's calling! Put it on the table!"

Kayley tosses it on the table and backs away. The projection comes up, and sure enough, it's Danny. She's back to wearing her bodysuit and short jacket, and oddly, she's got a familiar-looking bowl in her hands and is taking a sip from it.

"Oh, hey guys!" Danny says. "Sorry about the other night! I went a little overboard because I'm really missing my hubby. You do still owe me for that suit, though."

Danny picks up the spoon that's sitting in the bowl and spoons a thick cream-colored liquid into her mouth. I frown as I recognize what it is—congee. My body goes tense as something occurs to me. We've left a seriously big hole in our defensive line.

"Are those goji berries?" Grady asks, getting close to the projection and squinting.

"Yep! Ginger and chives too!"

"Danny...where are you right now?" I say, keeping my voice as controlled as I can. If she's where I think she is, then that's not going to last.

"At home, of course!" Danny replies. She gets momentarily distracted by a small amount of the rice porridge that slides down the side of the bowl. "And let me tell you, Rance honey, your mom is the best cook I've ever met!"

"You...you're at Rance's house?" Kayley asks, her voice trembling.

"Yes, why do you ask?"

There's pandemonium as everyone jumps to their feet, sending chairs skidding in all directions. A collective cry bursts out. Jaws go slack, and there's the general feeling that someone just dropped a live electrical wire into the pool of calm we were all swimming in.

Danny's bowl nearly falls out of her hands, but she catches it. A bit of the congee spills on her hand, and she has to suck it off her fingers to clean them up. She notices all of us staring at her through the AIC and glares at us.

There's silence after that. A stand-off that is making me sweat more with every second that passes by. I don't want to give her any sort of hint that she's got us where she wants us, but I really want to know if my mom is unharmed.

"Where is my mom, Danny?" I ask.

"Downstairs, her bedroom," Danny replies, continuing to eat—in my bedroom. "Sleeping, obviously."

"Is she...okay?"

"No..." Danny's pause is enough to make me want to dive through the AIC device and strangle her. "She's had a backache all afternoon, so she went to bed a little early to read and rest."

"Did you hurt her?" Kayley uses her most dangerous tone. It does not come out often, but when it does, watch out. She is on the hunt and will kill whatever she catches.

"Don't be silly," Danny replies. "I don't hurt old ladies. And definitely not ones that cook like this!"

"What are you doing there, then?" We all know the answer to this already, but it was the best I could come up with while I'm freaking out about my mom.

"Eating. What does it look like to you?"

"Enough of this game," Kayley says. I step back and let her go for it. My attempt to get her to lay down her demands failed, so I let the special forces take over. "You either tell us what you want, or you leave there right now."

"Honey, I thought it was obvious what I want. *My hus-band.* Get him, bring him here, and then we can all be happy."

"Why don't you get him yourself? You've got that power suit. Just use that."

"Not anymore! Your little fuzzy friend fried the main processor unit! But I'll forgive him because one, he seems really huggable, and two, you're going to do what I want!"

"Who are you?" I ask, trying to buy us time to figure something out. "Why come to us to ask for help?"

Danny gasps and covers her mouth with a hand.

"I didn't tell you? Oh." She looks for a place to put the bowl down. To my horror, she uses my bed as a table, tossing it there. "Well, I don't have to tell you my name again, but I'm a hand-hunter, you know, from Canis Ludis."

"Never heard of it," Parrish says, which I know is a lie. We've all heard the nutty rumors. For instance, their queen has ten husbands, and if any of them get into a fight with her that she doesn't win, she'll kick him out an airlock. Of course, as a full member of the

Commonwealth, that planet can do whatever they want, provided they pay their share of the Empire's heavy tariffs. I heard they're the sole source of a rare element that starships use, so no one messes with them.

"You're hand-hunter?" Kayley asks. "I would never have guessed that."

"Come on!" Danny stomps her foot. "Didn't you hire a hand-hunter to get your man?"

"I didn't need to hire anyone. Rance and I have known each other all our lives."

"Oh, well." Danny rolls her eyes. "So sorry the rest of us are not as adorable as the two of you."

"She's got that right," Afton mumbles.

Hiring someone to hunt down the man you've fallen in love with is the accepted way—on most of the Commonwealth planets, anyway. It started when an Imperial princess was spurned by her love interest, and so, being the spoiled brat daughter of the Emperor that she was, she hired the toughest mercenaries in the Empire to hunt him down and bring him back. The dude was so overcome that she would do all that just to get him back, he immediately asked for her hand in marriage. Once the word got out, all the eligible ladies of the court sprang into action. But they didn't wait to be spurned. They just picked their target and sent the hounds after the poor unsuspecting bachelor. This turned out more than a few solid marriages, apparently.

"Rance," Grady whispers behind me, "keep her talking. I'm sending the constables to your place."

I nod as I listen to Danny tell us about her most recent score for the daughter of the richest baron of industry on one of the central worlds. That's all I really hear, though. I'm way too focused on what Grady might be doing at the moment and whether or not he can be seen doing it. If this berserk woman catches a clue, my mom might be in big trouble.

"Rancy baby, are you keeping up with all this?" Danny asks. "I know it's a lot, so I'll try and use simple words, okay?"

"Oh, no, I'm fine." I push my mouth to smile and tilt my head. "Keep going. This is really interesting stuff."

"Really?" Danny's eyebrows lift. "Well, let me tell you of this other time when I had to get two hands at the same time...for one woman!"

I poke Kayley to get into the act, but she pokes me back—she's already there, eyes wide and mouth open, doing her best imitation of someone interested in Danny's story. What's important is that Danny is falling for it. She's getting into her storytelling with as much energy as she's putting into making my life a major hassle.

"And that's how it went!" Danny bursts into an uncontrolled fit of laughter. "So funny, right?"

"Definitely!" I say.

"Oh, I love that one!" She makes a big sigh that starts on a high pitch and drops. But then all sense of enjoyment disappears from her face, and she stands up straight. "Now, if you would please ask Mr. Sugiyama to stop doing what he thinks I don't know he's doing."

"What are you talking about?" I ask.

"Rance honey, hello? You can't deceive a hand-hunter. I've heard all excuses a man can come up with. Trust me, your gender isn't all that creative when it comes to deception."

"I'm not making excuses," I reply.

"You really wanna try me, don't you, mister?" Danny shakes her head and puts her hands on her hips. "Okay...but if something happens to your mom, it's not gonna be my fault."

"Hey," Grady says and slips past me with his hands raised. "I'm here. I'm here! See? Nothing going on."

"Tried to call security to come over here, didn't you?" Danny asks, wagging a finger at us. "And don't lie to me!"

"No..."

"Did you just lie to me?"

"No... er..." Grady sighs and drops his head. He was never great at lying. "Okay, I did."

"Didn't I just tell you not to do that?"

"You did."

"Great, now we're getting somewhere!" Danny claps her hands and walks in a circle. "So, now, kiddies, here's how this is going to work. Mom and I will spend some time together on my ship."

"You have a ship?"

"Of course. How else did you think I travel around?" Danny doesn't wait for me to answer. "So as I was saying: Mom, me, maybe a nice little vacation. I'll even hire a Reiki expert for her."

"Reiki?" Afton says in a sour tone. "No, she needs an Ayurvedic expert!"

"What in the sixth hell is that?" Danny responds. "Forget it! I'll find out, but you little brats need to hold up your end of the deal."

"Who said we had a deal?" Kayley challenges.

"Kayley!" I hiss as I turn to her, motioning with my head for her to not play tough right now.

"Listen, Little Miss Sassy Strawberry, this is the health of your darling's mom we're discussing here. Now, I can be nice and treat her well, or I can make sure you regret your terrible choice for the rest of your life. Which is it going to be?"

Kayley's face turns a bright red, not unlike the aforementioned fruit. She's building up to something, and my forehead gets sticky with perspiration. I really want to trust my girlfriend here, but...it's my mom. With as much time as KayKay has spent over at my house, she's practically Kayley's mom too.

The moment I see Kayley inhale, I throw my hand over her mouth. I can't let her say something that gets my mom in trouble. She squeaks in surprise and rips it off, breathing hard and glaring at me.

"Danny, wait, please!" I say. "Don't do anything. Just give us five minutes to talk it over, okay?"

Danny steps closer to her camera, her mouth twisting and her eyes narrowing.

"Five minutes, not a nanosecond more," she says, raising a finger, "and if you try to mess with me, I will give you the worst spanking of your life, young man."

"I understand, Danny. Thank you."

"Your time starts now!"

Chapter Eleven

WE GATHER AROUND WITH our backs to Danny's projection. We speak in hushed tones, our heads bent together. I don't know if that's enough to keep her from hearing us, but we don't have a lot of time to figure that out.

I don't know what Danny might be capable of doing to my mom. She said she wouldn't kill her, but there's plenty of things worse than death, and I don't want to think about any of them happening to my mom.

"Grady, did you get through?" Afton asks, with a quick glance back at Danny's image. She's busy making her way through the drawers of my desk—embarrassing, yes, but I'll take that over her watching our every move.

"I connected to them, but she caught me before I could put in a report."

"Well, we can't count on them, then," Kayley says. "We'll just have to find another way in."

"Way in?" I say, my eyes widening. "No, we don't do anything that risks Mom!"

"So, you're fine with this crazy lady kidnapping her to who knows where?" Kayley shakes her head. "No way, Rance. We can't take that kind of risk. It's too dangerous."

"Well, then what?" I respond. "We don't have time to figure out a new plan. She's too sharp for us to try to sneak one by her."

"Rance is right," Parrish says. "We have to say yes and then find a way to either do what Danny wants or figure out how to save her."

I give Parrish a short smile. If anyone was to back me up I knew it would be him. He knows what it's like to live with a single parent, and a mom at that. Just like me, he wouldn't want to do anything that would put her at risk.

"Four minutes, kiddies!" Danny calls. "Oh, and Rance, I'm a bit disappointed that no handwritten love letters are hiding in here. That's what the ladies like these days. Hint, hint!"

"Goddesses, I'm going to knock her out the next time I see her," Kayley says. Afton stares at her and slowly separates herself from her friend. I'm beginning to wonder if the time on tour didn't make my girlfriend a little less gentle than she used to be.

"What if we could get Teddy in the house?" Grady asks. "He could sneak up on her...then *bam*, popsicle!"

"Too risky," I say. "If she hears him coming, he might get shot."

"If we could get her out of the house, just for a moment, that might work," Afton suggests.

"Good idea!" Grady says. "Keep Teddy safe, and we don't even have to move."

"Okay, but what's going to get her to come out of the house?" Kayley asks, glancing around.

"What if we went there and asked her to come out just to talk?" Parrish asks. "Maybe Rance could do it. She seems to like him."

That gets a murderous stare from Kayley. Parrish shrugs, naïve to the underlying context there. Which, to me, is odd. He should know what she might be sensitive to. Either that or Kayley really has changed.

"No, dummy," Afton says. "She'll see that play coming a light-year away."

"Set a fire in the house?" Grady says. "Just a small one? She'd have to come out then."

"Dude!" I hiss. "That's my *house*! And definitely not with my mom inside!"

"How about that sinus irritant?" Grady says. "As a gas, it's invisible, silent, and doesn't have any scent."

"Dude," I growl. "Maybe you don't like your own parents all that much, but *I am not gassing my mom*."

"Yeah, second that," Kayley says.

"I love my parents too," Grady mumbles. I know he does, but we're in a tight spot, and there's no room to make a mistake. We all learned the hard way what happens when someone screws something up.

"We know you do," Afton says and pats him on the back, "but face it, buddy, your ideas right now are pretty crap."

Grady frowns at her, seeming confused about how she just comforted him and insulted him in the same sentence.

"Yoo-hoo!" Danny calls. "Three minutes, teenie-boppers. You are going to give me an answer on time, aren't you?"

"We will!" I stand up and turn on her. "But maybe you could help by not interrupting us!"

"Fine." Danny shrugs with one shoulder. "I'm enjoying checking your stuff out. And by the way, Rance..."

"What?"

"Buy yourself some new undies, hunh?" To my absolute horror, she holds a pair of my underwear up close to the camera for all to see. "What's Kayley going to think if you wear these to an intimate evening together?"

Kayley reaches over and pulls me back into the huddle. I catch her gaze, and it's intense. There's only one other time, maybe two, that she's gotten this way.

"Don't talk to her, Rance," Kayley says. "She's messing with your head so you can't think straight and come up with a way to stop her."

"It's working," I say.

"Then help us figure something out."

"I don't know," I reply. "Maybe we should start discussing how we can get her husband back for her."

"I'm in if we do," Afton says. "I want to see the nutball that said yes to marrying her."

"Not helping, Surela!" Kayley says, stunning Afton silent. We all go quiet—Kayley never brings out the "S" word. "Now, let's get back to it, or we're going to run out of time."

A few more ideas get tossed around, but our hearts aren't really in it. We realize that the five of us have gotten bested by an immature thirty-something woman. We who saved the planet and the Empire from total destruction. It's taking the game out of all of us.

"Hey there," Danny sings. "Don't mean to pry, but you guys have been awfully quiet for the last minute and a half. Hope everything's okay?"

"Are you serious?" Afton pops her head up. "You're just lucky we're not there right now."

"Well, let's think about that for a second." Danny puts a finger on her cheek and glances up at the ceiling. "If you were here, then I would have to do something rash, and that would likely cause some trouble for you-know-who's mother. So, I would have to say—"

"Oh, can it already!" Afton shouts.

"So rude! I'm going to have to remember you."

Before Afton can reply, Parrish throws an arm around her and pulls her down, giving her a side hug. Afton shakes it off and glowers at the floor. I have to give Danny credit. She's got some skills in the mental warfare department. I wonder if she ever worked in the intelligence ministry.

Time is ticking down, and everyone gives off their little tells of unease. My worries are not just for my mom but for my promise to help the Teddys. This is going to put a serious dent in the effort we can give to that mission. After all they've done for us, we might not be able to repay them this time.

"Hey, Danny?" I call out to her as I pop up.

"Yes, sweetums?"

"Rance," Kayley hisses and tugs on my shirt, but I push her away. Gently, of course.

"What's your husband in jail for?"

"Oh! You see, he was protesting the formation of a new military base on the moon of Viridi Silvanus by hacking into the troop ship's navigation and sending them cruising around in a circle...and well, the Emperor didn't like that too much, so he got tossed into the political section on Exodus."

Kayley grabs my shirt again and this time she keeps a hold on it so I can't go back up.

"Tick-tock, tick-tock, my little pretties! Time's almost up."

Kayley squeezes her eyes shut and keeps them closed. Her breathing is slow but forced, and I know she's trying her best to come up with anything. I'm ready to fall on my knees and beg Danny to let us save her husband just so she doesn't hurt my mom.

But only Afton said she'd support me so far, and if we're going to be successful, I need the entire gang to help with this. Kayley's the key to that. The others will do whatever she decides, so if I can convince her, I'm set.

Even though I have about a negative percent chance of doing that.

"KayKay," I whisper. She opens her eyes and looks at me with no expression. Whether that means she's out of ideas or that she's already made up her mind, I can't tell, and that makes the back of my neck itch.

It's worse, actually. I realize that I'm going to do whatever I need to do to protect my mom. If that means going against Kayley, then I might just do that. I don't want to, though. I remember what happened the last time. Kayley might not forgive me a second time, and the fallout would be worse because now we're in a relationship.

Being in a relationship...hmm. That means you trust your partner, doesn't it? That means you're honest with them and share stuff, right? I should do that with Kayley, but I'm terrified of what she's going to say.

"What is it, Rance?" she asks gently. Her hand relaxes its viselike grip on my shirt and slides up to touch my face. She must see that I'm struggling with this. Oh well. No time like the present to tell her how I feel.

"I don't know what to do, KayKay," I say, my voice trembling, "but I really want my mom to be safe."

"I know." Kayley smiles. "Don't worry, we'll figure it out together, okay?"

"*Bzzzzt!* You're out of time, kiddies. What's it gonna be?"

As Kayley and I share a moment, I see her jaw set and her eyes become steel. She glances at the others, then inhales and stands up. A shiver runs through my body as she turns to face Danny's image, her shoulders back. As comforting as she just tried to be, I still don't know what she's going to say. There's just enough time to get in a quick prayer to the Three Goddesses before she answers.

"You promise not to hurt her?" Kayley asks.

"Absolutely!" Danny replies. "She'll get the best treatment! I promise!"

"Okay then." Kayley turns back to me with a small smile. "We'll get your husband."

Chapter Twelve

I WANTED TO RUN home the moment we disconnected with Danny, but Kayley quashed that idea straight off. She was right to make that call. It would be too dangerous. Instead, we waited for the cover of darkness and brought Original Teddy with us. I privately hoped they were still there so I could see my mom once more before she was gone, but that wasn't to be. When we arrived, all the lights were out. Usually our kitchen lights are a beacon in the neighborhood's evening calm.

Everyone decided to crash at my place rather than go home and come back first thing in the morning. I'm glad they did, but I warned them that there wouldn't be anything special for breakfast, but I think they had already curbed their expectations. Afton and Parrish decided they would go get something for us, which would work out for them since they could get a morning run in at the same time. That left the rest of us to sleep in late.

When I opened my eyes, I found Kayley already awake. She was propped up on one arm, lying on her side next to me. I didn't remember us crashing together, but to wake up to her warm blue eyes gazing at me is something I hope to experience many, many times over.

"Good morning, darling," she says, brushing the fallen spikes of my hair out of my face.

"KayKay, did you sleep okay? I didn't wake you up in the middle of the night, and you couldn't get back to sleep, did I? I gave you enough space, right?"

Kayley giggles and presses a finger to my lips. It warms me to see her smile so brightly, especially after all the craziness of the past few days. That she still smiles when she sees me is a big lift to my spirits when I need it most. It doesn't absolve me from all the work I have to do to keep up with her, but at least I know she still cares for me, even in my current lowly state.

"No, silly, you didn't bother me. It was really nice to sleep somewhere familiar. I can't remember sleeping so well in…" Kayley's voice drifts off as she glances wistfully up at the ceiling. Her whole mood falls after that, and her gaze drops to the bed.

Something is bugging her, and if she's unhappy about something then so am I. We do have a lot to be worried about, my mom only being one of those things. There are two whole missions to plan, and I don't know how we will achieve either.

"KayKay?"

"Hmm?"

"Everything okay?" I watch for her reaction, but she's doing a good job of hiding it if she has one.

"Sure," she replies. I'm not convinced. There's got to be something she's not telling me. I'm sure of it. Sullen Kayley is not the normal mode for her at all.

Oh gosh, is it because of…? I'm such an idiot, worrying about myself so much. I nearly forgot about her feelings.

"KayKay?"

"What?"

"I'm sorry."

"Why?"

"Well, because of Danny. I really thought we were going to get our first client. Before I knew it, she was so close…and—"

"Stopping you right there," Kayley says, raising her hand. "I don't need details. I know it wasn't your fault. Let's leave it at that."

"But?"

"But what?"

"There's more to it, isn't there?"

"No, there isn't," she replies, but the small amount of distance she puts between us says something different. KayKay is hiding something, and I want to find out what that is. We're alone right now, so this would be the best time to get it out of her. She's going to revert to leader mode later when we're all together. There won't be any way to get her to talk then.

"Then did you want to tell me something?"

"Forget it, Rance. We don't need to have a discussion about it."

"What discussion?" Oh, now I'm onto something. I'm going to pursue it and hope I don't get my head bitten off.

"It's over, okay?" Kayley sighs. "What happened, happened, and I really don't want to get into the whole thing."

I'm guessing "the whole thing" means Danny. But what if there's something else? Kayley never let on that something was bothering her during our nightly post-speech calls, but now that she's here with me I can read her body language, and it's telling me she's upset.

Likely, in my wallowing over my sans girlfriend existence, I missed it. I mean, she was always all smiles, talking about all the amazing people she met that day. All I was thinking about was the day she would return. How I'd feel. Not about how she was feeling.

I won't make that mistake again. Kayley means way too much to me. I'm going to do better, give her the chance to talk, and then really, really listen. That would raise my level a little too, wouldn't it?

"KayKay," I say, "If you can't tell me, then who can you talk to?"

"Afton?"

"You're kidding, right?"

"She's a good listener."

"Well, I'm at least as good as her!" I give her a hopeful smile. "Or, I can be. Just give me a chance. I don't want you to keep something in that's bugging you. Even if that thing is me."

I take her hand in mine and give it a squeeze. But she looks away, a sure tell that she's hiding something. I know about it because my mom first called it out ten years ago when Kayley had rummaged through her makeup and made a mess. My mom is allergic to disorder and knew immediately that someone had touched her stuff. It could have been me, but Kayley was over that day. When my mom asked, I didn't move, but Kayley did. My mom condemned her right on the spot.

"KayKay," I try again, "I really want to make our relationship great, so if you've got something on your mind, get it out so we can talk about it. I don't want it to be rubbing on you all day. We're going to need some focus for when we make the plan to get Mom."

That moves her. In what direction it's hard to tell, but I think I found the right button to press. She shifts her position and sits up to lean her back against the headboard of the bed. I do the same, angling myself towards her.

Kayley clasps her hands together in her lap and gazes out the window at the foot of the bed. I give her a moment so she can collect her thoughts or gather the courage to talk to me. It doesn't matter to me which one it is—she can have eternity if she needs it. I'm not going anywhere. We do have to get Danny's husband at some point, however.

"When we were in school," Kayley begins, "it couldn't have been simpler. Everyone liked me...at least I think they did...and I liked them. Being class president was fun because I could help other students and make school life better for them. When I wanted something to happen, I asked one of the teachers to help me, and it was done...but everything's different now, isn't it?"

Kayley sniffles and rubs a sleeve across her face. It's a bit surprising to see her get emotional like this. It's not like she never has before, but it's a stark contrast to the imposing authoritative figure she was only last night. Now she's just like the little girl I remember who would cry when someone didn't pay attention to her. Often that someone was me.

"How is it different?" I ask. I think I know, but I want to make sure I'm not assuming anything.

"The people that come to see me on tour," she responds. "Sure, they were excited to see us, and my speech went great every night, but after they took their photos with us and made me stamp everything they could shove in my face, they changed."

"Changed, how?"

"It was like...that's all they really cared about. Their little piece of proof that they were somehow connected to a celebrity. To me. They didn't care about me. Not really. They just cared about what I could give them. And then, to hear what happened with you, when I'm on the other side of the planet with no way to do anything about it..." She sniffles again. "That really hit me hard."

My heart rises in my chest to where it feels like it's about to fall out. As I listen to her, I begin to understand, really understand, what's been eating at her. And for me to be part of the reason for her anguish and frustration—well, I should just sacrifice myself to the Three Goddesses for my sins. It's a good thing human sacrifice is not part of our religion.

"Sorry," Kayley says and sighs. "I didn't want to burden you with that. I did really miss you, and you were trying to be strong for me, listening to me tell you all about the people I met every night when I know you were missing me too."

"But now you're here. We're together."

"Only for two weeks...less now. With all that you've got on your mind—"

"The only thing on my mind right now is you, KayKay."

Kayley smiles at me. Not just any smile—the kind that girls give a guy when they're thinking *I could spend the rest of my life with him.* At least, that's how I see it, and my opinion is heavily biased.

"So tell me." I slide closer to her and take her hand. "Now that we're together, what can I do for you? How do I make you feel better?"

"You can't, darling. This is for me to take care of...if I can." Kayley slides her hands against mine as our eyes connect, and I fall for those amazing sapphire eyes of hers once again. "Right now, I just want to be the best leader that I can be. For you and for the rest of the gang."

"But, there's got to be something I can do?"

She reaches out, her hand going behind my neck. She pulls me close and gives me the warmest and sweetest kiss I've ever had. It's like a strawberry dipped into honey that's just been taken from the hive. We stay connected for what I'm sure is at least a millennium, and I don't do anything other than focus on how her love for me radiates through my body, giving me more joy and more hope than I've ever had before.

Of course, it's me who has to cut the eon short. It's me who realizes that I haven't yet said those three words to her. She must be waiting for me to tell her how I feel. I mean, she *knows* how I feel, but there's just something about saying those words that makes it official. And I do want to make it official. This isn't the situation I imagined, but it's as good a time as any.

I gather up my courage and lock my eyes on her eyes—her amazing, beautiful, perfect eyes. I could become a singularity within them and wouldn't be any less happy than I am now. If she could carry me around in her eyes and I could see the world the way she sees it, then I could see how she sees me. I can only hope that I am worthy of her in her eyes.

There I go again, procrastinating. Not intentionally, of course, because I have every intention of saying those words. It's just hard to focus when...well.

"Kayley," I say, sliding my hands up to caress her arms. She watches me in anticipation with one side of her mouth lifted. I think she knows what's about to happen. After all, I am making a huge effort to build up to it. "I...I wanted to tell you something."

"What is it?"

"I..."

I can tell Kayley has a grin prepared for when I release those three words from my lips.

"I..."

There's a pounding on the door that shocks us out of our serotonin stupor. We both jump, our heads spinning towards the door.

"Dude! Hope you're up!" It's Grady. "Someone is here to see you, and you won't like who it is."

I absolutely cannot believe my horrid luck.

Chapter Thirteen

I THROW MY ROBE on—the only thing I can find that seems appropriate—and leave Kayley behind in the guest bedroom. We let Afton have my mom's bed, and Parrish had mine. Grady was on the sofa in the living room and, save Original Teddy, he was the only other one home when whoever it was rang the doorbell.

And that person turns out to be someone I never expected to see again.

"Well, hello there!" Mr. Brownrigg says. "Are you Renton He'?"

He seems to accept my blank stare as an answer. I'm hoping that's enough to hide the fact that my entire body is screaming.

"Apologies for the small deception concerning my profession. It was necessary, as I am here on a special investigation. You already know Brownrigg is my surname, but to be more specific, I am Special Deputy Warwick Brownrigg." He glances around as if he's searching for something. "I'm here to discuss your security issue...may I come in?"

Shoot. I knew this guy was going to be trouble.

He's already in, so I try to stay relaxed and motion him into the kitchen. Grady hasn't wrapped up his blankets and pillows on the sofa yet, so that's not an option. At least Grady made him take off his shoes. Mom would have a fit if she saw dirt on the carpet. Dirt doesn't exist in my house. The moment my mom lays eyes on some, she executes it with extreme prejudice. I'm hoping nothing else is about to get executed.

"I just made tea," Grady says, coming out of the kitchen.

"Oh, excellent!" Mr. Brownrigg says. "Tea would be wonderful."

Grady presses his lips together and glances at me with eyes narrowed. I don't think he was offering to Mr. Brownstuffing there, but I just shrug. Anything that keeps the deputy distracted will do for now.

As the deputy steps into the kitchen, I realize I may have just made a grave error. Original Teddy was in the winter garden room in the back. This guy cannot know that he is here. A quick wave, and Grady comes over.

"Dude," I whisper. "Where's Teddy?"

"Out back," Grady replies with a yawn. A microsecond later, he also realizes the problem and nods vigorously. He's gone before I can even tell him to be careful.

We take a seat at the breakfast table in the kitchen. Really, it's a dining table that wasn't big enough to be called one and so we relegated it to use here. It's usually just my mom and me, anyway. And Kayley. That's why there are three chairs around the table instead of two. Sometimes when Kayley's or Parrish's mom visits, they sit in here and chat, though lately my mom's been making use of her new winter garden now that there's some wicker furniture in there. It's comfortable but bright. I'm surprised that Original Teddy likes it. At this moment, I wish he didn't.

"So, Mr. He'...may I call you Renton?"

"It's Rance, really."

"Very good, Rance then. So, Rance, how are you holding up?"

"What do you mean?" I frown.

"You reported that someone had kidnapped your mother last night, did you not?"

"Well, I—"

"Ah, ah." He holds up a hand. "No need to go into details. I know this is a difficult time for you. Now, I don't usually get involved with cross-breeds—"

"Sorry, what?"

"Colonials. People not of the pure blood of the Empire," Brownrigg explains with a frown. "You see, I am only here to confirm some details so we may begin our investigation, which will result in the safe return of your mother."

"What government agency did you say you were from?" I ask as I feel my forehead begin to take on a few wrinkles. I could be wrong, but I think I was just insulted. No way do I want this jerk anywhere near my mom, but I don't know if I can stop that from happening. So, I pour the tea because that's the only thing keeping me from freaking out.

"Ah, well, I am the director of the Imperial Ministry for Anti-Sedition Action."

"Strange that a director would come to gather information about a colonial's mother. Don't you have minions for things like this?"

"Well, as you know, I've been in town attending to other business. It was convenient for me to come by."

"What other business do you have in town?" I turn back to him, mugs in hand. His lanky frame is hunched over the table, and if he's making an effort to appear shorter, it's being thwarted by the fact that the chairs are a little too high for the table. My kitchen isn't small by any means, but he's like a giant in a shoebox.

"Thank you," he says as I place the mug down in front of him. "Unfortunately, I can't share that. That's, ah, a matter for the Crown that must remain securely in their trust."

"I see. So then, what did you want to confirm?" I ask, taking a seat on the side that faces the window. I really hope Grady's got Original Teddy under cover somewhere.

"Has the kidnapper identified themselves to you? Have they claimed any association with any known group or faction?"

"Not that I know of," I reply. It's the truth. Danny never said she belonged to any group. She didn't say her husband did either. I don't think either of them are terrorists, but what do I know? The only terrorist organization that anyone on Angelcanis has had experience with is a hidden faction within the Imperial government that murdered hundreds of us. This guy better not be one of them, or I'm going to spill my hot tea all over his face.

"No? No name at all?"

"Nope." I'm not telling this guy anything because I'm not going to put my mom at any more risk than she already is. Plus, he seems to think we're somehow lesser than full citizens. Angelicans don't kill each other for their own profit, so I can't see how that's possible.

"How unusual. Well, if this is a true kidnapping, they'll be in touch...and when they do, I hope you'll be willing to contact me."

"Sure."

"Thank you." He lifts his mug to express his gratitude and takes a sip. A curl of the side of my mouth is all I'm giving him in reply.

"This tea is delicious. Is it a local product?"

"Yeah, I think so."

Deputy Brownrigg continues to exalt the benefits of the soil on Angelcanis—as if I didn't know—but a thin shadow flies past the windows, pulling my attention away from whatever nonsense is coming from his mouth.

I think I just saw a tentacle slide across the windows. I confirm my assumption when I watch Grady streak by, headed in the same direction—the front of the house. Great. My nerves fire off in rapid succession, starting at my fingertips and racing around my back until they hit my spinal cord. I adjust my seat until I can get a better view of what's going on outside.

I can only imagine how the deputy's escort, waiting out front, will react when Original Teddy comes into view. We might be getting used to them here, but a pink alien with sharp teeth and tentacles would disturb anyone not expecting to see such a sight.

"Don't you think so?" Deputy Brownrigg asks.

"Sorry?"

"I asked if you thought tea leaves would become a major export here. As a colony, I'm sure you're eager to join the Commonwealth as soon as possible."

"Oh, I know nothing about that." I just blow the question off. I've got bigger worries than some political issue. For instance, Original Teddy, and whether he plans to exhibit himself around the neighborhood. That would be less than a pleasant situation.

"Your friend, the young lady...what was her name? Ah, yes, Kayley. Kayley Garmon...Garmonnik...Well, she certainly had a lot to say during her speeches."

"Like what?"

"You mean, you never watched one?"

"Well, yeah, of course I did." I wonder where he's going with this, and why he's not asking more questions about my mom.

"Some interesting conclusions she came to, don't you think?" the deputy asks. "Imagine, an entire faction of the government and the military in collusion against the direct orders of Parliament and of the Emperor himself. Of course, it's pure nonsense."

That really makes me burn, but before I can give this guy a serious telling off, Original Teddy's tentacles zip past the windows again, with Grady right behind. At least this time they're headed in the opposite direction.

"Say." Deputy Brownrigg leans towards me. "She wouldn't be here right now, would she?"

"No, she's not."

"Rance!" Kayley calls down from upstairs. "Can you get me a towel?"

I have to force my entire face to freeze along with the rest of my body. The only place I can think to look is directly into my mug. I bow my head and pretend to take a huge sip of my tea. I cringe as the scalding liquid burns my throat on the way down.

"Oh, well, who's that, then?"

"That's...my cousin," I spit out as fast as I can. "Yeah, she's come in from out of town after she heard about my mother."

"She arrived quickly, then."

"Well, she's only in the next town over."

"Oh? What side of the family is she on?"

"My father's."

The moment I realize the negative potential for my answer, my toes curl. If he knows anything about my father, he's going to get suspicious. Not that my dad was a terrorist, though some might call what he did terrorism. Myself included. But it wasn't as bad as all that. No, the worst thing he did was to leave my mom and me. Now *that* was an act of cruelty, and I won't ever forgive him for it.

"I wasn't aware that your father had any extended family on the planet here," Deputy Brownrigg comments. He's watching me closely now. I wonder if he can see the perspiration forming on my forehead. He must be able to because I can really feel it starting to collect up there. I don't dare touch it. He might take it as a clue that I'm nervous and then start accusing me of things I haven't done.

"Well, she moved back here to get an apprenticeship," I reply, trying to sound casual. "Yeah, or something like that."

The deputy leans back in the chair and crosses his legs. His attention is on me fully now, his eagle eyes observing me over his beak of a nose. We sit that way for a moment, he and I. As his current target of prey, I'm afraid to move lest he notice something off about me and dive in for the kill.

I can't let that happen. I want to protect the Teddys, but to get under suspicion by any government ministry is bad. This anti-sedition office must be looking for a problem—real or imagined—that they can sink their teeth into. If I want to get out of this without stepping on a land mine, I need an excuse for an out.

"Rance! Towel, please!" Kayley's voice comes at the perfect time.

"Uh, sorry, I should go help her," I say. Then I add, for some stupid reason, "We can continue talking when I get back."

"No, that won't be necessary." The deputy stands. "I think I've confirmed enough already. No need to trouble you further. However, if you do get a call from the alleged kidnapper, do make sure you contact my office along with the local authorities."

"Of course." I stand as well and show him out, as fast as I can, without making it seem I'm desperate to get rid of him. He nods to me, then ducks, unnecessarily, on his way out the front door. As he walks to his vehicle, I see not one but five military vehicles waiting for him. Not tanks, but armored enough to let you know they mean business.

That's when it becomes clear to me. This Deputy Brownrigg doesn't care about my mom. He's after something much more valuable to him, and there's only one thing I can think of that would bring him snooping around here.

Teddys.

Chapter Fourteen

"TEDDY, WE NEED A ride," I say as all of us, Doc Elizabeth now included, sit in my living room, awaiting the reason that I've called them here. It's been a long, exhausting day, and even though I'm ready to go back to bed and cuddle up with my girlfriend, I'm also too wired to do anything but go.

We've spent the better part of the afternoon coming up with a plan, and we did well—with what to do once we've figured out how to break into the Exodus prison. Then, of course, there's how to get back out, and then how to get away. Before all that, we need to figure out where Freddie Espy is on the moon-sized prison base.

"Conveyance is ready," Original Teddy replies, sitting on the floor in front of me.

"We're all ready to go, Rance, but where are we going?" Parrish asks.

"One problem at a time," I reply.

"No, that *is* the problem," Afton says.

I glance over to Kayley for some support, but she just shrugs and motions for me to go on. I think she might be punishing me for the delay in getting her towel earlier.

"We need to get off-planet first. That's not as easy as it sounds," I say. "First off, we've got that one armored vehicle sitting out front that's been here since this morning."

"Afternoon," Grady corrects. I wave a hand at him to dismiss his statement of fact.

"It doesn't matter since when," I say, "what matters is that deputy dude told them to stay here without telling me he was going to do that. What do you think that means?"

"It means you're a terrible liar," Afton says, then shrugs and glances around when I glare at her. "What?"

Another look over at Kayley confirms that she's still content to let me run this meeting, even if I fall flat on my face doing it.

"So, I figure the beach is the best place to get a lift?" I ask, glancing towards Grady and Original Teddy, who would be the ones in the know. Or at least the ones to make the best guess.

"That is accurate," Original Teddy confirms.

"Yeah, sounds good," Grady adds, "but how are we getting there?"

"We're walking." Afton is really on a roll tonight. She's not wrong, but I could describe her comments as being less than helpful at the moment.

"No," Grady tries again, "I mean, how are we going to get there without being seen?"

"Relax, Mr. Grady," Doc Elizabeth says, "I'm sure our team leaders have a plan in place to evade detection."

Grady looks between Kayley and me. I glance at Kayley, and Kayley glances back at me. Then I look at Parrish, and Parrish turns to Afton. Afton responds by placing a finger on the tip of her nose and pushing it upward.

"Say yes, Rance," Kayley instructs. So I do.

We're out the back doors of the winter garden five minutes later. We set the timer on the house automation so that the lights will go off in a staggered way, simulating all of us going to bed. Of course, if they cared to investigate, they'd know that every house in the entire Empire has house automation, and faking still being home is more than easy to do. They could be doing the same to us. Maybe no one is even in that armored vehicle.

Thirty seconds later, we're hopping the fence into the narrow walkway between the barriers of my neighbor's yard. It's where all the trash collection goes and not the most smell-friendly space to be climbing through.

We try to be as quiet as possible, but six humans of varying dexterity and one fuzzy alien are not the best combination for stealth.

Grady and Afton muttering their discontent just adds to the clamor of fourteen feet crunching through a mountain of refuse.

"Couldn't we have gone through someone's yard instead?" Grady grumbles.

"No, dude," I reply. "You'd have multiple fences that you'd need someone's help to climb over instead of one."

After that, Grady keeps his mouth shut.

It's not that far from the beach, but it's getting late, which means the town constables will kick people off the beach soon. There are, of course, plenty of places to hide from them, but we still have to get to one of them and then get onto a Teddy shuttle as fast as we can before that less-than-inconspicuous object gets spotted.

There's another alleyway on the next block, and I direct us down it. It's not as full of garbage as the last one. That's good since it means we can move through it faster. I take it at a trot, but Afton and Parrish sprint down so they can hurdle over the low fence at the end. Original Teddy must like what he sees because he does the same and gets a high five for his successful attempt.

A huge clamor explodes behind me, followed by a shout—Grady's shout. With a sharp inhale, I spin around to see him entwined with a trash bin and an old lamp cord that's still connected to the lamp.

"Dude!" I hiss and charge back towards him. Kayley and Elizabeth are already there, helping him up.

"Hey! Is someone there?" a man calls from the adjacent house. The four of us drop to the ground and freeze. He gets closer, then pauses. I don't dare move to check what he's doing. The composite slat fence isn't tall, but at least it's solid. Still, if he came to the edge and peeked over, he'd see four people lying in his trash. Not exactly what a couple of newly made celebrities want to be caught doing.

"What is it?" a woman's voice calls from farther away. It sounds familiar, and I realize there's a good chance someone will recognize Kayley if we're seen. All it would take then is for that deputy dude to ask around and hunt us down. Then he'll really be suspicious of us.

"Aw, maybe just someone's pet," the man replies and begins to turn. I see Parrish and Afton keep an eye on the man until they think it's okay to move. Once they give the signal, we move.

As we jump up, someone knocks into a trash bag that slides from a nearby pile and crashes to the ground. Kayley responds instantly and takes off towards the end of the alley. Doc Elizabeth is next, and I'm stuck shoving Grady up and forward.

"Hey, you!"

Those two words are enough to put Grady into overdrive. He separates from my shove like the second stage of a rocket engaging its thrust and bolts as fast as he can towards the end of the alley. I have to admit it's hard for me to keep up with him at that speed.

"It's those kids!" the man yells and points as I get my first leg over the fence.

"What kids?" the woman replies. Both of them lean over the edge and watch us as we make our escape.

"From the vid! The ones who saved the planet! I saw that girl with the red hair!"

"What are they doing in our garbage?" The woman frowns and glances down at their bags. She shrugs and looks up again as I land on the other side of the fence. By now, other neighbors are coming out of their homes to find out what the noise is about.

This has got to be the most excitement they've had in six months. Good for them, not great for us. The more of them that come out, the more that will know who we are. We weren't exactly unknown in our town before, but after everything that happened, we became ultra-known. Most of the regular people in our town have been considerate and left us alone, but as Kayley did more and more events, we've gotten handfuls of brave youngsters coming to town to try to rub elbows with the celebrities.

We've been careful to keep a low profile...until now.

"We've been recognized!" Grady cries.

"Not you, dummy, just Kayley," Afton replies.

"Goddesses!" Kayley groans. "I should have covered my hair!"

I gasp for air as we round the corner, hitting the street that goes to the beach—the wrong beach. We're going to hit White Orchid, the one everyone goes to. We need to get to Break Beach. Nobody's there at this hour, which makes it ideal for boarding a Teddy craft.

As we get nearer to the boardwalk, I catch lights, music, and a ton of people. It's some kind of festival or event, just the very thing we want to avoid.

"Oh great," Afton growls. "The moon festival is tonight!"

"Once we hit the boardwalk, just keep going!" Kayley directs. "Don't stop or pause for anyone. Not even the constables! It's not that far to Break!"

"I don't think I'm going to make it to the boardwalk!" Grady whines. Poor guy, blessed with tons of brains and not an equal amount of muscles to carry them around with.

"Ship is waiting," Original Teddy says. Down on all fours, he's having no issues with keeping pace. In this dim light, I hope he just looks like a pet. We don't have time to explain why a random alien is running about at the moon festival.

As we power down the boardwalk, we pass by many humans: couples, families, and the occasional single out for a stroll to enjoy the full moon. They comment as we pass by, but these are locals. None of them are going to think it too strange to see us around, even if we're running like escaped psychopaths.

Our luck slowly declines, however. We hit the thick of the crowd, and it's slowing us down to where we're going to be in trouble if we're noticed. The crowd is getting younger and less familiar as well. That means we're going to come across a horde of out-of-towners, likely hoping to catch a glimpse of one of us.

And here we all are, right in the middle of everyone.

"Hey, look! It's her!" someone cries.

"Oh shoot," Kayley says and takes off. Afton is right behind her.

"Hey! Everyone! They came! They're here!"

The steady murmur of the festivalgoers takes on a new character. It's full of gasps and shrieks of joy, and it only gets louder as we rocket by. We're close to breaking out of the crowd, but then there's that one person who has to ruin it for us.

"Hey, Kayley! You're so sexy! Can I have your autograph?" A guy a few years older than us gets in our way, but not for long. Parrish and Afton sprint forward ahead of Kayley and remove him from the boardwalk with a well-placed side-check. He goes spinning into the sand and lands on his back.

"Oh wow, it's really them!" someone else cries. It's echoed by another and another. Soon enough, a throng of kids is making a beeline towards us.

Now, they're a few years younger than us, and unlike us, they've been standing around for the past fifteen minutes. They're full of energy and getting a boost from the frenzy surrounding us. Needless to say, they're going to catch us if we can't figure out a way to stop them.

A pair of constables notice the commotion and head down from their patrol vehicle in the parking lot. They put their hands up to halt the growing crowd on our tail...but these aren't the polite citizens of our town, and they've found something more interesting than a full moon to check out.

Grady cries out and falls. I stop and turn back for him, scrambling to pick him up before the crowd overtakes us. Most of them are after Kayley, but Grady's got his own fan club. If they find him, then we're never getting out of here.

"Dude, I can't run anymore," Grady moans as I strain to get him on his feet. "Just leave me. I'll sign autographs, take pictures. Whatever... I just gotta rest."

"No way, dude," I reply. "This is worse than exploding buildings. You're going to get hugged by preteens, and everyone will want you to give you their love letters."

"Is that so bad?"

"Maybe not, but we've got a ship to catch and my mom to save."

I get him to his feet and we begin to move, but his legs buckle and he crashes down into the boardwalk again.

"It's him, it's him! It's Mutsu!" a girl cries, but then she yelps as a boy a few years older elbows her out of the way and charges for Grady, arms wide. He's almost on top of us as two other girls cut him off and barrel towards us, screaming.

I get my arms under him, but he's so exhausted his legs won't work. I'm near the end of my limit too, and there's no way I'll be able to save us both. Parrish is fighting his way through the crowd to get to us, but he's never going to make it in time. I think I should just cover myself over him and protect him from the attack. Not that it really matters—they're going to get to him, even if they have to rip me to shreds. By the time they're done with us, Deputy Brownrigg's men will be here, and that'll be the end of our little rescue mission.

Sorry, Mom. We tried.

As hands grab at me, trying to pry me off so they can get at Grady, a low, sustained tone blasts through the area. It's followed by a deep hum and a bright light from above. All the rabid fans scatter with cries and screams, and the area around us clears out.

I glance up and sigh as a familiar sight comes into view. Original Teddy descends on a black disk like an otherworldly deity and lands just next to us. By now there's a wide space between us and our rabid fans. Well, Grady's rabid fans, anyway. Their faces are strict clones of each other: eyes wide, mouths open, and stunned to disbelief at the cine show they're getting.

"Rancid, Gratin. Conveyance is available," Original Teddy says. "Departure is recommended."

Yeah, Teddy, I'll take that recommendation.

Chapter Fifteen

"THIS IS THE IDEA you came up with?" Afton asks as she crawls through the shrubs just behind me. "Don't you think the Empire would have secured their systems more tightly after our last break-in?"

Here we are, making our way into another brilliant idea that one of us came up with. I guess whoever came up with it thought we were capable because we've got prior experience breaking into a data storage system. That was on a ship, and even though we got what we were after, it didn't go all that well.

"Well, I think that it should be—" I begin, but she cuts me off.

"We *told* them how we did it. You do remember that, right?"

"Knock off the chatter!" Kayley hisses as she turns back to us.

I know it was my dumb suggestion, but I'm still wondering how Kayley picked me to go on this routine while able-bodied Parrish got to hang back with Grady and the doc. I guess four was enough, or should I say, three and one Teddy.

We're scratching up our hands and knees on the hard-packed ground just so we can sneak into the campus of the repository of legal records on Pruinonis, the closest planet to our own. There are quite a few repositories scattered about the Empire, and there's duplicate data on every Commonwealth world, including Angelcanis. It gets updated once a year there, but you have to get yourself to a repository if you really want the most accurate and up-to-date information.

It *is* a nice night for a robbery. The air here is as warm as on our own planet but much less humid, and the trees here are much taller and more fluffy than the sharp-leafed flora we have at home. They also give off an amazing scent. I can't quite place it, but it's somewhere between a citrus plant and a cherry tree.

The forest is alive with sound: avian calls and primate hoots. I'm hoping all that noise will cover our crunching of leaves and twigs as we make our ungainly way towards the facility's fence. It's doubtful there's going to be a ton of security, but we've come prepared in case of a contingency.

"Grady, do you copy?" I call through the Teddy comm.

"I'm here. What's up?"

"Anything happening inside?"

"I can't see that, dude. There are no cameras in the facility. Why don't you just look?"

"I am looking," I mutter, "but I can't see anything, which is why I'm asking. Don't you have a Teddy cam you can use?"

"Maybe if you stopped staring at your girlfriend's curvy backside, you'd see more," Afton says.

"I am not doing that!"

"Why not?" Afton replies with a chuckle. "I am."

"Keep your perverted eyes off my girlfriend!"

"Knock it off, you two!" Kayley turns around to face us. "We're about to reach the fence, and if you two are making noise, we are going *to get caught!*"

"Sorry," I say. Afton lowers her head and averts her eyes. It's an acceptable enough answer for Kayley, and she turns back around. I notice she attempts to adjust her position so that no one can ogle her from behind.

Kayley demanded that she come on this mission and wouldn't take no for an answer. I'm a bit concerned about her level of insistence. It's like she's on some kind of mission to convince someone she's up for the task. That someone wouldn't be me. I think she's perfect as she is. Compared to her, I've got a lot of leveling up to do.

We come to the clearing that separates the woods from the supremely tall fence surrounding the facility. It's a good thing we won't be climbing it—we'd never make it. A patrol makes a routine circuit around the main building, but since we're not playing at being cliff climbers, we won't be too concerned about them. Once they've passed, we'll have a healthy amount of time to get in.

How we do that, well, we're not exactly sure yet.

"Okay." Kayley turns back to the three of us. "Now we wait. Grady, have you found us a way in yet?"

"Er, through the gate? And then the door?"

Kayley sighs and leans back to sit up against a tree. I find my own and do the same while Afton and Original Teddy come up next to us. We've taken a calculated risk bringing him with us. It's unlikely that there's an alien life form detector system here in this facility, but they may have installed one after our last pilfering of classified information. I wouldn't blame them if they did, but it does make our work harder.

"Need something better than that, Grady," Kayley says. "How about a window or an air duct?"

"You've been watching too much cine with your boyfriend," Grady responds. "You can't go through an air duct...well, maybe *you* can, but Rance and Afton will never make it."

"Did you just call me fat?" Afton snarls.

As it turns out, Grady does have a Teddy cam. One that flies, apparently. I grumble that I'm not sure why he can't use that to take a peek ahead of us to see if anything is coming.

"Because then I couldn't keep an eye on you guys," Grady explains.

"We'll be fine," Kayley says. "Go ahead and see when the patrol is coming."

"No need," I say, pointing at the small open vehicle rounding the near corner, "there they are."

"Everybody down," Kayley orders, pushing herself behind a tree, "Teddy...camouflage!"

"Nonsense," Original Teddy replies.

All three of us humans twist to stare at him. He's standing up, tall and proud, and not making any effort to hide from the patrol.

"Teddy!" Kayley hisses. "They're going to see you!"

Teddy wraps his tentacles around the nearest tree and rockets up the trunk. A few seconds faster than we would ever expect him to, he's traveling down a long branch towards its tip.

Our fuzzy friend vaults from the end of the branch and onto the fence, barely rattling the chain links. I inhale sharply and hold my breath. Original Teddy is about to ruin our effort to get our hands on the sensitive data we need to save Danny's husband.

"What is he doing?" Kayley asks, staring with eyes wide. "Teddy, come back!"

It's too late to try and stop him. Kayley bows her head and plants it into her palms. We can only watch as he traverses the fence and climbs down the other side. At least the security patrol is turning the other corner and heading out of sight. That's one less thing we need to panic about.

"Hey, he's headed to the guardhouse!" Afton says—and a moment later, Original Teddy is bounding into the small shack. I don't know if I really want to see this disaster unfold before me, but I can't tear my eyes away.

As we contemplate the complete failure of the mission, I catch the body of a uniformed guard fall out of the booth and land in the grass. Once down, he doesn't move and doesn't make any attempt to stand back up. I share glances with Kayley and Afton, their jaws dropping as we all realize what's just happened.

"Infiltration is welcome," Original Teddy says, leaning out of the guardhouse and waving.

"Whoa," Afton mutters. "Thank the Goddesses for popsicle."

A second later, it occurs to the three of us we need to take immediate advantage of this occurrence. We spring to our feet and fly over to the gate.

"Keep inside the treeline!" Kayley orders. "And watch for the camera at the gate!"

We do our best to remain stealthy, arriving at the gate by paralleling the fence until the very last moment. There we drop behind a sizeable tree and wait for Grady's all clear.

"Good to go," Grady says.

"Teddy, open the gate so we can get in!"

Our fuzzy friend pops out of the booth and comes to the gate. He examines the lock and makes a bunch of pops and clicks that I can only guess are Teddy sounds of frustration. He tries to manipulate the lock with his tentacles but only ends up shaking the thing and making a bunch of noise.

Then Original Teddy makes a sound like a composite box ripping apart. I don't know what that means, but it's not making him move any faster to get the gate open.

"Teddy, there's got to be a key!" I say. "Check the guard."

He buzzes and goes to check the man frozen on the ground.

"That is not accurate," Original Teddy says.

"Maybe in the guardhouse," Afton suggests.

"Hurry!" Grady says. "You've only got a few minutes!"

He waddles over to the booth and spends a good amount of time rummaging through whatever is there. An occasional pen or other random item comes flying out.

"Hey, how long does popsicle usually last?" I wonder out loud.

"Don't know," Grady replies. "Maybe fifteen minutes?"

"You never counted?"

"Kinda hard to count when you're frozen, dude."

Teddy chirps and comes out with a key pin dangling from one of his tentacles. He strolls over to the gate and unlocks it, and we come pouring through. I check the building for a door and take off towards it the moment I spot it. We've no time to waste. The patrol is going to be coming back soon.

"Rance, wait!" Kayley says. I turn and frown at her until I see her point to the guard. "We can't just leave him like this."

"Why not?" I say.

"Because when he wakes up, he'll know someone broke in."

"Only you can fall asleep in the grass and forget you did it, Rance," Afton says, walking towards the guard. She steps around to his head and motions for me to grab his feet.

"Prop him up in his chair, and put his feet up on the desk," Kayley directs. "Make it look like he fell asleep."

"Do we have time for that?" I ask, leading Afton to the guardhouse.

"We don't *not* have time for that," Kayley says. "Teddy, help me gather these other things."

"Guys, you've got like one minute," Grady says.

We get the guard set up in a position that would be feasible to wake up in. We don't have time to debate whether he would have fallen asleep in the first place or if he would sleep like that at all.

"Bring the key!" Kayley says, and we blast across the yard to the door. I hope that the guard's security rights are high enough that it'll open for him. At least it doesn't take long to find out. The door swings open, and we pile through with Kayley in the lead.

Suddenly she stops, and the rest of us have to catch ourselves or bowl her over.

"We've got to return the key," Kayley says.

"We will," Afton replies, "but we don't have time now. The patrol is almost back."

"No." Kayley turns towards her. "If that guard notices his key gone, the place will go into lockdown."

"Maybe not," Grady says, "but he'll be more vigilant once he wakes up. Also, if you're going to do it, you'd better do it now."

"We have to return it," Kayley repeats, holding it out to Afton.

"Why me?"

"Because no one else can cover a sprint in record time."

Afton sighs and snatches the key from Kayley's hand.

"Be right back."

We duck down and watch Afton's impressive sprinting ability in action. She covers the distance in mere seconds that took us half a minute before. Through the window in the door, we see her drop the key in the guard's pocket and turn to make her way back.

"Afton, wait!" Kayley says into the Teddy comm as lights flash on the guardhouse and then continue sweeping towards us as the patrol vehicle turns the corner. We shut the door and slide down to the floor to keep out of sight. But now we can't see what's going on.

"Afton?" Kayley calls.

"Grady, can you tell what's going on?" I ask.

"I see the patrol, but not Afton," he replies. "Shoot, they're pausing by your door. Someone's getting out...they're headed your way...no, wait, they're just checking something outside. Stay down."

"No kidding."

"Okay," Grady says after a harrowing minute, "Afton, you're clear. The patrol is leaving."

"Afton," Kayley says, "get back here now!"

Chapter Sixteen

WE SLINK OUR WAY down the hall of the repository, pressed against the institutional blue of the near wall. The passage is dark in parts, and it's easy for us to hide in the shadows created by a neglectful maintenance worker. There are quite a few overhead lights that need the filaments replaced, and while they're at it, they can take care of the crumbling and yellowed ceiling tiles as well.

Footsteps are coming from somewhere in the intersection just up ahead. Kayley motions us to stop and drop in the deepest shadow we can find. It's not too hard to pick one, but we get settled just as someone walks through the junction. We hold our breath as they pass, but we shouldn't have worried. The administrator that walked by was so involved in their tablet they didn't even look up, much less glance down the hallway.

"Grady," Kayley whispers, "we're at the first intersection. Which way?"

"Right, then down a bit, then left, and left again, and you're there."

"Got it. We'll be silent for a while until we know we can talk again. If you don't hear from us in thirty minutes…"

"Burn the place to the ground," Grady says. "No worries. We're prepared."

"Dude, I wish you wouldn't describe it like that," I say. "Don't forget, we'll still be in here, likely getting tortured."

We waddle forward, still in a full crouch, towards the corner of the intersection. As far as we can tell, no other human is coming, and I doubt this place is high enough on the Imperial budget to get automated security or worker bots. They don't even have the funding to hire a decent maintenance person.

The first left is only a quick jog down the hall after we turn right. Kayley signals us to wait and then hops down to scout that turn. She's really getting into this, playing her part as mission leader with a healthy amount of enthusiasm. Afton is as bored as she ever is when there's no sign of a challenge. I'm somewhere in the middle, not particularly excited to be here, but happy that Kayley is getting into the moment, especially when she seemed full of self-doubt yesterday.

Kayley turns back to us and waves us up. I follow Afton as close behind her as I can without getting kicked, and Original Teddy brings up the rear. At least, I hope that's what he's doing. A quick check behind me confirms it, but his unannounced initiative back at the gate was more than unexpected. It was totally out of character for him. Who knows if he'll decide to go do something else without consulting us first.

"This is it, right?" I ask. Kayley nods, but her eyes are a little wider than usual. She directs my attention down the next hallway we need to travel through. I glance around, but I don't notice anything out of the ordinary.

"You don't see it?"

"See what?"

"The gigantic animal feet sticking out of the second doorway?"

I blink and look again. Sure enough, she's right. There's a pair of fuzzy legs there, belonging to some domesticated animal. A *big* domesticated animal. It must have a horrible sense of smell and bad hearing because it hasn't taken any notice of our arrival. Now, we've got cats, dogs, foxes, and pandas on Angelcanis, but this isn't anything I recognize.

"You go first," Kayley says, getting behind me and giving me a gentle push. Not expecting it, I fall forward onto my hands and knees. Not unlike the scary beast lurking in its lair.

"Whoa!" I turn to stare at her. "Why me?"

"Leaders don't ever go first."

"That's not true! Think about—"

"Well, I'm in charge, so I say you go first."

"You're scared, aren't you?"

Kayley wrinkles her nose and sticks out her tongue—absolute confirmation that she is petrified of trying to pass by that death machine on paws. I can't blame her. I've got a strong image in my head of that monster making chopped meat out of my face.

I could refuse, but that's not going to accomplish our mission. Maybe Afton is brave enough to try it first. I glance back at her, but her eyes are saying *not a chance in hell*. Well, I guess I could try to think positively about this and say that doing it—successfully, that is—could elevate me in Kayley's eyes as someone who isn't afraid of the big bad animal with teeth and claws. That's if I live, of course.

Kayley thrusts her finger down the hallway, her face resolute. That's my challenge—here goes nothing.

"Don't worry," Afton whispers. "We've got a fuzzy of our own, and I'll bet ours is better."

"That is accurate," Original Teddy adds.

I say a short prayer to the Goddesses and duckwalk towards my destiny. As I inch closer, I notice the rumble of the large-throated animal's breathing. I pause to ensure that I didn't just wake it up. A large throat means a large mouth, which also means big teeth. What did I just get myself into?

"Rance, get going!" Kayley hisses, spurring me on. I press against the wall farthest away from the sleeping beast and slide forward.

I peer into the deep chasm that is its lair and realize it could be watching me, getting ready to pounce. Those thumb-sized toes contain finger-sized claws, I bet. I'm not waiting around to find out.

The moment I slip by, I motion for the others to follow. Then I motion again, this time with more urgency. It takes them twice as long, with half of that time taken in deciding who would go first. After they waste a good deal of precious time, we finally make it to the archive. But the door is open, and the light's on—not a good sign.

"Rance, take a peek in," Kayley orders. Again, me with the risky moves. I'm beginning to believe my girlfriend may have it in for me. And all because of a towel that didn't arrive to her on time.

It doesn't take long to spot the clerk working at the terminal. She's got her back to us and is deeply invested in whatever task she has at hand. I reach back and give Kayley a thumbs-up and continue to watch. If I can understand how to navigate the system by watching her access it, we can get Freddie's location as soon as she leaves.

As I step back, I bump into something warm and fuzzy and nearly jump out of my skin. Original Teddy must be right behind me, trying to peek into the room as well.

"Teddy, let me know before you do that," I say, pivoting around to face him.

What I see is fuzzy, but not pink in the slightest. A big black nose sits in front of a pair of brownish-yellow eyes and just above two stiletto-length teeth. Its ears are tall and alert, and it has no trouble staring me in the eyes from my semi-crouched position. As it sniffs around my head, I realize that this domesticated predator could remove my face if it was so inclined.

"Stevie, is that you?" the clerk calls. "Come on in, boy, I've got a snack for you."

I make no attempt to stifle my sigh as the big cat pads around me and into the data room. Kayley and Afton grab me and yank me away from the door to place me between the two of them.

"That...is not to be messed with," Afton says. I nod in agreement, and she gives me a pat on the chest.

"Okay, now what?"

"Don't worry," Kayley says, "I have a plan. We wait until those two are close together, then we get Teddy to zap them, and we get what we need and get out of here."

"Great, but where is Teddy?" I ask, scanning around. Our fuzzy friend is nowhere to be found, and now I'm back to getting perspiration on my perspiration.

Something taps me on the crown of my head, and I angle my head back to look up. He's there, suspended from the ceiling from his other tentacle.

"Teddy, what are you doing up there? Come down!"

Original Teddy makes a motion that's an approximation of a human response in the negative.

"Teddy. Come on!"

His lack of movement tells me he's not going to listen. I wonder if he's as afraid of the big cat as we are. They are both on the top of their respective food chains, so I wouldn't expect him to be scared, but who am I to judge?

"Who are you?" It's the clerk, standing at the doorway and frowning. "What are you doing here? This is restricted access."

"Um, Teddy?"

"What? Who's Teddy?" She puts her hands on her hips and glares at the three of us.

"Teddy... popsicle!"

The moment I call it out, she becomes the very personification of Teddy's ability. She's also very off-balance, and her frozen muscles can't keep her standing. The three of us jump forward to catch her and stop her from falling face-first onto the floor.

"Get her inside and close the door!" Kayley says, and we comply as fast as we can before we realize our serious oversight. There's little we can do, as our hands are full of clerk and we have yet to find a place to put her down.

The mega-feline makes a sound like someone scraping hard metal across glass. It stares at us with some sort of expectation. We've all stopped moving.

"What does it want?" Afton asks.

"Maybe it's still hungry," Kayley replies, her tone implying we might be its meal.

"Wait, what about the snacks?"

"We didn't bring any food with us, dummy," Afton says.

"No, I mean, the cat went into the room because she offered it something to eat. That's got to be around somewhere, right?"

"And who's going to feed it once we find it?"

"Rance, you do that, and we'll get the information," Kayley decides.

"Why me?"

"Because I'm in charge, and I type faster than you."

"KayKay, you can't keep using that as a reason."

"Yes, I can. I'm the leader."

We lay the clerk down on the row of chairs that Kayley puts together. The big animal comes over to its owner and sniffs the popsicled woman. Another wild cry comes from its mouth, and it approaches the three of us.

"You got this, Rance," Afton says, and the two of them scamper away to the terminal, throwing a few chairs in between them and the animal and effectively blocking me in with it. Even Original Teddy hops over the tables and joins them.

"Teddy, don't tell me you're afraid of this cat too," I say. "Come help me. Maybe you can talk to it."

"Nonsense," Teddy replies and stays where he is.

"Great, thanks, buddy."

The animal comes over to sniff at my hand. I pull back, but it continues to press forward, looking for the promised snack. If I don't come up with something, it might decide I'm a good enough substitute.

"Hey, guys, is there some kind of...animal protein over there? You know, something it might want to eat?"

"Eww, no," Afton says. "I wouldn't touch it even if there was."

The tall feline jumps up again, landing its front paws on my shoulders. I stumble as I try to steady myself from the sudden weight pressing on me. My heel catches on the edge of a chair and I fall, landing on my back. Now I have a large, hungry cat on me, and I really think I'm going to be its next meal.

If I yell for help, someone might come, but then we'll get arrested. I can't make any quick movements that this sharp-clawed animal will take for aggression either.

Wait...what if the clerk had something in her pocket that was the cat's snack? Can I even reach her pockets?

As I stretch my arm out to reach for her jacket, the deadly feline licks my face. I shut my eyes and bear it, but now I can't see, and I'm only guessing where her pocket might be. I keep trying, but I'm hitting air. I have to get closer.

With the sedate cat on top of me, I try sliding myself closer to the chairs, but I'm not pushing hard enough. I have to give it one hard shove, and I'll be there.

The big cat doesn't like that and jumps off me with a growl. I peek with one eye to see it watching me warily, one paw off the ground with its killer claws sliding out.

"Doing fine, Rance," Afton cheers me on. At least now I can move, and I slide as fast as I dare over to the clerk and check her pockets.

There's a bag there—success!

I pull out the bag and find that my prize was better left unseen. It's a clear pouch full of raw, bloody bits of flesh and muscle. My first reaction is to gag hard. My second one is to get dizzy at the putrid smell of dead animal in my hands. I have no idea how I'm going to wash that off.

The cat comes over instantly and bumps its nose right into the bag. I can't get it open fast enough, but its large muzzle won't fit inside. It bares its teeth at me as if it blames me for its inability to have a snack.

As the bag comes open, I grab it by the bottom and fling carcass bits about the room. The cat follows the first one and chases it down to gulp it up in one bite. Blood and animal fluid are getting everywhere as I toss the snacks around. Most of it is on me.

"Rance, we got it! Let's go!" Kayley says, standing and turning towards me. Her look is one of shock and horror as she takes in my bloody outfit.

"Don't worry, I'm fine. It's the snack bag."

Kayley nods at me silently, eyes wide.

"Oh, nasty," Afton says and wrinkles her nose as she catches sight of me. "You're riding in the back with the cargo, and the moment we get back you're hitting the shower, or else I'm opening the airlock to space as you're walking through it."

It's so nice to have friends who care.

Chapter Seventeen

"YOU CHECK OUT JUST fine, Rance," Doc Elizabeth says, patting me on the head as I lie in her examination chair. "No danger of you contracting some strange feline disease, and the raw flesh was likely free of microorganisms. You know, that animal's mouth is probably cleaner than your own."

"Hey, I'm proficient with oral hygiene!" I reply.

Afton made good on her promise to ensure I did nothing but get clean the minute I walked through the airlock of the Teddy ship. Kayley didn't even bat an eyelash to back me up or assist me in any way. It's a good thing Afton didn't have any weapons, or she would have marched me at gunpoint directly to the shower in Elizabeth's room. It's the only one on the ship, as Teddys don't shower. They clean themselves, but not by wasting a bunch of water spraying it all over a small enclosed space.

"That's not what I'm implying," Doc Elizabeth responds. "Many pets have been modified so that their saliva is a powerful antiseptic. Before that, they would easily spread disease, and an epidemic on a ship is a very bad thing."

"Wow, where'd you learn that?"

"Some of us have made good use of our free time," she replies. There is a definite implication there. I think it's about me. I should probably be insulted.

There's a buzzing in my pocket, but it's not from my Sergo—they don't work in space. So there's only one place it could be coming from. Danny. I jerk and try to reach into my pocket to grab the capsule, but my arms are held down, and a second later, I realize my legs are too.

"Hey, why am I strapped into the chair?" I cry. "Did you drug me?"

"Of course. It's normal procedure," Doc Elizabeth replies, "I think."

"For an examination? Let me up! I can't miss this call!"

"Relax, Rance, when did I ever do harm to you?" Doc Elizabeth comes over and unbuckles me. "On purpose, that is."

As soon as I'm free, I grab the capsule out and toss it on the counter. Danny blows a kiss and wiggles her fingers at me as her image appears.

"Hiya, honey! How're things? Make any progress yet?" Danny clasps her hands together and tilts her head towards me with a bright smile covering her face. Wherever she's connecting from is bright as well. That's fairly unusual for a ship...if she's even on one.

I blink when I realize her regular tight-in-all-the-wrong-places jumpsuit has been replaced with a bright yellow two-piece beach outfit that is so tiny it should be illegal.

"Where are you?"

"Oh, we're taking a short holiday on Littus! The water here is so lovely! None of that saltiness like on the other planets."

"My mother hates the beach," I comment, not knowing what else to say. I was expecting that I'd find my mom locked up in a tiny ship's cabin with nothing to do but read the poorly written romance novellas that I imagined Danny having on board.

"Oh no, she does not!" Danny corrects. "Don't you know your own mother? You live with her! She's having the time of her life right now. Why did you never take her on a nice holiday, Rancy? She's your mother, after all."

I open my mouth, but the nonsense detector in my brain is fast enough to stop me from responding to something so ridiculous. I'll admit she does have a talent for turning words around on me.

"Could you at least cover up, please?" I ask.

"Why?" Danny pouts. "It's just you and me, honey bunny. I don't mind you looking. Everyone here on the beach is."

"He's not alone, actually." Doc Elizabeth makes an appearance, stepping into the camera's view.

"Oh, heya, blondie." Danny is quick to change gears, but I notice a brief slip of her bubbly persona when she sees Elizabeth. "What are you up to? Playing doctor?"

"I do not *play* doctor," Elizabeth replies, folding her arms in front of her. "I am one."

"Where's my mom?" I demand. "Put her on!"

"Sure thing, snookums."

She picks up her device and takes it over to a small cabana where my mom is reclining on a daybed. She's got her typical tan summer shorts and peach-colored shirt on, but she's covered her head with the largest visor I've ever seen. The sunglasses and refreshing drink in her hand round out the outfit.

"Mrs. He', it's your son calling!" Danny shouts at her as if she's half-deaf, which she's not. My mom may have better hearing than I do.

"Rance?" My mom squints into the device—I'm guessing it's a Sergo of some type—and tries to find me on the screen. "Are you home?"

"No, Mom, I'm away at the moment. Are you okay?"

"Sure, just fine. Having a wonderful time," she replies. "Listen, don't forget to water the garden, and tell Kayley's mom I won't be over tomorrow, but I'll bring the marinade over on the weekend. Oh, and the toilet's acting up again. Can you replace the plunger? I forgot to get one the last time I was in town."

Leave it to my mother to only worry about the house. But if she thinks she's on holiday, fine. I'll play along. I don't want her to get scared. At least she seems okay. I don't trust Danny, though. She might have created some elaborate cover-up to hide what she's really doing to my mom.

"Yeah, sure, Mom, but you sure you're okay? Is Danny taking care of you?"

"Of course! Never better. Danny is a nice lady. She should stop dressing like she's in some type of racy cine, though. Even if she's got the boobs for it."

"Mom!"

Danny snatches the device away from my mom and makes sure she shows me how she beams politely at her before turning the camera back on herself.

"See? She's loving it. Now, when are you getting my man?"

Of course she'd get down to business right after I get to talk to my mom. This woman is all about leverage and manipulation. I guess it comes with her job, but I don't have to like it when she uses her hunter skills against me. At least this time I have something I can give her.

"Yeah, we found out where he is on Exodus. We're on our way there now. You'll have him back before the weekend."

I don't know if that's true, but I'm desperate to stay on Danny's good side while she's got my mom hostage.

"Oh great! Nice job!" Danny's voice is full of excitement, but her face is closing down into a frown. She rubs her chin and glances up.

"Is something wrong?"

"No...I mean...I'm trying to remember. Where did you say he was?"

"I didn't, but we got the record from a repository on Pruinonis. He's in seventh division, building 72-D, block H, cell 56." I'm proud of my ability to remember that after only hearing it once when we were on our way back to the Teddy ship. I'm even more proud that I heard it while confined to the cargo hold. That was a good thing too. Original Teddy was licking my shirt as we waited for the shuttle to pick us up.

"Oh!" Danny shouts and hops. "I remembered!"

"What is it?"

"They moved him!"

My jaw drops. All sorts of thoughts go rushing through my head. What does that mean? Did they move him off of Exodus? If so, where did they move him to? Did we get the wrong information?

"Why didn't you tell us?" My voice is pitched and edgy. Doc Elizabeth puts a hand on my shoulder—a reminder to keep my cool.

"Sorry, honey bun, I just found out. One of my friends on Exodus just called me."

I can't even begin to speak. Her statement leaves so many questions to be answered that I'm about to smash through the ship's hull and go swimming in space because that would be more enjoyable. I take a deep breath and try to think rationally about this total bonfire of a situation.

"Did they find out where?"

"No. Just that he was moved somewhere new."

"That's really not helpful!"

"Actually it is, Rancy darling—"

"Stop calling me pet names!"

Danny glares and clears her throat.

"As I was saying before someone *rudely interrupted*. At least now you know not to look for him in building 72-D, block H, cell 56."

I need to find a wall to go bang my head on several thousand times. That's an easy task compared to this nightmare quest from this crazy woman.

"Still, I'll give you an A for effort. Your little team is capable of something after all." Danny hugs herself and rocks back and forth. "That makes me feel all warm inside, you know. And for that, I'll give you the name of my contact over there. Give her a call, and I'm sure you'll be able to find out what you need."

I shake my head and shut the capsule back in its case. I can't talk to her anymore or I'm going to explode. Danny is in total control of me, and she knows I can't do anything about it.

"Well," Doc Elizabeth says, the side of her mouth turned down, "I suppose we need to go have a chat with the others, then."

Chapter Eighteen

I'M HAVING MIXED FEELINGS about being back in the Teddy canteen. We've only known Teddykind for less than the time it takes Angelcanis to revolve around its sun, and yet this space has become the center of so much drama. Among other emotional situations, it was where I betrayed Kayley and then found out that she really cared about me as much as I did her. When I went against her wishes, she was furious, but we got the data, and didn't die, so it all worked out.

And here we all are again, amid Teddys enjoying their daily murder ritual for nutrition. We're used to it now, but most Teddys still avoid eating close to us. We've been considerate too, by choosing a table off to the corner so they can have plenty of space to gobble down innocent little creatures. This also helps us avoid the smell that comes after they eat.

"So, there's a good chance he's still in the same building?" Kayley asks, setting a breakneck pace for wearing down the layers of the smooth dark floor. Her boots might give out first, the way she's clomping around. The rest of us try to keep out of the way so we don't get run over.

"That's what Danny thinks," I reply. Kayley sneers at the mention of her name. At least she hasn't directed her anger at me. I could stand to have a day without taking abuse from someone.

"This contact of hers, what does she know?" Afton asks, leaning on the wall.

"We didn't talk to her yet," I say. "Doc and I came right here after we talked to Danny. She's supposed to know Freddie's new location and will give it to me when we contact her."

"And you said Mom was okay, right?" Kayley asks again. I give her a thumbs-up, and she's content to get her concern confirmed…a third time.

"I can get a subspace call through once we get the address," Grady suggests as he leans onto the table. It's closed at the moment, so we don't have to worry about little fuzzy things scurrying about as we discuss. We still have to deal with the occasional squeals of terror from the other tables, but like I said, it doesn't bother us vegetarians as much anymore. Not that any one of us is going to try eating a live creature. It was bad enough I had a dead one all over me.

"Danny promised to get that to us soon." I don't want to add that she was going to go for a swim first. No one would receive that very well.

"Rance, are you sure? We can't have any delays here. Your mom—"

"Yeah, I got it." I'm glad Kayley's worried about her, but no one's more worried about her than me. I don't trust Danny's bubbly façade at all. That woman could drop poison into my mom's drink and still be wearing a smile.

"So, once we get that, we'll have a location, but that doesn't change any other part of our plan. We'll need to sparkle in and then get into the station," Kayley says.

"Let's not try another space transfer again," Parrish says. "That was dangerous enough last time."

"We can't," Grady says. "We trashed those suits during Rance's rescue. We don't have any substitutes."

The suits Grady is referring to came from Colonel Nelson and his team. I lost mine when I got caught on the *Mursilis*, and the other three, as Grady mentioned, probably were full of holes from weapons fire. We left them on the station where I was rescued. I bet there's quite a few holes in the station too. Not from us—Teddys don't have guns.

"We'll have to find a way to bring a shuttle up to a back door somewhere, then," Kayley says.

"Teddy, can the shuttles camouflage like the ship?" Parrish asks Original Teddy, who's sitting on the next table over with his Blue Buddy. BB, as we now call him, was really happy to see us when we first came back. Most of the Teddys that we met were. The captain was the only one who held his excitement in reserve. That's not so unusual. I don't remember him ever being overly expressive.

"That is accurate," Original Teddy replies. "Camouflage is supplemented."

"Great, half a problem solved," Afton comments. "Just ten million more to go."

"Maybe you'd like to give some input then, Surela," Kayley says as she spins towards her on the return part of her pacing. Afton blinks and squints at her as if she didn't hear what Kayley said. I'm hoping she didn't. We're doing good so far, keeping the drama level down, and I'd like to keep it that way.

"Hey, KayKay," I call, trying to help maintain the calm mood. "Come sit down for a bit."

My girlfriend just glances at me and continues on her back and forth warpath. Afton is still trying to figure out what she did wrong. She didn't miss the fact that Kayley used the S-word again, and once was already strange, but twice? I get that Kayley's anxious to get Mom back. So am I, but if she gets any more upset, she's going to wind up making everyone crazy.

"Guys, come on," Grady says. "We've done this before. We know what to do. I've even got a few more ideas on how to apply some Teddy tech I just found out about. It's going to be like snapping our fingers."

Grady tries to snap his fingers to prove his point, but he fails to make any sound. It's like an ominous sign. He even tries again, then stares at his fingertips, frowning.

"Like what?" Kayley stops for a moment, right in front of Grady, putting him on the spot.

"Well, I've got this new scout device I'm working on. It'll be able to hear footsteps and map the location of guards in your vicinity. I've got a few other things that hopefully I'll be able to get the Teddys to prototype for me before we get there."

"You've got tonight," Kayley says. "We're going tomorrow."

"Wait," Grady says, sitting up straight, "why so soon?"

"You want Mrs. He' to spend any more time with that insane woman?"

Grady presses his lips together and dips his head. He wouldn't want anything to happen to her any more than he would his own parents. At least my mom is willing to hug him when she sees him. His parents, not so much.

"And Rance, you're sitting this one out as well," Kayley states, turning to me. "You're too emotionally attached to this. Parrish and I will go with Original Teddy and BB. That's more than enough for this kind of mission."

Did I just hear that right? I'm off the mission to get my own mom back? I think I can find an infinite number of things wrong with that decision.

"Wait a second, KayKay!" I stand up. "That's not fair."

"Well, that's my decision, and I think it's completely fair."

Doc Elizabeth speaks up. "It could be argued that you are too emotionally attached to this situation as well."

Kayley turns to her with an eyebrow raised. "How am I emotionally attached?"

"She's basically your mom too," Afton grumbles, as unhappy as I am to get pushed aside.

"Exactly my point," Doc Elizabeth adds.

Kayley shakes her head as her eyebrows crash together. There's a bit of a red tint forming on her cheeks as well. It's subtle, but as I know every color and line of her gorgeous face, it's easy for me to notice. I can only imagine what bloody color mine is at the moment. At least Afton and the doc have my back. I'm glad to have Kayley here instead of away on her tour, but she's going too far with her decisions. It's my mom, and I should go. If I can't, I might just have to pull the plug on this whole thing.

"So you think I can't be objective about this, is that it?" Kayley confronts her accusers, putting her hands on her hips and shifting her stare between Afton and Elizabeth.

"Yes, that could be an issue," Doc Elizabeth says. "Perhaps it might be best to let Parrish lead this mission, along with Afton."

"Not interested in leading anything, really," Parrish comments, holding up his hands. He makes a great team captain and looks after his teammates well, but for anything outside of sports, Kayley is the default leader.

"Well, *I* am leading this mission, so I get to decide who goes and who stays, and my decision is final. Rance already got locked up once —"

"That wasn't my fault!"

"I didn't say it was."

There's a collective sigh from all of us. Or should I say, most of us. Kayley stands firm, and the Teddys don't express themselves like that. Doc Elizabeth, too, is unshaken. She's a doctor, so I would expect not much affects her, but the rest of us find ourselves in a predicament; my girlfriend seems hell-bent on reversing the roles that we were in last time we were planning a *go and get something* mission.

The records repository was just a warm-up compared to what we're about to do. It may not be as dangerous as sneaking onto the SIR *Mursilis*, but there could be some serious consequences if we get caught trying to break someone out. Kayley and Parrish could become permanent residents of Exodus, and I'd prefer not to just see her during visiting hours. If they even have them.

I catch Kayley's look. There's fire behind her eyes, and she's breathing a little faster than normal. The sight of her twists my stomach into knots, forcing me to take a few of my own heavy breaths. I need to back her off a bit, or we're all going into cardiac arrest.

"KayKay, honey, would you at least take another day to think about it? Mom seems fine..." I shrug, although I'm not in full agreement with my assessment. Danny's too much of an unstable element to know for sure. Maybe I shouldn't have told her we'd be done in two days.

"No, Rance," Kayley responds, with more aggression than I think she wanted to. So she takes a moment to take a breath and maintain her own sense of mental sanity. She walks over to me and crouches down before me, her hands clasped together in her lap. Then she reaches out and takes my hand, her voice calm when she speaks.

"Rance...darling, you've done plenty already, and we're still going to need you to do more. It's okay for you to take a back seat for once. I know you're not good at it, but"—Kayley glances down at the floor and swallows—"now that we're together, it's not good for both of us to be taking risks at the same time. What if something happened, and neither of us were around to take care of your mom?"

"I'd do it," Afton says. "Your mom is awesome."

"Yeah, me too," Parrish adds. Grady nods in agreement, and so does Doc Elizabeth.

I get a little teary-eyed as I glance around at my buds. They all look back with smiles on their faces. I don't ever want to worry about my mom being alone, but now I know I won't have to. How lucky I am to have friends like these.

Kayley's calmed down, and I should too. When I look into her eyes, the nuclear furnace that was there has cooled into a warm and sunny disposition. If she can do that, then I can trust she's got everything under control. Maybe I shouldn't have doubted her to begin with.

"Okay, then?" Kayley asks softly, giving my hand a squeeze.

I smile at my amazing lady. It gets rid of a few of the bumblebees bumping around in my stomach. I'm still going to worry about her until she returns, safe and unharmed. I'll worry about all of them, the Teddys included.

"Okay, KayKay," I say.

Chapter Nineteen

I'M STILL NOT PERFECTLY fine with sitting this one out, but I'll play the supportive boyfriend and try to see the benefits of this arrangement. I will get to watch Grady in action, and that's always exciting. Captain Teddy assigned us a special room with little space but lots of light and all the communication tools we could ever need. He also allowed Grady access to all the Teddys and resources we asked for. I think he was getting irritated that we were disturbing his ship operations when we were on the bridge. Bribery is apparently not just a human tactic.

The one thing that isn't exciting is all the waiting. We're stuck in this closet we call our command center while Kayley, Parrish, and the Teddys fly through space in relative luxury on the shuttle. The stagnant air and heat in here aren't helping either.

"So, Grady," I say, "just to review the plan again, they're going to dock at an obscure part of the station, right? And that will provide them the cover they need to get on the station and off with little to no interaction with station security?"

"What's the matter?" Afton asks after glancing at me. "Worried?"

"Not really."

"Liar. They'll be fine. It's just a simple pickup."

"Hey guys." Grady throws up a hand. "Hush up, they're almost at their entry point."

"Put it on speaker," I say.

"What speaker?" Grady replies, looking around. I'm stunned. I would have expected that we'd at least be able to listen in on their progress. Are we really going to have to do nothing but sit here and listen to a one-sided conversation?

"Stop trying to be funny and turn the speaker on before I bash you," Afton warns.

Grady sighs and reaches over to flick on the speaker. Had I just taken a quick glance to his right, I would have seen it and not just had a small heart attack.

"Just trying to lighten the mood a little," Grady moans. "Ease up… Surela."

"That's it!" Afton goes to jump to her feet, but the cramped space slows her down just enough for Grady to slide his chair back so she can't get up at all. That only enrages her more, and she grabs the back of his chair and pulls. Grady lets out a cry as he and the chair go tumbling backward, and he falls into the space suddenly evacuated by Afton and me.

Afton doesn't stop there. She licks both of her pointer fingers and jams them into his ears. Grady yelps and flails about, trying to get up, while Afton laughs maniacally at him.

"Grady, can you read?" Parrish comes on the Teddy comm, and we freeze. Afton and I share a wide-eyed look, and we grab the back of Grady's chair and turn him upright.

"Hey, Grady, you reading us?"

"Uh, yeah," Grady replies, fumbling to key his mic. "Sorry, just getting things organized here."

"Oh, okay. We're extending the tube now. So far, so good."

"Got it. Don't forget to turn on your telemetry devices." Grady types furiously on a keyboard while a blur of code lines go flying by on his screen. Another screen above him flickers on and begins to display data from the four infiltrators.

"Do we have a map?" I ask.

"No. Didn't get a chance to build that one," Grady replies. "They've got cameras on them, so we can see that, at least."

"I knew we should have waited," Afton mutters. I poke her in the shoulder for making me freak out more than I already am.

"I can fill in the gaps when they can't talk," Grady suggests. "I don't have a map, but I have positioning data along with the vid so I can guesstimate where they are."

"Good enough," I say.

"We've connected the tube," Kayley says, "just waiting for BB to give the okay that we've got positive pressure in there. Then we'll open the airlock and approach the door."

For me, this is the scariest part. They've dropped this ad hoc tube on the side of the shuttle so they don't have to spend half an hour to put on suits just to take them off five minutes later. I can't trust something so...temporary. Especially when it comes to the health of people I care about.

"Here we go. Turning our cameras on."

I glance up at the screen, eager to see Kayley. At first the vid is dark, but then she steps back from Parrish, and now we can see the two of them facing each other. Kayley turns to the inside of the shuttle, and BB is there, fiddling with some small device. He flips it over in his hands a few times, then turns to Kayley and does the best impression of a thumbs-up he can manage.

Kayley turns back to Parrish, and then they both head down the walkway to the tube and approach the outer airlock door on the station. It's not a standard human airlock—we couldn't have used those. They're way too guarded. This one is a leftover from the construction of the station. It was supposedly used to get supplies in and out but doesn't get used anymore. Hopefully it still works.

"Okay, Grady, so I just hit the top key, then the code, and then the green key?" Kayley asks.

"Yep. The same company that builds star cruisers does stations too." Grady chuckles. "Since no one has learned it in fifty years, they're too lazy to use a different code."

"Well, here goes nothing, then."

Kayley gets her hand near the panel, then jerks it away.

"It's freezing. I can't touch that with my bare hand!"

"Oh, yeah, that's a good point," Grady says. "Sorry, forgot about that."

"Here, use these," Parrish says and hands her a pair of suit gloves. I don't know where he got them from, but I'll give him points for thinking ahead.

There's silence while we watch Kayley type in the code. Her video flickers for a moment, so we don't know if she completed the first attempt properly. Kayley stares at the panel as if she's expecting something to happen. Then she keys the code in again.

"Tell her to hold down the seven and the eight while she keys in the other numbers," Afton says, jogging my memory of the last time we tried to do this. Points for Afton, too, for remembering that.

"Another good point." Grady keys his mic to explain the procedure to Kayley.

"How am I supposed to do that with gloves on?" Kayley asks, then tilts her head to examine the panel while she maneuvers her gloved hands around it. "Oh, got it. I can do it like this."

She presses the two adjacent keys down with one finger on her left hand while she types in the other keys. When she hits the final key, the screen lights up for a few seconds, then goes dark. Kayley watches it in anticipation, and we're all right there with her.

A half minute goes by, and still nothing. Afton groans and turns away while Grady scratches the back of his head.

Kayley tentatively tries a button. Then another. There's no response from the panel. Kayley growls and pounds the panel with a gloved fist.

"Hey, hey, easy! We need that to be in working condition," Parrish says, moving towards her with an arm outstretched.

"It's not in working condition," Kayley responds, "that's why I'm hitting it!"

"Is it dead?" I ask.

"Maybe," Grady mutters.

"Oh boy," Afton says and sighs.

"Examination is requested," Original Teddy says, his voice getting picked up by their microphones. Kayley and Parrish back away and let Blue Buddy step in. He gets up close to the panel, and from there it's hard to tell what he's doing. I think he might be sniffing it, but I'm not totally sure.

A few minutes later, Blue Buddy also pounds the panel, then turns away to reenter the ship. He pops and clicks to Original Teddy, who flings a slurry of tones back to him. Blue Buddy repeats what I think is the same set of sounds, and then Original Teddy turns to Kayley and Parrish.

"Conductivity is not available," Original Teddy says.

"No power," Grady translates and lands a heavy hand on his table.

"Did he say anything else? Like how we could fix it?" Parrish asks.

"That is accurate. Human construction is not welcome," Original Teddy replies.

"What does that mean?" I ask. I turn to Afton when she chuckles.

"That means he thinks our manufacturing is worth less than space junk," Afton says, "and he's not wrong."

"Okay then, ideas?" Kayley asks, looking around and trying to keep the mission moving forward. I overhear the Teddys having a spirited conversation, their pops and whistles increasing in intensity until Blue Buddy turns away and heads towards the back of the shuttle. Kayley takes notice and turns to Original Teddy. I'm sure she's expecting an explanation.

"Aggressive entry recommended," Original Teddy says.

"Aggressive, as in..." Kayley pauses to consider his meaning. When she figures it out, a small gasp leaves her mouth. "You mean you want to blow up the airlock?"

"That is accurate."

"Isn't that dangerous?"

"It's *really* dangerous," Grady says, "and I don't recommend it. An explosion could damage the tube or rupture the seal on the station, and you definitely don't want to be around when that happens. Besides, an explosion will get noticed, and that ruins everything."

"Then, what?"

"Then we go back to the drawing board and figure out a better way to get in."

"You mean," Kayley says, her voice measured, "call the mission off, then come back once we've gotten another solution?"

"Exactly."

"No way," Kayley replies. "We don't have time for that. Rance's mom is in danger, and we don't have the luxury to just approach this like it's a hobby. No, we have to figure this out. Now, let's start from the top. What can we—"

"Uh, sorry to interrupt you, KayKay," I say, "but Grady, what's that blue light shining into the tube near the seal?"

"Huh?"

Both Parrish and Kayley turn to look that way, and the blue light comes in more clearly through their cameras. It's moving around as if it's attached to something that wants to find a way into or through the tube.

"What is that?"

"It's a maintenance bot," Grady says. "It's come to fix the panel."

"Great, why don't we just let it, then?" Kayley suggests. I think that could be a good idea. Afton shrugs her assent when I glance at her.

"Because it's not automated," Grady replies, in a matter-of-fact tone, then mutters a curse when he realizes what he just said. Someone is controlling that thing, which means that any second now, humans will notice the big tube stuck to the side of the station, and that will end any attempt at getting in.

Before Grady can issue a warning, we hear the hiss of air moving. Parrish and Kayley scan around, trying to find the source of the sound.

The airlock opens, and a fully suited repair worker steps out. He is so interested in the tube that he doesn't notice the ship attached to it. That doesn't last long.

So much for the rescue mission.

Chapter Twenty

"WHAT THE HELL?" THE man says the moment he catches sight of Kayley and Parrish staring back at him.

"Shut the airlock!" Parrish yells, backing away. At first the maintenance worker frowns at him and points to the station lock as if Parrish were talking about that one. His mouth opens to make a comment, but the door to the Teddy shuttle shuts in his face.

"Teddy, disengage the tube!" Kayley shouts. Afton and I get restless on the floor, and my stomach churns something fierce. If they were back on the ship with us right now it wouldn't be soon enough. I can only imagine what high-ranking security official the maintenance man is calling to either arrest or shoot our infiltration team.

The cameras go dark, and I rise to my feet. Afton follows, and we both grip the back of Grady's chair as if we'd fall off the ship if we didn't.

"What's happening? Are they okay?" I cry.

"Telemetry is still working, but they've gone silent," Grady explains. "No need for them to make chatter that might get picked up by the station."

My fingers are curling themselves into knots as we wait for them to get clear of the station's sensors. Then we'll be able to speak with them again. Then I'll know they're safe.

"How long, Grady?" I ask.

"Not sure, but it shouldn't be more than a few minutes."

Even a few minutes is hard to bear. Afton becomes the physical personification of my emotions. First she tries standing, then she sits back on the floor, kneels, and finally decides on a crouch. I have to stand, but if it wouldn't be distracting for Grady, I'd be jumping up and down in panic mode instead. I have no idea how he manages to stay calm staying back like this.

"Okay, we're clear," Parrish whispers into his mic. Not sure why he feels the need to speak quietly, but I'm so glad to hear his voice. "We should be back in about two hours."

"No, we're returning to the station," Kayley says, her voice hard. At least that's what I think she said. I glance down at Afton for confirmation, and she's as slack-jawed as I am.

"Wait," Grady says, "repeat that. Did you say you're *going back?*"

"Yes. Teddy, turn the shuttle around."

"Wait, wait, wait, wait." Grady holds up a finger and shakes it every time he speaks. "Kayley, that's a really, *really* bad idea. If they see you coming, they might just attack, and even if you get to the station, you can't get in the way we planned. They'll be watching all of the old airlocks now."

"Then we won't go that way," Kayley replies. "Is Rance there? Tell him to get in touch with Danny's contact again, and tell her to get us in the front door. We'll figure another way out once we're inside."

Of course I'm here! Where did she expect me to be? More importantly, what in the holy names is she doing? My girlfriend is sprouting some crazy talk, and I've got to stop her before someone gets hurt.

"Let me talk to her," I say, moving next to Grady to get access to the mic. He gives me the space without question and slides the mic key over to me. "Kayley? Are you there? It's me."

"Oh good," Kayley says. "Yes, Rance, call Danny's contact. Tell her to find a pair of security badges and meet us at the main entrance."

"KayKay, that's not going to work! Even if she agrees to do it, you guys already triggered security, and they'll be looking for you. The moment someone notices you, it's over. You can't take that chance! Please, come back. We'll figure out another plan."

"This is the best time for us to just walk in," Kayley says. "Security will be so focused on the airlocks, they won't think to put much effort into the main entrance. All we need to do is get in and get to the right building. Once we do that, we'll find a back way out, and the Teddys can pick us up."

"KayKay, no. You haven't had a chance to think it through. There are too many things that can go wrong that you won't be prepared for."

"You mean like, going the wrong way and getting caught?"

It hurts, but I can forgive my girlfriend for the cheap shot because she's really stressed out at the moment and trying to make the best choices she can. But her decision is totally reckless, and I have to make her see that. Besides, I went the wrong way on purpose.

"Kayley, honey," I say, as gently as I can. "I'm sorry, but I can't do what you ask. You're not thinking straight, and that's going to get you into trouble. I don't want anything to happen to you, so please, come back?"

There's silence from her side, and I worry that she's shut the Teddy comm off and is going back without our support. I glance at my buds, hoping they have an explanation. Grady just shrugs and shakes his head. Afton offers nothing more either. She can't even meet my eyes, deciding to stare at the floor instead. I sigh and say a small prayer to the Goddesses that they'll show a little mercy to me and bring Kayley back.

"Rance," Kayley comes back, her voice flat, "if you want us to be together past this moment, you'll do as I say. I'm getting this guy, and then we're getting your mom back safe. I told you that's what I was going to do, and I don't want to hear you try to stop me any longer. Now, call that contact, and if you don't want me dead, you'll make sure she's waiting for us when we get back there."

Did I just hear that correctly? There's no way she just threatened to break up with me. That can't be right. I know she's trying to be a strong leader, but this is over-the-top nuts. I don't know what to be more afraid of—Kayley leaving me or her getting hurt. Or worse.

"What the hell should I do?" I ask out loud, my eyes getting wet. I'm surprised at myself for being so emotional, but when it comes to KayKay, I'm a total puddle.

"Call Danny's contact," Grady suggests. "There's no way she can get badges so quickly, and that'll be the end of it. They'll have to come back."

"Do one better," Afton adds. "Tell her to say she couldn't find badges fast enough, and then they'll just turn around."

"Yeah," I say, running a hand through my hair and taking a breath. "Yeah, good idea. I'll...I'll do that."

Grady taps some keys and gets us hooked up to the local Sergo network via subspace carrier wave. It's only text, but it'll do. He gets up and lets me sit down in the chair so I can get my message across.

The only number Danny gave me was for Quinn. Danny kept saying "her," so I assume it's a woman. I don't really care either way, as long as this Quinn agrees to play along with my ask.

RANCE: Hey Quinn, I need your help!

QUINN: What you need?

RANCE: We've got two of ours arriving on station. Can you get two security badges so they can get through the front door?

QUINN:

RANCE: The thing is, I don't want you to actually do it. There's too much buzz around the facility right now, and I'd really like them to just come back before they get into trouble.

QUINN: So that was yous that set off the alarm?

RANCE: Yes.

QUINN: Big trouble, that.

RANCE: I know! That's why I want them to come back. Can you do that for me?

QUINN: Danny said give you what you need, so yes. It done.

RANCE: Thank you! We owe you one.

QUINN: Nope. This paid by Danny.

I sigh with a light feeling as I sign off. They'll have to come back now. I'm sure I've done the only thing I can to protect Kayley. Parrish, too. And the Teddys. I don't know how I could handle it if any of them got hurt. Of course, I should have thought that through before we decided to put this little team of ours together. There's always a risk when you're in the problem-solving business.

All we have to do now is wait for them to get back on and tell us that they're coming back because the mission failed—a second time. If that's not enough to get Kayley to realize she needs to call it quits, then I've no idea what'll reach my girlfriend. We'll get Freddie, and we'll get my mom back. I know we will. Besides, Danny promised to take good care of my mom. She might be loony, but I don't think she wants to hurt my mom. I hope that doesn't change.

"What do you guys think?" I ask after I tell them what Quinn said.

"It's the best you could have done," Grady says, sounding confident. "Don't worry, they'll be back soon enough."

I glance at Afton, and she bites her lip as she looks back at me. She's not admitting it, but I know what she's saying. I feel the exact same way. I'll relax once they're all back on board, safe. Hopefully that will be soon.

The moments click by, and the three of us return to our routine of waiting while imaginary bugs crawl all over our skin. None of us can be still for even a moment, and we wind up standing together in the icebox-sized space. But it's not cold at all, of course. My cheeks are burning, and I could almost slice the air in here, as thick as it is. Even so, I don't dare leave. There's no way I'm missing their call.

"Damn, this is torture," Grady says.

"Worse," Afton says.

I can't breathe, and as I look at my two buds, I notice they can't either. It's not the air, which is bad enough. It's the waiting.

"Grady..." Kayley's voice comes on, but it's not forceful like before. She's gasping for air as if she just ran from one side of the station to the other without stopping.

"I'm here," Grady says, keying the mic and hopping into the chair at the same time. "What's happening? Everything okay?"

"We're returning," Kayley says, and the three of us remove the atmosphere's worth of air from our lungs in record time.

"Thank the Goddesses," I say, setting a reminder in the back of my brain to do a super-merit at the nearest temple the moment we touch back down on Angelcanis.

"Parrish's been shot. Inform Elizabeth." It sounds like her mouth is on autopilot. She got the words out, but there's no hint of emotion connected to them.

All the feeling goes out of me, and everything becomes distant. Parrish...shot? I don't know how to respond to that. The last hour has been nothing but a nightmare, and it's about to get worse. We've waited for casualties on this ship before. Two people died at the end of it.

"Come on," Afton says, grabbing hold of my arm. I don't know whether it's for my support or hers, but it doesn't matter. We need each other in this awful moment. She won't let go of me, and I won't let go of her.

All that matters is that we do everything we can to ensure our friend survives.

Chapter Twenty-One

WE HUDDLE TOGETHER, AWAITING the shuttle's return with bated breath. Neither I, nor Afton, nor Grady want to enact any of the routine motions of life for fear that a simple hand gesture or inhale will cause irrecoverable damage to our friend.

As I replay the situation in my head, I keep thinking how stupid I was to panic at Kayley's threat. I shouldn't have believed her, but at that moment, she was so convincing. Now that I've had time to consider it, I realize she couldn't have meant what she said. There must have been something more I could have done or said to convince her not to go through with it.

Why am I such an idiot when it comes to her?

"Let me in there first, okay?" Doc Elizabeth says as she arrives in the shuttle bay with a small bag of medical stuff. We nod affirmation and step aside, wishing all the power in the universe to her to save Parrish. It's at that moment I have my first doubt. I know Elizabeth is an actual doctor, but I have no idea how much experience she's had healing weapon wounds.

Afton and Grady push closer to me as if they just read my thoughts. They care for Parrish as much as I do. They care for Kayley too, but she's the unknown variable at the moment until we know what happened. I hate thinking it, but if she endangered Parrish in some way, she's got to take responsibility for her actions.

I hear the hiss of the inner airlock door and drive my focus there. It dissolves, and there stand Original Teddy and Blue Buddy, suspending Parrish above them. I didn't know their tentacles were so strong, but at this moment I am supremely thankful they are.

Doc Elizabeth rushes over to give Parrish a quick triage examination. I await her determination, clenching my hands together so tightly my thumbs go numb.

"He's been hit in the thigh and the arm," she says, glancing over at us, "not mortal wounds, but serious enough. Don't worry, I'll be able to take care of him."

They proceed through the shuttle bay and head to Doc Elizabeth's room. I really want to go with them, but my feet won't move. I need to see if Kayley's okay first.

"Hey," I say, seeing Kayley step through the airlock. Her face is a mask, and she takes no notice of me. So, thinking she may want some comfort, I go to embrace her with my arms wide, glad she's returned safely. But Kayley sends her arm straight out and shoves me away. She stomps down the hallway without a word, and she's gone.

I'm dispatched to purgatory by her action. I had pumped myself up, expecting to console her as needed, but my girlfriend has shut herself into a dark place. Maybe I'm not the solace she needs, but I can't even begin to say how much it hurts me to think that.

"Go help Elizabeth," Afton whispers in my ear, "I've got Kayley... and don't worry. That's the best thing you can do for her right now."

With a squeeze of my arm, she sprints off after Kayley. I don't like it, but I have to trust that she's right. If there's anyone who can function somewhere near normal right now, it's Afton.

"I'm going to help Elizabeth," I say, turning to Grady. "You coming?"

"No, dude," Grady replies, pressing his hand to his stomach. "I...I gotta review the recordings...see what we can do better...you know, for next time."

I know it's an excuse, but if that's the best therapy for him, then who am I to stop him? I drop a hand on his shoulder, and out of nowhere, Grady wraps his arms around me. I stiffen at his motion, surprised. Grady isn't a touchy-feely kind of guy, but the rest of us are, and I think it's starting to rub off on him. If that's what he needs, I'm okay with that. I need it too.

Grady pulls back, rubs a sleeve across his nose and then takes off, leaving me as the sole human in the shuttle bay. The few Teddys here go about their business, doing whatever they need to do to power down the shuttle and secure it. They're aware I'm here and give me a wide berth. All that does is remind me that I'm alone.

But I have a friend who needs me, and that's where I should be.

"Ah, Rance," Doc Elizabeth says as I open the door to her room, "thanks for showing up. I do need some help. Kayley should be the one assisting me, but I expect she's not in the best frame of mind at the moment, is she?"

"Forget it," I reply, pushing in. "What do you need?"

"First things first." She nods over at the table. "Grab that green bottle and rub that stuff on your face and hands."

"What is it?"

"You might have touched something dirty without knowing it, so we're just making sure you can't spread any microbes into your friend here. The ventilation system will take care of anything else."

I do as she directs and stand opposite her on the other side of Parrish. He's lying unconscious on the exam chair, which the doc has raised and flattened out to resemble something more like a table. She's got a respirator on his face and some kind of tube stuck into his good arm. As I take him in, a host of bad thoughts rush through my head.

"Ouch!" I glare at the doc as she retracts a needle from my arm. "What's that for?"

"Checking compatibility. We may need to give Parrish blood." She turns around and slides the syringe into a small box on the table behind her. "Ideally, it'd come from a relative, but since there's none of those on the ship, we'll have to take some from one of us."

"So?"

"So." Doc Elizabeth watches the readout on the box. "Not an exact match, but his body can still receive blood from you."

"Whatever he needs." I hold out my arm to her. "I'm ready to give as much as you need to take."

"Not yet." She holds up a hand to me. "He's stable now, but that may change when we try to clear up any of the damage."

My eyes go wide as I envision her slicing into the body of my friend and shoving her tools into his wounds. This is going to be pure anguish for me if Parrish starts to feel pain. If he can just lie there, like he's just sleeping, and wake up after we're all done patching him up, that'd be for the best.

"Are you sure you can save him?" I ask after I hear Doc Elizabeth exhale long and slow.

"Save? Of course, but that's not what's worrying me."

"What, then?"

"Let's just start, and then we can talk, okay?"

I try to remain as attentive as possible and listen to every direction that Doc Elizabeth gives me. I'm still afraid, though. I have to fight my hands from shaking when I hold some tool or device for her. She talks gently to me, and that helps. I just have to focus on whatever task we're doing, and then any thoughts about our procedures going wrong will stay away. I don't want to accidentally kill my friend because I have no idea what I'm doing. I can only trust that Doc Elizabeth will keep me from making any mistakes.

"You're doing fine, Rance," she says, "going slow is fine. We're almost done with his arm. Just need to assure the connective tissue is secure enough, so it'll heal on its own."

"Glad to hear that."

"Alright then, let's get on with his leg, shall we?" Doc Elizabeth looks at me with lips pressed. Her current mood isn't creating any level of enthusiasm in me. We're half-done, so that's something. Parrish didn't move or flinch all the time we were working on his arm, so that's good too. But something is bugging the doc, and I have to know what it is, or it'll bug me too.

"Why are you worried about his leg so much?" I ask.

"Well, considering where he got hit, just above the knee like that. There's a lot of important stuff there," Doc Elizabeth answers. "And given he's an athlete..."

She just waves a hand at him but says no more. She doesn't have to. I understand the consequences of doing a bad job here. None of us would ever want to tell Parrish that he could never run again. I'm helpless to do anything more than what Doc Elizabeth tells me. I have to trust that she's got his best interests in mind and that we won't have to make any compromises to get him on his feet again.

"Hold that here"—Doc hands me a suction device and moves my hands exactly where she wants them to be—"and don't move. I need the space to fix what I can."

I hold the device in both hands, putting all of my brainpower into making sure it does not move one micrometer from the spot where Elizabeth placed it. She grabs a fresh set of metal tools from her tray, one sharp and one not, and gets to work.

Creases and perspiration form on her brow as she manipulates the devices inside Parrish's leg. I'm hypnotized by her intensity. The rest of the room dissolves around me, and all I see are my hands, Doc Elizabeth and the wound. She works quickly, making minute movements with her hands only someone with years of skill could manage. I wonder how that's possible, given she's only a few years older than me.

"Rance!" Doc Elizabeth shouts, shocking me back to reality. My whole body flinches, and I watch helplessly as my hands shake and move the suction device outside of my allotted space.

"I'm sorry! I didn't mean it!" I cry.

"Don't worry, it's alright," she says, glancing up at me. "You didn't hurt him. Just stay vigilant, okay?"

"Yes, definitely, absolutely. Anything!"

Blood bubbles up and spills over the side of Parrish's wound, running down his knee. When the doc notices the panic on my face, she looks down.

"Oh, dammit. Not now!"

"What? What's going on?"

"There, go there." She grabs my hands and moves them again. "Stay there until I tell you to go back, okay?"

"Yes, got it!"

I'm desperate to know what's happening, but I don't want to interrupt her. She's working more furiously than before, and even though she said I didn't, I can't help but think I messed up. My buddy is bleeding out because of me. He must be. Doc Elizabeth would never tell me if I did something wrong, but the guilt is swelling up in me, and it's making it difficult to keep steady.

"Now back," she commands with a firm tone. "Move slowly...a little more...almost...stop there. Good. Now hold it."

"What happened?" I ask again.

"No talking," she replies.

It's a long time before she says anything again, leaving me to stew over my actions. It was just a second. Less, even. Could I have just caused Parrish to lose his ability to walk, much less run? When I think about it, I can't breathe. I regain my breath again, but the guilt remains.

Doc Elizabeth sighs and steps back to lean on the counter behind her. She rubs a hand across her forehead and, just for a moment, looks up at the ceiling.

"Okay, you can take it out. Slowly, very slowly. That's good. Just lay it down there."

"Is Parrish..."

"I don't know, Rance. Honestly, I do not know."

"But his wound?"

"I'll seal it shut in a moment." Doc Elizabeth's body sags as if she's just run the marathon that Parrish was hoping to complete. "The rest is up to him, but now, I'll be having your blood."

I sit and watch my blood drain from my arm and seep into Parrish's. Except for the small pinch of the needle, I feel nothing and wonder if this lack of action on my part will really save his life. If that's true, I can do nothing all day long, if only for the survival of my friend.

"Good, Rance," the doc says once the transfusion is complete. "I couldn't have done it without you, and I do mean that honestly. Go rest. You're going to feel tired with all the life I just sucked out of you. It was a bit more than I expected, but you'll be alright. Make sure you drink some water too. I'll finish up here and come find you later."

"Thank you, Elizabeth. If you weren't here—"

She stops me from finishing the sentence and shakes her head. She may not want praise, but I'm ready to heap it on her by the starship load.

"Go rest, okay?" Doc Elizabeth says, patting me on the back.

"I will, but, just like you, I've got something to take care of first."

Chapter Twenty-Two

I ARRIVE AT THE door of Kayley's and my berth and slump on the wall. Doc Elizabeth was right—I am not up for anything other than lying down, closing my eyes, and sleeping until we're back home. But as much as I want to do that, I can't. I need to talk to my girlfriend, or at minimum, listen to what she wants to say.

Hesitation sets in as I'm about to open the door. What if she's not ready to talk to me? Kayley might just shut me out like she did down in the shuttle bay, and right now, I don't have the emotional capacity to handle that. I have to trust that Afton did what she could and Kayley will be ready to talk.

I try knocking instead of barging in like a thoughtless human being. But after I do, I realize that's also problematic. If Kayley answers and she's not ready to see me, that's going to be supremely awkward for the both of us.

As the door dissolves, it's Afton who answers. I sigh in relief and give her the best smile my lethargic face can create. Afton curls an edge of her mouth, then glances back inside. She ushers me away from the door so she can step out and shut it behind her.

"What did you do to yourself?" Afton asks, her mouth curl turning into a grin. "You look terrible, buddy."

"I think I just gave Parrish half of my blood."

Afton's mouth drops open. I don't think she expected that answer.

"How is he?" she asks quietly.

"Still unconscious, but Doc Elizabeth fixed him up." I don't want to say more. Afton would take it hard if she knew there was some question about Parrish's future physical fitness. The two of them have run across half our planet together.

"Can I see him?"

"Sure," I say with a shrug. I'm not about to tell her no, or give her some concern about why that's not a good idea. She should go see him. Even if he might not be aware she's there, I get the sense that he'd know, somehow.

"Okay." Afton turns to go, but then pauses. "Rance."

"Yeah?"

"She'll see you, but go gentle, okay?"

"No worries. I don't have the strength for anything else."

I shut my eyes for a minute, preparing myself for the potential Kayley onslaught that happens once I step inside. I can bear it, whatever it is. As long as she doesn't push me away again. That I couldn't handle.

I take a breath, press the button, and step through. Kayley's there, lying on the low futon mattress—another Teddy installation. I don't know where they got it from, but I'm very much looking forward to collapsing into it.

Kayley lies on the far edge, her back turned towards me. I shuffle over, drop myself down, and swivel towards her. It's not anywhere near as graceful as I intended, and it shakes the entire futon and Kayley with it. She doesn't react, and I wonder if she might be asleep.

"Hey," I say, testing the waters. I'm met with only a sniffle. I have no idea what it means, but I know she's awake. Should I say something more, or do I just keep quiet and let her speak when she's ready?

"Parrish?" Kayley asks, her voice broken and weak.

"Resting and safe," I reply, thinking of the best way to answer her. My brain won't find a best way, so I give her whatever words my mouth will form. "Elizabeth did an amazing job."

"Did you help him too?"

"I hope so."

Kayley sniffles again and goes quiet. That wasn't the response that I'd hoped for. Maybe I should have been more confident and told her he would be fine, but I don't know if that's true. I won't lie to her. She doesn't need that right now.

"It's my fault, isn't it?" she asks, and every sense in my body goes on full alert. My answer just made things worse. She's putting the blame on herself, and whether that's the truth or not, I can't let her go down that deep, dark hole.

"No, KayKay," I say. "The person who shot him is guilty. Not you."

"No," she counters, "that guard was only doing what they were trained to do. I put Parrish in danger."

I swing my feet up onto the futon and roll over to her. I go gently, as Afton advised, and just for the moment, only touch her shoulder so she knows I'm here—that I support her—and that I'm here to stay.

"Why don't you tell me what happened?" I suggest. "We can talk it through and figure it out together."

"What's the point?" Kayley rolls onto her back and covers her eyes with the palms of her hands. "Parrish is hurt, badly...maybe permanently. We weren't even close to getting in, and Mom's still with that...psycho."

Her hands clench over her face, and she digs her palms into her eyes as if she wants to stop herself from ever seeing anything again. As she falls deeper into her darkness, my heart breaks. I feel a welling in my chest, and I want to cry out as if that alone would break her from her misery—but it won't. I have to step up and figure this one out, or she will hate herself forever.

"KayKay, Mom's okay. I talked to her. She asked me to make sure all her plants were watered. No one does that if they're scared out of their mind."

"It doesn't matter," Kayley says. "I promised you that I'd get her back, and I failed."

She slides her hands down and sniffles again with a shaky breath. It's then I realize she hasn't looked at me since I came in, and that's grinding on me. I know she's upset, but I could really use some hope to know if I can help her get out of her dark place. Maybe I can't. Maybe I'm just selfish—I don't know. I'm not her equal in so many ways, and I've never had self-confidence the way she's had it. I just wish Kayley would look at me. Then I'd know I can care for her.

"It's not the end of the world, Kayley. Parrish will be okay, Mom will—"

"How can you be so sure?"

I pause to take a breath. I can't fudge this answer, or she'll shoot it down faster than this ship can jump. The problem here is that I have no idea what the answer is. I'm just trying to give her a little comfort so she doesn't blame herself for everything that's happened.

"Well, I think it's because..." I have to pause to think. My brain isn't cooperating the way I need it to, and I really need it to.

"You don't have any idea, do you?" Kayley wasn't meeting my gaze before, and now she's averted her eyes to the farthest possible corner of the room from where I am. If Kayley wants to discuss failure, we could talk about how I'm totally screwing up this conversation.

"Honestly, no," I admit. "But if we're all together, I think we can solve this. We'll find a way to get Dan—her husband back, and my mom safe. That I'm sure of."

"Well, Parrish is out," she says. "He's not going to be able to help."

"Yeah, but he's—"

"And you should count me out too."

Did I just hear that right? Did she just speak the worst possible words she ever could have said? I've never known Kayley to quit anything, and I can't believe that she would start now.

"Kayley, no! Please, we need you!"

"No, you don't. I've already proven that I'm not capable of being a good leader. You don't need me to screw anything else up. I'm done, Rance." Kayley drops her gaze. "I don't think I'll even go back to the tour. Angelcanis doesn't need to listen to a screw-up."

"Well, then, I need you."

"Why?"

"Because...I love you."

That turns her eyes my way, though not with the look I was hoping for. This is a glare, a narrow-eyed, smoldering glare. I'm guessing that my timing is off. I wasn't even planning to say it. The words just came out, and maybe I only meant to say how much I care about her, but it's too late to take it back.

"No," Kayley says, her voice low.

"No, what?"

"You don't get to use those words as some free pass when you can't think of what to say. I don't accept them." Kayley turns her back on me and lies back down on her side.

Goddesses help me. I'm in trouble now. Not only did I mess up, but Kayley's shut down, and unless I come up with something, this could be the end of her as our leader. There's no way I could replace her. Only Parrish has leadership experience, and he's out too. Nothing against Grady or Afton, but the three of us are not command material.

The team will fall apart if Kayley's not our leader. It'll crash completely. And if there's no team, we'll eventually get lost in our own pursuits and stop hanging out altogether. This is the very thing I didn't want to happen, and part of the reason I begged everyone to become a team—so we didn't have to go our separate ways.

"I'm sorry, KayKay," I say and slide next to her so I can wrap my arm around her. She doesn't object, but she doesn't react either. I shake as I pull in a breath. I've no more energy to keep my emotions down any longer. They come pouring out of me as if I'm a pitcher of water, tipped over. "You're right. I didn't know what to say. I'm not thinking straight. Doc said that might happen when I gave Parrish my blood."

"You did what?" She presses against me and turns her head. She's not looking at me directly, but it's better than getting a full-on cold shoulder.

"Elizabeth said Parrish had lost a lot of blood and that I could donate some to him so he could recover faster. I'm not like you, KayKay. I don't know anything about medical stuff. I just wanted to help in any way that I could. I mean, that's what we do for each other, right?"

"Of course," Kayley says and turns fully around to face me, putting a hand on my chest. Her other hand goes to my forehead and watches my face for a moment. "Do you feel sick at all?"

"No, but I don't care even if I did. If it helps him, then he can have all my blood."

"It doesn't work like that," Kayley says. I know I'm just dripping words out of my mouth at this point, just mind to mouth with no filter in between.

"But it does, KayKay. That's what you're like to our gang. You're like the blood that gives it life. You invigorate us, give us the will to accomplish things we never thought we'd be capable of on our own.

You understand what we can do and bring out the best in all of us. No one else can do that, and if you quit, well, we'd lose our lifeblood, and we can't live without it."

Kayley looks down at the bedding, pensive. Her delay in response gives me hope I may have said something that made sense to her. I have no idea what that might be since I can't remember a single word I just said.

"Kayley?" I ask, hoping for something more than silence.

"Lie down," she commands and pushes me, so I turn to lie on my back. Kayley snuggles up to me and puts her head on my chest. I respond by wrapping my arms around her, but I'm not yet comfortable. There's still a little itch inside my head that will only get scratched with some kind of a response from her.

It doesn't come right away, and even though I'm fighting to keep my eyes open, no way will I sleep until she says something—anything at all that might give me hope that our little team isn't over. Because if that happens, then what I'm really afraid of could happen. The end of the team could also mean the end of Kayley and me. She'd go off somewhere far away to forget about all this, and I won't be able to follow.

"No promises," Kayley says, her voice a soft vibration on my chest. "I need to sleep on it, at least. I still have too much doubt in my head."

"Okay. I understand." My hand brushes through her scarlet strands, sliding through them without the slightest bit of effort. It's not the answer I wanted, but I can't push for more.

"But...Rance, I want you to know..."

"Yes?"

"When I'm with you, I'm exactly where I want to be. I have no doubt about that."

Chapter Twenty-Three

IT WAS TWO MORE days to get us back to Angelcanis. I wanted to save time and sparkle-drive back, but Captain Teddy said it wasn't good to overuse the drive. Well, that wasn't exactly what he said. There were a lot less words that amounted to his usual "not recommended." Personally, I think it's not working again.

Kayley stayed mostly in our berth and slept, and I didn't push her to do more than that. She did come out to have a few meals with us, though I noticed the wistful look she would give everyone when they laughed and joked around together. I'm sure she was thinking the same thing I was—it wasn't the same without Parrish. I tried to organize a meal or two up in Doc Elizabeth's room so we could eat with him after he woke up. The doc was cool with it, but Kayley wouldn't go.

I saw the disappointment on Parrish's face when I tried to come up with some excuse for why she didn't visit. I'm sure he knew the real reason. He didn't blame her for his wounds, and I knew he felt bad that Kayley was ashamed to show her face to him. We'll have to figure that one out, or we won't ever be a team again. First, Kayley has to give me her answer, which she hasn't yet.

Once we got back, Parrish wouldn't go home. He didn't want his mom to freak out, so he just told her he was staying over at my place for a few days. Doc Elizabeth decided to stay too, along with Original Teddy and his Blue Buddy.

"Hey, Rance, someone's at the door," Afton says when the doorbell rings. She's sitting at the kitchen table watching me while I'm attempting to figure out how to cook breakfast. I got picked to do it because it's my house, and other than the guy who can't walk, no one else offered their assistance.

"Yeah, thanks. I heard it. You did notice I'm kinda busy, right?"

"Fine, I'll get it." Afton gets up and heads out of the kitchen. But before she exits, she freezes and her eyes go wide. "Shoot."

"What? Who is it?"

"Brownjerk."

"Dammit! Him? What the hell does he want?" Then I remember our little escape. "Do you think he's going to arrest us because we gave him the slip?"

"Nah." Afton glances at me with a smirk. "Don't worry. If we were being arrested, he wouldn't have pressed the doorbell."

"Go make sure the Teddys are hidden," I say, wiping my hands on my mom's apron.

"Ah! Mr. He', good morning!" Deputy Brownrigg is all smiles as I open the door. So far, Afton's right. He doesn't want to arrest us, but then, what is he doing here?

"Tea?" I offer, just because then I can cook and talk.

"Thank you, but no, not this time," Brownrigg replies. "I'm in a bit of a hurry, you see."

"Oh? Why's that?"

"Well, the very thing I came here to ask you about."

I stare at him. If he's trying to trigger a thought or make me suggest something he could use against me later, it's not happening. I'm not falling for that. I'm well wise to that play since Afton has tricked me with it once too often. She doesn't even bother with that tactic anymore.

"We think," Brownrigg explains, "there was an attempted break-in, or breakout...well, that's what we're trying to determine...at one of our penitentiary stations."

"What's that got to do with me?"

"Ah, well, two things, actually. One, we can connect a prisoner there to your mother's kidnapper, and two, a maintenance worker recalled a young woman matching the description of one Kayley Scarlett Garmonuke...Garminock..." Brownrigg sighs. "You wouldn't happen to know where she is, would you?"

Oh, crap. If they have someone who can actually identify Kayley, the entire Empire will be looking for her—she's the one getting arrested. I've got to get this guy out of here as soon as possible, and then we've got to get off-planet.

"Kayley's not here," I reply in my attempt to shut that line of questioning down. Then I try to change the subject by asking about his first statement. If he already knows who Danny is, then we've got even less time to get Freddie than we thought.

"No one to trouble yourself with," the deputy replies, smiling, "but we're closing in, and soon we'll have found her. Your mother will be home before you know it, and you can go back to farming or whatever it is that you people do here."

"I'm not a farmer," I reply, my eyes narrowing as I remember another thing from his last visit—what a complete jerk this guy is, making assumptions about me and everyone on Angelcanis. We love our farmers, but we're not all growing things here.

"No, of course you're not." He leans down towards me with a hand on his chin. "What, could you say, is it that you *do* do, Mr. He'?"

"We help people in need," I reply, lifting myself up to my full height.

"Oh? What kind of need? Financial perhaps?"

"No...we find and rescue people." I should add that we haven't rescued anyone yet, but I don't want to make the government think I don't have an actual job. They'll conscript me to some Imperial office and chain me to a desk so I can file forms all day long.

"I see...and, have you done any work recently? You know...rescuing someone?"

"No," I reply flatly, reacting to his mocking tone. "I've been too worried about my mom to work."

That's sort of true. I have been worried about my mom, and getting her back has been the team's main focus, so we wouldn't accept any new work right now. Besides, I can't rightly tell him he might be one of our jobs.

Deputy Brownrigg returns to his full height. He reminds me of a tree in his wrinkled brown office fatigues. Just give him a green hat, and he'd be all set.

"Now then, a few more questions before I go."

As the deputy is about to begin his inquisition, a flash of red coming into the living room hits the corner of my eye—Kayley. The moment she sees Brownrigg, her jaw drops open, and she retreats back up the stairs.

Kayley trips and cries out, crashing onto the middle landing of the stairs. That's what it sounds like, anyway. It's enough to make both the deputy and me jump. He turns towards the sound with a raised eyebrow.

"My goodness, who was that?" He takes a step towards the stairs, and I panic. How do I stop him without rousing his suspicions? It's not like I can smack him over the head with a frying pan.

But, if it came to it...

Afton pops out from around the corner to save our skins. She's wearing an embarrassed smile and walking while holding her knee, which makes her limp. Brownrigg examines her curiously, then backs up a step to allow her to enter the living room.

"Oh, so is this your cousin, then?" Brownrigg asks.

"Oh, no!" Afton giggles in a very high-pitched tone. It's very un-Afton, and I don't know what she's planning to do, but I can feel the perspiration already forming on the back of my neck. "No, no. I'm Rance's girlfriend, and so sorry to interrupt, but I just fell down the stairs! I'm so clumsy! Right, darling?"

My gaze is aimed at her, but I can't believe what I'm seeing. Or hearing. The squeaky, nasal voice that comes from Afton doesn't match any concept that I have of her. I'm impressed.

Deputy Brownrigg is a bit unsure as well. He scratches his chin as he peers at her.

"How interesting," he says, "and here I thought Ms. Garmon...um, that she was your adored."

"Oh, you're so funny, mister!" Afton snorts and throws her head back in a laugh. Then she wraps her arms around me and gives me a smooch on the cheek while kicking up a foot behind her. She's overdoing it, and that sweat is going to be dripping down my face really soon. "He wouldn't date someone like that! Not my Rancy!"

Brownrigg makes another quick examination of Afton with narrowed eyes. He turns to me with the same glance, then back to her. This is it. He's got us now. Any second he's going to call on his agents to tear the house apart, looking for any tiny clue that gets him to Kayley.

"Well, then, I don't suppose you've seen her today, have you Ms., uh…"

"Jee. Surela Jee." Afton beams. "But now I gotta go put some ice on my knee, 'cause I kinda bumped it."

"Ah yes, well, of course, please don't let me keep you. There's only one other matter I need to discuss with Mr. He' here."

"Oh, what's that?" Afton asks in her squeaky voice.

"The matter of the recovery fee."

"Fee?" I blink. "Fee for what?"

"Well, naturally, the Empire will want to recover any funds exhausted in the search and recovery of your mother. We certainly have the right to do so when we extend our services to non-citizens."

"You want to charge me to save my mother?" Forget sweating. My face is so hot that it's going to boil off any perspiration that comes out.

"Well, if you were a citizen," Deputy Brownrigg replies, "there'd be no fee, of course. Your taxes would already cover such services."

I glance at Afton, who's become surprisingly silent. I can imagine she doesn't want to break character. There's also her father and brothers to consider. If Brownrigg doesn't already know who they are, I think he's going to find out.

"In any case, we still need to recover your mother before I can assess any charges. Let's focus on that, shall we?" His patronizing smile makes my stomach sick. I just glare at him as he waits for an answer.

Deputy Brownrigg seems to take my lack of response as his cue to leave. and walks out. I take a moment to remove my fingernails from my palms. My whole body shakes in anger, and I forget I was even nervous during that entire conversation.

"He's getting nothing," Kayley growls, stepping out from the stairwell into the living room. "*They're* getting nothing. Not one single jorin!"

Kayley looks out the front door window to watch the deputy get in his car and speed off. She's bristling like some rabid animal. Thank the Goddesses Afton stepped in when she did. Though, I wonder who would have had the worse end of it should Kayley have confronted the deputy.

"We're going to get that Freddie and get your mother back *without* any of their greedy hands touching anything we've worked hard to get. Then they'll know they can't mess with Angelcanis!"

"KayKay," I say and turn to my girlfriend, a hopeful smile forming on my face, "does that mean you're not quitting?" I'd give anything to have her be the leader again. Still, I think it's too soon. I don't want her to rush back into it if she's not ready. I also don't think I'll have much say. Here's to hoping she's one hundred percent.

"Damn straight it does," Afton replies with a grin. "I'd better go get some breakfast for us all. We're going to be busy today."

I raise an eyebrow at Afton's statement.

"Well, whatever you were making in the kitchen turned into a black mess a long time ago."

Chapter Twenty-Four

WE SIT IN A hire vehicle, staring out the windows as it proceeds down a winding path through darkened streets. Grimy concrete walls and ductwork large enough to swallow a human go on and on with no end in sight. Add the black of night to that and you've got the perfect backdrop for cine noir.

"Where are we?" Grady leans across me to ask Kayley.

"Canis Ludis," Kayley replies. "You do remember that you helped get us here, don't you, Grady?"

He sighs and rolls his eyes. "No, I meant where are we in the city?"

"Look outside. It's the industrial quarter."

Kayley is right, of course. We're traveling through the seedy, smokestack-filled section of Os, the planet's second-largest and most coarse city. It's got its share of beautiful architecture—sprawling plazas and historic buildings—but we're nowhere near that part of town. It was pure luck that we found someone to take us to the outskirts like this. Our driver thought we were joking for the longest time before we could convince him we weren't.

"So then," Grady goes on, "what are we doing here?"

"Dude, you were there when we discussed it," I say.

"You were there when we called Danny to ask for help, dummy," Afton adds, sitting on the opposite side of Grady. She leaves off the part about how we were actually calling the hand-hunter to beg her for more time.

"Yeah, but when you guys were blabbing away with her, BB and I were discussing my engine design. He's really a brilliant engineer, you know."

"How is that even possible?" I ask. "Blue Buddy doesn't even speak a single word of Common!"

"Teddy translated for us," Grady explains.

"That must have taken forever," Afton says. "No wonder you've got no brain left."

"Alright." Kayley lets out a slow breath. "Grady, for you, I'll explain this one time. We're going to meet someone who used to work with Quinn. Billie Morgan. She's a hand-hunter like Danny now, but she still has connections at Exodus. She may have a code we can use to get in."

"Don't know why we'd need a code," Grady mutters, "I've got plenty."

"Because"—Kayley leans over me to glare at Grady—"*this* code will get us in the front door and then out the back one. So we won't have to find some old, broken airlock to squeeze through."

"Supposedly," I add, and Kayley turns her glare on me. I raise my hands defensively. "I mean, she wasn't exactly clear on how it worked."

I'm not wrong. Danny had no idea what Quinn's friend has for us, only that it was guaranteed to work. None of us believed it, of course, but it's all we have to go on. I personally have a good feeling about it. That's because we have to run through this nightmare of a location to get what we need. Nobody has to go through a graveyard like this without coming back victorious.

That's what I'll keep telling myself.

"We're here," our driver says. "So if you wouldn't mind getting out...quickly. I don't want to hang around to get my bus stripped while I'm still in it."

He makes good on his statement the moment we're out, not waiting around for us to even say thank you. I expect that's why he demanded payment up front.

"Too bad we couldn't bring Teddy along with us. He could have been helpful," I say, my gaze wandering around to examine all the filth and grime that cover nearly every wall, beam, and column that surrounds us. It's like someone just wiped all the dirty grease they had on their hands over everything. It's a slimy contrast to our own well-manicured town.

"He would have made us stand out," Kayley counters, flinching away from a column. She checks her sleeve to make sure nothing got on it and presses a hand to her heart when she finds out she's safe.

"Oh, like *we* don't?" Afton says. Something catches her eye, and she glances up.

There's an old—and likely inoperable—rail line that runs above the street. All the lights there are dark, and the scant few underneath that are working throw pale light across the pavement, washing the street in an eerie desaturated hue.

The one beacon comes from the glaring red sign for the Sin & Bone, the establishment that's our destination. It looks as deserted as the street, save for one man, one very large man, standing outside. He eyes us warily as he plays with a lollipop stick in his mouth.

"Well, good eve' there, children. A little lost, are we?" he says as we approach.

"No." Kayley steps up to him, making herself as tall as possible. "We're looking for someone."

He frowns at her claim, but a moment later, his eyes pop open, and he points the lollipop stick at her.

"Oh, I bet you're here to get yourself a hand-hunter, aren't ya, sweetie?"

My girlfriend wrinkles her nose at the "sweetie" and I can tell she's about to respond in the usual Kayley fashion, but Afton's well-timed elbow in her side cancels her attempted retort. Not one to be slow to catch on, she brightens and smiles at her would-be opponent.

"That's right!" Kayley replies in an unusually chipper voice. "May we go in, please?"

"Sure, honey." The door guard nods towards the door. "You'll find most of 'em in the far corner to your left."

Kayley over-cutes herself when she gives him a coquettish side smile, squeezing her shoulders together as she holds one hand with the other. She glances back at us and motions with her head towards the door, then skips towards it. We follow her, not anywhere near the same level of chipper as she's faking. But then the door guard holds out an arm, barring our way in.

"But the rest of you gotta stay out here," he says, shaking his head.

"What? Why?" Afton asks.

"Only brides-to-be can go in. This is an industry-only establishment, sorry."

Oh, great. Kayley won't go in by herself. She'll want backup in there to—

We share a look as Kayley slips through the door, still on her pretend nuptial high. If I didn't know better, I'd say she's enjoying her part-playing a bit too much.

"What if we were all looking for someone?" Grady asks. The door guard raises an eyebrow at him. I think he's trying to calculate exactly what my buddy meant by that.

"It doesn't work like that, kid," the door guard replies. "Hand-hunters find men, not women."

"Well..." Grady drops his gaze to stare at his shoe, clutching a finger of one hand with his other. I'm impressed. I didn't think he had it in him to act.

"Oh!" The door guard shoots up, his face getting red. "I'm so sorry! You should have said something before. Go in, go in!"

"Way to go, Grady," Afton says, patting him on the back as we slide past the door guard. "Didn't think you had it in you to pretend like that."

"Yeah, well," Grady replies, still holding on to the bashful attitude, "sometimes you find out things about yourself that seem useless at first but then help you later on."

The inside is as smoky as it is dark. Various smells, ranging from sweet and spicy perfumes to the stale and bitter stench of spilled beer, smack me in the nose the moment we walk in. If I had to describe it to someone, I'd say it smells like Danny Lecker. That means we're in the right place.

Kayley comes shooting out of the haze and stops, holding her hands out and shaking her head.

"What happened to you guys? I thought you were right behind me."

"We couldn't get in unless we told him we were all looking for someone," I explain.

"Oh." Kayley nods, but I don't think she understands. "Anyway, you're here now. I found our contact. Come meet her. She's cool."

Ms. Cool is exactly as described. She's reclining in a booth, with her arms stretched out and one booted leg up on the seat. A cigarette or some other smoking apparatus hangs from her reddish-brown lips. She's got a shiny black bodysuit like Danny's, only hers ends in short pants with netlike tights underneath.

"And who is this?" Ms. Cool asks, regarding us over the pair of sunglasses hanging off her nose.

"Well, this is the team that's going to help Danny Lecker out."

"Don't say that name here," she says, "and I when I asked 'who is this,' I meant who is that?"

Ms. Cool flicks a finger right at me and stares me down as she takes a puff off of her smoke stick. She's evaluating me like a coffee buyer might select the quality of the beans they will purchase.

"I'm Rance. I'm the one in contact with Dan...with you know who."

"Are you married, Rance?"

"No." I glance at Kayley, who's becoming more irritated with every passing moment. At least it's not directed at me for once.

"Do you want to be?"

"Listen, we're in a bit of a hurry," Kayley interrupts. "Do you have the code? Then we'll be out of your hair, and you can go back to... whatever."

Ms. Cool takes the smoke stick from her mouth, puts it down on the edge of the table, and picks up a bottle to take a long swig from it, her gaze never leaving me. I'm a bit unnerved by it, as she's got nearly the same color eyes as Kayley does. It reminds me of the question she just asked me.

I would want to be married. To the right woman, and of course, Kayley checks and double-checks all the right boxes for me. We've never talked about it though, and I would never press her into anything. We are still fairly young, and if she chooses me—which I hope she does—there will be time to talk about it later. But I'd want my mom to come to any wedding I had, and for that to happen, we need to get her back.

As she puts the bottle down, she makes a grand show of wetting her lips with her tongue. Not in an erotic way. She's not trying to seduce me or anything, like the other hand-hunter I know. This seems more like the way she prepares to do something. It's very kick-ass if you ask me.

Ms. Cool takes a breath and puckers her lips together. What comes out is a flurry of notes in a sequential pattern, all through one of the most beautiful whistling tones I have ever heard, and I've heard a lot. My mother used to take me to regional whistling contests where she competed. She was really good, but she got bored with it after winning a few times and quit.

"So, are you going to give us the code or not?" Kayley says.

"I just did," Ms. Cool replies.

"You mean that tune you just whistled was the code?" I ask, though I'm not really asking. It's more of a statement confirming it.

"Right you are," she replies and winks at me.

"Can you do it one more time?" Grady asks, pulling out his Sergo and setting it to record. She obliges, and once again I'm thankful for my quick-witted friend. I haven't given him points in a while, so I'll give him an extra ten on top of the two he should get today.

"Got it?" she asks Grady, who bows in thanks to her and steps away.

Well, this is going easier than expected. See, I knew traveling through the gauntlet of Grime City was going to put us out on top. Next stop, Exodus.

Chapter Twenty-Five

"NOW THAT PART'S DONE," Ms. Cool says and turns to Kayley, who is cooling herself down after getting what she wanted, "we need to talk about my price."

"Your what?" Kayley asks, her eyebrow rising.

"Hey, I am not doing this one for free," Ms. Cool says. "That woman already owes me plenty. She's got a way of getting you to do stuff for her."

"You too?" I ask. Her eyes float over to appraise me, a purple fingernail touching her chin. She confirms with a single nod.

"We can pay," Afton says, even though she's not the one with the rich parents, "but we don't have the funds with us."

"Never said it had to be cash, girly," Ms. Cool replies, spreading her arms out on the seat back. "Besides, I'd prefer to get this transaction over with now, so I can get back to work."

"Well then," Kayley steps in, "what else do you want?"

"He'll do." Ms. Cool tips her chin in my direction. "I've got this one client he'd make an excellent match for. Her Plan A got hitched before I could get him. Sneaky bastard."

Wait a second. This lady really wants to use *me* for one of her clients? Doesn't she realize that I've got someone to go break out of a high-security prison? Hasn't she been listening to anything we've said?

"I don't have time to get married," I say, picking one of a trillion reasons why I don't want to do that for her.

"There's always time for that, precious."

Well, this is a problem we didn't expect to come up against. Danny talked about her as if she was the most generous person in the world. She might be, but not today.

"We'll come back with the money," Kayley says, "how's that?"

"I'm thinking...mmm, nope," she replies, putting her feet on the floor and leaning forward. "You've already got the code. If I let you go, there's no guarantee that you'll come back. I don't know you well enough to trust you, so we're taking care of this here and now."

"And if we refuse?" Kayley asks, folding her arms.

"Well." Ms. Cool chuckles. "Then I'll just have to do my job...for the client that's already paid me, and on top of that, I'm going to have to give Mr. Gadget over there a nice hard zap too. That'll erase whatever recording he's got."

Kayley's tough-girl routine falls apart, and she takes a step back from the hand-hunter. I would have expected her to come after me, but to zap Grady just to destroy the recording isn't very nice. My buddy is already a shade paler than he is normally, and he's moving to hide behind Afton, who remains silent.

We do have one advantage here: we've already got the code. If there's a way for us to depart without getting zapped—correction, if there's a way for us to depart without *Grady and me* getting zapped— we're safe. Now, looking at her, I'd have to say this lady is at least as strong as Afton, which means she might be as fast. Running seems like the obvious way out, but definitely not the one guaranteed to get us home free with the least amount of trouble. If we could—

"Rance, run!" Kayley shouts. She snatches a drink from a table and blasts the liquid right into Ms. Cool's face. The hand-hunter sputters and shoots to her feet, gasping.

All of the nearby tables go silent and stare, and I join in. Kayley has to grab me and turn me around before my legs start moving. We bolt to the door, picking up speed. Afton and Grady are just behind us.

"Oh, don't run!" Ms. Cool whines. "I'm not warmed up yet!"

A weapon blast strikes the wall next to my head as we fly out the exit, throwing sparks everywhere. I feel the burn of one on my cheek, and I push Kayley out the door even faster than before. This lady is serious. More serious than Danny, even.

"Hey, how did it go?" the muscle-bound door guard asks as we zip by. "Did you hire someone?"

"We're still deciding!" I call. "We'll have to come back!"

"Okay, hope to see you soon!"

We find a dark alley and duck down it. We'd never choose to go there in a normal situation, but the danger is behind us, not in front of us. We've got to find a place to hide. Then get off-planet as fast as possible.

Kayley cries out as she stumbles. I catch her just before she splashes into the black muck covering the ground. There's no telling what it is. It might be worse than a zap from Ms. Cool's gun. We're not going to wait to find out.

"Split up!" Afton says. It's not a bad idea. "I'll take Grady, and we'll try to find a way back to the spaceport. You guys…"

"Yeah?"

"Don't get caught!" Afton pushes Grady down a side alley, hopefully one that goes back to the main street.

"Don't get lost!" I shout back.

Kayley and I pause for a breath. Neither of us has done much running as of late, and we're not in any shape for a long-distance chase. If we get out of this, I promise the Goddesses that I'll wake up early and start training every day.

"You okay?" I ask her as she's catching her breath. Kayley nods and smiles tightly.

"You only got this far?" a voice calls from the end of the alley—it's Ms. Cool. She stands at the alley's entrance, her body backlit by the bright red light of the sign. "This is going to be over in no time, then. Just stop now, and we'll all go back inside for a drink. We won't have to get sweaty then, right?"

Our answer is to take off. I knock a pile of boxes over as I brush by them. It's not going to stop her, but it might slow her down. Might.

We hit a right turn, but Kayley slides and smashes into the wall. I grab her as I go by, giving her a boost so she's in front of me again. This alley is cleaner than the last one, so we dig in and pick up speed, heading towards the next turn. Wherever that is. This alley is dimmer than the last one. It's going to be hard to see anything soon.

We're nearly there when I hear a crash of metal impacting the wall behind us. I can hear her booted feet squishing through the slime on the ground. It's slowing her down, but it's doing the same to us. No advantage there.

"Hey!" Ms. Cool shouts. "Where's your friends?"

"They went home!" I shout back.

Kayley slides to a stop and spins around. She points frantically to the turn we just missed and shoves me in that direction. I over-rotate, and I slip. Yuck. At least the muck is thick enough to cushion my fall.

Ms. Cool picks up her speed and raises her weapon at us. A few rounds fly past and spark off the walls. The sound of the gun is tremendous, echoing through the alley.

I vault up and race down the alley after Kayley. We're running blindly at this point, with no thought about where to go other than away. I'm hoping we can get back to the main street. Maybe get up on those tracks I saw before. They'll take us back to town—I think. All we need to do is give her the slip.

Ms. Cool's footsteps go silent. Did we lose her? I dare to glance behind me and see nothing. She's not there, and I'll take it as a blessing. I keep up my pace, but to where I don't know.

The alley opens up into a yard behind one of the old factories. It's full of rusted junk and piles of trash. A single light hangs down from a pole, creating dark shadows in the corners of the yard. It could be a good place to hide if we were planning to do that.

"Wait," Kayley says, breathing heavily, "stop for a minute. I need to catch my breath."

I do too, but it's not a good idea. We could get caught out in the open. Kayley puts a hand on my shoulder and bends over, negating my wish to keep moving. Looks like we're going to break, no matter what.

"KayKay," I say through my panting after a minute. She nods, and with one last deep breath, stands up straight.

But we've waited too long.

Ms. Cool steps out of the shadows, a big smirk across her face. Her eyes are dead set on me as she approaches, patting her hand with her weapon. Kayley gasps and reaches for me, trying to grab hold of my shirt, but all the muck stuck to it makes her fingers slide off.

"They always run, you know. No matter what," Ms. Cool says, coming closer. "It's kind of insulting. As if all these dudes think we're not good at our jobs. I worked really hard to be good! Ha! No respect whatsoever. I mean, did you guys think I don't know this area? I practically grew up here!"

I back up and spread my arms out, keeping Kayley behind me. If someone's going to get shot, it's not going to be my girlfriend. Then I realize Ms. Cool has no reason to shoot Kayley. She's gunning for me. Literally.

"Rance, this way!" Kayley grabs the back of my pants and tugs. She lets go fast enough so I can turn around and follow. A jolt of adrenaline races through me as I catch where she's headed—Kayley's found an exit out of the yard! We push ourselves hard to reach safety before I get shot.

"No! Not that way, guys!" Ms. Cool calls after us, her voice tinged with disappointment. I grin to myself. I'll bet she's getting tired and doesn't want to chase us anymore.

All that talk from her about how good she is. Well, maybe she's good, but she's lazy. Doesn't want to even break a sweat to catch me and help her client. Too bad. We're getting out of here!

Kayley comes to a screeching halt and I slam into her back. My arms wrap about her reflexively, ensuring I don't knock her into the nastiness on the ground. But now I'm wondering why she stopped.

A quick glance forward, and my heart sinks—a dead end. No wonder Ms. Cool didn't give chase. There's nowhere for us to run. I can already hear her sigh as she comes up from behind us.

"I was trying to save you the embarrassment of running into a wall, but well, here we are," she says. "Now, are you going to come quietly, or do I have to zap you?"

"Even if you get me, my friends have already escaped with the code! And you haven't gotten me yet."

"Oh, no, they didn't," Ms. Cool replies. "I called my friends for a little favor, and well, that's over. Your tall friend put up a good fight, though. She'd make a pretty good hand-hunter, I'll bet."

There goes that bargaining chip. We could still find a way to get around her, but it seems unlikely.

The pop of her gun goes off, and a second later, I'm on the floor. My entire body tenses and shakes with the electrical stimulation the dart fired from her weapon. Kayley cries out and drops down next to me.

"Serves you right for making me run in this gunk," Ms. Cool says, leaning over me. "Don't worry, precious. She's a nice lady...a few years older than you, but that shouldn't make a difference."

"No." My voice breaks. "My mom...I have to get my mom."

"It's a *wedding*, not a jail sentence. Your mom will definitely be there."

"No, you don't understand..."

"I understand plenty. It's always like this when they get caught. Always the begging and the pleading. Well, stop being such a wimp. She's beautiful, and you're not some ugly duckling, so she's bound to like you. Is that so bad? Let's go!"

Ms. Cool brushes off Kayley's attempt to keep her away by giving her a hard shove. Kayley falls back, and then Ms. Cool pulls me up by my arm. I try to struggle, but the electric dart exhausted all the strength in my muscles. I'm like a floppy doll in her clutches.

"No," I say again weakly. "No, I don't want to marry her! Don't make me, please!"

"Ugh! You are such a whiner." Ms. Cool sighs. "Alright, why can't you?"

"Because the girl I want to marry is right here."

Ms. Cool blinks and tilts her head sideways. Her eyes swing up to take in Kayley, my muddy girlfriend, and now possibly my fiancée?

"That's quite a strange way to propose, precious," Ms. Cool says and takes another glance at Kayley. "Did you hear what this guy just said?"

"W...what?"

"So are you gonna accept or what? If you do, I can't take him. He's used goods at that point, which makes him worthless to—"

"I accept," Kayley says so fast, Ms. Cool can't even finish her sentence. The hand-hunter sighs and holsters her weapon.

"Well, there you go. How nice for the both of you." She turns away with a wave. "Have a happy life together!"

"Wait!" I call after her.

"What?"

"What about the code?"

"Consider it a wedding present." She gives us a soft smile and a wink.

Chapter Twenty-Six

I JUST PROPOSED TO Kayley, and she accepted.

Those words keep repeating in my head as we wind our way back to the street to meet up with Afton and Grady. Afton blinks at the two of us, covered in alley muck.

"What the hell happened to you two?" she asks, shaking her head, her mouth open.

"She let us go," Kayley replies, keeping her arms wrapped around mine as we walk.

"What?"

With the help of the nice door guard, we get a hire vehicle to come pick us up. As we head back to the spaceport, where the Teddy shuttle awaits, Kayley explains our harrowing chase and our poor decision to stop in the yard. And then how our next stupid idea was to run down the dead-end alley. Afton and Grady listen, but they frown through the whole retelling.

"Something doesn't add up," Afton says, rubbing a finger on her chin. "She had you cornered, and she just let you go?"

"Well, no. I got zapped first," I reply. "And then she let me go."

"What are you not telling me?"

Kayley and I look at each other, and my girlfriend's mouth opens, but no words come out. She's as stuck as I am how to explain what happened. If the words weren't stuck in my head, repeating over and over, I wouldn't even be sure if it happened.

"She let us go," I say finally, "because I proposed to Kayley."

"Why would you do that?" Afton shoots back, eyes narrowed, sounding like she's accusing me of something.

Kayley sighs and explains why I said what I said. That it wasn't a proper proposal, just one to get us away from Ms. Cool, aka Billie Morgan. I got the feeling she would have let us go anyway, but I prefer the thought that my declaration of commitment to my girlfriend saved us.

It bugs me a little that Kayley dismisses it so easily. Like it was nothing. Of course, we've never discussed it. Not really. A joke here or there, but nothing serious. But even though Kayley's murdered any possibility of it being a real marriage proposal, she *has* been clutching on to my arm for an unusually long time.

"Hey," Grady says as we climb aboard the Teddy shuttle and get locked into our seats for launch. "While we've got the chance, we should talk about our next step."

"We go get Freddie, right?" Wow, Grady really fried his brain talking to BB. Either that, or Billie gave him a zap that we were unaware of.

"No, dude," Grady corrects. "We're not going in half-stupid again. We need an actual plan this time."

"Yeah, but now that we've got the code, we should be able to just walk in the front door."

"Uh, no," Afton says. "We've got to find out what exactly happened at the entrance, so we know how to avoid that problem again."

Afton's got a point. We haven't talked about what happened in full. That's mostly because I was overprotective of Kayley and didn't want her to relive what must have been a horrific experience. But we will need to get the facts, and Parrish is the best man for that job. He's the one with the first-hand experience...unfortunately.

I make a silent comment to Afton and Grady by moving my eyes down to glance at Kayley. They both nod their understanding and go silent. We do need to talk about this. However, with Kayley here, this might not be the best time to do it. She seems fine at the moment, but I'm still unsure how much she's being honest with us and how much hurt she's hiding.

"It's okay, guys," Kayley says, putting on her smile. "Let's talk about it. We need to discuss it."

Afton and I share a glance. Kayley is apparently a mind reader. She knew we were talking about her when we were not talking about her. Either that or I'm horrible at hiding my feelings from her.

"Why don't we get Parrish on the line?" I suggest. "He's bound to be wondering about what's going on, and I'm sure he could use a little conversation. Doc's good to talk to, but…"

"We get it," Afton says, "not all there, right?"

"No more than any of us," Grady murmurs.

I ask Original Teddy to call the ship for us, and he obliges, dropping the small vid globe from the ceiling for us. We gather around and watch as first Doc Elizabeth gets on, then Parrish. He's got on a huge smile, and his eyes are practically dancing. Boy, if I didn't feel bad before about leaving him behind, I sure do now. He's missing us so much that he doesn't bother to ask why Kayley and I are pretending to be the inside of a sewage pipe.

"Hey, dude," I say, apologetically. "I don't want to rub salt on your wounds, but we need to know about what happened at the station."

"I thought I told you never to use that saying again," Afton grumbles. I just side-eye her and she sneers back.

"It's okay," Parrish says with a curl of this mouth, "Doc and I have been doing a lot of talking, and she's been a big help."

"Make sure I get at least a few points for that, Rance!" Doc Elizabeth calls from behind him. I give her a thumbs-up, and she waves.

While we talk to Parrish and the doc, I hear a metallic plunking. It keeps repeating at regular intervals, and I think it might be coming through the vid.

"Hey, what's that noise?" I ask. Maybe it's a glitch or bad reception.

"Oh." Parrish holds up the corn husker thing. "It's this. Doc suggested I use it to keep the muscles in my arm and hand moving."

"You left it here last time," the doc adds. "It looked like it could work for rehabilitation, so I put it to use. I do wish he'd play another tone, though."

"Go ahead, Parrish," Kayley nudges, getting us back to the conversation. "Tell them what happened at the station. I'll add anything that I can."

From the start, their return was in peril. The alarm that was triggered locked down the entire facility, and there was no way they were going to get in, with Quinn's help or not. The moment Parrish stepped onto the dock, an army of armed guards greeted him, and they were more into shooting than talking. All he could do was run, and he didn't get very far before the Teddys had to drag him back into the shuttle.

Parrish wound up telling the entire story while Kayley shrank more and more into her seat as he went on. I realized I was squeezing the life out of my hands, watching her squirm on the opposite side of the cabin. I didn't want to crowd her, so I took the seat next to Grady. Now I'm paying for my decision because I really want to be next to Kayley, but Afton's in the way, and if I called attention to that fact, Kayley would tell me to stay where I am. That would ruin the quiet, supportive tack I was going for.

"So the lesson here is: don't trigger the alarm, and if you see guards, run like hell," Afton says. "Good. Got it."

"Glad you get it," Kayley replies, "because you and Rance will be the ones going in next time."

"What did I do to deserve that honor?" Afton asks as her mouth twists into a pout.

"Yeah, I second that question," I say.

"I'm on the bench this time, which means you two are the only ones capable of going," Kayley replies. She's dead serious, and this isn't the time to argue the point.

"We'll need some Teddy backup," I say. Everyone nods in agreement.

"Teddy is available," Original Teddy says from the cockpit. I forgot how good his hearing is when he wants it to be.

We discuss a few finer points but come to no other conclusions. There are still a few holes we need to figure out, but we don't have all the information we need. The other problem is we don't know what information we need because we don't have any of the other information to know what it is we're missing.

I'm about to think out loud about that idea when a buzzer goes off in the cockpit. It catches our attention, and our conversation goes on hold.

"Pronouncement incoming," Original Teddy says. Before I can say anything, the vid globe flashes and the screen changes to an Angel-3 broadcast. There's no sound, but it's obvious that it's a news report from our town. A brownside house is being overrun by an army of government officials. And there, in the middle of all of them, a reporter is speaking to a lanky man wearing a crumpled brown overcoat. In fact, all of his clothes are brown.

"Brownrigg," I growl.

"Dude, that's your house," Grady comments. I blink and get closer to the screen—Grady's right. I can see Mom's green curtains in the front bedroom window.

"Oh, boy," Afton says. "I guess we're going to be staying for a while with the Teddys."

We watch a little longer, and it becomes obvious that they're searching my house. For what, I have no idea. There's nothing there they can take—no suspicious devices, no secret data, not even my wallet. Nothing is there, and unless he's back to steal my mom's good tea, I don't get what he's doing there.

"Isn't it obvious?" Kayley says after we switch off the broadcast. "He's the anti-sedition director. He thinks you, me, and anyone associated with us are a bunch of insurgents. He's convinced that we're up to something bad."

"We *are* up to something," Afton replies. Grady shrugs in agreement.

"We're trying to save my mom!" I cry. "How is that bad?"

"Because, dummy, we're going to break into an Imperial prison facility to do it." Afton didn't need to state the obvious, but it puts things into perspective. Once again, we're in a tough spot, and that tough spot involves an Imperial official on both sides of it.

"This is ridiculous!" I say. "It's not our fault we're in this position!"

"It kinda is, actually." Afton, ever the destroyer of dreams, once again smashes mine with the truth. At least she gets a filthy elbow in her ribs from Kayley for it.

"That's not fair," I shoot back. "How was I to know that Danny was going to turn into an insane woman? We tried to get away from her, but she wouldn't take no for an answer, and now we, the most famous people on all of Angelcanis, are being labeled as terrorists! All because Deputy Brownbagg wants to pursue some agenda against us! He might even be part of Crowley's conspiracy for all we know."

"We do know," Grady says, "or at least, we can guess. We're high-profile, and he wants to make an example of us so that the rest of Angelcanis snaps in line. Also, I thought his name was Brownrigg."

"No, it's Brownjerk," Afton says.

"So now we either get arrested for trying to save my mom, or we fess up and put our hopes in the Imperial police doing something about it." I sigh and lean over to stare at the floor. We're already two days past our deadline for getting Freddie, and there's no solution in sight. We can't trust the government either. Brownrigg may just be one of many looking to get revenge on us for uncovering ex-minister Crowley's treachery.

"Rance," Parrish says, back on the vid. "We're doing our best. Famous or not, that's all we can ask for. It's your mom we're talking about here, so I'm okay with whatever you want to do, but if it was my own mom, I'd already be heading back, gunshots or not."

Parrish has a point—he would do anything for my mom too. He already has. I'm not worried about the legal aspects of this whole situation. I've already been in jail once. I'd argue it was unfair imprisonment, but we did do something illegal, even if it was for the right reason. I guess justice doesn't always agree with law.

"Yeah, I'd be right there for your mom too, dude," I say. "Sorry again about what happened."

"No need to apologize," he replies.

"I just wish we could get this Brown-noser off our backs, so we could operate without him sniffing around our every move."

"What if we could?" Grady asks, catching everyone's attention.

"How?" Afton asks.

"You guys know I'm famous, don't you?" Kayley asks. We all turn to her, confused.

"We're all famous," Grady says, though I do think Kayley's way more accurate here. We *were* famous. Grady still is with a certain group of teenie-boppers, while Afton, Parrish, and I are likely more infamous than famous at this point.

"Not as famous as I am," Kayley replies. "How many speeches and public appearances did you do?"

"What are you thinking, KayKay?" I ask.

"We use my fame to trick Deputy Brownrigg and send him off on a wild chase that'll keep him tied up until we can get Freddie. Then we get your mom and find a safe place to lay low for a while."

I can see the grins forming on everyone's faces as the possibilities of an idea start forming in their twisted little minds. My own face is stretching into a hopeful smile as I turn to Kayley.

"Great," I say, "how do we do that?"

Kayley just beams at me. I don't know exactly what she's got planned, but I am glad to see her in a positive mood.

"Okay," Kayley says with a grin, "this is what we'll do."

Chapter Twenty-Seven

IT'S SO GREAT TO be back home—back on our home planet, anyway—and breathing fresh air. I'm glad to not be drowning from a lungful of industrial waste every time I breathe. Our industry here doesn't make slag. We've got produce and high tech. No petrochemicals, no hexachlorocyclopentadiene. No nasty stuff at all, ever. That's why the Empire doesn't get us. We only make what's good for the planet.

And right now, we're fixing to make big trouble for Mr. Lanky himself, the Empire's *Deputy Anti-Sedition Lackey*.

The first thing is to get him to come to us. That's why we picked Yeomanry, Angelcanis' second-largest city. We're sure to get results here, and if Deputy Brownrigg is at the capital, he'll be here in no time. That's exactly what we want him to do.

"All set?" I ask Kayley as she walks away from the organizers of the event. They put together her world tour. I couldn't believe how disappointed they were when Kayley canceled the last week of her tour, but when she offered to make it up to them by doing this big show here in Yeomanry, they got excited. Then, when we added the sweet stuff on top—to have all of us make a showing—they went through the roof.

"Almost," Kayley replies and gives me her infamous smile. My knees get weak, and I'm reminded of why I fell for her in the first place. And then I measure myself up against her and still find myself majorly lacking. Ah, well. I can't have everything.

"Hey, check this out," Afton calls, waving us over. She's got a tablet that she turns towards us. The screen is chock-full of numbers, charts, and graphs, and I have no idea what they're about. "This is the total attendance estimation for today's event."

"That's ten times the size of my other events!" Kayley stares wide-eyed at the screen.

"Yep." Afton grins.

"Hey, where'd you get that tablet?" I ask. Afton shrugs and nods towards the tent that's clearly marked Head Office and Employees Only.

"Found it over there," she replies.

"You didn't find it! Put it back!"

The rest of the morning went faster than a Teddy ship at full speed. There was a lot to go over and a lot to rehearse before the show started. Now we've got an hour before we're up, and everyone, except for Kayley, is getting the itch. Other than the one time the Teddys first met the people of Angelcanis, I'm not well acquainted with facing a large crowd. None of the Riding Kayley's Coattails team are. That's why KayKay has the biggest and most important part. I know she's going to knock it out of the park.

"Sergeant Cortell!" I exclaim as our *Mursilis* co-conspirator comes walking up, totally spiffed out in his officer's uniform. That's when I remember I've got to stop calling him Sergeant. He's got his own command now. He's a lieutenant.

"Rance, how's it going?" Lieutenant Cortell asks, holding out a hand. I take his hand and give it a hard squeeze. He does the same and nearly crushes my hand. "Looking good. You've gained some weight back."

"Yeah, my mom's been spoiling me. Kayley too."

"Hey," Kayley says, "thanks for doing this. It's going to be a big help."

"Of course. I'm always up for a chance to hit back at the subversive element in the Empire."

"So, everything's in place?"

"Couldn't get as many as you asked for, but what I've got should work."

"Let's hope so. We can't allow him to get free."

I don't know exactly how this is going to go down. I mean, Kayley explained it to me. Then told me again, and then again just to be sure. I still don't get it, but I trust her. She's not one to miss details.

As we get close to showtime, I notice that the throngs of people promised in the estimate haven't arrived yet. A handful of passersby saw the banner that we put up and stuck around, but other than that, plenty of green grass in front of the stage is still visible. The event crew and Lieutenant Cortell's men outnumber them by at least a magnitude.

I catch Kayley pacing backstage and recognize the signs of her anxiety. My own leg starts to bounce as I sit next to Parrish and Doc Elizabeth. We need this crowd for the plan to work. If they don't come, we become fruit ripe for Deputy Brownrigg's picking.

"What do you want to do?" One of the organizers has come up to Kayley. He's wearing a bit of a grimace but trying not to show it. It's obvious that he didn't expect this to happen.

"It's not a holiday, right?" I ask Parrish, watching KayKay discuss the issue with the man.

"No," he replies, "but that shouldn't matter."

No, it shouldn't matter. Kayley's on top of the "it" list right now, and that means anyone on this planet would kill to meet her. Here we're offering a free chance of a meet and greet, and nobody's taking us up on this once-in-a-lifetime offer.

Kayley walks up to me, her head cast down and her hands planted on her lower back. She pauses before me and stays silent.

"What do you think, Rance?" Parrish asks.

"I think we're being too negative," I reply. "We haven't even started yet, and we're ready to admit defeat? No way."

"Well, as you can see, darling," Kayley says, waving a hand out to the peppering of people around the square, "our promotion has failed to bring in the numbers we expected."

"Maybe we didn't have enough time to promote," Parrish suggests. It makes sense, but my girlfriend doesn't want to hear it.

"Well, if we don't get a big enough crowd before I go on, we're going to call this off and get off this planet before we get arrested."

As Kayley walks away, the three of us share a moment of alarm. She's not one to give up so easily, so if she's already thinking about it, then we need to get our act together and figure something out.

"We're not going to solve this sitting on our hands," I say to them. "I'm going to see what kind of people I can find."

"I'll go with you," Parrish says. "It's better than sitting around here."

"You'll still be sitting on that gurney chair when you go out there, my friend," Doc Elizabeth says to him, "but I'm willing to give you a push."

The three of us head out on our quest to find a ridiculous amount of people in a minuscule amount of time. We first chat with the people waiting for the show to find out how they heard about the event. They didn't hear about it at all, as it turns out. They were just walking by and saw the sign. They hadn't heard about it on any of the regular Angel channels or even on Sergo link. We plead with them to reach out to their friends to get them down, which they promise to do, but with no guarantees.

Talking to people in the area results in the same outcome. They're interested, and some even Sergo their friends to come down, but after wasting half our time doing this, we have barely made a dent in our huge personnel requirement.

"Let's try the park," I suggest.

"Do we have time?" Parrish asks.

"All we'll have is time if we don't make this happen."

I shuffle my feet as I push his floating gurney chair, another Teddy invention. It's unlikely that our trip to the nearby park is going to account for much. It's not the weekend, and most people will be at work or school. It'll be a miracle if we find anyone.

As we walk down the primary thoroughfare, a group of young people around our age pass by. They don't notice us at first, but then one kid turns around and calls to Parrish. With I sigh, I stop and turn his chair around.

"Hey, aren't you that guy that was with Scarlett Kayley?" he asks, ignoring Doc Elizabeth and me completely.

"Yeah, I guess," Parrish replies with a shrug. I'm confused about why they're using her middle name first. Unlike Afton, Kayley doesn't even like her middle name. Maybe it's a new nickname.

"She's so amazing!" a girl in the group says. "I wanna be her when I get older!"

I glance at the girl. She's got to be like a year younger than we are.

"Well, she's going to speak in Nelson Square in like two minutes." Parrish, always knowing when to play or pass, gets in the plug with perfect timing. "You should go."

"Are you joking?" the kid who first stopped us asked.

"No, not at all. Go see for yourself."

"Holy toast, dudes!" the kid says. "If it's true, I'm blasting it all over my feed!"

"It's about to start, so you should go now," I say. "In fact, we have to get back too."

"But first," Doc Elizabeth says, "do you know where we can find a million people?"

"A million?" He thinks for a second, the massive number not fazing him at all. "Maybe in the meadow. There's usually a bunch of people there."

They wave and head off. Not in the direction we want them to, but that was to be expected. Kids are flakes these days. They never do what they say they're going to do. A handful of annoying teens weren't going to make a difference, anyway.

We come upon the edge of a clearing and find about twenty or thirty people spread out on picnic blankets. Some of them are playing karaoke with a makeshift speaker system. I cringe as the murder-worthy off-key singing gets louder.

"I think we'll pass on that group, yeah?" I say. Doc Elizabeth nods.

"Then let's head back," Parrish says.

"Wait, no," I say, but I've got no reason to stop them. I drop my gaze, and my jaw tightens. I don't want to give up, but we're out of time. If we don't go back now, we're going to miss Kayley's decision, and we're just wasting time out here now.

"Let's go this way," Parrish says and points deeper into the meadow. "It's faster, I remember."

"How could you remember?"

"I've been here a few times on away games with the team."

"Which team?" Doc Elizabeth asks. "For that matter, which sport?"

I sigh and dig my feet in to push Parrish through the meadow. At least it's a nice day, and he's getting some fresh air. I've heard that's good for healing. Still, I can't help but hang my head and sigh. We've wasted the remaining time we had and have nothing to show for it. What I feel worst about is letting KayKay and my mom down.

"Goddesses," Parrish says out of the blue, "look at that."

"Hunh?" I glance up, and my mouth drops open. I even have to blink a few times to really understand what I'm seeing. A vast ocean spreads out before us—an ocean of all shapes, sizes, and colors. It ripples with motion and is alive with sound like a roaring waterfall. I peer across its span, and still I don't think I can see the ends of it.

"It's a sea of people," I say, my mouth beginning to salivate.

"But we can't talk to all of them in time," Doc Elizabeth says in despair. "Not in a millennium could we do that."

"We've got to try," I say and step around Parrish's chair. Doc is right. No way we're going to talk to them all individually. This calls for something more drastic.

I cup my hands over my mouth and yell: "Hey everyone! Scarlett Kayley is speaking in Nelson Square right now!"

Only one guy looks up, stares for a moment, then returns to his friends. I glance at my companions, who encourage me to try again. I do, and now I get around five people reacting to my shout. Their reception is anything but positive. Some just squint at me as if they didn't hear what I said.

"I've got to be louder," I say, glancing around. Right! The karaoke system! That'll work perfectly! I'm bolting over to it in a matter of microseconds. Parrish calls after me, but there's no time to explain. Either this works or it doesn't.

With a little effort, I get the speaker arrays spun around towards the mass of people. One guy—I bet he owns it—watches me with confusion, but at least he isn't trying to stop me.

I don't have any idea how to use this system, but I can find the microphone and the control that says "output." After that, it's all a guess. I hope it's powered up, at least.

It is.

"ATTENTION," I say and immediately pull the mic away. Wow, this system is way more powerful than I would have guessed.

"Hey, what are you doing?" The guy watching me gets up and starts coming towards me, a scowl forming on his face. I'd better get this done before I lose my chance.

"LADIES AND GENTLEMEN, WE INVITE YOU TO HEAR SCARLETT KAYLEY GARMONICHNYY NOW SPEAKING IN NELSON SQUARE! HURRY, THERE'S NOT A LOT OF SPACE LEFT!"

Oh, that got the reaction I was looking for.

Chapter Twenty-Eight

WE RACE BACK AS fast as we can, hoping to catch the end of Kayley's speech. We don't want to miss our own chance either. More than any of that, I want to see the look on Brownrigg's face when Lieutenant Cortell does his thing.

As we hit the square, we skid to a halt. There's a shuttle sitting on the ground right in front of the stage. Five men, including a tall one in a wrinkled brown overcoat, are escorting Kayley towards it. They've handcuffed her and are not making any attempt to be gentle. Afton and Grady are there, but their efforts to intervene are failing.

"Oh feck," Doc Elizabeth exclaims.

"How'd he get here so quickly?" Parrish curses, unusual for him.

"We've got to stop him before they get her on that shuttle," I say, but before I can head off, Doc Elizabeth grabs me by the wrist and holds me back. That gives Parrish enough time to grab my other arm, and now I'm definitely stuck.

"No, they'll just arrest you too, Rance," Doc Elizabeth says.

"But...Kayley..."

"Nothing we can do about it."

"Not true!" I insist, trying to shake their grip. "What about Lieutenant Cortell?"

"He would have already if he could have," the doc replies. That's true, so I stop struggling, and the two of them relax their grip.

I rip free of the two of them and charge towards the shuttle. They call after me but I'm not stopping. I can't let him take Kayley, or else our whole mission dies on the spot. With Parrish's wounds and Kayley gone, we'd be a lame-butt team.

I have no idea what I'm going to do when I get there. I have no weapons, no plan. Shouting at them won't do much. I'll need to come up with something fast, but today is one of those days where my brain just isn't working the way I need it to. I thought I got enough sleep, but I was a little anxious about today, so maybe I didn't.

"Brownrigg!" I yell as I get to the shuttle. I stop on the far side to catch my breath and really think about what I'm going to do to get Kayley free. Of course, I shouldn't have shouted out his name because here he comes to see who's calling him.

"Ah, Mr. He', there you are," he says and motions to someone out of sight.

"Why are you arresting Kayley?" I ask, still breathing heavily.

"What? No, she's not under arrest."

"She has restraints on!"

"Merely a precaution," he replies and glances around the side of the shuttle again. "We are bringing her in to answer some questions. As I've said, Rance, we have some concern about the message she's been presenting to the population here. They have certain...anti-Imperial overtones."

"Kayley's not trying to overthrow the Emperor!"

Two guards bring Kayley around to our side, with Afton and Grady flanking them, turning every step they take into a stomp. My girlfriend is hanging her head and doesn't see me, but the others do. All of them pause at Brownrigg's command.

"Yes, likely not, but I would be remiss in my duties if I did not explore every possibility, especially from someone so...popular with the people of this planet."

This guy is delusional if he thinks Kayley is some sort of insurgent. That's the complete opposite of what she looks like at the moment, slumped forward and letting the two guards hold her up.

"Let her go!" I cry as I feel a fire building up inside of me. No one treats my girlfriend like that.

"Rance!" Parrish says, catching up to me with the others. "What are you doing?"

"Getting this idiot to release Kayley," I reply.

"That was uncalled for, Mr. He'," Brownrigg says with a small pout. "Now, you are welcome to come with her, and then you can take her home once we are done."

"Done with what? Torturing her? No way I'm gonna let you do that."

"Rance, careful," Doc Elizabeth warns.

"Did you just threaten me?" Deputy Brownrigg takes on a different persona when he asks this. He's no longer the bumbling government official that he's pretended to be. His face loses that naïve demeanor, and his forehead gains a few lines.

I'm not stupid enough to fall for his trap, but I do really want to tell him to jump off the planet. He thinks he's got the advantage because he's a government official. Well, I've got something to say to a jerk like that.

"It's you who's threatening me!" I say. "Extorting money from me to save my mom, and now arresting my girlfriend because you're worried about a few words she said? I bet she's more loyal to the Emperor than you are!"

"And what is that supposed to mean?" Brownrigg's eyes narrow, and he leans towards me. I realize I just messed up too. I told him Kayley was my girlfriend. Ah, well. He probably didn't believe Afton's silly act, anyway.

"Easy, Rance," Parrish says, but I'm done with being cautious. This is about the girl I love, and I can't stop so easily when it comes to her.

"It means that you just might be in with Crowley!" I shout, and out of the corner of my eye, I see Parrish bury his face in his hand. That's fine. I'm just getting warmed up.

"As in Minister Crowley?"

"*Former* minister."

"Well, I see where this is heading..." Brownrigg says.

"Yeah, that's right, me uncovering your big deception!"

"What I see is that it will be necessary to bring you in for questioning too." Brownrigg waves his hand, and three of his officers walk from around the side of the shuttle. I can tell by their casual gait that they've been waiting there, ready for this moment. This means Brownrigg was planning to arrest me this entire time. Shoot. I should have considered that.

"Now, Mr. He', if you would step over here and put your hands on the side of the shuttle. These men will restrain you for your safety and ours, so please do not resist."

"He didn't do anything!" Parrish yells. "Leave him alone!"

"On the contrary," Brownrigg says. "He's threatened a government official and his statements about former ministers are suspect. I think that qualifies him as having done plenty. Now, hands on the shuttle, please. These men would prefer not to use force, but they are well trained in the art and will use it if necessary."

The energy goes out of me, and my shoulders sink. I should have had a plan. Even if it still resulted in my arrest, I would feel better about my efforts. I've sent the success meter plummeting off a cliff. No crowd for Kayley's speech, no freeing my girlfriend from an unlawful arrest. It's a wonder I woke up on time.

There's a sudden commotion to my left, loud enough for me to glance that way.

I catch my breath when I see it. It's a flood. A massive flood of people. It's like they all just picked up and brought their day in the park over to us. Some are pointing at the stage with awe, while others are staring at us and excitedly talking to each other. I bet they're wondering if the redhead in restraints is the Scarlett Kayley they've come to see. I bet they'd be furious if they knew the truth.

Wait a minute...

"Hey!" I shout. "These Imperial jerks are trying to arrest Scarlett Kayley!"

There's a murmur of confusion from the crowd. Brownrigg throws a nervous glance between them and us. He knows exactly what I'm trying to do. His finger comes up, and he shakes it at me in a warning. But honestly, I don't care.

"Hey! It *is* Scarlett Kayley!" a girl yells. "They've got her locked up!"

A thousand cries of outrage and disbelief erupt from the crowd. Some pick up their pace towards us, shaking fists and pointing fingers. As the word spreads around, the energy from the horde turns dark. Deputy Brownrigg and his men all take reflexive steps backward.

And as I'm also faced with this angry mass, I quickly follow.

"Rance," Doc Elizabeth says quietly, "what did you do?"

"Get those bastards!" someone yells, and a mass of angry people roars and charges. Doc Elizabeth is the first to bolt, grabbing on to the back of Parrish's chair and shoving as hard as she can towards the stage. Next are Deputy Brownrigg and his men. They pile into the shuttle faster than I've seen anyone move.

I dart towards Kayley. Grady and Afton are there first. They snatch her from the hands of the guards, who are more than glad to let her go. They even toss the restraint key to Afton. The three of them rush around the side of the shuttle, heading towards the stage.

The ground rumbles beneath my feet. It's a tremor of enraged Kayley fans, and they're not slowing down. I'm last to escape to the high ground before the flood of people hits.

There's a heavy boom as the horde impacts the side of the shuttle. They smash into it with such power that one side lifts, rocking the entire ship on its skids. It's a sight to behold, as the ship likely weighs as much as a house.

We watch from the stage as the shuttle is surrounded. Fists pound on its hard surface. The heckles and shouts coming from the crowd reach a fever pitch. I can only imagine what it must sound like inside the shuttle. When I try, my stomach gets tight, thinking of what might happen if that bloodthirsty mob gets in.

"Lieutenant Cortell, I think you're up," Parrish says, once again calling a timely play. Point Parrish.

The lieutenant and his thirty or so heavily armed men storm to the front of the stage, weapons out. For the moment, they're not aiming at the mass of people, but if this doesn't work, they might have to.

"Attention! This area is now under the supervision of the Angelcanis military! Stand back from the shuttle! I repeat, the Angelcanis military is asking you to stand back and let us handle this!"

"Not until we hear Scarlett Kayley speak!" someone cries. It's seconded by a thousand more voices, and that's echoed by ten thousand more. I glance over at my girlfriend, who's been watching the entire incident with a passive mask on her face.

The crowd's not exactly at a standstill. If they decide to charge us, there's little we could do about it. Lieutenant Cortell reads the situation and turns an open palm towards Kayley, inviting her to take up the mob's request. Kayley puts on a sly smile. I know she's been waiting for this moment. Of course. She was born for this.

"My friends, thank you for your concern," Kayley says, stepping up to the podium. "I'm not hurt, thanks to you, and I don't want anyone to be harmed today, so please, allow our great military to take charge of the situation."

As I watch, she blossoms into the world-famous celebrity they all want her to be. This crowd is under her spell, just like I've been under her spell. They'll do anything she asks of them.

"And," Kayley says and turns back to smile at us, ending on me. Her eyes are filled with such warmth, and I wonder why. Her gaze lingers, and then she turns back to the crowd. "If you stay calm, I'll introduce you to my friends...and my fiancé."

There's a rising cry from all of the women in the crowd and some disappointed sounds from some of the men. I grin to myself and shrug, trying to be cool, but I'm a total wreck inside. Does she actually think of me as her fiancé?

We need to talk.

The crowd pulls back from the shuttle, and Lieutenant Cortell knocks on the hatch. It opens to reveal a shell-shocked, wide-eyed Deputy Brownrigg.

"Sir, this area is now under the protection of the Angelcanis military," Lieutenant Cortell says. "For your safety, my men and I are going to be taking you to a secure facility. Come with me, sir."

"Yes, and I hope that it will be permanently secure," Doc Elizabeth says under her breath.

And just like that, we're free to carry out our mission without some government flunky getting in our way. I take in an elated breath and smile.

Things are finally coming together.

Chapter Twenty-Nine

EVERYTHING IS FALLING APART.

We're here in the drama hall—I mean, the canteen—of the Teddy ship, attempting to put the final details of our jailbreak plan together. So far, we have about two things agreed upon: who's going and how we get in.

After that, our plan is nonexistent.

We haven't put all that much thought into it. I would guess that's because we were too busy whipping up small armies and nearly getting sacrificed. Still, we're here now, and we've got the time.

Well, not really. Danny called to say she was getting bored and if we didn't get this done in the next two days, she would sell my mom to the queen of Canis Ludis. She also threatened to dump poison into my mom's drink if she couldn't make the first threat happen. I'm praying to the Goddesses that neither happens.

Despite all that, the others are riding the love-fest high they got from a hundred thousand cheering Yeomanry residents, and we're not nearly as focused as we should be.

"Hey guys," I say, trying to pull everyone together, "can we start from the top? Let's talk about how we're going to get there and back."

"Easy," Grady says, "this time, you get there by standard shuttle, and then a Teddy shuttle picks you up."

"Yeah, but we can't just have a Teddy shuttle show up at the main dock," I reply. "I mean, they're becoming known around the Empire, but any Teddys walking around will attract a lot of attention."

"Don't worry, dude, we'll find another way out."

"Isn't that why we're here talking?"

"Of course." Grady shrugs, and all I can do is send my eyes for a roll around their sockets. I sigh and get to my feet.

"Hey, I know we're all tired, but we have to get this done. Are you guys with me?"

"I am," Parrish says as he plunks out a small melody on his corn husker thing. I give him a smile of thanks.

"So am I, Rance," Doc Elizabeth says. "Though I do hope you won't be needing my brand of help this time."

"Kayley?"

"You're doing great, darling," she says and gives me a thumbs-up. "Don't forget I'm only backup."

"Wait, what? I thought you were going to help!"

"I am helping, and I'll jump in if you need me to, but you got this."

I throw my hands up, shaking them in the air. "We cannot have a repeat of last time!" I cry, stomping my foot. "Can at least one of you take this seriously? What about you, Afton? Afton?"

Afton stands along the wall, her hands together, eyes closed. One leg is pulled up with the knee bent out, and she has her foot pressed against the opposite leg. A serene smile touches her lips, and for once, I feel no wariness towards her.

Still, she looks ridiculous.

"Hey! Stop messing around and get over here!" I say. "You have an important part in this mission! What are you doing, anyway?"

"Calming my inner self so my thoughts can move freely," she replies in a soft voice.

"Does it help?" Kayley asks, touching a finger to her lips.

"Absolutely."

"Can you show me how?"

"Sure."

I watch in horror as my girlfriend joins her. Now there's two of them along the wall trying to imitate a tree.

"Darling, you should try this," Kayley says. "I feel calmer already."

"Not surprisingly, I don't."

"Maybe Quinn can help?" Parrish suggests.

I had forgotten about Quinn. Our mysterious contact should still be willing to help. I hope. She, or he—I'm still not clear about that—

was open to helping last time, and that wasn't a big ask at all. Unlike my team, she was totally down with supporting me.

RANCE: Hey Quinnster!

QUINN:

QUINN: Who dis?

RANCE: Danny's friend. Rance...the one with the special pickup requirement.

QUINN: Rance.

RANCE: You got it.

QUINN: You some kinda idiot?

RANCE: Why?

QUINN: My name not Quinnster and I not you friend. Don't message that again.

RANCE: Sorry.

QUINN: What you want?

RANCE: We still need to pick up the package. We've got a new code, and we're planning to come through the front door this time so we don't set off any alarms. I'm coming personally this time. Me and one other.

QUINN: You stupid, Rance. Nobody come back here, not even prisoner.

RANCE: I have to. Danny's making me.

QUINN: Danny still? Fine. She owe me double, then. What you need?

RANCE: An escort once we're inside.

QUINN: Fine. Arranged. But it you own neck if you lose it. I don't do cleanup.

RANCE: Understood. We'll give you a heads-up when we arrive.

I sit down with a sigh. At least that's something. One more piece of the puzzle added. We know how to get there. We can get around inside, and we have a ride home. All that's good, but there are important details yet to be figured out. I'm not stepping foot on that station until we get those solved.

"So, what's next?" Parrish asks. Thank the Goddesses for him. Really. He's the last person I would expect to want to be involved in this again. But that's Parrish. When he sees a goal he can achieve, he doesn't stop until he makes it happen.

"I guess...we need to find a way through security," I reply. "We're going to need some sort of security clearance."

"What about the code?" Doc Elizabeth asks. "How do you use it?"

I stare at Parrish blankly, and he stares back, an exact mirror of myself. We never found out how it works because we were running from Billie Morgan when we should have been asking her that question. There was that minor issue of her wanting to snatch me for one of her clients that kinda got in the way.

"You don't know, do you?" Doc Elizabeth folds her arms in front of her and presses her lips together. I find a nice spot on the floor to watch while her disapproval targets me for assassination.

"We had a small misunderstanding with our contact," Grady says. "It's no big deal, though."

"No big deal?" I lean into Grady with my mouth hanging open. "How many times did *you* get zapped, dude?"

"Hey, she threatened she was going to do it to me too," Grady replies.

"Would you like me to show you how it felt?"

Grady opens his hands and curls the corner of his mouth up. There's got to be a few puffs of steam blowing out of my ears by now.

"Okay, boys," the doc says, "how about we take it down a notch or two, yeah?"

I shake my head and sit, but then stand again. It just got overly warm in here, and I have to move. I start to pace back and forth while the others are...actually, I have no idea what they're doing. I do know what they're *not* doing, which is helping me figure this out.

We've got a code we've no idea how to use, a contact who gets insulted at friendly overtones, and no known way to get off the station after finding the person we need. All in all, it's a major mess. Sure, we got one thing—no, wait, *I* got one thing accomplished, but until we fill in the gaps, there's still no plan. And without a plan, my mom becomes a scullery maid for a nutty royal.

"Fine," I say to whoever's listening. "So if we can't use the code, let's think of another way."

"Uniforms?" Parrish suggests.

"Uniforms aren't going to do us any good if we don't have passes."

"Maybe the Teddys can whip up some fake passes for us," Grady says.

"How are they going to do that without a pass to copy?"

Grady shrugs. "Maybe I can hack into somewhere and find an image."

"Yeah, but that only gets us the card, not the specific info that's on it, right?"

"Hmm." Grady itches his chin. "True. To get that, we'd need to hack into the company that makes the machine that prints the cards."

"And how easy do you think that's going to be?"

"Not easy at all." Grady shakes his head. "Okay, scratch that idea."

We're back to the beginning...again. Without a way through security, this is going to be the shortest mission we've ever done. For me, it's the most important mission we've ever done—saving my mom. It's got to happen. There is no other option. Her life is over if we fail.

It's even warmer than before. I wipe my brow with my sleeve and wonder if I should have worn something lighter. Teddy ships are set to cool compared to human normal, yet it feels nearly tropical in here. My lungs also feel tight. Maybe something is wrong with the environmental systems?

When I glance at my buds, they're not perspiring one bit. Then I turn to Kayley and Afton, and my internal furnace burns white-hot. I can't believe that they're just going to pose like that while we stress it out over here.

"Hey!" I shout. "Would the two of you *please* wake up and help us? And Parrish? No offense, dude, but could you knock it off on that thing for a bit?"

I hear a content sigh come from Afton, and I spin on her, ready to give her a piece of my mind. She stretches her arms out and plants her foot back on the ground. Before I can step up to get in her face, she bends herself in half from the waist and plants both hands on the ground. Then she comes back up again, breathing deeply. Kayley follows suit, and all I can do is stand there watching, feeling my eyebrows make every attempt to meet in the middle of my forehead.

"Ah." Afton opens her eyes and smiles serenely at me. "That was perfect."

"I'm glad! Can we save my mom now? Please?" My heart thumps hard, and my breaths get short. Doc Elizabeth glances at me with concern. I feel like I'm about to combust.

"Rance." Afton puts a hand on my shoulder. "You really need to find your inner peace, and then answers will become clear to you."

"What are you talking about?"

"Wow, that was wonderful," Kayley says and rubs the side of her head on my shoulder. "Okay, let's get to work. You need my help, right?"

If I was a rocket, I'd blast off, smash through the hull, and fly back home. I'm really getting to the end of my fuse, and exploding Rance is not something that anyone wants to see.

"We were discussing the code," Grady answers for me because right now, I just...can't.

"Oh, right," Kayley says, nodding. "So, Billie said there's a kiosk where we play in the tones of the code, and it'll create a temporary pass for you to get through security."

"Wait, when did she tell you that?"

"Before you guys came in." Kayley looks at me, not getting the fact that I've been racking my brain to figure out what she already knew. I hang my head, totally and utterly defeated. At least we've got a solution.

"Kayley?" I mumble.

"Yes, darling?"

"Can you take over, please? I'm going to go walk out the airlock."

Chapter Thirty

AFTON AND I SIT side by side in perfect calm inside Exodus Station's visitor shuttle. As a way to get to the station, this is by far the most relaxing. We have Teddy comm for when we need it, but we can't have anyone hearing us discussing the mission. This is a passenger ship we're on, and so the best thing for us to do is sit back and enjoy the view.

"Hey, how are you and Kayley doing?" Afton asks.

I get a chill down my back as I stare out the porthole of the shuttle. I'm not sure I have an answer for that. Afton might even know more than me, which makes me wonder why she's asking. Then I get an itch from considering that.

"Fine, I guess."

"You don't need to pretend with me. I'm her friend too, or did you forget that? I know she's been all over the place since the last time... you know."

Afton means the last time we tried to break into Exodus. Since that day, over a week ago now, Kayley's swung hard between despondent and euphoric. It's hard to tell how she's really feeling, and I worry she's going to make a poor decision just to convince herself that everything is fine. Her reception in Yeomanry lifted her spirits, I'm sure. I just hope not to a false level, where she'll come crashing back down again.

"Yeah, she's been, and she...well, I mean, I..." It's hard for me to get my thoughts straight. I've got so many when it comes to Kayley.

"Have you told her you love her yet?"

"Of course, we say it to each other all the time."

"Yeah, right. Listen, you"—Afton pokes a finger into my chest —"you better get your act together and just *tell her*. Then you can worry about what comes after. You left her hanging, and she's been waiting ever since. So, stop being a wimp and tell her already."

"I told her!" I look down. "She just didn't accept it."

"Oh, and why's that?"

"It's complicated."

"No, it's not. Here, watch me." Afton turns my head towards her with a finger on my chin and locks eyes with me. She's got her not often seen happy-girl face on, and I know I'm about to be properly schooled.

"Rance, I love you," Afton says in the sweetest voice she can conjure. It's not Kayley's dulcet tones, but I have to admit Afton's got some skill. It's very believable.

So much so that the old woman sitting across the aisle from me bats me with her bag. I jump and spin to face her, eyes wide.

"What's wrong with you?" The old woman frowns. "That girl just bared her heart to you, and you can't say it back? Don't be a wuss!"

"See?" Afton chuckles and, when I turn back, pats my cheek. "No need to wait."

"Okay, I get it," I mutter. I sink into my seat, properly chastised. It's not like I don't want to say it. I *did* say it. I just messed it up. That's all. Is it too much to want the moment to be special to show Kayley just how much she means to me?

I'm saved from any more lectures by the docking announcement. That also means I need to switch gears and get focused on the job ahead. That's going to be tough now that Afton has stuck a major guilt complex on me. I'll be hard-pressed to keep my full attention on the mission every time I hear Kayley's voice.

We wait for the artificial gravity to engage and then shuffle out onto the visitor's dock. This is not the main one for the facility, but a smaller one built strictly for the lower security required for people coming on to visit prisoners. There's only about ten guards here, and most of them are so bored, they're barely paying attention to what's going on around them. Still, they are enough to get the hundred or so shuttle passengers lined up and ready to go through the security system for an initial scan.

We'll have to wait to turn on the Teddy comm until after we get through security. Our Sergos are run through a special device that looks for extra components inside the casing. It's a good thing that Teddy comm doesn't require our Sergos to work. Just the earpiece is enough, and that doesn't look like anything more than a hands-available device. Inside or out.

"So, where do we get our pass?" Afton says, glancing around.

"Not sure. Why don't you put your girlfriend face back on and go ask that guard that's been checking you out for the last minute?"

"Hey, I'm not just something to ogle," Afton says with a pout.

"And I'd be the first to back you up on that, Surela, but right now, it's your face that's going to go get the answer we need."

"Rance, buddy, I think if you were going for a compliment, you failed miserably. Still, I appreciate how you recognize you need my gorgeous looks to help us out here."

Afton skips off towards the guard, whose smile grows to gigantic proportions as she approaches. I have to admit, Afton has an amazing ability to adapt to the situation, whatever it is. She's rarely stuck in one particular mindset. It's gotten us out of quite a few situations in the past, and not just times when we were messing with the authorities. Though, Afton's got her share of those experiences too. I'm still trying to get her to tell me about the time she got arrested...by military police.

"Okay, got it," Afton says, coming back. "The kiosk we should use is just to the side of the office over there. He recommended we use that one because it's more private."

"Did he ask you on a date too?"

"Would you be jealous if he did?"

"Hey, I have a girlfriend already, or are you suddenly believing your own words?"

"Are you?" Afton smirks, knowing she's won our little verbal spar. I don't understand how she can relax enough to joke around. I've got this funky tingle on my back that I know will only go away once we're off this station.

We're through the initial security check, and we make our way to the kiosk. Now we can switch on the Teddy comm and let the team know we're here.

"Oh! Great!" Grady says, leaving his mic open. We can hear him call the others, and there's a bit of a scramble as I hear a pair of feet slap their way towards the mic. That's got to be Kayley.

"Rance? Afton?" There she is. "Are you guys alright? Was there some delay? We've been standing by waiting for you to comm in."

"Teddy also standing by," Original Teddy says. It's good to hear his voice, however odd and warbly it is. If he and his Blue Buddy are on the case, I know we're in excellent hands for when we're ready to make our exit. Now, all we have to do is...everything else.

"No delay," I reply. "We just couldn't use the comm on the shuttle."

"Yeah, an old lady beat Rance up," Afton says with a snicker.

"What? What happened?"

"Never mind," I say with a quick glare at my partner-in-crime. "We're at the kiosk, and we're about to put the code in."

"Remember to put the earpiece up close to the mic on the kiosk. Otherwise, it won't hear the code when I play it back," Grady says. "Let me know when you're ready."

I start the process on the kiosk. As expected, it's self-explanatory, so that's one less itch I need to scratch. There's a few screens to run through, but once I'm there, I pull the earpiece out and hand it to Afton. She accepts it, holding it far away from her body with just her finger and thumb. Her overreaction of disgust is not lost on me.

"Okay, I've handed my earpiece to Afton, and she'll let you know when it's in place. Also, Afton may need an anti-cooties shot when we get back."

I keep an eye out for any guards as we wait. What we're doing is illegal enough to make us permanent residents here. I'm not even sure a free and fair trial would be part of that equation. Then again, the guards here are as likely to use their trigger fingers as their mouths and ears.

Afton hands me my earpiece back, and I pop it in. My hand drops quickly as Afton's new boyfriend glances over at us. I smile and wave, and he nods back but continues to watch me until another guard interrupts him. I turn away from him so he doesn't see the guilt on my face.

"What's it say now?" Grady asks.

"It says...'please wait,'" Afton says.

"It's processing the code. Shouldn't take long."

The sudden clip-clop of boots on the hard floor catches my attention, and my heart stops. I try not to move too fast, but the sudden panic takes hold of me and I jerk my head up to look.

Fortunately, it's only a guard headed to the office just around the corner. I let a breath out and share a relieved glance with Afton, whose eyes are about as wide as they'll go. We get back to waiting anxiously for this dumb machine to give us access.

"Everything going okay?" a voice says behind me.

I yelp and turn. It's the guard who was watching me before. He had a friendly smile on, but now that I've gone and freaked out, his smile is fading and his eyebrows are rising.

"Oh! You startled me...us...or..." I glance at Afton, who appears calm outside, but I know all of her internal alarms are screaming.

"Sorry about that," Mr. Friendly says, "but it doesn't usually take this long, so I came to check on you. What's the screen say?"

No use trying to hide it. I take a step back and let him take a look. He makes a thoughtful sound and nods. Then he turns to examine the two of us for the longest ten seconds I've ever had the pleasure of counting.

"The two of you ever been here before?" Mr. Friendly puts his hand on his belt...right next to his weapon. If he's trying to intimidate us, it's working. I really wish this stupid kiosk would hurry up.

"No," Afton replies in a small peep. It's the shortest sound I've ever heard her make.

"And who are you going to see?"

"His..." Afton says, pointing to me.

"Her..." I say at the same time, pointing to Afton.

We both stop when we hear each other speak and share an awkward glance. Afton motions to me to continue answering.

"My...dad, her father-in-law," I say.

The guard slumps a little at my answer, then glances between the two of us as his eyes narrow.

"The two of you are married?"

"Yep," I say and force a toothy smile onto my face.

"Our parents arranged it," Afton says with a nervous chuckle. That gets an understanding nod from the guard as he adjusts his belt and gives me another hard look. I'm shrinking under his heavy gaze and hoping he doesn't shoot me just because he wants to go on a date with Afton.

The machine beeps a saving tone, and a series of fast clicks rattle off inside it. It's a sure sign of something printing, and I'm tallying up all the merits I'm going to need to make once I get home. Mr. Friendly's eyes dart down to the machine, and he nods again, turning to go.

"What's his name?" He stops and turns halfway back.

"Who?"

"Your father." He catches my jaw drop and turns fully to face me. His face is impassive, but his eyes say he's just waiting for the chance to shoot me down. As if that wasn't terrifying enough, I need to make up a name on the spot.

"Benicio Cavalcante," I reply, taking a chance that he's never heard of my father before. I couldn't think of any other name to use, so I just used his real one. That wasn't the wisest choice. If he recognizes the name, we're both about to get a few holes put in us.

The guard stares at me for an eternity, and my lungs freeze and fracture into thousands of pieces.

"Be careful once you're inside," the guard says. "This is a high-security facility, and there are many dangerous prisoners here. Stay with your escort and keep your eyes open."

We both murmur a thank-you and remain imitations of Teddy popsicles until Mr. Friendly is well out of earshot before we both let out the shakiest breaths of our lives.

Chapter Thirty-One

WE'RE THROUGH SECURITY.

I don't know how we both didn't have heart attacks after the final documentation check. The code and the pass it created were real blessings. Without them, we would never have gotten this far. I would totally give Billie a hug if I saw her again, as long as she didn't zap me for it.

The guards told us to head straight down the corridor to the tram, but we have to meet up with Quinn first. They said they'd meet us at the nearest intersection, but as we approach it there's no one there. Afton and I duck around the corner and wait, just out of sight from the guards at security.

"Did she say when she'd be meeting you?" Grady asks.

"Not exactly, no. We said we'd be arriving soon last time we chatted, but the shuttle was late," I reply.

"We don't even know what she looks like, do we?" Afton asks. "Why does she have to be so secretive?"

We can't stay here long. At some point, we're going to have to go to the tram station and take it wherever our pass tells it to go. That might be right to Freddie, or it might go straight to the station superintendent's office. If Quinn doesn't show, we'll have to take that chance.

"Contact her," Afton says.

"That might be a bad idea," Grady says, "and she might not even respond."

"True, but we've got little choice," I say and pull out my Sergo.

"No calls inside the station," a helmeted guard shouts and starts towards us—so much for that. I wave an apology and make a show of putting it back in my pocket. That doesn't convince him, and he unclips the safety strap on his weapon as he approaches. "You're supposed to head to the tram."

"We forgot which way it was," Afton tries, putting on an innocent grin, but if he's buying it, he makes no response to show understanding. Or caring.

"Show me your pass," he orders, and I hand it to him with both hands. He stares at it for a moment, then slides it into his shirt pocket. "Follow me," he says.

I give Afton a sidelong glance, and she returns it—no answers there. We've cast the die and now have no options but to follow along.

The guard heads to the tram station and waits for us at the gate. Once we're there, we look up at him expectantly. He watches down the hall for a silent minute, then nods towards a door marked No Exit. Afton and I share a confused glance. Could this be Quinn? If so, they are making my chest tighten.

"This way," the guard says, opening the door and motioning for us to go in first. I don't like it, but since we've no weapons and I doubt we could fight our way out even if we did, I do as I'm told.

It's just another corridor, so I guess I shouldn't have worried so much. It's a bit brighter than the tram area and pristinely clean. If a speck of dust found its way in here, it would likely be obliterated instantly. I hope we're not being considered specks of dust.

"To the end, the last door on your right. Go now," the guard says and then closes the door behind him.

"Did you guys find Quinn?" Grady asks.

"We don't know where we are," Afton whispers. "Better if we stay silent for now."

I examine the door before I open it. It's solid, so no way to get a hint of what's inside. I tell myself we've done this before, so it's no big deal. Nobody is threatening to shoot me or holding a gun to my head, so that's a plus. With a firm nod to Afton, I open the door and step inside.

Something cold and metallic pokes me in my temple, and I freeze.

"You move, run or yell, you dead. Got that?" a voice says, and I follow their direction to the word. Someone puts a hand on my back and shoves me deeper into the darkened room. I stumble and catch myself on the edge of a chair, doubling over it.

"You too, inside," the voice says. Then the door closes, and I'm blinded. A moment later Afton catches herself on my shoulder with a gasp. I hear her recover quickly as her clothes go taut with a sharp snap.

"You very lucky, both you," the voice says. A hand grabs the back of my shirt, pulls me up straight, then spins me around to face the owner of the voice. "If that guard didn't see you. You'd be off to the pit right now."

"Quinn?" I try, tentatively. The owner of the voice steps into the meager light, and my eyes almost fall out of their sockets. It's a woman, but I question the level of humanity that exists in her shiny metallic face and glowing eyes. There might be a human brain behind it all, but I'd even question that.

"What's the pit?" Afton asks, moving her face closer to Quinn's. Quinn eyes her warily as Afton's finger comes up to try to touch Quinn's face. A gun placed right between Afton's eyes puts a quick stop to that.

"You don't wanna know," Quinn replies, holstering her gun. "Let's go. No time to waste."

"Wait, what's—" I point, but don't touch.

"My face? That you wanna know?" Quinn gets close enough that I can see my reflection in her metallic skin. "It got ripped off by a prisoner from the pit. Now I got a new one. It better, right?"

"Yes, absolutely," I reply and nod with great enthusiasm.

"Must make putting on makeup hard," Afton comments. Quinn turns to glare at her, and Afton backs up two fast steps. But Quinn gives her a toothy grin and chuckles.

"Don't need no," she says and reaches out to squeeze Afton's cheek with a chromed hand. Afton's eyes dart down to watch the hand as it pulls away. I'm not sure if she's scared or curious. Maybe a bit of both.

"Come, we go get your man."

Quinn escorts us to a small room and ushers us into a translucent capsule waiting there, closing the hatch behind her as she steps in. I notice she walks with a limp and her motions with her arms are stiff and mechanical. This place must really be dangerous for that to have happened to her.

We hop inside and the capsule gets sealed into a tube. A second later, acceleration shoves the three of us back in our seats. It's so heavy I can't even lift my hands more than an inch off my body for a good minute.

"Whooee!" Quinn exclaims. "Always love this!"

"What is this?" Afton asks.

"Emergency loop," Quinn explains. "Pneumatic power. Better than that tram any day."

The pressure gradually releases, and I can take a full breath again without feeling like someone is sitting on my chest, but it doesn't last. The capsule decelerates and we all get slammed in the opposite direction. My harness digs into me, and I wonder just how many bruises I'm going to have tomorrow.

"We here," Quinn says and disconnects herself from her seat. She sees Afton having some trouble with her harness and gives her a hand. It surprises Afton, but she allows it as Quinn moves way faster than she ever could. In fact, she's inhumanly fast, and I rush to get mine off before her machine hands can touch me.

"Before we go." Quinn turns around to face us, blocking the exit. "You gotta be smart out there. You follow my direction ex-act-ly. This political prison, but that don't mean these couyons are genteel. I not clean your brain up if it gets mashed on the ground, right?"

Both Afton and I nod. I hear myself swallow, and I think I hear Afton do it too. I didn't want to picture my head in that ugly state, but it just popped into my thoughts, and now I can't get rid of the image.

"Hey, guys, what's going on?" Grady asks.

"Not now," I whisper.

"What that?" Quinn eyes me, but I just shake my head.

She unholsters her weapon and motions us out before stepping out onto a catwalk that hangs above a very deep chasm in the station. There's a fiery light down at the bottom, and I think I see some movement there.

"That the pit," Quinn says, the edge in her voice making it clear she's not excited to discuss it. "Keep moving."

We pass a few guards escorting prisoners along the walkway—a few nod to Quinn, but none even spare a glance at Afton and me. The prisoners do though, and their looks run the gamut of human expression. Some are merely curious, while others are confused. One smashes any amount of calm I had managed to regain after our shaky entrance. If he weren't fully restrained, I bet he would have torn me apart.

After walking in a long upward spiral, we stop in front of a closed cell. Quinn taps a button on her lapel and there's a click inside the door. She grabs the handle and gives it a twist, and the door begins to retract on its own.

"Go in," Quinn orders. "I be back."

My mouth drops open as I stare at her. Is she going to leave us in a locked cell with a criminal? I try to protest, but Quinn puts her boot on my back and thrusts before I can get my first word out. I fly forward and land hard on the metal floor. Afton gets shoved in as well, and the door clanks shut. I hear her shout and pound on it. We're locked in, and possibly for good. A sudden sense of familiarity comes back to me.

My mind races. Did she just trick us? Is she really even Danny's friend?

"Dammit, I knew we couldn't trust her!" Afton growls and pounds again.

"That's not going to help you." The voice floats out from the back of the cell. It's pitched high but light. I look up, and out of the dark, a blond-haired man steps forward and offers me a hand. "You okay?" he asks.

"Yeah, thanks." I accept the offered hand and get to my feet. It gives me a moment to have a good look at him. For a man, he's…pretty. Bright blue eyes and a smooth complexion, with not even a single hair on his head out of place. It makes for a curious image in this dimly lit cell. Even his teeth are perfect when he smiles at me. For someone who's been locked up for a while, he's in considerably good condition. I was a complete wreck after just a few days.

"The guards treat us all the same," he says. "It doesn't matter if we've murdered a million people or simply called out an injustice. So, what are you two in for? Saving the whales?"

"The what?" Afton asks, coming up next to me.

"Are you Freddie Espy?" I ask.

"Sorry, have we met? Perhaps when we stopped the deforestation on Albion by strapping ourselves to the trees?" He giggles and shakes his fists. "Ooh, that was such a good one!"

"Uh, no, we're not protestors," I say and lean in to whisper. "We're here to get you out! Well, we're supposed to, anyway."

"Here to get me out? That sounds wonderful, but how will you do that now that you're locked in with me?" He smiles and shakes his head. "No, I'm sorry, my friends. I think we are all in here for a long time."

"No! Your wife sent us to break you out!"

"Wife?" Freddie looks confused.

"You know," Afton says, "Danny Lecker. Your wife."

"Well." He throws his hands up. "Whatever you say. I am looking forward to leaving soon, but my friends, as I stated before, there is the slight problem of being locked up together."

Chapter Thirty-Two

"GRADY, YOU THERE?" I call, pushing the earpiece in.

"Dude!" Grady replies as if he's been desperately waiting for us to call in. "Are you guys alright? You cut us off so quickly before, we were freaking out!"

"Alright is a relative term," I reply. "We're not hurt, but some messed-up stuff is going on."

I explain our situation to him, making every attempt to not curse every human being directly responsible for putting us in this position. Grady and whoever else is listening on the other side are dead silent as they listen to our tale of woe. I know Kayley's there, and I hope she's not blaming herself for this debacle. It wasn't her who exchanged saliva with one very sneaky hand-hunter. Not that I did it on purpose.

Quinn is the unknown in this situation. I had no reason to doubt her until this point, but if you're trying to help someone, ramming a foot in their back isn't usually the way to prove that. She could be some kind of double agent, working for the government. I'm sure more than a few of those seditionists would be happy to know where I am.

"So, any ideas?"

"Hang tight for a minute. We're discussing," Grady replies. I can hear the apology in his voice, but it's not his fault we're in here. I was so focused on getting the job done that I didn't even consider the possibility that Quinn would dupe us.

"Freddie." I turn to him while we're waiting. If I can figure out why Danny sent us to get him, it might provide some leverage against her to get my mom back. If we ever get out of here, that is.

"How can I help?" Freddie asks.

"Tell me why you're in here," I say. He shrugs and turns his hands up.

"That's easy. Everyone knows that."

"We don't," Afton says, shaking a fist at him. "So out with it."

"Okay, okay. No reason for threats. We are, as you say, birds of a feather, yes?"

"I have no idea what that means," Afton replies. "Just spill it, already."

Freddie explains his role in about twenty different anti-government protests and how he and his organization saved an entire continent on Sordibus Prime. I remember hearing about that planet once—how it was so poor that the government there sold off half of the world so the Empire could build an industrial waste facility on it. That would have destroyed most of the native life there and turned the rest into a wasteland.

"You must see all the little animals there. They are just so cute. How could anyone want to destroy such a cute animal?" Freddie says and shakes his head. "I just don't get it."

"I do," Afton says. "It's always the cute and fuzzies that get saved. No one ever wants to save a reptile."

Freddie turns to her and frowns thoughtfully.

"Hey, Rance," Grady says, coming back on, "so this is what we've got so far. Teddy and BB will take the shuttle with a few other Teddys and fly to the southern end of the station. From there, they'll try to get on board and get to you."

"Okay."

If that's the best they've got, it'll have to do.

"Any ideas on getting us out of this lockup?" Afton asks.

"Teddy says they've got that covered. Just stay put."

"And what if we don't get to decide that?" Afton stands up and puts her hands on her hips, waiting for an answer, but one doesn't come.

"By the way," Freddie says, "who is this that you are talking to?"

"Our way out, hopefully," I reply.

The idea of waiting for the Teddys to rescue us is not one I have warm feelings about. I think they could do it, but it's not about if. It's about when. Depending upon what level of evil Quinn is interested in achieving, she could move us to another, more secure cell, like that pit place she mentioned, or she could just space us, and that would be it for Rance and company.

"What do you think?" I ask Afton. "Should we try something on our own?"

"I'm for anything that gets us out of here faster," she replies.

"Yes, I am also," Freddie says.

"Good," Afton says, "then keep an eye on the door and let us know if someone is coming."

We walk to the back of the cell and search around. There's not much here, save for a sink, a toilet, and a set of hard metal bunks. It's dark, so searching for something like a vent is not easy, though I do finally manage to spot one. It's way up high, and I can't tell how big it is from where I am.

"Get on my shoulders, and I'll lift you up," I say to Afton.

"Are you joking? You could barely lift little Freddie back there. You get on my shoulders."

I roll my eyes but do as she says, using the bunk to get up. If the bunks were closer, I'd just climb up on them instead of playing acrobat with Afton. She is stronger than me, but that doesn't mean I'm easy for her to handle. I've put on some weight being so idle for the last six months.

"So? What do you see?" Afton says.

"Nothing. I'm not high enough."

"So stand up, then...but slip your boots off first. I don't want heel marks on my shoulders."

Once again, I follow her direction, kicking my boots off and then using the top bunk to steady myself as I plant my feet on her shoulders.

"Goddesses, Rance, did you eat everything in the farmer's market for the last six months?"

"Hey, that's not very nice."

"Fine, I'm sorry, but as soon as we get back, you're coming out to train with me. You and Kayley both."

"Did you just call my girlfriend fat?"

"Forget it. What do you see up there?"

"It's still too high up." I scan around, looking for something to step on. "Get up on the toilet, then I should be high enough."

"Who the hell do you think I am? I can't do that."

"Try."

"Oh," Freddie says. I try to turn to see what he's doing, but I can't twist enough, and if I jerk around to look, both Afton and I are going down. It's bad enough that Afton is shaking me around as she tries to get her feet up on the toilet. I don't blame her for having trouble. I'm heavy enough, but the seat is metal and slippery, and that's just a terrible combination.

"Someone is coming," Freddie says. "Perhaps a good idea to get down."

"Yeah, easier said than done," Afton replies. "We just got up. Look while you can, Rance."

I put my hands on either side of the vent. It's wide enough for someone to fit through. All I need to do is figure out how to get the grate off, and we could slide out of here to...well, who knows where, but wherever it leads has got to be better than here.

"Someone is at the door!" Freddie hisses, and a second later, the latch clicks. I jerk around to look, but my motion pulls Afton off-balance. Her foot slips off the toilet seat and we go down. I reach out for the edge of the bunk but crunch my chin on it instead. I'm knocked back, and I bang into the wall.

"What the hell you do?" Quinn's glow-in-the-dark eyes peer at me from the front of the cell. She's come in and closed the door behind her.

"We didn't know if you were coming back!" Afton says, sprawled out on the floor. "You just kicked us in and took off."

"Well, now you got to go! Get up!"

"I've got to put my boots on," I say, mostly because I can't think of anything else.

"No!" Quinn shouts. "No time...they coming!"

"Who's coming?" I ask.

"If you keep lie there, you gonna find out." Quinn steps over to Afton and helps her up. "And you don't wanna find out."

I get up and push forward. Quinn taps on the door and someone outside opens it. She glances in both directions, then beckons to us. I've got just enough time to snatch up my boots, but Quinn grabs my hair and tugs as I attempt to put them on. Her metallic hands are not gentle.

"Forget the boot! Come on!"

The four of us skate across the walkway and take a ramp that leads down into a service tunnel. She stops and turns on us. Afton stops short, and Freddie and I bang into her.

"You go there, keep straight," Quinn says, pointing down the tunnel. "It gonna keep going down, but don't stop, don't ever stop. You get to the bottom lock. That you pickup spot."

"You're not coming?" I ask.

"No, too dangerous for me now. I'm done with you. You get yourself out."

I nod reluctantly, but start moving, anyway. Then, to my surprise, Quinn grabs my shoulder and stops me. I jerk back and spin on her.

"You tell Danny she owe *triple*," Quinn says. I nod again and start to move, but Quinn grabs me and pulls me back.

"Hey! What—" I stop, seeing the white edges of her synthetic eyes. I watch her take a tight breath, and I feel my chest respond in kind.

"You be careful. You going to the pit. Don't stop. Don't stop *ever*." Quinn spins me around and shoves. I turn back to say thanks, but she's already gone.

The pit. If there was a place I would never want to experience, this would be it. After seeing what happened to Quinn, I don't want to think about what monsters are down there. Literal monsters. Not human beings in any sense of that term. The most violent creatures known to the Empire are where we're going.

And that's just the guards.

Chapter Thirty-Three

OUR EYES ARE ALREADY well adjusted to the dim light of the station, but the service tunnel is only illuminated by a scattering of status lights on panels randomly spread about. It makes our travel through the narrow and cramped tunnel a challenge. Even on a Teddy ship we can stand straight up. Not here.

I can't help thinking about what we're going to see down there. It seriously freaked Quinn out that we were going there. I can still see her silvery face as she spoke her ominous warning. She had a first-hand experience with the prisoners down there and barely managed to survive the encounter. If all we have to do to stay safe is keep moving, we are definitely not going to stop.

Of course, she could have gotten us out another way, but I don't think she wanted to be involved in our jailbreak any more than she had already. Speaking of another way...

"Hey Grady, change of plans," I say, and wait for a response, but none comes.

"You getting anything?" Afton asks.

"No. The station must be interfering with the transmission."

"Yeah, but this is subspace, not radio. Metal objects don't block that kind of transmission. Why is it happening?"

"Well, I'd ask Grady if I could get him on the line."

The tunnel turns, and like the walkway, it winds downward. The red glow peeking through from behind the panels makes our descent seem like we're headed to the underworld. If Hades is down there, I really hope we don't meet him. He could be friendly, but I seriously doubt it.

"You know," Freddie says, "this is really exciting."

Both Afton and I give each other a side glance. It must be nice to be so naïve of the dangers we're about to face. Then again, if Freddie had a clue as to what we need to do to escape, he might not be so chipper.

In a place with the Empire's most violent criminals, you need an equally dangerous force to guard them. It'll be the guards that we'll need to watch out for most. They're the ones with the heavy standoff weapons. We don't plan on getting close enough to any of the prisoners for them to be a problem.

"Grady?" I try again, but I'm not expecting anything. "Are you getting us?"

"Rance." I sigh in relief as the voice responds. It's not Grady, though—it's Kayley. "Are you guys alright?"

"KayKay, listen. There's been a change of plans."

I describe to her our current situation and what we need to do to get out, leaving nothing out—especially the part about the pit and the major risk we'll be taking. Kayley stays quiet until I'm done.

"Okay, be careful. I'll see you soon," she says. She must not have heard the part about bloodthirsty criminals and equally savage guards.

"You heard the part where I told you the Albion Assassin is down there, right?"

"I'm listening," Kayley replies.

"You know, the monster who savagely murdered a hundred people by ripping their heads off? Your boyfriend could meet him if he's not careful."

"Then be careful."

"Are you not worried at all?"

"I trust you, darling."

Afton raises an eyebrow as I swear and pull my earpiece out. She's also fast enough to grab my hand before I throw it away. I take in a calming breath and nod my thanks. That would have been a dumb thing to do in the anger of the moment. At least someone besides me understands how tense the situation is.

We arrive at the bottom and halt. Our way is closed off by a heavy metal door. Part of the tunnel becomes translucent here, and the pit's fiery light blazes through it, illuminating the area in its hellish color.

"Let's take a peek," I suggest, examining the door for a key or control. It's Afton who finds that it's neither of those. She grabs the handle and triggers a latch that unlocks the door. If we were on the other side, I doubt we'd be so lucky. No one wants cold-blooded killers simply walking out of permanent imprisonment.

We crack open the sliding door just enough to get our fingers in. A frozen breeze pours in that sends a simultaneous shiver through the three of us. That was unexpected. We're not dressed to handle anything cooler than the inside of my house on a hot day. If we have to go through it to get where we're going, we all might lose a few fingers and toes.

A shout and a scream echo through the area, followed by the squeal of powerful energy weapons discharging. There's the smash of something heavy against the wall we're behind. A deep rumble vibrates through the floor and up into our bones, shaking our bodies and our nerves. Then, after that, silence. The only other hint that a violent event just happened is a trickle of red fluid that leaks into the tunnel access closet. It could be blood, it could be hydraulic fluid, but either way, it's proof that something savage just happened.

"What do you see?" I ask Afton, not really wanting to know the answer.

"Machines," Afton replies. "Machines controlling men."

"Mechanized security," Freddie says. "I've encountered them before. Yes, very dangerous."

And likely not something that's going to be affected by a Teddy popsicle attack.

"Still think this is exciting?" Afton asks Freddie, who gives her an emphatic shake of his head.

"What about the airlock?"

"Not here." Afton pauses. "But I see a sign. We'll have to go through there to get to it."

"Through...there?" Freddie asks, his voice pitched higher than usual.

I sigh. Here we go again.

"We need a diversion," I suggest. "Something that's going to get those bots looking elsewhere while we sneak through."

"You sound like you've got an idea already," Afton says. "Great, go for it. I'll get in touch with Grady and meet you at the airlock."

"No."

"You'll be fine."

"Gee, thanks, *Surela*. I'm going to remember this...if I make it out alive."

My next sigh is exponentially larger than the one I just let out. I've got no idea what kind of distraction I can make that won't end my life in some horrible way. I hunch down and drop my boots—wait—*my boots*. I can use those. Somehow. I just need to think about it.

"Kayley? You there?" I call after returning the Teddy comm device to my ear. How glad I am that Afton stopped me from tossing it.

"Where else would I be? Grady's back and Parrish is here too, and the Teddys are standing by. They're just waiting for you to give the okay, and they'll bring the shuttle down to the airlock."

"Great, but first, I need some help. We need a diversion so we can slip by some of the big meanies down here. What can I do with boots?"

There's a few moments of silence before Parrish gets on.

"Hey Rance, can you throw them at something that would make a big noise? Like break glass with them or something?"

"No glass down here, dude. Glass doesn't exist in a penitentiary."

I was really hoping for more than that, hoping that Kayley would take charge and give me some direction, but she's really overdoing this "staying out of it" thing. I regret even calling them now. Break some glass? Give me a break. Those security bots would target me in an instant and I'd perish in plasma fire.

"Wow, look at that," Afton gasps. "That guy has to be like the size of four of you."

"Yeah?" I perk up. That sounds like an opportunity to throw something at. "Does he look like the kind to get angry if he got hit in the head with a boot?"

Afton spins on me, wide-eyed, her jaw dropping. That's exactly the image I had of her in my head when I was saying it. I can imagine my face looking like that if she suggested it to me.

"You're completely nuts, Rance." Afton shakes her head, but the side of her mouth is curling up. "But I like it. Honestly, I would never have expected you to come up with it. Just make sure we're well out of the way before you do it."

"Then get going." I grin. "You've got five seconds."

"I'll tell Kayley how brave you were at your memorial," Afton says and slides the door open just enough to get herself and Freddie through. They take cover on the opposite side of the tunnel entrance, just deep enough into the dark that they're out of sight. I slide through after and turn the opposite way, hiding behind the edge of the wall that juts out.

It's difficult to see in the red light, but the massive man that Afton mentioned is not. He towers over the security robots—four of them—that surround him. A block of steel binds his arms at the wrists.

As I ready one of my boots, I enter the realm of the surreal. I can't believe I'm about to do what I'm about to do. We've been in rough spots before, but I'm about to create my own disaster.

With a nod, Afton and Freddie go, keeping to the edge but headed right towards the airlock passage. My arm winds back, and I aim for the back of the big man's head. The cold is already numbing my muscles, and I shiver. I hope I've got enough strength to make this work.

In two seconds, they'll pass me, and I'll let my boot fly. I squint, and not just to aim better. It feels like my eyeballs are freezing. Why is it so cold? One second to go...then...

I let the boot fly. It arcs out but completely misses him. Shoot! Not even close. It hits a table before knocking into the wall. Two guard machines turn to examine the sound but don't investigate further. A small knock like that won't alarm military spec'd security drones.

At least I have the other boot, but my hands are shaking so much I can barely grab hold of it. No time to wait. I aim for his back—I can't miss that. But before I'm ready to release it, it slips from my hand, tumbling off in a high arc.

And hitting the big man exactly where I had planned to the first time—square on the side of his head.

I've never heard such a roar from a human being before. If I wasn't already shivering, I'd be shaken to my bones. I cringe, pressing myself against the wall and hoping he didn't see where the boot came from. Now I really understand why Quinn was terrified to come down here.

There's a clank of metal on metal, and a screaming klaxon goes off. The shattering of polycarbonates and the whine of energy weapons comes next. With my last bit of energy, I get up and ready myself to burst out into the horror just on the other side of the wall. The terrible sounds the man makes are enough to freeze my feet to the floor, but just down the hall is freedom. If I don't go now, I may never get the chance.

When the first security bot goes flying through the air, that's my cue. I take off, my socks sliding on the shiny floor. I get my grip again and rocket towards the door marked with the airlock sign. I do exactly as Quinn advised. I don't stop and don't look back. Not ever.

Chapter Thirty-Four

"WOOHOO! MY FRIENDS, WE are free!" Freddie exclaims and jumps up and down until Original Teddy comes back from the cockpit. Then he cringes and backs away. "My goodness, what is that?"

"Not what, who," I say, slouched down in one of the seats. "Freddie, meet Original Teddy. Teddy, this is Freddie Espy, the guy we came to get."

"Greetings. I am Teddy," Original Teddy says, holding out a tentacle. He must have learned that on his tour around Angelcanis. I wouldn't have taught him that—no one would have accepted it for a handshake.

"So you are," Freddie says, chuckling nervously. "How adorable."

"Like those cute fuzzies on Sordibus Prime?" Afton asks with a smirk. She's in a similar reclining position, except she's propped her feet up on the back of the chair in front of her. Also, now, like me, she's bootless.

"Well, not exactly, but," Freddie tilts his head, examining our fuzzy pink friend. Original Teddy tilts his head in mimicry of him. "I can see their appeal, yes?"

"You are okay too," Original Teddy says, then turns to me. "Rancid, transmission has been received. Viewing is recommended."

"Thanks, Teddy." I raise a hand up, and he slaps his tentacle on it. Now that, I'm proud to say, I taught him. "Yeah, let's see it."

"Transmission is unavailable. Summary is available."

I blink at my fuzzy friend.

"Okay, let's see the summary, then."

The shuttle's small globe drops down, but instead of a vid, there's only text. It's a message from Lieutenant Cortell.

And it's not good.

"Oh, hell, no," Afton says, reading over my shoulder.

Kayley and team,

Unfortunately, I tried my best, but I could not hold Deputy Brownrigg for more than a few hours. I even tried to requisition the general in command of my group, but he wasn't willing to go against the Anti-Sedition Ministry. Now that man's on the warpath, and I wouldn't be surprised if he comes straight for you.

Be careful.

Lt. Cortell.

P.S. Attached is some data you might want to look at. I obtained it from a friend in the general accounting office. There's a chance it may help us find a way to put Brownrigg away.

"Forget him," I say and wave my hand at the globe as it rises up again. "He's not going to find us on the Teddy ship. All I care about is my mom."

As I say it, I realize Brownrigg will be a bigger problem for us than I just stated. Even if we can get my mom back, we might have to spend a very long time hiding away on the ship. If he's got the authority to push Lieutenant Cortell's group around, he could easily block us from ever setting foot on another Imperial planet again. That includes home.

I take in a deep breath. I wish that lanky jerk would just go away, but that's never going to happen, and my mom is still Danny's captive. So Mom comes first. We make the swap, and then we figure out how to deal with Brownrigg.

"Freddie, do me a favor and go hide in the back for a bit," I say.

"Okay, but why?" Freddie blinks at me.

"I need to call Danny, and I don't want her to know we have you yet."

"Ah, I see! Yes, I am happy to play the missing persons." He mocks sneaking to the back storage hold on his toes.

I drop the comm unit on the table and wait for Danny's image to appear. I hope for my mom's sake that this is going to be an easy swap. She could be fine, but she might also be scared out of her wits and pretending to be fine for my sake.

"Long time no hear, buttercup!" Danny says with a big grin, pressing her face close to the camera. "I was thinking you'd abandoned your poor mommy. So whatcha got for me?"

"We got something for you, alright," I say. "But first, you're going to let me see my mom, and then you're going to answer a few questions."

"No problem, honey bun. She's right here. Say hi, Mom!" Danny turns her camera, and, sure enough, my mom is there, in some ship's cabin. She waves and goes back to watching whatever vid is on. If she's watching the new episodes of *My Doctor, My Chef* without me, I'm going to be pissed.

"So then," Danny says, swinging the camera back to face her, "you got someone to show me, Rancy?"

"Not until you answer some questions!" I reply, sitting up. "We just risked our lives for you, only to find out you've been lying to us this whole time!"

"Never did I do such a naughty thing!" Danny pouts and feigns hurt, her chin trembling. It's a pretty solid act, I have to say.

"Yeah? Then why did your buddy Quinn almost lock us in a cell to rot? And she says you owe her triple! That doesn't sound like a friend to me!"

Danny gasps, placing a hand across her chest. If I didn't know better, I'd think her shocked reaction is as authentic as it gets. She even throws in a few blinks as her eyes well up for good measure. I almost feel bad I caught her in a lie.

"Oh, I'm so sorry, pumpkin! Quinn is totally my bestie! She was there that day when I met my husband-to-be! That day on Vaudvilla...of course, back then she was still a total hottie." Danny leans into the camera. "What do you think of the whole...metal thing? It's okay, right?"

"Yeah, sure. It's fine."

"Now." Danny's eyes narrow. "Where is my Freddie?"

Freddie steps out of the cargo hold—just like I told him not to— and twinkles his fingers at Danny's hologram with a shy smile.

"Oh, hello there! So you are Danny, yes?"

"Who the frack are you?" Danny asks. "Where's Freddie? Where's my darling?"

"Wait." My head spins between Danny and Freddie, and I think all the blood in my body just dropped to my feet. "Isn't this him?"

"Hell no, that's not him! My honey has dark hair!" Danny seethes. "What kind of sick joke is this?"

"Um," Freddie says, "I think I can help to explain."

Afton and I immediately flash each other a wide-eyed stare and go stiff. What I've just heard in the last few seconds is going to give me nightmares for the next century. I can't even comprehend what I am hearing. How could we have just risked our necks for nothing? How could Parrish have gotten shot for the wrong person?

We rescued the wrong guy? I mouth to Afton. Her only reply is to shake her head in minute movements.

"I am Freddie Espy," he says, pointing to himself. Danny flinches and takes two steps back from the camera.

"No! That's not possible!" Danny cries.

"You see, I was not at Vaudvilla that day. I was too far away to make it, but the People Against Imperial Neglect still wanted to make use of my likeness to rouse the crowd. If you met someone that day claiming to be me, then you would have fallen in love with Jurgen, my assistant. It's true—he is a handsome fellow."

"I..." She glances off-camera, then back. "I fell in love with your *assistant*?"

Now I don't feel all that bad for Danny. You fall in love with the people you fall in love with, and that's that. You don't have any control over it. Even if you make the mistake of falling for someone you thought was someone else, you still fell in love, and that's not a bad thing.

"Wait a second, Danny, didn't you ever try to visit him on Exodus?"

Danny stares through the camera and blinks. Then her whole body shakes in rage as if I just asked her if I could keep all of her weaponry on a permanent basis.

"Of course not! Political prisoners don't get visitors!"

"It is true," Freddie adds. "I was not allowed to have visitors."

I'm getting worried that Danny is about to renege on our deal. She could just claim we didn't hold up our end and then do something heinous to my mom. I need to jump on that before she does.

"Danny, listen," I say, giving the best polite smile I can. "I know this is all a big misunderstanding, but well, we *did* get who you asked us to, from where you asked us to get him, so how about bringing my mom home?"

"N...n...no! No way!" Danny points a finger at me. "You were supposed to get *my* husband and You. Did. Not! That's a fail on you, Rancy pants! So until you get me *my* man, Mom is staying with me!"

"He's not your husband, because you never actually married him," Afton mutters. "Not that you're getting that."

Okay, so she's upset and not accepting reasonable suggestions. I'm a bit agitated myself. This is her mix-up, not ours. Though I am wondering: if we rescued the real Freddie Espy...where is this Jurgen guy at?

I can wonder later. Right now, Mom.

"No!" I say, taking the polite mask off. "We got you who you asked us to get, and that's all we needed to do! Now give us back my mom, or I'm going to get the entire Imperial Anti-Sedition Ministry after you!"

"Why him?" Afton asks in a whisper, flashing me a glance. I just shrug. It was the only organization I could think of at the moment that sounded scary.

"You do that, and Mom gets a free ride outside the ship! With no suit on!"

"You wouldn't dare!" My heart jumps just thinking of the possibility. I really need to get Mom away from this crazy woman before she really hurts her.

"Rancy boy, you've got no idea what I would dare." Danny puts her hands on her hips and glares at me. "I don't make fake threats."

"It's not fair! We don't even know where he could be!"

"Not my problem," Danny replies. "That's why I hired your team in the first place."

"You are unbelievably cruel," I say. "All this for a man you love? I should just space him out the nearest airlock the moment I find him. How would you like that?"

"Hey! No copying!" Danny shouts. "Find your own threat!"

This is getting me nowhere. Mom is still a hostage, and now Brownrigg is free to come after us again. And he will, with a vengeance. That means any search for Danny's love interest is going to have to be done at a distance. One step on any Imperial planet, and we'll get locked up so quick, we won't even have time to get our luggage.

I wish I hadn't been so greedy. All it's caused is a massive mess. Mom's in danger, Parrish may never run again, Kayley—

I have never been so unworthy of her, ever. It's my fault she's in the state she's in. She tried to help me and ended up making a big mistake...and for what? We didn't even complete the mission—any mission.

"You got one day, Rancy boy," Danny growls. "One day to find me *something* about my man, and if you can't, well, I hope you got Mom's funeral urn all picked out, because I'm done playing around."

"Danny, wait, we—"

"No excuses! Do it...or else!"

Chapter Thirty-Five

I KEEP FINDING MYSELF in the same place and feeling the same way when I'm there. The place is the canteen on the Teddys' ship, and the feeling is that I'm totally exhausted from sneaking into and then escaping a maximum-security space station. I really need to break out of this vicious cycle.

The Goddesses have a name for this which roughly translates to "downward spiral." It describes a situation where every action taken by an individual is self-destructive and only serves to speed up their race to the bottom. Naturally, being the goddesses of wisdom, compassion, and strength, they also have a solution for breaking the tragic loop.

Stop being such a dumbass.

"How quaint everything is here," Freddie says, looking around the canteen with a brilliant smile. "It is chilly, though."

"Teddys can't help their fuzziness," Doc Elizabeth says, munching on a bit of black celery. "Ergo, they need it to be cooler than us furless humans."

As if on cue, Original Teddy enters, a small cylinder in his tentacle. He wobbles over to me and holds it out.

"Transmission is available."

"Great." I take the cylinder from him and examine it. This must have been what Lieutenant Cortell sent us. "How do we watch it?"

"Introduction of prior information is paramount," Original Teddy replies.

"So, you've got something else to tell us first?"

"That is accurate. Identification of menace is available."

I sit up with a jolt, startling Kayley, who's been leaning on my back. I share an anxious look with her and Afton, though Kayley's level of interest comes nowhere near Afton's.

"What? How did you find that out?" I ask. I feel Kayley settle on my back again and wonder why she isn't more interested in Original Teddy's statement.

"Menace was available at disembarkation."

"Disembark..." I frown, trying to grasp what he's saying. Original Teddy's mastery of Empire Common is on par with that of many humans, but sometimes he leaves out important bits of information that are critical to understanding him.

"Maybe he doesn't mean this ship," Grady suggests.

"That is accurate, Gratin."

"Oh! So you mean he was at another Teddy ship when they were docking?"

"That is accurate."

"But," I say and chew on my lower lip, "how could you have identified them? It's not like they would have just introduced themselves to you as 'the Teddy Menace.'"

"Menace is unaware that Teddy has connectivity."

Right. I get it now. This person or persons have no idea about Teddynet, and so showed up multiple times when Teddy ships were docking somewhere. It wouldn't take much for them to get suspicious of someone for doing that.

But even Teddys wouldn't jump to conclusions. There's got to be more to it than that.

"So, Teddy, you said you've identified them. Do you have an image?"

"Unnecessary," Original Teddy says. "Rancid and Gratin are aware of menace."

"We know who this person is?" Grady asks, turning to me.

"Of course we do," I say and sigh. My fist slams into the table as I growl out a curse. I don't know why I didn't realize it before. Now that I think about it, everything he did was so obvious. He was never after us. It was the Teddys that he wanted.

"It's Brownrigg," Grady says, seeing the rage in my face. "He's got to be one of Minister Crowley's minions."

"That is accurate, Gratin," Original Teddy says.

This just complicates things to the thousandth degree. We've got less than a day to rescue Jurgen, which isn't going to happen. It's not like we could step on any planet or station if we found him, anyway. That brown-bag bastard is watching every port and orbit for Teddys. All we'd have to do is show up somewhere with the only method of transport we have, and he'll be on top of us in a second.

"In that case," Grady says, "I'm going to look at that data the Lieutenant sent over. If we can connect him to Crowley, or something worse, we'll have something to strike back at him with."

I nod at Grady. I might have been ready to dismiss Brownrigg before, but now that he's become a complete blockade we've got to get him out of the way before we can move in any direction. I'm sure he's got some dirty secret somewhere, but I haven't got a clue what that might be. Hopefully he can turn up something.

"Visual of transmission is now recommended," Original Teddy says and points at the cylinder. I glance at it in my hands. There's no obvious buttons or switches on it, so I've got no idea how to turn it on.

"Tap the edge of it and lay it flat," Doc Elizabeth says.

A projection shoots from the edge of the cylinder and produces a two-dimensional image. It's the text of an Imperial transmission. An All-Points Bulletin, which is usually meant for government and law enforcement.

And it's got images of me, Afton, Freddie, and Kayley on it. I don't expect that's because they want to discuss how attractive we all are. As I read the copy connected to the images, I understand that this is anything but gossip. This is a warrant for our arrest, with an option to shoot to kill should we fight back.

"Oh...boy," Freddie says, leaning over my other shoulder. "Out of the black hole, right into another gravity well."

"Simultaneous data also collected," Original Teddy says, and the globe drops from the ceiling and plays a vid. A vid with Deputy Brownrigg on it.

"My fellow citizens, these insurrectionists are the scourge of the Empire. They have no care for law or order, and they will do anything to get what they want. We must stop them at all costs, and if we cannot bring them to justice, then termination is the only answer."

"Great, he's calling for our execution," I groan. Kayley wraps her arms around me and puts her head on my back. It's comforting, but I'd prefer it if the Queen of Speeches would say something and then take charge. We need to get organized against this guy.

"To that end, we at the Imperial Ministry for Anti-Sedition Action will utilize all of our resources to bring these seditionists to justice. If necessary, we will use force. The safety of all citizens is paramount, and protecting citizens must be our priority. If you have any information on the whereabouts of these people, please inform our ministry immediately. Your lives may depend upon it."

"He makes us sound like we're a bunch of murderers," Parrish says, hanging his head. I glance at my buddy and sympathize. He's fought hard to earn everything he's gained, and for someone like Deputy Brownrigg to just strip it away on a misunderstanding...that I just don't accept.

"My ministry has been hard at work ensuring your safety, and I am proud to announce that we have captured the leader of these anti-Imperialists, one Freddie Espy. An appointed jury will try him and swiftly convict him. Then he will be executed in a legal and humane way. Rest assured, citizens, you will be safe soon enough."

"Oh, hey," Freddie says. "That's Jurgen!"

"You got to be kidding," Afton says, leaning in to peer at his image.

The transmission ends, and everyone performs their own personal version of defeat. Of all the people in the Commonwealth, the last person I'd expect, much less want, to be holding the key individual that gets my mom free is this brown-paper jerk.

"Well, at least we don't have to search for him anymore," Grady says, and immediately gets yelled at by every human in the room. Every human save for Kayley. She hasn't really moved, except to raise her head at the shouting. I'm about ready to shout at her.

"This is going to be a problem," I say, and win the award for understatement of the millennium. Afton frowns at my unskilled use of words, and Grady just sighs.

Even if we were to use every Teddy trick in the book, I don't know how we could get this done in time. Jurgen might as well be in another galaxy. It might take us forever to get there, but at least Brownrigg won't be there. Then we'd have to get back, and by then a millennium might have passed by. Danny, or my mom, would be long gone, and that just puts the perspective on how impossible this is going to be.

I just wish we had more time. Time gives us space to plan or investigate. If we could find out what really makes this guy tick, and if we could really connect him to Crowley like Grady thinks he is, then we'd have a ton of ammunition to fight him with. He might even give us Jurgen willingly so that we don't blab out his secrets.

I turn my head to ask Kayley for advice, but before I can get a word out, Parrish speaks up.

"Call Danny," he says.

"Now there's a bad idea if I've ever heard one," Afton says.

"Yes, I think this is the bad timing," Freddie comments.

"Why call her? We've got nothing to give her." I wonder what Parrish has in mind. It could be good, but I'm trending towards agreeing with Afton and Freddie. Still, I'm open to hearing anything that will get us more time to plan.

"Tell her what we just found out. Maybe she'll give us more time," he says.

"I take it back," Afton says, "that's not a half-bad idea after all."

I'm inclined to agree. I can't think of any negative outcome if we tell her. Danny will see we're trying, and maybe, now that she's calmed down a little bit, she'll be more generous with her time. And my mom's life.

"KayKay, what do you think?" I ask, turning my head towards her as she rests her chin on my shoulder.

"Sounds good," Kayley replies. She plants a kiss on my cheek and stands up. "Do it."

That's more than I've gotten from her ever since we returned, so I'm going to take it as the best advice she's going to give. I'm desperate, so I'm not going to question her suggestion. I'll just take it as a command and do exactly as she says.

Chapter Thirty-Six

I PULL THE COMM unit out of my pocket and place it on the table. The device powers itself on, and a moment later Danny's image appears before us on top of the table, as if she's a goddess poised on her altar.

"Hey, peaches," Danny says, smiling. She approaches the camera, hands on her lower back. "I didn't expect to hear from you so soon. Got something for me?"

"Is my mom okay?"

"You know, you're so sweet, bubby. Of course she's okay." Danny tilts her head at me. "That's not the reason you called, is it?"

"No! We have something for you."

Danny's eyes light up, and I see the woman in love behind the mask of the deadly hand-hunter. I don't want to be cruel, but I'm going to take as much advantage of that as I can.

"So," she says, her voice filling with hope. "What is it? Did you find him?"

"Kind of," Afton says with a snort.

"What do you mean by that, girly?"

"It means we know where he is," I say.

"Well, don't keep it a secret, honey bun. Tell me!"

"He's under the custody of Deputy Warwick Brownrigg, director of the Imperial Ministry for Anti-Sedition Action."

"Oh, that's bad." Danny's eyes grow wide. She paces away from the camera and back again. Then, after a pause to look at us, she returns to her pacing. "Very, very bad."

"Yes, it is terrible," Freddie adds. "The deputy thinks he is me."

Danny runs a hand through her hair and shakes her head. I think she might even be talking to herself. Her lips are moving, but I can't hear what she's saying. I really hope our news didn't just make her crack. Not while she's still got my mom. That would be a truly horrible thing to happen.

Then she stops and pivots to face the camera. Without warning, Danny stomps forward and leans in. She curls her lips and runs her tongue brusquely across them. I also notice she's breathing faster.

"Where are you?" she asks, staring into the camera.

"We are here," Original Teddy replies.

That wasn't the answer she was looking for. Danny's already blush-tinted cheeks get even redder. It goes all the way to her ears as she grits her teeth and digs her fingers into her hair, pulling it back.

"No," Danny says, her jaw tight. "Give me your coordinates. I'm coming there."

"Uh, why?"

"Because I'm taking charge. This mission just became too big for your little gang. If I'm going to get my honey back safely, I'm going to be the one to do it, and you're going to help."

"Absolutely not!" I shoot back. Afton wanted to call out a bad idea before? This is it. This is definitely it. I've seen how she operates, and that couldn't be further from the way we do things. Her total disinterest in safety is going to get someone killed, and that someone is *not* going to be one of us.

"You want your mom back, safe and sound, Rancy boy? You're going to tell me where you are!"

I turn around to get Kayley to back me up, but she's not there. Shoot, that's right. She walked out just as we were calling Danny—why? This is a critical moment, and Kayley's not around. If we don't get some backup, Danny is going to squash us like a twenty-ton roller.

Everyone turns to me as if I'm the one with the answer here. I get that it's my mom and all that. It'd be nice for once, however, if someone else stepped up. Not that I can blame them. They don't for the same reason that I don't. None of us are Kayley.

Which gives me the exact answer I need.

"Okay, okay, Teddy, you can give her the coordinates," I say and jump to my feet. "See you when you get here, Danny!"

I race towards the canteen's exit, my mind running through whatever words I can find that will make sense to Kayley once I put them together. Then, after she hears them, hopefully she'll agree with them.

"Wait!" Danny shouts after me. "Where are you going? We're not done yet!"

I catch the nearest Teddy lift, startling two red Teddys I haven't met. They quickly give me space and the three of us go hurtling up to the living quarters level. I'm out with a wave of thanks and burn down the corridor, trying not to bang my skull on the ceiling while smashing words together in my head.

"Darling, hi," Kayley says as I burst into our berth, out of breath. "You called Danny already?"

"Er, no," I reply. "Well, yes, but..." I suck a breath in. "The others will finish with her. She's coming here."

Kayley's sitting cross-legged on our bed, her hands in her lap. There's not much room to sit anywhere else, so I just lean against the wall and try my best not to appear annoyed.

"So then," Kayley says with a grin, "you just had to tear yourself away from such an important discussion because you missed me, right?"

"You could say that," I reply with a smile. She's not wrong. I did miss having her there—not exactly for the reason she's thinking, but I'd be a liar if I didn't admit that I want to have her with me every second of the day.

But Kayley wouldn't be Kayley if she didn't know my every nuance. I can't hide anything from her, even when I try my best.

She puts her feet on the floor and her hands out to the side on the bed. "Why do I get the feeling that's not the reason you're here?"

"Well, I *am* here because I was missing you," I reply, her stare forcing me to shift my position. "Not just as my girlfriend, but as team leader."

"Oh." Kayley drops her eyes to the floor, and my stomach drops down with them. I hate myself for causing her any pain, but I needed to tell her and hopefully get her out of this rut she's in.

"But"—Kayley's whole mood changes in a moment, and any hurt that she's feeling gets covered over by the cheerful mask she puts on —"if Danny's coming, that's good. She's got experience handling stuff like this, I'll bet. Mom will be home in no time. You guys don't need me."

This is exactly what I had feared. Kayley's trying to pretend she's fine when she's not and using Danny as an excuse. I know she's really saying that she's got no confidence in herself, and she doesn't believe she can be the amazing team leader we all know her to be. I wish I had the time to help her get back on her feet, but I don't.

There's got to be a way I can convince her to try again. As if things weren't difficult enough, it hits me that my own confidence entwines with hers. If I can't help her, what does that say about me and my worthiness to be her boyfriend?

Kayley's got to get down there.

"That's not true," I say. "You've always been able to get the best plans together. If Danny leads this, she's going to wind up blowing us all up. You're the one to find the best ideas."

"What do you mean? Grady's got great ideas," Kayley says, keeping her emotions hidden behind her mask.

"Because you inspire him to come up with them!" I counter. "You bring out the best in us, KayKay, because you know us. Danny just wants to smash stuff with two guns blazing. She's not interested in having the best plan. She just wants to make the biggest and scariest noise, so no one notices just how fragile she actually is."

"When did you become an expert on her?" Kayley asks, her eyes narrowing. It's a warning—I need to be careful stepping through dangerous territory. I try to shrug it off, and amazingly, Kayley lets me. Now I'm really worried about her.

I don't know that much about Danny Lecker, but I have noticed a few things that make me think she's much more of a softy than she pretends to be. Take her chosen profession. Danny is a cupid in synthetic patent pants, not an assassin. She brings people together for romantic relationships, and even if her methods are a little... rough, what she really wants is to make people happy.

When she found out her Freddie wasn't the real Freddie, I could see how crushed she was. The man who she was in love with wasn't who he had pretended to be. I think she's just going through with this because she's hoping he'll live up to the fantasy she had of him.

"Kayley," I say, trying another angle, "do you realize this is going to be our first real rescue? We're doing this because we chose to. No one is forcing us to. That means we need you to make the big decisions. You're the only one that can do that."

"Do what? Make more decisions that will get someone else hurt, or killed?" Kayley says. The mask slips just long enough that I see how truly tormented she is. The positive energy I had built up drains from my body. I'm very much doubting myself now, but I have to keep trying for Kayley's sake.

"We believe in you, KayKay," I try. "We'll follow you, whatever you want us to do."

"That's what scares me." The mask is off fully now. She's avoiding my gaze too. I'm praying hard that she can break free of her insecurities.

"KayKay." I get down on my knees before her, taking her hands in mine and hoping that she'll look in me the eye. "Please. As your boyfriend and your friend, please come back down. We're not a team without you."

"No," she says in a small voice, turning her head to the side, "I can't."

"Yes, you can!" I give her hands a reassuring squeeze, but she doesn't react to it. "You are absolutely capable."

"I'm not—"

"Please, KayKay."

"No."

"Kayley, give it a chance!"

"I'm not ready!" Kayley tears her hands from mine and turns away fully. I let my hands fall to the floor, my body sinking with them. All I can do is stare at the floor—the dark floor. I wish it would become a black hole and swallow all the suffering in the room. Especially Kayley's. That way she could regain her confidence again.

It's a nice thought, but I know it's not going to happen. I haven't given up on her. I just need to find a way to bring her back. I hope I can do it soon.

Meanwhile, we're likely going to run some insane plan with Danny, because that's the only way I'm getting my mom back. Mom has to come home, even if it kills all of us.

Chapter Thirty-Seven

"WE ARE SO GOING to get killed," Afton says, hunched down next to me. "This is really what you came up with while I was sleeping?"

"Not me," I say, "I was talking to Kayley."

Afton gives me a side-eyed glance. "Mighty convenient for you to be elsewhere while all this was happening, wasn't it?"

"Yeah, well, don't blame me either," Grady says over Teddy comm. "You heard my ideas."

"And promptly ignored them," Parrish adds, also via the Teddy communications tech.

Danny trots back to us where we're huddled, just across the street from the Emperor Richard the Equitable Institution for Criminal Justice and Reformation. She gives us a thumbs-up as Freddie comes up beside her. The knots in my stomach make more knots.

The place is as large as its name is long and an imposing concrete wall taller than Grady's four-story house surrounds it. It's smooth and angled out, making any attempt to climb up it impossible. We're here because, as everyone will freely admit, Danny insisted on doing this. Grady and Parrish were afraid that she might do something bad to my mom if they said no, so they avoided getting into conflict with her. If I had been there, I would have stopped it. At least I think I could have, but there's no way I'll ever know. Still, I'm kicking myself for being where I thought I could help the most, rather than being where I could actually make a difference.

The four of us are about to do something stupid because I couldn't be in two places at the same time. I'll have to ask the Teddys if they have any cloning tech so I can make that work.

On second thought, that's a bad idea.

"So, we're just going to blow up the wall, rush in, get this Jurgen guy and rush out?" Afton asks for at least the tenth time. I think she's hoping that if she says it enough, Danny will realize how insane the idea is and call it off. Now that we're here, each holding a large satchel of explosives, I can guarantee that's not what's going to happen.

"Yeppers, girly," Danny replies, pressing a switch on her recently rebuilt armored suit. "They won't be expecting us at all!"

"Who would?" Afton mutters. I'm in total agreement. No one would be stupid enough to attack a place that's got to contain several thousand well-armed guards behind a fairly impenetrable wall. But then, there's Danny.

"It really is so exciting to be here," Freddie says, taking in a deep breath and pumping his fists. He was the only one that didn't just pretend to go along with Danny's plan. "The fresh air is so... stimulating!"

"Isn't it?" Danny beams at him, and the two of them share a moment of bliss. Afton and I can't help but share a distinct moment of our own. One that involves a simultaneous roll of our eyes.

"The gate that you want is just on the other side of the block," Grady says. "It leads right into the storage facility that's next to B Section."

"That's where you said Jurgen was, yes?" Freddie asks. "Oh, I can't wait to see the look on his face! He's going to be so shocked!"

There still might be time to stop this insanity. I think I should try, and I think my buds should back me up. I also think that I'm in trouble if they don't. Yes, we need to get this Jurgen guy. If I'm ever to see my mom again, that is. We also need to keep ourselves alive. That would also be an important factor in seeing my mom again.

The question is, what do I offer Danny that is more compelling than retrieving the one she loves? As a recently attached person, I get where she's coming from, even if my methods might be a bit more reasonable. I want to help her get him back. I just don't want to get blown up in the process.

We duck through an alley that gets us centered on the gate we're looking for. It's two seriously solid metal doors that could easily crush one of us if they toppled over. With the amount of demolition pack we've got on us, there's no doubt in my mind they will do more than fall.

No guards out front, which is good. Hopefully none on the other side as well. As much as I'd like to protect my own life, I don't want to take anyone else's either. Hmm—that might be an angle I can use with Danny.

"Hey, Danny." I shuffle up next to her. "You know there might be people on the other side of that gate…if we blow it up, they may get hurt."

Danny turns to me, her eyes widening and darting back and forth. She presses her tongue against her lower teeth as she considers my statement with some concern.

"Well, shoot, I sure hope not," Danny says, then shrugs. "But even if there are, they'll be fine. This amount of det-pack should just be enough to blow the hinges off."

"How many times have you used it before?"

"Well, none, of course, sweetie," Danny replies. "I just picked it up on the way here."

Even though no one says anything, I know my buds are groaning internally. I avert my eyes so she can't see what I'm thinking.

"Um," Grady says, "do you really know how to use these things, then?"

"Of course, smart guy! The trader I got them from—marvelous story that, by the way. She was so happy when I picked her man up for her, and they are *madly* in love now—she taught me all I need to know." Danny places her pack down on the ground. "See, it's easy. Just flick the power on like this, set the timer here, and then press this button."

I back up so quickly that I smash into Afton, who's also distancing herself from the bomb as fast as she can. Afton falls back into a seated position, and I sit down on top of her, my backpack pushing into her face. Afton yelps and shoves me to the side.

"Can we *not* turn them on now, please?" Afton says, her voice shaky.

"Oh, girly," Danny giggles, "you worry too much. You can just cancel the timer by pressing this button here, see?"

"Yeah," Grady says, "probably a good idea to not do that until they're planted on the door."

"Not even probably," Parrish adds. "That's a minimum requirement."

"You guys, don't you know we won't have time to do that when we're up there?" Danny asks, as if that was common knowledge already. "There are cameras all over that area. They'll see us if we stick around too long."

"That's what's worrying you?" Afton asks, incredulous.

"Everything will be fine," Freddie says, waving a dismissive hand at us. "I'm sure lovely Danny has it all under control."

"Did you just call me lovely?" Danny turns to Freddie, a pink tone forming on her cheeks.

"Yes, I did," Freddie replies with a grin. "It is very true."

"Can we get on with this, please?" Afton says, her voice taking an aggressive edge. I'm right there too, standing up and dusting myself off before I offer Afton a hand up. She declines my assistance and pushes herself up instead.

"Sure, girly, we—"

"You can call me Afton, by the way."

"No..." Danny puts a gloved finger to her lips. "That doesn't describe you at all. But don't worry, I'll come up with something better."

Afton sighs and shakes her head.

"Okay then, let's do this!" Danny says with a cheerful smile. "Rancy honey, you're with me on the left, Freddie and..." Danny purses her lips and points to Afton, who just motions for her to get on with it.

"Power up your det-packs, set the timer for five minutes, and engage it. Then we'll charge up there, place our packs, and come back for cover!"

"Thrilling! I love it!" Freddie says.

"Remember to place the outside of the pack towards the wall," Grady says. "The charge inside focuses its blast in that direction."

"Oh, and," Danny says, "important safety tip. Don't fall or drop it when it's armed."

Well, if I ever had a chance at stopping this from happening, I've failed miserably. I blame myself, mostly, as I got caught up running away from a live det-pack and forgot what my strategy was going to be. If Kayley was here, this would never have happened.

My thoughts drift to my scarlet-headed girlfriend. I told her what was happening, but she didn't even acknowledge it. I'm more worried for her than I am for myself at this point. If something happens here, I can just run away. Kayley can't run away from herself.

"Guys, is Kayley there with you?" I ask.

"No, dude," Grady replies, sounding apologetic about giving me that information. "I think Elizabeth is with her right now."

"She's fine, Rance," Parrish says, trying to stop me from worrying. It's a nice try, but a little late. "Concentrate on the game in front of you, so you can come back to her safely."

"Right," I reply. It's excellent advice. I tighten my jaw and put my game face on. I don't have much of one, but I try to imagine Parrish's appearance when he's in the final quarter.

"Okay," Danny says, "here we go. Speedy Girl and I will go first, and when we're halfway there, you guys hit it. Okay?"

There are nods all around. Danny and Afton crouch down, planting their hands on the ground like they're about to race. They are, and so am I. We've got less than five minutes now to get there and then seek cover. After that, who knows what will happen. Hopefully not all that much.

The two of them take off faster than I could ever hope to go. I watch a moment, then take my mark as well. Freddie drops next to me and gives me a tight-lipped nod of confidence. He might be enjoying this. I'm sure not.

We're off. All I see is the gate in front of me. It looms larger as I race towards it. My pace isn't as fast as I'd like, but the pack is weighing me down. It's like I'm running with half my body underwater. I push harder and glance over at Freddie. He's got me by a few strides.

My breathing gets faster and deeper. Soon my intake won't be enough to keep my speed up—I was never much of a runner. I'm already struggling not to fall. Maybe I should accept Afton's offer to train. I'll have that chance as long as I stay upright.

Danny's already secured her pack to the wall and is flying back. Afton, too, I'm sure. Now it's just up to me. I hit the wall next to the gates, swinging the pack off my back and ripping off the adhesive cover.

I scan the doors. Danny's put hers down low, so I've got to put mine as high as I can reach. I lift the pack over my head and aim it towards one hinge. Right on it, or right next to it, Danny said.

My toe catches on the strap to Danny's pack. I stumble forward, the pack slipping from my hand, but I catch it just in time. That was close.

My pulse throbs in my forehead, and I get dizzy. I still manage to place the pack where it needs to go. Someone must have seen us by now. In a second, guards will be on us—I can't think of them. I need a moment to catch my breath.

How much time do I have left?

I look down at Danny's pack—less than a minute—I need to get out of here. Now. My body hits me with the adrenaline, and I rocket back to where the others beckon me, wide-eyed and anxious.

"In, in, in!" Danny says, bending a door open with her suit. We pile in, falling over each other to get out of danger. Afton and I grab each other and find a spot to hide behind a large piece of machinery. I don't know about Danny and Freddie, but they must be doing the same.

I share a glance with Afton as we calm each other down. The silence around us helps. After that rough minute of total terror, it's a strange contrast.

"Hey," I whisper to Afton, still taking in deep breaths, "do you thin —"

The detonation is so sharp it knocks any air from my lungs. The building shakes and shudders like it collided with a star cruiser. Glass shatters, bits of metal fly out in a deadly arc, and the large piece of machinery before us rocks on its foundation. Insulation falls from the ceiling and rains down on us, pelting us with its dense structure.

Afton reacts faster, dropping and covering her head. I take another second to move. My brain has lost all sense of thought. It's like I just got hit in the face with a sofa.

Then, just like that, it's over. Dust wisps through the air, filling it with a chalky haze. I push myself up, unsteady, using the chassis of the machine for support. Afton follows, and we stumble our way towards the door, seeking uncontaminated air.

Danny and Freddie are there, coughing from the dust. Blood drips down from the side of Freddie's head—not seriously, I think. I can only imagine what I look like.

"Guys, are you there?" Grady asks, his voice small but insistent.

"We're here," I reply in between coughs. I catch the sight of red on my arm, and I touch it to check the wound. No pain, but that will come later.

"Did it work?" Grady asks. I try to rub the dust from my eyes and squint across the street, but it's hard to see farther than my own fingers.

When the smoke and dust clear just enough to see, I blink and check again.

Then again.

I'm not sure I can believe it. Where the two doors of the gate used to be, there's a gap in the wall large enough to fit one side of my house. The doors themselves are impaled into the side of the building —a building made from reinforced concrete that's got to be two meters thick.

"Did it?" Grady asks again.

"Oh, you could say that," I reply.

Chapter Thirty-Eight

"NO TIME TO WASTE!" Danny says. Her voice is hoarse, but her spirit is undiminished. She pounds a button on her suit and a high whine emits from it. With a grin, she turns and pounds towards the breach in the wall and leaps onto the loading dock with a single hop.

"Here we go!" Freddie says, trying his best to keep his enthusiasm up, but the blast has knocked all the energy out of us. I can't find much will to dash into the middle of a disaster zone anymore.

Danny waves and coaxes us to come forth from our dusty shelter. We obey, striking a pace only a turtle would call excited. Freddie's making the most valiant effort, but he just doesn't have it in him to run. Afton and I, on the other hand, aren't going to push ourselves.

My head still feels like someone squashed it from both sides. My ears are ringing, and I can't hear anything below a near shout. I don't know how we're going to remain vigilant on any level. If guards sneak up on us, they might have to fire a few rounds before we know they're there.

"Okay, which way? Right?" Danny asks, making a move in that direction.

"No!" Grady says. "Tell her to go left! Left!"

I shake my head and point in the opposite direction. Danny spins in her suit and dashes off that way, once again leaving us behind. That wasn't the plan, but neither was destroying half the loading dock.

Freddie glances at us for instruction, and I motion him forward. He manages a weak smile and then trots off after Danny, leaving Afton and me to bring up the rear.

"Didn't we give her a comm?" Afton asks.

"We did," I reply. "She must not have turned it on."

We make our way around fallen warehouse shelves and over smashed crates that have spilled everything from sanitary paper to office chairs, and then we find the exit. We know it's the direction Danny went because a pair of guards are lying, immobile, on the floor there. I swallow hard, dropping next to them to check their pulse. Good—still alive. I sigh and keep going.

Afton and I turn right, following after Freddie. His pace has picked up, and now ours needs to as well—our luck so far has held up, but it won't forever. Soon enough this place will be crawling with guards and emergency workers.

"Grady, what's the cell number again?" I ask.

"B-412."

"There!" Afton points to numbers on the wall, directing us straight ahead. She goes to dash off, but I grab her arm and slide her to a stop. She spins on me, confused and looking ready to shout something she might regret later. Then again, knowing Afton, perhaps not.

"We can go the other way too!" I say, pointing to another set of numbers on the far wall. "It might be faster, even."

"No, don't split up!" Parrish yells through his mic. Afton freezes, glancing between both sets of numbers. She grabs my wrist and drags me in the direction I pointed out.

"We're not splitting up," Afton says, "we're all meeting at the same spot."

Afton and I dash down the hall, yellow emergency lights flickering above us. We cross paths with a handful of staff, but they're so focused on getting to the scene of the explosion, they don't bother with us. I'm definitely adding a few merits to my next temple visit for that.

"Right!" I shout as Afton overshoots the turn. She skids to a stop and heads back towards me, her boots slipping on the smooth floor. I wait just a second before pushing on ahead, picking up speed as we move down the hall.

I glance back to make sure that Afton is behind me, but I shouldn't have. She's a much stronger sprinter than I'll ever be, and she'll be catching up to me in no time.

Also, I would have avoided the guard coming around the corner at about an equal velocity.

We plow into each other like two asteroids in Albion's ring. My shoulder slams him under the chin, and his pistol jabs into my side. I twist in pain and spin into the wall, bouncing off, but the guard gets the worst of the impact. He's knocked off his feet and lands hard on his back with a loud grunt.

Afton is on him in a microsecond, pressing her knee into his chest and grabbing his weapon. She rips it over his head and steps back from him, covering me as I get my senses back. The guard does too, nearly at the same time.

"No, please! I have a family!" the guard cries.

"Tell us where to find a cell, and maybe I'll just shoot your knees out," Afton snarls.

"Okay, okay! Which one?"

"B-412, please. We're visiting a family member."

"This is a hell of a time—" He cringes and covers his face with his arms when Afton presses the barrel of the weapon into it. "Second turn on your right! Don't shoot, please!"

"We were never here, got it?" I say in a gritty tone. He nods as many times in a second as is humanly possible, and we take off.

Danny and Freddie are already in front of the cell door as we round the corner. Danny steps back then charges the door, throwing her shoulder into it. The suit makes a serious dent in the door but doesn't knock it down. She moves back again and kicks twice. The pounding of metal on metal rolls like thunder. I glance down the hall, the muscles in the back of my neck twitching.

"Keep an eye out," Afton warns, and she turns to watch the other way while Danny continues to hammer away at the door. Every time she pounds it, I jump. We're going to get caught before she ever gets in. There's got to be a better way.

I turn back to give the door a quick examination. Sure, Danny's made it look like a vertical bathtub, but she's got a lot more to go before the hinges and the bolt give way. Let's see...the hinges are right there, on the outside. So is the bolt—

We are all so totally stupid.

"Danny!" I shout, getting her attention. "Go for the hinges! Like we did with the gate!"

"We don't have any more det-packs," she replies with a frown.

"Kick the hinges off!"

"Oh." Danny turns back to the door and gives it a once-over. She spots the hinges and grins. "Got it...step back, Freddie."

Danny drops into a stance, takes a short hop, and spins. Her leg kicks out and her heel smashes the top hinge, snapping it right off the door. It flies past Afton's head and whistles down the hallway to finally clank down on the floor.

"Hey!" Afton shouts. "Warn me before you do that! Goddesses!"

"Don't blaspheme!" Danny shouts back, kicking the other two hinges off. Once the last one is off, the door leans out, making it easy for her to grab the edge of it and tear it from the cell.

Inside stands a tall man, long-haired and wide-eyed. He stares out at us, unblinking. We do the same, and for a solid awkward minute nothing happens.

"Danny?" He asks tentatively.

"Oh, honey bun! It's you! It's you!" Danny rushes towards him, her arms wide, but she misjudges the width and clanks against the edges of the door frame. She tries again, but Jurgen holds his hands up to stop her and walks out instead.

"So, you came to get me out, then?" Jurgen asks, then spots Freddie and raises an eyebrow. "You are also here? This seems unlikely."

"Yes." Freddie shrugs. "I am also here, with my gratitude to these younger people here and here."

Jurgen puts a hand to his chin and nods as Freddie pseudo-introduces us. He might have done more, but Danny entraps him in the arms of her suit and begins to place soft kisses all over his face. I blink as tears pour down her cheeks. Well, she didn't trick us this time. She really loves this guy.

"It came from down here!" a man's voice shouts from around the corner on my side.

"Okay," Freddie says and claps his hands together, "this is our signal to be going, yes?"

"Absolutely," Afton says, turning the rifle in that direction. I quickly move out of the way and slide over to her.

"So," Jurgen says. "We are going, then?"

"Yes," Freddie replies.

"This is a good idea, yes?"

"I think so, yes," Freddie says.

"So then, let's go?"

"A good—"

"Move it!" Afton screams. A rapid burst of fire shoots from the barrel of her weapon. A host of bodies hit the floor behind me. I glance back and see five guards taking cover as bolts of plasma shoot over their heads.

We whirl away and bolt down the hallway. Afton's still firing as she stumbles backward, trying to keep up with us. Plasma darts ricochet off the walls and floor, keeping the guards pinned down. As she empties the charge clip, we round the corner and take off towards the exit.

"Thanks, girly, but I can take that now," Danny says and snatches the weapon from Afton's white-knuckled hands. Afton stares at her and lets it happen. I don't blame her. She just rammed all her nervous energy into that gun. I grab her arm and tug to the right. Soon enough she's got her senses back, and we run together.

"Guys," Grady says, "just thinking about this, but it might be good for you to find another way out. That spot has got to be covered with personnel by now."

"Really? This just came to you now?" I cry.

"Well, I didn't expect you guys to blow the world up."

"Too late. We're almost there."

As we slide around the corner, Grady's idea manifests. The corridor that leads to the warehouse is chock-full of emergency crew. I even catch sight of a construction supervisor before we all duck behind the corner again.

"Okay, point for you, Grady," I say. "Any ideas?"

"How about I just smash through them while I'm firing? The rest of you can follow," Danny suggests. Afton glares, and Danny sticks out her tongue at her.

"No way," I say.

"Got something," Grady says. "There's an emergency exit close to you, but you'll have to go through some offices before you can get to it."

I repeat for Danny and Jurgen's benefit, as they don't seem to be paying attention to Grady.

"Great, let's go!" Danny says and pops up. She offers Jurgen a hand, and he accepts with a smile. "Which way?"

Grady gives us the directions, and we're off, away from the warehouse. It's just a few turns, and we're nearly there. I inhale and grin to myself. This was a wreck of a mission, but we'll be successful —our first real rescue! Save for mine, of course, but that doesn't count since we weren't officially a rescue team at that point.

We're so close to succeeding that I can smell the fresh air from outside. It's got this wonderful floral scent, though there are some undertones of rotting grass in there too. It doesn't matter. We did it!

As I revel in our success, Afton jerks to a stop and grabs me before I shoot past her. Inertia keeps me going forward, but the moment I see it, I plant a hand on the wall and freeze.

"Whoa," she says, "what the hell is that?"

Chapter Thirty-Nine

I TAKE IN THE sea of green slime covering the floor. The walls too. The way it bubbles and glistens, it almost looks like it's alive.

"What do you see?" Grady says.

"Oh, bummer," Danny says, "security foam."

I'm going to have to trust Danny on this one, but I've seen nothing like this sticky, slimy mess. It's truly nasty. Even if I were still five years old and playing in the mud, I wouldn't be able to come up with slop like this.

"Don't go in it," Grady warns. "It's got a friction coefficient of near zero. There's no way you can stand up—you'll slip instantly. That's the whole point of it."

"So why did they put it *here*?" Afton asks.

"Probably an automatic system, programmed to go off during emergencies," Grady replies. "Your detonation must've set it off."

"Great." Afton chews on her cheek. "No walking out that way, then."

"What if we don't walk?" I ask, cringing at my own suggestion.

"What do you mean?" Freddie asks.

"It's just slippery stuff, right?" I ask. Everyone nods. I point. "So, there's the doorway that we need to get to. We just aim ourselves for it and slide."

Everyone considers this for a moment, and when the vision hits their brains, big smiles abound.

"Wow!" Freddie says. "Sliding! How fun!"

"Are you really going to try that?" Grady asks, his voice pitching up. "The only way to stop yourself is to grab on to something. If you miss, you'll keep going, even past where the foam ends."

I scan everyone's faces to get their reaction. I want to try, but I don't know about anyone else. It's got to be like moving around in zero-g. It might take a little practice, but eventually everyone will get the hang of it.

"If we don't do this, then where else can we get out?" Afton asks.

"Well," Grady says and sighs, "there might be another way, but it's back the way you came."

"We've got another option?" Danny asks. I shake my head. "Well, then. Let's slide! I'm first, of course. Then, honey bunny, you and Freddie can come after, followed by you two."

She smirks and points at Afton and me. Not sure why she needed to do that. It would have been the logical order, anyway. We were the only two left.

"Oh, boy," Grady mutters.

"Take it slow," Parrish warns.

"Help me aim," Danny orders, flopping down on her belly. In the quiet after they turned the alarm off, her armored suit smacking down on the floor is a bit louder than I like. I check behind us just to make sure no one is coming to investigate. Those guards are going to find us at some point.

Jurgen and Freddie get to either side of her and set her up like a curling stone, and just like that bizarre game on ice, they launch her into the slime.

It turns out to be better than ice—Grady wasn't joking. The moment that Danny begins to move, she instantly picks up speed and starts to rotate. Only her fingers grinding on the floor stop her from going into a full flat spin and missing the doorway entirely. She fires off a small grappling hook from her suit to stop her from overshooting, but even still she swings right into the wall with a heavy thump.

"Okay, Jurgen, you next, snookums!" Danny says as she pulls herself through the doorway and spins herself around. "Keep your feet up, like I did!"

It's a good idea. We don't want to have this stuff on our feet when we try to stand in the safe zone. It's going to be all over the rest of us already. We'd get nowhere fast with it on our boots.

Danny retracts the grappling hook and shoots it into the wall across from the doorway—another good idea. If she's got it low enough, then nobody will slide past and fly off down the corridor.

Thanks to Danny's clever thinking, there's no problem getting Jurgen and then Freddie to the doorway. They struggle a bit to pull themselves in but make it without much difficulty.

"You next, Afton," I say, but she glances at me sideways, then shakes her head.

"No way you're going to get down there by yourself," she shoots back.

"Oẳn tù tì?" I suggest, and she nods. It's only fair.

"Guys, you do not have time to be playing games!" Grady says. Danny gives us a dirty look and beckons so aggressively at us Freddie has to duck out of the way to avoid getting hit by her powered hand.

"Just one round," Afton says. We both hold out a hand, palm up, and raise our other in a fist. We count to three as we pound our fists into our palms. On "three," Afton sticks out two fingers and grins... until she sees my hand is still in a fist.

"Best out of three!" she begs, but a commotion from down the corridor ends her appeal, and she drops on her stomach, hands and feet in the air. I drop next to her and grab her legs, aiming her at the door. Hopefully.

"Hey, buddy! Watch the hands!" Afton growls.

"I didn't—" I say, then shake my head. "Someone is coming! No time to mess around."

"I'm telling your girlfriend what a pervert you are."

"Fine." I give Afton a shove, but harder than I meant to. Afton yells as she slides like a pro hoverboard racer down towards Danny's safety cable. She slams into it, yanking Danny forward. Danny falls, knocking Jurgen down and falling halfway through the doorway.

That's the perfect time for those guards to show up.

"Hey!" one guard shouts at me. "On the ground, hands on your head!"

"No problem!" I shout back, placing my hands on the back of my head and diving forward. My chest impacts on the floor, blowing the air from my lungs. I'm skidding towards Afton and Danny, *and* I can't breathe. Also, I'm spinning. Fast. I have no idea which way I'm heading, and I don't really care. Air comes first.

The rapid *prat-prat-prat* of automatic fire booms through the corridor, and plasma sparks fly everywhere. A few even skim the foam and ricochet until they find something to burn into. Danny fires back at them, hitting something or someone.

I also hit something—Danny's wire. It digs into my shoulder and into the side of my head. I grab at it until it's firmly within my grasp. Then air flows back into my lungs.

Hands slap down on my back as the corridor fills with a heavy volley of shots and smoke. Two shots scrape across my back, and I cry out as a thousand little burning needles jam themselves into me.

"Rance!" Grady shouts into the comm. "What's going on? Are you okay?"

In desperation, I make the mistake of trying to grab on to the arm that's scooping me towards the doorway. It's full of slime, and I get covered in the stuff. But that's not as bad as the fire coursing over my back.

"They're in the office! Go around!" a guard shouts as I get hauled through the doorway. Hands go under my arms and lift me up. Afton's face meets mine through the haze of agony. She watches me for a moment, then spins around and takes off, Jurgen and Freddie just behind her.

"Up you go, Rancy baby," Danny shouts, backing into me. She grabs my legs and leans forward, lifting me onto her back. I throw my arms around her neck and she jets after the others.

We break through the exit and power towards the side gate. Afton and the others are just ahead, doing their best to avoid the attention of the single guard that stands between us and escape.

Our stealth mode disappears when the other group of guards pop out from nearby. They shout at the gate guard and point at us, too far away to aim effectively at a run.

"Don't stop!" Danny shouts at the others and then at me. "Head down, honey. We're smashing through."

I chance a glance at our intended ramming target, feeling the hair on the back of my neck stand up. If she slams into that metal composite door, Danny's not the one who's going to get hurt. Her armored suit just formed a helmet to protect her head, while I am guaranteed to get a lot more than a scratch.

The guard at the door screams a warning before he fires off a few rounds, but Danny's racing at an inhuman speed, using the suit for all it's got. The guard shouts a curse, and the next thing I hear is the door being blown off its hinges and flying across the street.

Danny pauses and waits for the others to clear the exit. They rush through, but the other guards have closed the distance, and they're raising their weapons towards us. She spins and heads after the others.

"Let me down, let me down!" I shout as the guards fire after us. I don't want to be the target on her back they're aiming for.

Shots scream by my head. A few hit the pavement and bounce. Danny takes evasive action, zigzagging in leaps and bounds until we find cover in the darkness of an alley.

"Grady," Afton says, panting, "we're ready for our ride!"

"Thirty seconds away," Grady replies.

"Everyone here?" I ask.

"Where's Jurgen?" Danny says, dropping me to the ground.

"He was just with us..." Freddie says. "At least until the alley."

"No!" Danny wails, turning around to head back.

"Danny, no!" I shout after her, but there's no stopping her. I couldn't do it even if I wasn't in searing pain. I do hope she finds him and gets back to us instantly.

"Hey, where are you hit?" Afton asks. I grimace and point to my back. She puts a hand on my shoulder and checks it out, inhaling sharply between her teeth when she sees it.

"That bad, hunh?" I ask.

"Ten seconds," Grady says. "Meet them in the clearing just behind the building...and hurry, those guards are going to be coming any second."

"Shall we go?" Freddie says, attempting to maintain his cheerful demeanor but failing big-time. He might not be hurt, but this little rescue has taken a lot out of him. It's taken a lot from all of us.

"Wait," I say, "we've got to wait for Danny and Jurgen."

"No," Grady says. "You don't owe her anything, Rance. If she can't get back on time, you get on that shuttle. We'll get your mom another way. Afton, tell him!"

Afton looks at me with her mouth open but stays silent. I know she wants to leave, but I think she understands. Danny's trying to save the one she cares about. That's no different from what any of us would do.

All I want to do is collapse on the shuttle the moment it arrives. But I saw how Danny looked at Jurgen. It's the same way Kayley looks at me. The idea of abandoning them makes my heart ache. All Danny wants is to be happy. I don't want to be the one to deny her that.

"Shuttle's here!" Afton shouts. A breeze blasts down the alley towards us as it sets down. I blink to keep the dust out of my eyes, and as the air clears, I notice Afton is looking at me, an expectant look on her face. She wants me to say it's okay to go, but I'm not ready to do that yet.

"Go, guys!" Grady says. He pounds the desk so hard I can hear it come through his mic.

I sigh. I can't risk Afton and Freddie waiting for something that may never happen.

But before I open my mouth, the ground vibrates beneath my feet —it's got to be Danny. Sure enough, she appears, Jurgen lying limply in her arms. Tears cover her face, and her mouth is twisted in agony.

"The doc," Danny whimpers, "she can save him, can't she? She can, right?"

"Grady, tell the doc we're going to need some serious help when we get back!" Afton shouts.

I look up at Afton, surprised, but when I turn back to scan Jurgen, I notice the side of his head is a dirty red that drips down onto Danny's gloved fingers. My gaze turns to Danny again, and her eyes are begging me for help as she sobs.

"Get to the shuttle," I say to her, "get him somewhere comfortable. We're right behind you. I promise we'll do what we can until we get him to the doc."

I really hope there's something we can do. For both their sakes, I really hope so.

Chapter Forty

JURGEN DIDN'T MAKE IT back to the Teddy ship. Doc Elizabeth called his passing before we even got out of the atmosphere. We tried everything she instructed us to do, but with no real medical equipment, there was just no way to save him. Perhaps even with the right life-saving devices it might not have been possible.

Danny was inconsolable. The moment the doc offered her condolences, she completely broke down. All we could do was watch while she huddled over him, kissing his face as her tears fell onto his cheeks. I was seeing a very different woman than the one I had first met nearly three weeks ago.

There was not a dry eye in the shuttle's cabin after that. Even the detached and self-confident Afton was wiping moisture from her eyes. I could not hold it in at all. I bawled like a baby, as much for Danny's loss as for fear of the same thing happening to me.

At one point, Original Teddy came back to see what was happening. When he saw all of us in such a state, he made a gurgling sound, then turned around and went back to the cockpit. Teddys don't cry, as far as I know, or at least the ducts around their saucer-sized eyes don't release moisture when they're sad. I'm sure that little noise he made was for our benefit—some kind of sympathetic lament.

That time in the shuttle is what keeps repeating in my mind as I lie on my stomach in Doc Elizabeth's room. Kayley's here too, assisting while the doc takes care of the "extremely serious burns" on my back. That's how she put it, at least. I can't see them, but I definitely do feel them. At least I did until Doc gave me something for the pain. I'd really like to know where she got the stuff from.

Kayley's been mostly quiet, only responding to Elizabeth when required. She's crouched down next to me so she can look into my reddened eyes. Her own have a forlorn glaze, and her chin rests on her hand at the edge of the exam table. She draws her fingers through my hair with a soft touch, and I feel warmth at the contact. I smile, hoping it cheers her a little.

I am comforted to be here in the care of my loving girlfriend and the amazing Doc Elizabeth. I wouldn't trade the two of them for the best doctors on Albion. Though, all is not calm here. There's a rift in our relationship, and we really need to talk it out, or it will widen into a chasm.

"Did the best I could, Rance," Doc Elizabeth says, her voice gentle but confident. "There may be some scarring, but we won't know for a while."

"Will it heal fully?" Kayley asks.

"It should, but the area might be tender for a while." Elizabeth chuckles. "Perhaps no more rescue missions for a while, yeah?"

"Yeah," I reply. "Sure."

"Now, I'm starved," she says, "so I'm going to leave you two alone here for a bit if that's alright. Maybe I can bring you back something?"

"No, I'm good."

"Thanks," Kayley replies with a shake of her head and a small smile to the doc, who gives us both a wave before she heads out.

I close my eyes and let the quiet moment soothe me. I imagine we're at the beach, and Kayley's fingers are a soft ocean breeze running through my hair. The sound of the air rushing through the vent is the ocean waves crashing on the beach, and the sun is the big exam light over my head. It's a stretch, but I'm still happy.

"Rance, I'm sorry." Kayley's small voice pops the bubble of my dream, and I open my eyes. It hits me in the gut to see the earnestness on her face. If I could melt into the table for a while, I would. She always seems to be caring for me when I mess up. I truly love her for it, of course. It just lowers my state of self-worthiness when we're in this position, which seems like always.

"What for, KayKay?"

Kayley drops her gaze from me. She's either considering her words or gathering the courage to tell me the truth about something. I'll have to be patient, even though I feel absolutely awkward with my cheek pressed against the table like this.

"I let you down." She presses the tips of her fingers against my lips before I can object. "I should have been there. I should have gotten involved. Then you wouldn't have gotten hurt, and then…"

"I'm glad you weren't there," I reply, but she takes it the wrong way and pulls back. I can only smile and try to explain better. "No, I mean, it was a total mess from the start. It's amazing we got as far as we did."

"Still," Kayley says and looks down, "I wasn't there for you. Or Afton, or even…her."

"Help me sit up," I say, but she clucks her tongue at me and shakes her head.

"You're better lying down."

"Yeah, but it's really weird to look at you this way. Please?"

She begrudgingly does what I ask, rolling me onto my side and then helping me to sit up. The room spins once I'm upright, and I realize that Doc's painkiller is way stronger than I expected. Kayley has to hold me by my shoulders until my head gets off the carousel. She grabs a chair and slides it over so she can keep a steadying hand on me. Her other hand finds mine, and our fingers wind together.

"I know you're going through a lot, KayKay," I say. "If there's some way I could help you, I wish you would tell me. I hate seeing you trying to do this by yourself. Couldn't you just lean on me a little?"

"Not while you're like this," she replies with a smirk. I get her point, but she's avoiding the question. I press her again, and I see her shoulders stiffen.

"I'm okay," I add.

"No, you're not, Rance. You could have died, and I wouldn't have had the chance to do what Danny did. I wouldn't have been there to say goodbye."

"You were thinking about that too?"

Kayley leans forward to lay her head on my leg, wrapping her arms around my waist. I reciprocate by laying my hands on her back. It's a clumsy hug, but it's the best we can manage at the moment.

"When I was away," she says, "all I could think about is what if something happened to you...to all of you. I was a day away from everyone, and even though Teddy and Lieutenant Cortell were there, they weren't really there. Once speeches and greetings were over, they went to their rooms, and I went to mine. Then there was no one around."

"No one invited you to dinner?"

"Sure, there were plenty of invites. But political dinners are boring and stiff, and they just...left me empty. The only part that I loved was being in front of the people, not the politicians."

"I'm sorry, KayKay, I didn't realize it was so hard on you. But you're here with us now, right?"

"Yeah." Kayley snorts and slumps in her chair. "And look what's happened. That crazy woman got you hurt and someone else killed. You and Afton are probably wanted for execution in twelve different systems by now. All this happened because I wasn't there."

"You can't blame yourself, Kayley. That's not right. None of us can be on it all the time. We're not...Teddys. We aren't connected by some crazy cool technology that allows us to share our memories."

"But we *are* connected, right?" she asks, catching my eyes. I nod and curl the side of my mouth. "So when you get hurt, I feel it too."

She's not talking about some strange psychic connection. My girlfriend just means that she worries about me. She worries about all of us. If one of us was to be labeled the parent in the group, it would be her. She's the boss, the leader, and the unofficial mom. We love it that way.

The same goes for our concern for her. *My* concern for her. Forget my own feelings. I'm feeling a lot of pain on her behalf right now. Not because I've got two long gashes across my back, but because she's my Kayley, and my love for her knows no bounds.

Maybe what she needs is to get right back into the role that she's most comfortable with—being in charge. If I can get her to just try it. Even for a day. She would realize that's where she's meant to be and —hopefully—fall right back into it.

"Kayley, I know you don't want to hear this, but we really miss you. Me, Afton...everyone. If you would just want to try, you know, one day, just come to a meeting and take up your spot at the head of the team..."

"Yes," Kayley says, so I continue, hoping that I'm making some impact. I don't really know what I'm saying, but if I bumble out some perfect phrase, then just maybe she'll reconsider.

"We really need you there, KayKay," I say, dropping my head to stare at my hands. "It's not just this last mission. None of us is the leader you are. I've tried to make decisions, but I just can't see things like you do. Danny's too strong-willed for the rest of us, and she doesn't listen the way you do. I know you already said you weren't ready, and if you need more time, I'll try to understand, but—"

"Hey." Kayley squeezes my cheek with a single hand to stop me from talking. "I already said yes."

I stare at her, blinking. I heard her words, but for some reason they weren't registering in my brain yet.

"What? You think your pretty face and a few nice compliments were going to get me to change my mind?" Kayley grins like Afton would, and the realization of everything that she was saying hits me. "That's cute, darling, but I had made up my mind the moment they brought you in here. You guys need me."

She's coming back to us. Kayley's going to lead us again!

I'm filled with a joy that could only come from her. I return to my beach dream, but this time Kayley's the sun, and the strands of her fiery hair are solar rays reaching out to me and blanketing me in their warm caress.

"You're really serious? You're ready?" I ask, double-checking in case the painkillers in my system are causing me to hear things.

"Honestly, there's still a lot of doubt in me, but I can't let you down anymore. I'm here for you...and yes, I could use someone to lean on, once in a while."

It's strange to hear, but Kayley sounds like me begging her for forgiveness. Our roles have reversed, and I understand exactly how she feels. I'm the one always letting her down. I'm the one always trying to reach up to her level and the one that's always failing.

"You don't let me down, KayKay. Never. You're perfect at everything—"

"I'm not."

"And I'm the one always messing up—"

"You don't."

"Really, I don't know how I could ever be truly worthy of you."

Kayley sits up, her eyes searching mine. Her lips go stiff, and fire ignites in her gaze—uh-oh. In my desire to be honest, while I was making sure she didn't put herself down, I annoyed her.

"Don't do that," she says, her voice edgy. "Don't you ever say that again. Listen to me. *I* decide who and what is worthy of me, and if we're together, that means that *I* cherish *you* as someone that is truly and deeply important."

"I know, KayKay. I just want you to understand..." As her hard gaze softens, I get lost in her eyes, and my words float away. She reaches out, her hands clasping mine.

"Rance, that means that you are absolutely worthy of me. So please—"

"Kayley," I say to stop her. I don't want to see her beg. My heart thumps hard in my chest, and I feel my breaths get shallow. I'm okay, I think. Just a little emotional. All this time I've been worrying over something I should have never wasted a second on. Kayley accepts me for who I am—mostly—so why can't I just do the best that I can for her and forget everything else?

"What is it?"

"Do you know how much I love you?"

"No," she replies with a frown. But then all the toughness in her eyes evaporates, and a coquettish smile forms on her lips. "Why don't you tell me?"

Chapter Forty-One

IT WAS THREE DAYS before I felt comfortable enough to get up and out of Doc's space. Kayley was there most of the time and stayed late through the evening, until Elizabeth kicked her out and told her to go get sleep. Everyone else spent time with me, even Original Teddy and a few of the blue buddies.

Everyone but Danny, that is. She locked herself in her ship where it's parked in the Teddy ship's hangar. Not even Freddie can get to her. My mom might be there with her and that worries me. If Danny's not taking care of herself, then my mom isn't getting taken care of either. And what if Danny's gone and done something more drastic?

We've got to get on that ship and talk to her.

"Looking forward to sleeping in your own bed tonight?" Parrish asks as he and Grady meet me just outside Doc's room. I'm glad to see him standing on his own two feet. It's too soon to tell how much his wound is going to affect his athletic abilities, but this is a start, at least.

"It's not really my bed, but I am looking forward to it."

"You in pain?" Grady asks.

"Not too much. It's just sore at this point...don't think I'll be doing any heavy lifting for a while."

"You never did any heavy lifting!" Parrish jokes and goes to slap me on the back. He stops himself just in time. "Whoa, sorry."

Instead, he just lays a hand on my shoulder and helps to keep me steady as we move down the corridor.

"Afton, Freddie, and Kayley are in the canteen," Parrish says. "We'll take you down there."

"Sure," I reply. I am hungry. My stomach has been growling since yesterday. Doc said I could eat anything, but it's not all that easy to eat and drink lying on your stomach. She found out that Kayley sat me up and had a complete fit about it. Next thing I knew, she strapped me into her chair for a day and only released the belts when I promised not to move.

While food is the priority, it's not the only thing on my mind. I want my mom back, and I'm sure everyone wants the same. To do that, we need to crack the gigantic safe that is Danny's ship. Then, if everything is okay there, we can figure out how to get my mom home.

Or if that fails, we could just send her back to Littus.

"Hey, Kayley wants to discuss your mom too," Grady says as we walk. It's as if he was reading my mind. I wasn't thinking to bring it up until after I had a full stomach, but I see the wisdom in starting the discussion now.

"Yeah, dude," I say. "We've got to get Danny and my mom off that ship...for both their sakes. Whatever environment is in there right now can't be good for either of them."

"Well, I'm sure that the systems on the ship are fine. A scout class like that's got long—"

"I think Rance meant the mental environment," Parrish says.

Grady shuts his mouth and looks up at him, a small frown running across his face. The moment he gets it, his eyes pop open, and he inhales an "oh." I'd laugh harder at my genius friend, but anything more than a brief chuckle hurts.

"Yeah, that too," Grady adds.

"There's got to be some kind of emergency access on the airlock, right?" I ask, trying to give my bud a chance to redeem his intelligence.

"Sure, but I wouldn't put it past her to set a trap on it."

"Maybe we can get the Teddys to scan it, and check before we try?"

"But she'll know the moment we open the airlock, won't she?" Parrish asks.

"Yeah, true." I hadn't considered that. Danny can't be thinking straight right now. She might shoot us as we're coming in. There's my mom to consider too. I don't want it to be a race to see who gets to her first. That's more risk than I can handle.

We take the circular lift down to the next level. I glance down at the floor and remember stepping on a similar dark disk not all that long ago. That was the first time Grady and I boarded this Teddy ship. It's amazing how much we've all been through since then.

"Any other options?"

"If I can get my hands on the specs for that ship class," Grady replies, "I might be able to find another way."

"We could try to call her again," Parrish suggests. I'm sure he's thinking that it worked last time, so why not try it again? The problem is that last time we had something Danny wanted. Now we don't.

I tell Parrish it's a no-go. Grady agrees. They've already tried that a hundred times already—individually, and as a group: on Teddy comm, on thelittle device that she jammed down my throat, and then finally by tapping on the cockpit canopy. At least the Teddys can see that there are likely two living beings aboard. It gives me hope we can still get to her.

Then comes the hard part.

"You guys realize that we're only working on half the problem, right?" I lift my head as I ask, though I'd rather keep it hung. The hard reality of the truth makes my head spin.

"You mean Brownrigg?" Parrish asks.

"Exactly."

We arrive at the level below, and as the door dissolves, I see Original Teddy standing there. That he knew we were going to be coming down doesn't surprise me. What does is Kayley's there with him, a disapproving look on her face.

"Whatever it is, Kayley, I didn't do it," I blurt out.

"No, you didn't," Kayley sighs. "It's this message we just received from Lieutenant Cortell."

She folds her arms and nods in the direction of the canteen. My eyes follow, but I hesitate. While I know it's the place where I can get my badly desired nourishment, it's also the place where we've had all levels of angry disagreement. I've got a feeling our upcoming conversation will fit right in with my bad memories of that place.

I open my mouth, but my rumbling tummy stops any protest I was about to make.

"Come on, dude," Grady says. "Better to be bothered on a full stomach."

Once we arrive, there's a quick greeting and a "I am glad you are not dead" from Freddie. Kayley halts any other small talk when she hands me a tablet with the message on it. Grady and Parrish gather around me and the three of us get to reading, lumps in our throats.

Kayley and team,

Likely, you've seen Deputy Brownrigg's all-points bulletin and his general statement to the Commonwealth. As I suspected, he is making good on all his threats. Apparently, some group they've labeled as terrorists attacked an Imperial prison and freed Freddie Espy. Whoever it was, and I hope it wasn't any of you, did some serious damage to the facility. They're claiming that forty-five people died in the explosion.

Brownrigg now has the authority to appropriate an elite arm of the military to hunt down and capture these terrorists. Dead or alive. He's already raided a nightclub on Canis Ludis, and a few locations on Angelcanis. I checked to see if any of them were your homes, but so far, it doesn't seem so.

Wherever you are, I fully recommend hiding out there until this blows over. At some point, he'll tire of looking and just find someone to arrest, and that will be the end of it. But under no circumstances should you go to Angelcanis. Your parents are safe for the moment, and your arrival may risk them unnecessarily.

I'll be in touch once I know more.

Be careful,

Lt. Cortell.

I catch Kayley's gaze as I look up. Her face is devoid of any emotion, but I know she's got a nuclear furnace burning inside. My own is coming up fast. We didn't kill anyone—amazingly. But Brownrigg will use that lie to poke his nose around anywhere he wants to. With a specialist military team behind him, that nose just turned into a muscular leg that can kick anyone around he so desires. And to add to that the possibility he may be after everyone's parents? Or our homes? This is not something we have time for.

"What do you want to do?" Kayley asks, watching me.

"Go to bed," I reply.

"That's not an option."

"Then I'm going to talk to Danny, and if she doesn't respond I'm going to bang on her hatch until she comes out."

Kayley nods, Afton stands, and Freddie smiles. So do I. They're all behind me and I know Grady and Parrish will be too. There's no more waiting for Danny. We're out of time. If we can't do a simple thing like get my mom out of a ship, we're never going to stop Brownrigg.

And we have to stop Brownrigg.

"Let's go get Mom."

Chapter Forty-Two

FIVE OF US MARCH down the intensely dark corridor to the hangar, our faces set. I'm getting my mom out of that ship no matter what. Danny has kept her there for too long, and I can't trust that woman anymore. Not that I ever really did.

I feel no anger towards Danny for what she's done. In fact, I might be grateful. Despite her threats, she's taken care of my mom, and even shown her a good time. If anything, I might be jealous that Danny did something for her I couldn't.

As we near the turn to the hangar, Doc Elizabeth shoots around the corner, her eyes wide and her hands beckoning us with a frenzied motion.

"Guys!" Doc Elizabeth shouts. "Guys, come quick, it's Danny. She's got a bomb!"

"Couldn't you have used the comm?" Grady asks with a raised eyebrow.

"Just come to the dock!"

"Why do we have to solve *her* problems?" Kayley's mutter is spiked with a bit of anger towards our nutty hand-hunter.

"Be easy with her, KayKay, she just lost the one she loves," I say. Kayley doesn't complain after that. She understands the feeling of loss.

We walk in to find a screaming Danny in her power suit, swinging a crate around. A group of Teddys watches from the far corner as she lifts the crate over her head and scans us. I hope that thing isn't about to be hurled our way.

"That bastard! I'm going to put a big hole in that scruffy head of his!" Danny says, shaking the crate over her head. Everyone takes a big step back.

"Hey, what the hell is wrong with you?" Kayley shouts, stepping right up to her. "You're freaking everyone out! Drop that crate and knock it off!"

"Get out of my face, Red!" Danny glares at her, but Kayley doesn't back down. "You chose not to take part, so you don't matter!"

"And you think you've got the right to terrify everyone?" Kayley shoots back. "What are you trying to accomplish with this tantrum of yours?"

"I'm going to take my ship and drive it right through that craphead's house! That's what I'm going to accomplish."

"Who?"

"The one who put my honey in jail! And then destroyed my favorite hangout!" Danny whines, dropping the crate. I know who she's talking about. There's only one government tormenter that's been on our case this entire time. "This is all his fault! He deserves to die!"

"You really think killing someone is going to change anything?" Kayley puts her hands on her hips and tilts her head. I'm glad she's not afraid of Danny, but if she saw what the woman was capable of, she might be.

"Enough of you. I'm not answering any more questions. Either help me or get out of my way!"

"No." Kayley stands steady. "You've already made enough trouble for us. I'm not letting you make it worse."

"Oh, yeah?" Danny pulls out a gun and aims it at Kayley's head. Kayley doesn't move, but I catch the whites of her eyes showing just a little more than they did before. "Try to stop me."

There's a shout, and everyone ducks or finds somewhere to hide, except for me. I'm too slow to react, and I don't know if I'd go run and hide while my girlfriend is in danger, anyway.

"Teddy, popsicle!" Parrish yells.

"No, wait!" Against my better judgment, I hold up my hands and approach her. Danny swings the gun at me, but hesitates.

"What are you doing?" Danny asks, the edge in her voice stepping down a notch.

"Well..." I motion with my hands and body to indicate her and the present situation. She follows my gesture, then snaps her attention back to my face with a glare.

"You going to try to stop me too? You and your perfect little girlfriend here?"

"Let her go, Rance," Kayley says. "Let her go blow herself up. That'll be one less thing on my mind."

"No, KayKay," I reply, then turn back to Danny. "I just want to talk to you."

"Forget it! Talking time is over, so if you're not going to help me, go away. The two of you remind me too much of..." Danny falters, her shoulders dropping.

"You and Jurgen?"

"Don't say his name!" Danny's lips press together, and I see them quiver. My heart aches for her. Every time I think of the two of them, it only leads my thoughts back to Kayley and me.

"Danny, I'm sorry. I don't want to see you hurt anymore, but revenge won't solve anything."

"Are you serious?" Danny gives me a manic grin. "It's going to solve everything! That government grub will be gone, and I'll have gotten justice for my honey."

"Danny, please." Freddie also steps up, hands up at shoulder height. "He was my friend, and I loved him too. Can we at least have a nice little farewell party for him first? You know, just so we can say goodbye properly."

"I can't do that yet." Danny shakes her head, but the anger is draining away from her. "I'm not ready to do that. This has to be first."

"Okay," Freddie says, "okay, I get it. But you're my friend too, Danny Lecker. I don't want to see you hurt."

"Too late for that!" Danny cries. "He took my sweetie from me, and that hurts! That really...really...hurts. He's got to pay!"

Then the bomb that the doc mentioned comes out.

Shouts from the humans and screeches from the Teddys echo through the hangar. I recognize it as the same det-pack that we used to annihilate the prison wall. This is just one of those, but if it goes off, it'll do way more damage to this ship, blowing a hole through the hull and sucking us all out into space.

My feet feel heavy, and I can't move. It's not for me that ice runs down my back. I don't want the last thing I ever see to be my friends dying. I swivel my head towards Kayley, and she glances at me. She's afraid too, but seems unsure of just how freaked out she should be.

"Danny," I say, my voice gentle as I approach her. "We want to get Brownrigg too."

"Then why are you trying to stop me?" Danny snarls at me, then gets quiet, turning thoughtful. "By the way, what's your reason?"

"He's been after the Teddys for their technology. We think he's part of a bigger conspiracy that was started by Minister Crowley."

"Okay...so? Why do you care about what the government does?"

"They're going to use it to take over the Empire!"

Danny's mouth opens, and her eyes become unfocused. She can take as much time as she wants to think about it. If it makes sense to her, then we're headed in the right direction. That she hasn't powered on the bomb is also good.

"We don't want that to happen, right?" Danny asks, her eyes rotating up.

"Of course not!" we all shout.

"So, getting rid of Brownrat gets my revenge, and saves your buddies...*and* the Empire?"

"Yes." I smile at her.

"Great, so let's go blow him up!" Danny powers on the det-pack and lifts it up to throw it on her shoulder.

"No!"

"Danny," Kayley says, pressing past me. "Blowing him up isn't the worst thing you can do to Deputy Brownrigg."

"Really?"

"Humiliation would be far worse." Kayley takes another step towards her, star-fire burning behind her eyes. "An explosion is fast... painless. It doesn't make him suffer. Is that the best way to get revenge? Right now, he thinks he's all-powerful. That he can do anything. If we get him arrested, put on a very public trial, and then thrown in jail, he'll suffer for the rest of his life."

Danny stares at her. We all do. Kayley's surprised us, and I am glad for it, even if I'm going to be a little more frightened of her than usual from now on.

"You're kinda scary, Red, did you know that?" Danny asks her, eyes wide. Then, to our relief, she powers down the bomb and sets it down. "But yeah, now that I think about it, that sounds fantastic."

"Let's get Brownrigg for Jurgen," Kayley replies with a small grin. "And the Teddys."

"Hey, by the way, we found something in the data!" Grady says with a smirk.

"You did?" I feel small pinch of hope surface in my chest. Not just because we're no longer going to die in massive fireball that engulfs the hangar, but because we may see some real justice done.

"Well, we didn't find any connection between him and Crowley, but I did find something just as juicy."

"Well, don't keep it all to yourself, Shaggy," Danny says.

"He's been skimming off his Ministry's budget and dumping the funds into a secret private account. I don't know where that money's getting spent but I bet it's not anything the Emperor or the Finance Ministry approved."

"KayKay," I say, "do you think Lieutenant Cortell could get what we found to some authorities we can trust?"

"He could," Kayley replies. I notice there's a lot of action going on behind her eyes. She's got something on her mind, but she's not ready to share it. I'll have to ask later.

"Good, then let's get him on Teddy comm and find a place to meet up. Let the Imperial Agency put the evidence together and throw him in jail for as long as he deserves. I bet there's a few people in the accounting office that would be willing to testify too."

"No," Danny says, "I want to catch him myself. I want to see the look on his rotten face when he finds out it was us that bagged him!"

"And how are we going to do that?" I throw my hands up in frustration. Here we have a perfect plan, and Little Miss Destruction wants to ignore it because she's still got some kind of overblown lust for revenge.

"We trap him," Kayley says. I spin on her, my jaw dropping. If she's thinking what I hope she's not thinking...

"KayKay," I say, putting a finger up. "Being around Brownrigg is dangerous. He's got that elite military group that we are totally not prepared to go up against."

"Don't worry, darling, you're not going anywhere," Kayley says cheerfully, then her face darkens. "You're on the bench with Parrish. There's no way I'm letting you get hurt again."

"Then how are we going to bait him?" Grady asks, glancing between the two of us.

"We'll use something he really wants," Kayley says, a grin coming back to her face. "Me."

Chapter Forty-Three

With my mom safe and happily roaming the Teddy ship in the company of a bunch of white Teddys who took an immediate liking to her, we set off in the Teddy shuttle on our mission. I'm camped out in the back of it, keeping Danny and Freddie company as they prepare to support Kayley in her bait game. This part of the shuttle is about as far away as Danny can get from Jurgen's death, which happened in the crew hold. That's where all the comfy seats are, but I think the three of us prefer hard crates to difficult memories.

This is also as far as I go, unfortunately. Kayley's relegated me to the literal back seat—Parrish and me both. We're walking wounded, so our dear leader has ordered us to sit this one out. While Parrish remained on the Teddy ship to assist Grady, I decided to tag along. As much love as I've got for my buds, I felt I needed to be here. Kayley begrudgingly allowed it because Doc Elizabeth came along too. I guess the doc felt that she might have a better chance to save a life if she was nearby.

"Danny," I say, watching her as she stares out into nowhere. She's completely spaced out. I catch Freddie's troubled glance as he scratches his forehead with a finger and looks away. Ever since her breakdown, he's spent the most time with her. It can't have been easy.

"Danny," I say again, and this time she blinks and turns to me.

"What's up, honey cakes?"

I smile. There's no point in asking her to stop with the pet names. I know it riles Kayley something fierce, but Danny will be Danny, and she won't change. Not now anyway, and it would be cruel of me to call her out on it.

"You ready?"

"What? Oh yeah, sure." She nods a few times. I think she's trying to convince herself more than me.

"What about your suit?"

"Not yet." Danny turns away. I catch a little tremor in her lips as she finds a stack of spare parts on a shelf to examine. At least they won't remind her of the terrible episode that just destroyed her life.

"Okay, I'm going to check and see if everyone's got their part of the plan ready," I say and get up, but before I can take my first step, Danny grabs my hand. I turn back to look at her.

"Hey, thanks," Danny says, giving my hand a squeeze, "I know you're just trying to help...and after all the bad things I did to you."

"Like what?" I deflect. "My mom was happy she could go on holiday."

"Sure she was." Danny grins for a moment, but then her face gets stony. "Rance, don't worry. I'll look out for Kayley. Nothing's going to happen to her down there."

I smile back and give her a thumbs-up. It's forced, but I can't let her know how much of a mess I am inside. Not just for Kayley—for the rest of the mission team as well. That includes Danny, Freddie, and the invincible Surela Afton Jee. I don't know how she stays safe all the time. The Goddesses must really have a thing for her.

It's Afton I run into on my way to the mid-cabin. She's reclining on one of the new benches the Teddys installed for humans. We've been getting a lot of use out of them. In fact, I think we've been using the shuttle more than they ever did. She sticks a leg out to block my path.

"Where are you going, cabin boy?" Afton says with a smirk.

"Do I really need to answer that?"

"Yes, if you ever want to see your girlfriend again. Tell me the secret password, and I'll let you pass."

"If you don't let me pass right now, I might just pop you one, Surela. I don't care if you're a girl," I say with a false sneer.

"Nice." She retracts her leg and lets me pass. I take a step, but then turn back to her.

"Go," Afton says, tapping my leg with her toes. "She's probably waiting for you."

"That'll be a change."

As I enter the front cabin, I catch sight of Kayley, and my jaw drops to the floor. There's my scarlet-haired beauty in full Angelcanis costume and regalia. Her dress sparkles like a vision in a dream. Its cinched bodice and A-line skirt make the perfect silhouette for her. The silvers and sky blues of her gown reflect the color of her eyes. I remember her talking about it for an hour with me when she first received it from the tailor. The vids I've seen of her wearing it do not do any justice to the beauty I see before me.

As she turns towards me, time slows down, and the shuttle disappears around me. I'm reminded in an instant of one of the many reasons I fell in love with her. For me, Kayley is the most beautiful girl in the galaxy, and I will fight anyone who tries to disagree. It might just turn out to be an arm wrestle, but either way, my point gets made.

"Rance, darling. Please stop drooling all over the Teddys' nice shuttle," Kayley says through her perfectly colored lips.

I blink and sigh, but I stare for a moment more, and Kayley blushes.

"What?"

"Nothing, I just wanted to make sure I remember how you look," I reply.

"Yeah? And how do I look?" She smiles and poses for me.

"Like you could defeat Brownrigg and his army by yourself. Could you...maybe wear that dress more often?"

"No," Kayley replies, making the emphasis with her eyes. "Do you know how complicated this is to put on? I swear whoever designed it enjoys punishing women. I can barely breathe in this thing!"

"You might be right," Doc Elizabeth says with a chuckle.

"What did you need?"

"Honestly, KayKay, I'm having some doubts about this."

"Now?" Kayley's eyebrows shoot up. "Why now?"

"Well..." I have to come up with something better than to blame Danny for being sad. "We kinda tried this already, right? Baiting him with your speech? Don't you think Brownrigg's going to be wise to that?"

Kayley fumes, but I can tell she's considering it. She doesn't want to make the same mistake as before, and I hate to make her think twice about our plan. I just don't want anyone to get hurt.

"No," Kayley says after a few minutes. "It's different. We might be doing the same thing, but Brownrigg's got an army behind him now. He's got a lot more to prove, and the mess you guys made at the prison will bring him running. We just need to make sure that Danny can get him away from those soldiers."

My shoulders relax. Kayley's got it right. Plus, what happened in Yeomanry that day wasn't our plan. It was just a lucky outcome, heavily weighted in our direction thanks to Kayley's superstar popularity.

I take another glance at the stunning visage that is my girlfriend, and as I think over our plan, something occurs to me.

"Can you actually run in that thing?" I ask.

She hitches up the skirt and kicks one of her legs out to show me her shoes. They're petite versions of Afton's running gear. When she drops her dress down over them, they're covered so no one can see what she's got on her feet.

"How about the others?" Kayley asks.

"I was about to go find out," I reply, and Kayley throws me a questioning glance. I lose about half a head of height as I shrink under her gaze.

"Why didn't you check before you came up here?"

"Uh...because I couldn't wait to see you?"

"Now, that would work any other time, but this time..." Kayley makes a circling motion with an inverted finger. I bow my head and turn to go, but I need to say one more thing to her. It's important, and it needs to be said. I take in a breath and pull myself up.

"KayKay?"

"Yes?"

"I just wanted to tell you how beautiful you look."

Her face gets a warm glow to it, and she smiles. Then she nods slowly towards the back of the ship, her eyes never leaving mine. I hesitate just long enough to take her in one last time, then I head back.

"How'd it go?" Afton says, coming from the back.

"She looks amazing," I reply, and Afton gets a sly look on her face.

"Is that all you went up there to find out?"

"No, but did you see how she looks?"

"Buddy." Afton folds her arms. "I have no doubt that she's going to make every warm-blooded human being within eyesight faint with desire. Did you check with her about the plan, or were you so overcome that you forgot?"

"Would you blame me if I did?" Afton only chuckles at my response. I continue, "She's good to go...what about you?"

"All I need to do is pretend I'm you," Afton replies.

"Huh?"

"Dummy. I don't take my eyes off of her. Then if she needs me, I'm there."

Afton wrinkles her nose at me because I must have some type of worry-face going on at the moment. She takes a step towards me.

"You know you can trust me, Rance," Afton says, her voice soft.

"I know, but really, watch yourself too," I say in a tight voice. "Both of us know exactly how dangerous this is going to be."

"I know," she replies. "Be happy you're not going this time."

"I wish I could. Half of everyone I care about is going."

Afton reaches out and pulls me into a hug. I embrace her back, feeling a little odd for wrapping my arms around my friend when I didn't do it to my girlfriend. Even though we're dating, Kayley will always be the girl who's out of my league, while Afton...heck, she's just one of the guys.

Freddie comes from the back, his brow deeply creased. He glances at both of us, a *please help me* look on his face.

"What's up?" I ask.

"You might want to see for yourself."

We enter the cargo hold and find Danny on the floor, knees tucked in against her body and her face soaked with tears. She sniffles and wipes her eyes, but the tears keep coming.

"Hey," I say, dropping to her side with Afton. "Danny...what happened? You were doing fine before."

"No, no, I wasn't," Danny sobs, "but I tried…I really tried."

"Hey, pull yourself together," Afton says, as gently as it is possible for Afton to say something. "We really need you."

"I know, I know…." But all that does is make Danny into more of a blubbering mess.

This is a problem. We need her and her amazing suit, but she won't be anywhere near useful if she can't keep it together. I look up at Freddie, then over to Afton across from me. Both of them are wearing the same doubtful frown, and they're watching me expectantly.

I look back at Danny, my heart aching for her, but I have no idea how to get her out of the total hopelessness she's feeling. I could remind her how she wants to get revenge on Brownrigg, but that might just send her deeper into her grief.

Maybe if we start getting her into her suit, she might agree to go through with it. She hasn't said she couldn't do it. I just assumed that she wouldn't be able to, given her current state.

"Come on, Danny, let's get up." I glance over to Afton, who gets my idea right away. We reach under her arms and slowly get her to her feet, but as I'm moving around to her front to look her in the eye, Danny throws her arms out and falls into my arms. My knees bend at the sudden weight, and I stagger back. Afton tries to help, but Danny is dead weight on me. Her arms are not so loose, however. They press on my back and into my burns so hard my eyes water.

Afton sighs and shakes her head. Freddie just looks lost, and here I am with the completely bereft Danny slumped on me while I try not to scream in pain. If only she was a little shorter, she might not be crushing my wounds, but no, she's my height, so—

My height? Goddesses! Danny's armor might fit me. I might have to suck my gut in a little, but it just might work!

I guess I'm going on this mission after all.

"Guys, I've got an idea you're not going to like…"

Chapter Forty-Four

DEENEEHAAN, A COLONY PLANET of a billion fiercely independent people with little love for the Empire or its overbearing desire to rule them. The original expedition tried settling on one of the Central Planets, but nobody wanted them, so they ended up here. Then the Empire started poking its massive nose around, looking for resources. Those early settlers quickly drove the government representatives off the planet, leaving only a tenuous relationship remaining between them.

It's the perfect place for a trap.

I crouch down in an alley around the corner from where Kayley is stirring up the hornets. She's giving it her all, and the crowd is really getting into it. Their cheers echo down the alley, bouncing around and repeating back to me as the sound returns from the back wall. This will surely get Deputy Brownrigg here in a flash.

Danny's suit is definitely made for a woman and not for me. It's loose in places where it doesn't need to be and tight enough in others that I'm starting to worry whether I'll be able to have children after this. While I can expand my chest enough to breathe, I have to keep my gut totally sucked in. And my shoulders are rubbing the armor plating in all the wrong ways. I am going to be very, very raw after this.

"Okay, check-in," Grady says. "Any sign of Mr. Scruff?"

"Nothing yet," Afton replies, "but it's a helluva show."

"I have also seen nothing," Freddie responds. He's in the back corner of the square where the stage is set up. I call it a stage, but it's nothing more than a riser and some speakers we picked up locally. Still, it's enough for Kayley to make her speech and rouse the locals.

"Negative from my spot," I say.

"Wait...Rance?" Grady says. "Is that you? Where's Danny?"

"Danny couldn't make it, so I'm playing dress-up today."

"Dude," Parrish jumps in, "you should have told me you were doing that. I'd be there right with you!"

"We didn't exactly plan this," Afton says. "If we did, we would have found a way to sneak you on the shuttle."

"So what happened to Danny?" Grady queries. I explain the situation, and they both express their understanding. She's better hanging with Doc at the moment.

"So, do you know how to use that thing?" Parrish asks.

"I kind of got a crash course, yeah."

"Crash being the keyword there, dude," Grady says, "as in, don't. You're going to be in enough trouble when Kayley finds out. If you get hurt again, she's going to kill all of us."

"Don't worry. I'm not planning on getting hurt again."

There's a huge uproar from the crowd and then shouts as sirens from local constabulary vehicles begin to pull into the square. People start to scatter and run as a familiar voice gets on his own public address system, calling for everyone to stay where they are and for Kayley to give herself up immediately. Like that would ever happen.

"It is the man we have been waiting for!" Freddie yells. It's Deputy Brownrigg, alright. I'd never forget that nasal voice—right on time.

"Okay, here we go," Afton says. "She's coming off the stage now and headed your way, Rance. Keep that helmet on and don't say anything to her. Or this mission is over and done with before you can say sorry."

"Got it," I reply. I glance down at the rifle I have in my hands and power it on. It's loaded with fizzy shot—balls that stick to anything and emit a really nasty shock. I'm not killing anyone today. Hopefully Brownrigg's team is on the same page.

All we have to do is cut the deputy off from the rest of his team, then give him a good dose of the rifle. Once he's down, we snatch him up and take him to Lieutenant Cortell. It's a quick, simple plan, and we're banking on its simplicity.

Kayley comes flying around the corner. I freeze as she sees me. Does she recognize me? I'm fully covered, so—no. Kayley gives me a thumbs-up and continues down the alley. Brownrigg should be next.

But it's not him. It's Freddie, running for his life. He pumps his arms and legs in a frantic race to escape. But from what? He knew I was here to protect him. As he passes me, I see how wide his eyes are.

Something is wrong.

I'm dying to ask, but if Kayley has put a Teddy comm receiver in her ear, she'll know what's up. I've got to be patient. If I can.

"It's a bit of a mess out here," Afton says. "Our girl may have done a better job than she thought she would."

"What's happening?" Grady asks.

"People are fighting back."

"Oh...boy."

"Some of them have weapons," Afton adds.

"Pull out of there," Parrish says, sounding worried.

"I would, but...I'm trapped behind the stage."

Gunfire erupts from the square. A bullet ricochets down the alley and hits the dirt next to me. I duck, not wanting to get hit. Then I remember I'm wearing bulletproof armor—not that the realization of it makes me want to get back up.

But Afton needs help, and she's not wearing anything that will stop bullets. I scan down the alley. Freddie's pink shirt is visible even in the dim light back there. Kayley's there too. If I go help Afton, they'll be unprotected.

An explosion rocks the square, and I jump. Afton! There are cries and screams from everywhere. I need to know if she's okay, but I can't use the comm. Did Grady hear it? He's not talking, so probably not.

People scatter from the square—some into the alley. They halt at the sight of me, unsure if I'm friend or foe. Oh, no. They're blocking the way, in or out. A slight motion of my weapon, and they turn and bolt. Problem solved.

"Afton, are you clear?" Grady says. "Afton?"

She could be badly hurt. That's it...mission or not, I'm going.

"I'm headed out," I say, adding new temples to visit to my already long list. "I'll get to her and bring her back."

"You stay where you are, Rance!" Kayley shouts. Shoot! She's on comm! "Let Danny get her. She's got the armor. Danny, can you help?"

Wait. Does KayKay think I'm still on the shuttle? I glance down the alley again to see Kayley staring right at me, her hands on her hips. Now I know she thinks I'm Danny, but I still get a shiver down my spine.

"Danny, do you copy?" she asks again as I crouch, motionless. She takes a few steps towards me, and I feel beads of sweat drip down the side of my face.

"Er, she's reading you, Kayley," Grady the wonder boy says, covering for me, "something's wrong with her mic."

To enhance Grady's fabrication, I tap the side of my helmet and give her a thumbs-up. She nods and gives it back. Phew. That was risky—ten points to you, Grady.

I turn and rip down the alley and out into the square. Before I can drop my head down, a volley of bullets flies my way. One hits the suit right in the torso and bounces off. Whoa, I felt that! My eyes drop to see if I'm hit, but there's not even a scratch.

I don't need any other proof I'm safe. I go all out towards the stage, pushing my way through the handful of combatants. They jump out of my way, unsure if I'm attacking them or not. I don't have time to tell them who I am. Afton's my goal.

When I slide in behind the stage, she's there, a little out of sorts but unharmed and staring up at me with a very wrinkled forehead. I tap the side of my head and turn my hand in a questioning motion. Afton just shakes her head.

Another explosion knocks me off my feet, and I crash into the ground and roll. The ill-fitting suit jabs me in my shoulders and ribs, and I grimace. I'm okay though, but...Afton?

Also okay. She's curled herself up in a ball for protection. Her arms are covered over her face, and her hands cup her ears.

I check the area to make sure I've still got a safe exit—good so far. My eyes turn to the red flashing lights of the constabulary vehicles. One of them is a complete wreck, but Deputy Brownrigg's men are not intimidated. They fight back with the ferocity of a small army.

I scoop Afton up in the arms of the suit and power back towards the alley, bullets and other projectiles glancing off the suit. It might be a strange time to worry about this, but I really hope Danny won't be mad if there's some damage to her armor. I mean, that's what it's for, right?

Kayley and Freddie jump up as I rocket towards them. Kayley gasps and covers her mouth with her hand, and her shoulders sag in relief when Afton swings her legs down and plants them on the ground. Kayley sighs and rests her head on Afton's shoulder.

"Hey, is everyone okay?" Parrish asks.

"Yes, thank the Goddesses," Kayley says. "But our plan is in trouble."

"So, what are you going to do?"

Kayley glances at me, chewing her lip. I can tell she's stuck. We really didn't have a plan B here. This should be simple: trick Brownrigg into showing up and then capture him. We got the first part right, but the second half of the plan has blown up like a kettle full of kerosene.

The weapons' fire has become more sporadic, but it's still there. To make matters worse, a few combatants have taken cover just inside the entrance. They're too busy fighting to notice us, but it could become an issue if they do. And of course, if we want out, we'll have to go through them.

"Kayley?" Parrish queries.

"Hold on, I'm thinking!" she says with a snarl. She wipes a hand across her brow and takes a deep breath.

A massive boom rings out in the square, followed by a blast that throws debris up into the air. The ground shakes and rumbles as chunks of wall crash down around us. We pull back under an overhang at the end of the alley for protection, but I honestly don't think it'll help much.

"Armor! Take cover!" someone shouts from down the alley.

"This way!" another one shouts—that voice was close. I take a protective stance in front of the others, preparing to raise my rifle.

But there's no rifle.

"Oh, shoot," Kayley says, saying exactly what I was thinking. I dropped the gun when I fell behind the stage! Instead of picking it up, I grabbed Afton. Now that's a trade I'd take any day, but a rifle full of fizzy shot would be really helpful. We're about to be overrun by two dozen men with questionable intentions and uncertain loyalties.

And there's a big armored vehicle behind them, aiming its main weapon our way.

Chapter Forty-Five

"HOLY SOPHIA!" AFTON SHOUTS out the name of her favorite Goddess. That's her special secret-weapon emergency call. If she's saying it, well, we're in big trouble.

Maybe there's a door I can smash through? No. I try to wipe the sweat from my face but only wind up scraping the glove over the helmet. A sharp sound ensues, and Afton gives me a side-glare.

There is a grated window nearby. It's small, but if I can punch it out the others can sneak through. The wall there is fairly thin and... hmm.

How strong is this armored suit? Can it smash through a wall? I just might have to find out.

I catch Kayley's attention and point to the window. She nods, understanding, and motions her permission. I don't know if she's realized what she's caused, but she must be freaking out as much as the rest of us.

The whir of the armored vehicle winds up to a scream. They're going to fire! The men are nearly on top of us too. We need to move. Now.

I take two steps back and, remembering my five-second training, I press the turbo in the glove's thumb. The suit blasts forward towards the wall, with just enough time to get my shoulder in front of me before impact. I close my eyes and dial up Afton's emergency Goddess for a quick prayer.

The impact never comes. Did I miss it? No way! How do you miss a wall? My eyes open in a dark space. I try to get my bearings, but suddenly I hear a loud clank, and the world spins around me.

There are vibrations behind me. Someone running past. A few someones. Then there's a boom, and the entire floor jumps, tossing me upward. I land hard—on my burns! Yeow! I groan, lifting my back off the floor, but the sweat makes my shirt stick to my wounds.

Kayley and Afton drop down next to me. They're shouting, but I can't hear anything with this dumb helmet on. I try to reach out to Grady, but Teddy comm isn't working. The only way I'm going to hear is to take the helmet off. That's a big problem, but I don't know if I have another option. Oh, well, here goes. I really hope my girlfriend doesn't punch me the moment she sees me.

"Rance?" Kayley cries out and jerks her head back as the helmet slides back. She's not surprised for long, however. She mouths some choice curses at me, and her eyes narrow. "You are in *big* trouble... *darling.*"

"I'm sorry, KayKay, but Danny just couldn't do it. She's just totally overcome," I say in my defense. "If I didn't, it would have ended our mission before it started."

Kayley tightens her jaw and clenches her fists. She really wants to pop me one. I wouldn't blame her if she did. Besides, my back is killing me so much more than any punch from her would. She's no weakling, but I'm already in agony.

"I am sorry, but a lover's quarrel is not something we have time for just this moment," Freddie says. "I think I hear boots."

"He's right," Afton seconds. "Get up, Rance."

If the suit wasn't powered, I'm not sure I could have sat up on my own. My head is spinning, and the pain in my back shoots stars across my eyes. We'll see what standing does.

"Hey, what happened to that gang of guys fighting the deputy's men?" I ask, rubbing my head.

"Long gone," Afton says. "They cut us off and ran away. So much for loyal supporters."

"How about Brownrigg?"

"Could still be outside," Kayley says and mutters another curse. Boy, she's really on it today. "Who knows at this point?"

There's a commotion behind me. I spin to see a bustle of government soldiers forcing themselves through a big hole in a wall

—a big hole that I made! We stare at them, motionless, as they shove each other through to get inside. One of them gets in, then scans the room, squinting. Right! His eyes aren't adjusted to the dark yet.

"Run!" I hiss. The sound catches the attention of a few soldiers, and they squint my way. But my team stays frozen. I've no idea what they're waiting for, but they need to get a clue *now*.

"Run!" I shout, dropping the helmet back on and charging the soldiers. A few of them notice me and raise their guns—too late. I plow into them, knocking them back. They blast out of the hole like a shaken bottle of fizzy water opened, and tumble back into the alley.

I'm there too, tripping over the puppy pile of men as I struggle to break free. They grab at my legs and try to pull me down. A few select kicks with the suit, and they quickly quit trying. I grin and chuckle to myself. I might be indestructible in this thing!

"Get that crazy woman already! Tackle her if you have to!" a voice shouts. A really familiar voice. It's Brownrigg—good. Time to clear this mission off the table. Maybe I should take the helmet off too. Then he can actually see who took him down.

I point at him and stomp forward. Brownrigg gets this look in his eyes as if he's just seen the god of death himself. He takes a few steps back, raising his hands and shaking his head—it's no use. I don't even have to walk fast to catch up with him.

"Get her, you fools!" the deputy cries, picking up his pace. He fumbles in his coat for something and pulls out his badge, a golden disk with the Emperor's crest in its top-left corner. "In the name of His Majesty the Emperor and the houses of Parliament, Daniela Lecker, I am placing you under arrest!"

He's really rubbing it in, but I'm getting bored. I press the button up on the collar and the helmet slides away. If he wants something to be scared of, let it be me!

Deputy Brownrigg goes still, his mouth falling open. He even takes a step towards me, fixing his spectacles and squinting. The moment recognition hits he jumps back.

"You! H...how did you get into that suit?"

"Not easily," I reply. "So don't make it any harder on me, and come peacefully."

"That..." Brownrigg's head wrinkles. "That's my line! And you should follow your own advice, Renton He'! You and Kayley Garmon...Garmonich...oh, never mind! Did you really think that I'd fall for the same trick twice? I came prepared this time! Now I'm going to arrest you for breaking every statute of the Anti-Sedition Code."

"Yeah, I don't think so." I laugh and fold my arms in front of me. "It's going to be—"

Something slams over my head, obscuring my vision in white light. I stagger forward, my hands flying up to cover my skull. Two pairs of arms wrap around my legs, while two more try to restrain my torso. Four more arms grab my own and pull them behind my back. I grimace as my shirt tears away from my burns.

"Surrender while you can, Rance," the deputy says, "and maybe I'll put in a good word for you."

"Forget it," I growl, pushing against the six men who are trying to take me down. "I'm not the one who's going—"

A seventh man jumps on my back, and we all tumble to the ground. They pin my arms and legs to the ground, trying to get restraints around them. I keep pushing them off, but even with the suit it's exhausting. Every time I fling one of them off another takes their place.

"What's that now? I don't think I heard all of that," Brownrigg says mockingly, cupping his ear at me.

"I said you're—" A hand squishes my face into the ground. That's it. I'm really done with this walking roll of toilet paper trying to repress me.

"Didn't hear you, lad," Brownrigg says and giggles. "Speak up!"

I roar and smash on the turbo, shoving with as much power as I can muster. The suit multiplies my action by a hundred. Or thousands. Well, I'm not exactly sure, but it's way more than I expect. I launch off the ground and climb into the air, just above the alley. My force hurls Brownrigg's men in all directions. They become screaming projectiles. Some land on top of the low-slung buildings, and others crash behind me and the deputy.

I come down with a heavy thud on the same spot. Brownrigg jumps back, covering his face. I stand up with daggers in my eyes for this paper bag of a man who thinks he's better than me. Better than everyone on Angelcanis.

"The truth is, Brownrigg," I shout, "it's you who's inferior!"

"What?" He frowns and tilts his head at me. "What are you talking about?"

"Pretending to be better than us when all you do is cheat the very system that pays you!"

"Oh"—Brownrigg fakes applause—"an excellent speech. You should run for office. I don't suppose you have any proof of this so-called cheating?"

"Actually," I reply and grin, "we do."

His smirk disappears as I approach. He knows I'm telling the truth. Brownrigg raises his hands again and steps back, eyes widening. This is how it should be. The good guys win, and the bad guys go to jail.

"You are going down, Brownrigg," I say. "We're going to take you to the authorities...*real* authorities who understand that skimming from their government is bad."

"No," he replies.

"No? That's your answer?"

"Yes." Suddenly he jumps out of the way and shouts, "Fire!"

An eerie whine emits ahead of me. I take my eyes off of Brownrigg and look forward. Oh, heck—the armored vehicle. Its cannon is aimed right for me. I pound the helmet switch, raising it just in time.

This is really going to hurt.

Chapter Forty-Six

I'M ALIVE...I THINK. I'M aching in every possible spot there is to ache, but hurting is a good sign. The Three Goddesses aren't floating over me, preparing to judge my life as worthy of being reborn. Unless I've been such a bad dude that I went straight to purgatory. Though, purgatory doesn't usually come with a massive headache. At least not that I've heard.

My eyes open a crack. Harsh light streams in and I wince. I try again, and as the light dims, I'm able to open them a bit more. That's when I see the shadow of someone looming over me—Brownrigg. He's got his hands on his hips, and even though I can't see it, I'll bet he's smirking at me too.

"Still thinking you're going to take me in?" He laughs. "All you colonists are the same...a little freedom to govern your own affairs, and then you think you have the right to do anything! Well, so sorry to drop this on you, but you will never be a full-blooded citizen of the Empire! You don't deserve it! You can't match our intellect, and you could nev—"

"Could you not?" I ask, grimacing and putting a hand to my head. That's when I realize that the arm of Danny's suit is disintegrating. I can't believe this thing was strong enough to absorb the power of a plasma cannon! But just barely. If the gun had been any bigger, I wouldn't be here to talk about it.

Brownrigg kicks me, and I jump, my attention snapping back to him. He kicks me again for no reason, and that's when the ache in my body turns to hot needles. I cry out, and Brownrigg laughs again. Another kick gets me dizzy, and I fall back.

"If you want me to boast over you, like some cine villain, I shall!"

"I love cine. Does that mean you're going to tell me your whole diabolical plan too?"

"No." He kicks me again. "You already know it, so what's the point?"

"True." I tilt my head in agreement, then realize I'm having a civil conversation with someone who just tried to blow me up and then kicked me three times. I should be raging angry, but I'm not. Some scent in the air is giving me happy thoughts.

"Now, where was I?"

"Something about being superior?"

"Yes, right, and this is where you need to understand your position of inferiority. Ever since our departure from our mighty homeworld —"

"Albion?" I ask.

"What?" Brownrigg frowns. "No! I mean, yes! Stop interrupting!"

"Albion is the Empire's homeworld, right?"

"Of course it is!"

"Did you forget?"

"Shut up, you colonist hick!" He kicks me three more times in succession, and I cry out, curling up into a fetal position. Brownrigg sighs and takes a moment to regain his composure.

"So, now this is what is going to happen. I," he says and points to himself, "the superior human being, will arrest you for whatever I want, and you..." He points down at me, pressing his finger into the center of my chest. "You, the inferior being, will spend the rest of your miserable life in the deepest prison I can find."

"You mean like the pit?" I ask, pressing a palm into my forehead.

"Yes! Like the—" Deputy Brownrigg stops, his eyebrows furrowing. "How do you know about that?"

"Because I was one of three people that escaped from there."

"You?" He pulls back, shaking his head. "That's impossible! No one escapes the pit! Especially not a rotten little half-breed such as yourself."

"Yeah, well, with a little help, me and two of my friends did, with not even a scratch on us."

"Which friends?"

"The two behind you," I say and point. Brownrigg's eyes go wide and he spins around. Afton and Freddie are there, and Kayley's behind them, grinning. With no warning, Afton socks Brownrigg right across the jaw. His head jerks back, his body twists, and he falls, crumpling to the ground.

Afton winces and shakes her hand. Kayley and Freddie rush over to me, dropping down to my side. Slowly and with much grimacing, I unroll myself from my protective position and lie on my back.

"This is exactly why I didn't want you to come," Kayley says, her eyes hard. "You should have just left it up to us, but I guess you're never going to change, are you?" She sighs. "Anyway, I've called in the Teddys to pull us out before anyone else gets hurt."

"What has happened to Danny's suit?" Freddie asks, pulling a chipped piece of armor off and examining it. "It has...crumbled."

"No one is going to ask me if I'm okay?" I whine.

"We know you're not," Afton replies, "so there's no point. And I don't see you asking about my hand."

I chuckle and grin, even though it hurts. We're all acting like we did before, and that's a good sign things are getting back to normal. Yes, I've got some resting up to do, but that's nothing new.

There's a cough from the deputy as he regains consciousness and turns over. Afton walks over to him and puts her boot in his chest, but he only laughs.

"You think you've won? You think you've gotten me?"

"Not think. Know," Afton replies. "You're going down."

"Why do you keep saying that?" he asks. "Is that some kind of heroic fantasy that you have?"

"Actually, I was the one who—" I say.

"Stay out of this!" Brownrigg hisses.

"Hey!" Afton presses hard on his chest. "You be nice to Rance. He just got blown through a wall."

"Well." The deputy grins. "There's more where that came from...fire at will!"

Plasma rifles pelt the building, bolts burning into the walls and ceiling around us. We scramble for cover, dragging Brownrigg with us. He resists, but Afton smacks him and he stops. With the dead weight of the suit on me, I'm having trouble getting up. At least I'm still somewhat bulletproof, as long as I cover the parts of me that aren't.

"What are you, stupid?" Kayley shouts at the deputy. "Your own men are shooting at you too!"

Brownrigg glares. "They won't hit me! They're my elite force!"

"They're not hitting *anything* at the moment," Afton says, peeking out.

With some effort, I roll to a safe spot. The firing dies down, and I hear the scuffle of boots getting closer. That's trouble, elite or not. We've got to act quickly before they're on top of us.

"Ideas?" Kayley asks.

"I am for escaping," Freddie says. "Yes, this would be a good idea."

"There's no escape for you, pink boy!" The deputy cackles. "You're all getting locked up!"

And here I was a hundred percent confident we had won. I'm not giving up, but all we've got is a broken power suit and a bunch of rubble we can throw versus several heavy rifles fired by skilled soldiers. That's not much of a matchup.

I really don't want to go back to jail. I've been there twice already, and it's not really a fun place to visit, much less stay for any length of time. Kayley and my friends don't deserve to be there. I'll do anything to stop that from happening, even die if I have to.

A scrape of something hard on the rocks outside catches my attention. This is it—I tense—we're going to be fighting with whatever we've got. If this suit around me has any use left, I'll throw myself on them and hope that's enough to slow them down so the others can escape.

A long shadow appears through the hole in the wall. It looms large. I'm ready for anything. I move into a crouch, preparing to spring on our attackers. Here they come.

"Failure to achieve proper camouflage, Rancid," Original Teddy says, climbing through the hole. Behind him is Blue Buddy and a white Teddy. "Further study recommended."

I let out an enormous sigh, nearly collapsing where I crouch. The others do the same. Thank goodness the Teddys got here when they did. We were done for otherwise.

"What is this?" Deputy Brownrigg cries, sitting up. "Well! I should have known! You are in collusion with the enemy! Traitors to your own people! Oh, ho! No jail time for you! I fully expect you will be tried and execut—"

"Popsicle, please, Teddy," Afton says. A second after, the deputy goes still, and Afton pushes his suspended body to the ground. "Goddesses, he's annoying."

"Thank you, Teddy," Kayley says, and Original Teddy gives her a salute with his tentacle. "We're glad you made it."

"Gratitudes are unrequired," Original Teddy says. "Mission completion is paramount."

"Can we get out of here, please?" I say. "This thing is giving me a rash."

"That's what happens when a guy wears women's apparel," Afton sneers. "You really have no idea what we go through."

"After wearing this suit, I think I might," I reply, gritting my teeth as the suit rubs against my broken body.

Chapter Forty-Seven

THE TEDDYS LIFT THE petrified Deputy Brownrigg up with their tentacles and raise him above their heads, preparing to transport him away. I push myself up and do my best to clean up the suit, but I know my efforts are in no way going to lessen the shock when Danny sees it. Kayley watches me and just shakes her head. I'm not sure if it's pity or if she's just fed up with me at this point—I'll have to deal with that later. Right now, I'm just glad to be alive.

We step out into the open air, though it's not clean or clear. Trails of smoke waft about, and there's the distinct odor of sulfur coming from somewhere. I sigh, but I'll manage. Soon enough we'll be headed home.

A sharp whine cuts through the air, penetrating the smoke. It rises in pitch, getting louder and more chilling. I know that sound—not only are we not safe, we're about to get barbecued!

"The armored vehicle!" I cry, grabbing Kayley and rushing forward. The others scatter to whatever cover they can find, leaving Deputy Brownrigg to lie frozen next to his men like logs in a lumberyard.

The gun pounds the surrounding buildings as I zigzag around the alley to avoid the deadly bolts that could easily cut both of us in two. I don't know why I'm charging towards a vehicle that's firing at us, but it seemed like the best idea at the time. They can't shoot us up close like that.

As the gun continues to add windows to the buildings around the alley, Kayley and I drop down in front of its wheels. She puts her hands over her ears and presses into me. That gun makes a big noise when it goes off.

"Grady!" I shout. "Call Grady! He'll know how to fix this!"

Kayley presses her ear against mine. Grady picks up immediately.

"Armored vehicle?" Grady asks. "What kind?

I describe it to him, and then there's silence. Did he hear me? Why isn't he responding? The gun goes off again, and Kayley jumps and yelps.

"Ah, okay, so I bet there's a power-down tone code for it," Grady says casually, as if he's discussing the latest specs of the machine at a social gathering. "All you have to do is find the input and put the tone sequence in."

"Grady! In the name of which Goddess are we going to make that happen?" I yell. The gun blasts off another round. I don't know if Afton and Freddie are safe, but if we don't stop this, the entire area will collapse.

"Like you did at the station, just hold the earpiece over the control panel and poof!"

The gun fires again, and Kayley and I wince. My ears are really ringing.

"Where the hell is the control panel?" Kayley asks.

"How should I know?" Grady replies.

"This is *your* idea!"

"Okay, okay, the panel is probably on the bottom of the chassis. You'll have to slide underneath to find it."

Kayley and I both cry out as the gun goes off and part of a roof collapses. It's right where we left—where Afton, Freddie, and the Teddys might be. Kayley and I share a horrified glance. Whether or not they're okay, there's only one way to solve this.

We scramble under the armored vehicle from opposite sides. I'm struggling to push the dead power suit around, but for my slim girlfriend it's quite spacious. The good thing is the bottom of the chassis is fairly flat, so we find the control box with ease.

Of course, it's locked.

"Grady, it's locked!"

"Break it open!"

"With what?"

"Your suit!"

That's not going to happen. Kayley and I share another glance. Her eyes suddenly light up, and she reaches down and rips her dress, pulling one of the metal ribs from the skirt. My eyes open wide, and I grin from ear to ear. She hands it to me, and out of sudden impulse, I kiss her. Kayley blinks and just stares. I shrug. I don't know why I did it, but she just made me really happy at that moment.

I'm about to turn my attention to the problem at hand when Kayley wraps both hands around my head and slides herself forward to plant a really deep one right on my lips. It's gushing with all sorts of passion and desire. My whole body tingles, and for once, it's for a good reason.

When she pulls back with a warm smile on her face, I stare at her in shock. She blushes and shrugs.

"I just wanted to say I love you," Kayley, my most perfect girl, says.

"I know"—I grin—"but right now, I love you more."

The power of the next shot from the gun rocks the entire vehicle, and I feel its weight crush what's left of the power suit's armor. At least it could protect me one last time, but now I realize that if we don't shut this thing down now, it's not just my friends who will be in trouble.

I jam the metal rib—I really have to find out why they make these things so strong—into the edge of the box, and the cover pops off from the leverage I put on it. Sometimes I really love physics principles.

"Okay, Grady, we've got the cover off, and I see the mic!" I say, putting my ear to Kayley's again.

"Great," Grady replies, "on the count of three, put the earpiece up to it, and hold it there for five seconds."

"Got it! Ready when you are!"

"Go!"

Three...two...one...I pull the earpiece out and jam its speaker up against the mic. I glance at Kayley, and we count to five. Then I hold the Teddy comm unit up so we can both talk to Grady.

"Did you do it?"

"Yes! What happened?"

The gun fires again, and I'm slammed into the ground. I feel something pop in my back, and I don't know if it was the suit or me. Kayley stares at me, her face frozen in fear. I smile to try to calm her—it helps—but I'm still on the verge of hysterics.

"Nothing happened, Grady!" I shout—good, I'm still breathing.

"Maybe there's another code?" Kayley asks.

"Sure, but I don't have a recording of it to play!" Grady replies.

"Sing it, then!" she says.

"What? No!"

"Parrish, what about you?"

"I can't even play an instrument," Parrish says, then drops off. Did Teddy comm go down? "Wait...Rance, I have an idea...be right back!"

"Parrish! Where are you going? We don't have time. Come back!"

There's silence from the gun above. Did they give up? No way. But that leads to another thought. If they gave up, that would mean they're going to move...with us under it.

I hear the squeak of a hatch open above us—someone's coming out! Kayley gasps and covers her mouth. She looks at me, the question clear in her eyes. I shake my head in reply and put a finger to my lips.

Boots hit the ground and walk around the vehicle. We stay as frozen as we can and hope they don't do the obvious thing. I hear footsteps move away from us and head down the alley. Happily, they don't look under the vehicle, but that means they're either looking for our friends or trying to rescue Deputysicle Brownrigg and his pals.

"Rance! Kayley!" Parrish is back on the Teddy comm. I fumble for the earpiece, trying to cover the speaker.

"Don't shout," I whisper.

"I've got the solution," he says. I hear a few melodic plunks, and I frown...but only for a moment.

"The corn husker!" I say, louder than I want to. Now I'm petrified and excited at the same time. Parrish's garbage picking is going to save us! I forgot he had it.

The boots scrape on the ground sand run back at us. They heard me! Very big, bad, nasty problem!

"They're still there!" a voice says. It's got to be the soldier running back to the vehicle. "Rotate five degrees left and fire!"

As his boots clank above us and I hear the hatch slam, I get a bigger fear—he's not after us, they've zeroed in on our buddies, and they're about to pulverize them into biological mush!

"Okay! Count of three!" I shout, forgetting about my own safety. "Do it now!"

The gun turret rotates and locks into place, the deep whine of the ammo recharge rising to a screech. I forget my count and just thrust the earpiece at the mic on the control panel. Kayley grabs my hand and holds it steady.

I don't want to think of my buds getting killed. It's too much. I'll offer all the money I ever make towards building a new temple to the Goddesses if we can save them. Of course, if this works, I'll need to start making money.

As if the Goddesses hear me, the engine of the armored vehicle conks out. The whine of the gun drops to a low hum, then dissipates. Soon after, the hatch opens, and we hear a pile of feet climb down, drop to the ground and start to run.

"It's those aliens!" one of the soldiers shouts. "They got some kind of death ray!"

I sigh and look at Kayley. Her face is covered in dirt and sweat, but she's never looked more beautiful. I know I thought that before when I first saw her in the dress, but this slimy version is even better.

"Guys!" Grady calls. We get back on the Teddy comm, once more putting our heads together. "Did it work?"

"Tell Parrish he's got some musical ability after all," I say and slump down, closing my eyes.

We did it.

Chapter Forty-Eight

AS WE STAND, ALL together in my backyard, I look around at all the faces before me, and my eyes get a little teary. It could be that the pain blocker Doc Elizabeth gave me is causing me to be emotional, but I doubt that. This feels real, like seeing the ocean for the first time or winning first prize at the school science fair. I never did, of course. It was always Grady, except for the one year when he had to travel so he didn't compete. That year it was Class President Kayley who won.

I think I'm just happy that everyone is here. Of course, Jurgen, Danny's love of her life, is not, but after two weeks with us, at least she's starting to smile again. She's really taken a liking to my mom, always complimenting her on every little choice of spice or cooking trick she pulls out. Everyone else has learned not only to tolerate her but to welcome her as a temporary member of the team.

"Don't worry about it," Danny says after I apologize to her for the trillionth time about her power suit. "I've got three more."

She and Freddie are leaving today. They're headed back to Canis Ludis. Apparently, Freddie lives there too—I should have known—and I think he's taken a liking to Danny too, but he remains aloof about it. Even I know it's too soon to jump into something. Danny's got some healing to do before she even thinks about love again.

"So," I say, fiddling with my fingers, "since we achieved not one, but two missions for you, I don't suppose there's any chance we could get that reward you offered us?"

"Payment?" Danny stares at me for a suspended second, then her face brightens. "Of course, honey bun, you've got some big bucks coming to you."

I hold in my excitement and refrain from jumping for joy. We got paid for a job! Our first real job. It was a hard one, for sure, but that just makes getting a reward all that much more thrilling.

"But I have to take it back for payments on a new power suit, so we're even," Danny adds.

"You just told me not to worry about it!" I cry.

"That's right," Danny says. "I said don't worry about it because I'm using the money from your reward to pay for the replacement."

My shoulders slump. It's exhausting to go from euphoric to totally depressed. We really could have used that money to get our world-saving business started. We need an office...equipment...a sign, even. Now where are we going to get the funds to do all that?

"Aww, don't pout, sweetie," Danny says, putting her hands on my face and mocking me by sticking out her lower lip. "I am so grateful for all of your help. You've done so much for me."

"Hey," Kayley warns Danny, "hands."

"But." I look down. "Jurgen..."

"No, no, honey." She slides her hands around the back of my head and pulls it down to her chest, rocking me gently. "You did the best you could."

"Hey!" Kayley shouts. Afton jumps in as well.

"What?" Danny asks, glancing at them both.

"Can you release my boyfriend, please?"

"I'm fine, KayKay," I say.

"Buddy," Afton says, shaking her head. "Do I really need to explain to you how that was the wrong answer?"

"You need to cool your heels, Red." Danny releases me with a huff. I stagger back and catch the three women having a stare-off. There's a few glares shot my way as well.

"Hey, by the way," Parrish says, trying to break the tension, "I found out what this thing is."

Parrish shakes the little corn husker box he used to play the code that shut the armored truck down. The others gather around to examine it. I keep back because, well, I've seen it, and also I'm currently in the penalty box.

"So, what is it?" Afton asks.

"It's called a Thom, more commonly known as a thumb piano," Parrish replies, "so it really is a musical instrument. We used it how it's supposed to be used."

"What's a piano?" Grady asks. Parrish shrugs. The obvious conclusion would be that it's some kind of musical instrument, but if Parrish didn't find out, it's unlikely anyone else will.

"Well, I'm glad we got some good use out of it," I say. "Now you can toss it back in the garbage where you found it."

"Are you kidding?" Parrish asks. "This thing was critical in the success of our mission! I'm gonna learn how to play it."

"Good luck with that," Afton says. "That thing is so old it looks like it'll break before you get very far."

Parrish wrinkles his nose at her, and I laugh. He's doing a lot better now that he's on his feet with no support. It's still a long way until he's training for marathons again, but Parrish wouldn't be happy just sitting around like I am.

"I am curious," Freddie says. "What's going to happen to Mr. Brownrigg now that your lieutenant has him?"

"Oh, he's done," Kayley says with a smirk. "Lieutenant Cortell has some fairly high connections in the Ministry of Justice. Brownrigg likely won't see the light of day ever again."

"Yes, this is good," Freddie says with a nod. "Very good."

"Still doesn't help us get another gig," Grady moans, dropping himself down on one of the lawn chairs next to where Doc Elizabeth is sunning herself in her two-piece skin suit.

"Well, you're welcome to come help me on Canis Ludis," Danny says. "With my skills and your, uh, various talents, we could make a great team."

"No thanks," Afton replies. "We're good."

"Alright then, my darlings," Danny says, "we're off. Come visit sometime! We'll have a great time. Love you lots!"

"That's not mutual," Kayley mutters.

"Oh, and you, tuff stuff." Danny points at Afton, who steps back and folds her arms. "You are a strong, confident, and totally sexy girl. You'd make a great hand-hunter, darling. Come look me up if you ever want to make some real money. I promise you...men will be falling all around us!"

"Yeah, not really looking to be surrounded by men," Afton replies.

"Surela? A hand-hunter?" Grady bursts out, giggling hysterically.

"Laugh it up, dork and a half," Afton growls. "You'll soon find that fuzzball head of yours so deep in the ground that you'll forget which way is up."

Grady holds up a hand, still doubled over with laughter. Afton's not having it, and she drops herself down on top of him, leaning back to crush him on the lawn chair. Grady yelps, but he's no match for Afton. She folds her arms and grins as he begs for her to get up. Doc Elizabeth makes a casual glance at them, then resumes reading her tablet.

I laugh. It's good to see my buds so carefree. It's really been a while since we've all laughed together. Kayley lets out a snicker as she comes to my side. We share a grin, and she kisses my cheek, putting her hands on my shoulder and leaning into me. I let out a sigh, her closeness warming me. I lean back into her a little too.

A transit vehicle picks Danny and Freddie up. We all wave to them as they take off. I'm not afraid to admit I'll miss the two of them. Even if one of them knocked me off my rails and made my head spin so much I wound up dressing like her. I've still got the scabs on my shoulders from all the damage her suit caused. There were some other...problems, but the doc says I should be fine. She also says she would love to be an aunt. Not really sure what that means, but I'm happy I'm okay.

"So, back to the beginning again?" Kayley asks, her scarlet hair falling on my face as she leans into me.

"Yeah," I sigh, thinking of all the energy we've spent, all the hurt we've been through. "Or maybe we just call it quits, instead."

There's a collective shout from everyone, consisting mostly of questions regarding my head and what's wrong with it. Afton jumps up in outrage. Parrish, too. Kayley even steps back to glower at me.

"You can't give up," Doc Elizabeth says. "So what if you've not made the money you'd hoped? You've helped a lot of people, Rance. That's a good thing, I'd think."

"She's right, darling," Kayley adds. "We haven't come all this way to give up now. But maybe we just need some downtime to figure things out. All of us have been through a lot. I know I wouldn't mind kicking back for a few months."

"Yeah, I guess," I say, dropping my head. "But what, then? Save some pets? Maybe we're just not cut out for this."

"Rance, look at me," Kayley says, and I obey. Her steel-blue eyes are the warmest I've ever seen them, except maybe for the first time we kissed. Nothing is going to beat that. "What you wanted to create is happening. Maybe not as fast as you'd like, but it *is* happening. There's no rush, darling. We're young, we're *famous*...well, I'm famous...and we don't have anything holding us back. What more do you want?"

I smile at my amazing girlfriend. Of course, she's right. Our whole future is ahead of us. That is, provided our names get cleared from a list of very dangerous seditionists that we definitely don't belong on. I think Lieutenant Cortell will help us with that, so hopefully that should be good. But I'm sure there's still plenty of bad people in the Empire that want to do us wrong, given how much trouble we've been causing for them.

A few months off would do us some good. We could remember what it was like to be ourselves again. Parrish could heal. Afton could spend more time with her dad, and Grady could get his engine design out there. Kayley and I? Well, let's just say we would perfect the art of doing nothing together. Yes, that would be the ideal situation, and of course, we could all spend time together. The Teddys too. They're becoming a familiar sight in the cities on Angelcanis, so that would be an easy add-in.

As I start to reply to Kayley, Grady's Sergo buzzes. He pulls it from his pocket and answers. Immediately his face collapses into a serious frown. Grady stands and starts pacing as he talks in short replies to whoever is on the other side.

When he disconnects, he turns around to look at us, his face hard. Everyone gets quiet and waits for him to say something.

"I have some news," he announces. "We've got a job...it'll pay well."

"Yes! Grady! That's awesome!" I say, feeling my mood brightening. "And big money! Great!"

Then I notice that he's not celebrating with the rest of us.

"Grady," Kayley says, tilting her head at him, "who's the client?"

"My parents."

About the Author

Marc B. DeGeorge has made every attempt in his adult life to maintain a balance between how much science and how much art he dabbles in. Sometimes, he's even successful. When he was young, he wanted to be an astronaut, and then an aeronautical engineer—he even went to Space Camp! But then he learned how to play guitar and his space dreams took a back seat. He spent a decade playing professionally in bands and studying music in college (university only took five years). These days, things have come round full circle, and Marc envisions the future by writing books that imagine what challenges humanity may face, and what we might accomplish together.

When Marc isn't writing, he performs traditional Japanese music on shamisen and writes, shoots, and edits performing arts photos and documentaries under the MuseMarc Studio name.